VENGEANCE IN THE MIST

COVENTRY SAGA
BOOK 10

ROBIN PATCHEN

Copyright © 2023 by Robin Patchen

All rights reserved.

No part of this book may be reproduced in any form or by any electronic or mechanical means, including information storage and retrieval systems, without written permission from the author, except for the use of brief quotations in a book review.

Cover designed by Lynnette Bonner.

CHAPTER ONE

Two breaking-and-entering cases, two assaults, one bribery and—Misty Lake flipped through the last few files—a couple of narcotics possession charges.

She'd returned from a bathroom break to find fresh files on her desk. So much for leaving work at a decent hour. It was already four forty-five, about the time normal people were finishing up on a Friday. A couple of summer interns wandered past her open door, laughing. One poked her head in. "Have a great weekend!"

"You too." She barely looked up from her desk.

How would she manage these new cases on top of the work that'd piled up? She'd already known she wouldn't see a weekend off for the rest of the summer. Now she'd have to forgo sleeping as well.

When a knock sounded, she was grateful for the reprieve. Until she looked up.

And here she'd thought things couldn't get worse.

Tate Steele stood in her open doorway, smiling in that irritating, charming way of his. The man was drop-dead gorgeous—and knew it. His perfectly cut suit—probably some Italian designer—showed off his fit physique. Somehow, though all the attorneys at the DA's office wore business attire, he managed to look overdressed. Tate was just a couple of inches taller than her five-ten frame, but he took up a lot of space. She blamed that on his oversize ego.

"Leland wants to see us."

She groaned, glancing at the calendar always open on her monitor. "We don't have a meeting on my schedule."

"Just you and me." Tate's eyes sparkled, bringing out specks of blue in the hazel.

No wonder he was smiling. Any opportunity to ingratiate himself with the boss.

She didn't bother to ask what it was about. The district attorney didn't need an excuse to summon his prosecutors.

"He wants you to bring your new cases," Tate said.

"Why?"

Tate, who was not burdened by mountains of files, just shrugged.

She gathered the paperwork and preceded him to the stairwell, their footsteps echoing on the wood planks. One story up, they made their way to the DA's suite, which was a lot fancier than the windowless offices where she and Tate and the other ADAs toiled their days away.

An administrative assistant directed them to a conference room, and Misty led the way through the open door. Rich, dark wood paneled three of the walls. The fourth had windows overlooking the neighboring buildings. Most of their meetings took place downstairs. She'd only been in this room once, when she'd been hired two years before. She still sometimes missed the slower pace of the suburban district where she used to work. Back then, she'd longed for more exciting cases. What was that expression? *Be careful what you wish for.*

District Attorney Leland Humphrey waved them in, a cell

phone pressed to his ear. He was in his early sixties with smooth, tanned skin, and despite the white hair, looked younger than his years. Seated at the far end of a long cherry table, he leaned back, nodding as if the person on the phone could see. "That's great, Damien." He indicated the space beside him, and Misty set the files down and rolled out the cushy chair.

She'd expected Tate to sit across from her, but instead, he slid into the seat on her opposite side.

Leland smiled at them and shrugged, his version of an apology, she assumed, for making them wait. "Let Cecelia know if there's anything we can..." A pause, then, "All right, sounds good."

He ended the call and slid the phone into his pocket. "My brother. Always got something going on." His jovial expression faded, and he gave Misty that intense look she remembered from their first meeting. "How *are* you?"

The question made her stomach swoop. She hated when people did that—emphasized the *are* with that annoyingly compassionate tone.

"I'm fine, thanks."

"After everything that happened," he said, "you must be dealing with some residual—"

"I'm working through it." Her recent kidnapping was the last thing Misty wanted to talk about. That was what her counselor was for.

How many people got kidnapped twice in their life? And by the same person, no less? But Vasco Ramón was now dead, along with most of his men. Those who'd survived were in jail awaiting trial. She prayed daily that the prosecutors assigned to their cases would care more about justice than expediency.

In other words, that they'd be more like her and less like Tate Steele.

"It can't be easy, but I'm sure you're handling it well." The expression on Leland's face—a smile dimmed by worry—told Misty that he was not sure at all. "Unfortunately, you're falling behind on your work."

"I've got it under control. Some cases take longer—"

"Which is why," Leland said, shutting her up, "I've asked Tate to join us."

She glanced at her coworker and saw a hint of surprise on his face. So, he hadn't known. This wasn't Tate's fault, but she glared at him anyway. As if she needed *his* help.

She forced a relaxed expression when she turned back to her boss. "I appreciate the offer, but I can handle the job."

"Nobody would blame you if you couldn't," Leland said. "You've gone through a trauma. It's no surprise it's affecting your work."

"It's not affecting my work." She tried very hard not to let her frustration show.

"Misty." Leland reached out as if he might pat her hand. She wasn't in the mood for a pseudo-father-figure patronizing her. He pulled back at the last second, but she could feel his desire to comfort her as if she were a damaged child. "I'm worried you're not getting enough rest. From what I hear, you're the first through the doors every morning and the last to leave."

He was calling her out for being a conscientious employee?

"I appreciate your dedication to the job," Leland continued, "but you need to take care of yourself, especially now." The DA's focus shifted to Tate. "Your workload is lighter right now."

"I've had a couple of cases dropped, a number plea-bargained, so—"

"I admire your efficiency. I'm hoping some of that will rub off."

Rub off? As if Misty should be more like *Tate?* Settling for plea deals, dropping cases he couldn't win—that was *admirable?*

The man cared nothing about justice.

"Since you two are friends," Leland said to Tate, "you already know about Misty's trauma."

Friends? Hardly.

"More than anyone else in the office," the DA continued, "you're aware of what she went through this summer."

Somehow, Misty managed not to growl as her boss talked about her as if she weren't in the room.

Tate said, "I'm sure it hasn't been easy."

"It's been fine." Misty didn't bother to look away from her boss. "I don't need help."

"You've got some free time." Leland kept his focus on Tate as if she hadn't spoken. "She needs a hand."

"Sir, I don't need—"

"—I'm happy to do what I can."

Of course he was. Sycophant.

Leland wore a pleased smile as if he were doing her a great favor.

In his defense, he was trying to help her. She should be thankful and gracious.

She felt anything but.

"This is not up for debate." Leland's fatherly expression only increased her frustration. He meant well, but she could do her job—and do it a lot better than Tate Steele.

"I'm worried about you," Leland added.

"I appreciate that, sir, but honestly, I'm doing all right."

"You'll be even better if you let yourself rest." Leland's eyebrows lifted, his chin dipped, and he gazed at her over his glasses. "And learn to accept help every once in a while." He pulled the stack of cases Misty had brought closer and flipped through them. In the silence, Misty tried very hard to hide her anger. She might not be the flatterer Tate was, but she didn't need to antagonize the boss.

Finally, he closed the last file. "These seem pretty straightforward. You shouldn't have any trouble dispatching them quickly. The two of you work together on it." He slid the pile back to Misty. "Tate's great at coming up with plea deals that satisfy all parties. Take the opportunity to learn from him." He pushed back in his chair and stood.

With no choice, she stood as well, plastering on a smile she was sure hid little of her brewing frustration. "Thank you, sir."

Tate led the way to the door and opened it, standing aside so she could go first. She usually didn't mind gentlemanly behavior, but it was the last thing she wanted at that moment. She sent him a look she hoped would scald as she passed.

If he noticed it, he gave no indication.

She was halfway across the plush reception area when Leland's administrative assistant spoke. "Misty, a call came in for you, and they forwarded it up here. Jeffrey Cofer?"

A defense attorney she'd gone up against more than once. "Which case?"

The woman held out a piece of paper. "Parks. Frederick Parks."

Misty snatched it.

"What's that?" Leland spoke over Misty's shoulder. She hadn't realized he'd followed them out. "You know the case?"

"It's from when I worked in Middlesex County. I'm sure it's nothing important." She pocketed the message. "I'll call him back." Later. When she wasn't seething with anger and burning with shame because her boss didn't think she could hack the job.

And he'd assigned her least favorite person in the office to help.

CHAPTER TWO

Tate followed Misty into the stairwell. As annoyed as Misty was, he was excited about the opportunity Leland had given him. He'd hoped that his hard work would be noticed, and apparently, it had been. If he could prove himself useful, maybe he could move into the opening in white-collar crimes, where he'd have a better shot at meeting the city's business elite. He didn't plan to spend the rest of his life slogging away as a prosecutor.

District Attorney Tate Steele... It had a ring to it.

Judge...?

Supreme Court Justice...?

Someday, maybe. He needed to focus on the here and now, even though the future was always beckoning him. God had good things in store for him. He trusted that, trusted that he'd be successful, that he'd be rewarded for his hard work and his integrity. His father had always impressed upon him the way the world worked, and Tate was doing his best to follow Dad's advice. Anything worth doing was worth doing well. Any job worth having was worth excelling at.

Tate had known Misty since law school, and she'd always been a worthy rival. But since her kidnapping, she'd been slipping. She needed to learn to hide her feelings better, especially in front of the boss. Leland had the power to direct both their futures, and Misty had done nothing in that meeting to ingratiate herself with him.

She reached their floor and banged through the door at nearly a run.

"Wait up," he called.

She didn't slow and didn't turn as she stomped to her office and whipped the door to close it between them.

He managed to catch it before it slammed in his face. "I'm glad we're being adults about this."

"Go away." She yanked the cord that connected her computer to the monitor and shoved her laptop into a leather bag.

"Where are you going?"

"It's"—she glanced at her watch—"five thirty on a Friday night."

"You haven't left the office before me since—"

"Well, I am today." She shoved the new case files—and a bunch more from the top of her messy desk—into the bag. Obviously, she intended to work from home.

"I'll walk with you. Just let me—"

"What part of 'go away' is unclear to you?"

"We have work to do."

She paused, took a breath, and glared at him. "I'm taking the night off."

"Big date?"

She flinched as if he'd wounded her, and maybe he had. As far as he knew, Misty didn't have a boyfriend. She kept to herself. She never attended social functions hosted by the other ADAs. And, by the expression on her face, she wasn't dating anyone.

"Look," he said, "I didn't ask for this, either. Okay? I have a life outside of work." Tate managed to stifle the next words that wanted to spill out. *Unlike you.*

"Some of us take the job seriously," she said.

"What's that supposed to mean?"

"What is it they call you?" She flipped the cover of her laptop bag closed and hefted it onto her shoulder. "The 'Plea Master'? That's the only reason Leland wants me to work with you—to get the cases settled as fast as possible."

"That's the job, Misty. We get assigned cases, we move them through the system."

"Really? I thought the job was justice."

"Oh, come on. You don't have to go all Atticus Finch on every drug arrest."

"Atticus Finch was a defense attorney. We're prosecutors, in case you forgot."

A deep breath kept his exasperation from leaking out. He took a second to get his emotions under control, then plastered on the smile that worked on almost every woman he'd ever met. "Let's not do this. You heard Leland. He wants us to get these taken care of."

"I'll take care of them."

Every woman but Misty Lake.

She crossed the room toward the door, which he was blocking. "Move."

"We're going to work on them together because that's what *our boss* wants us to do. Whether we like it or not."

"Heaven forbid you should disobey the boss. I saw a scuff on his shoe. Maybe you should have licked it clean."

Apparently, the gloves were off. "What is your problem?"

"Seriously. Move."

Another breath for patience. "Look, I get that you're angry.

I'd prefer you not take it out on me, since none of this is my fault."

Her shoulders lowered the tiniest bit. She'd shoved her hair into a messy ponytail, and little strands stuck out by her face. Normally, Misty was unruffled and put-together, her white-blond hair gathered in some sort of clip or bun thing. Her makeup was always perfect. Her clothing fashionable. But she'd ditched her suit jacket earlier, and her blouse was coming untucked.

He sort of liked this unkempt version. It reminded him that she was human. That her sharp edges could be smoothed. "You deserve a night off." Not that he'd have minded poring over the cases with her, maybe sharing take-out.

Sharing laughs. Sharing...

Ugh, why did his mind always go there with this woman? Sure, she was gorgeous, but she loathed him. And frankly, he wasn't her biggest fan right now either.

"I swear," Misty said, "if you don't get out of my way, I'll whack you with my bag and scream."

He couldn't help it. He laughed.

Bright red patches rose on her cheeks. He was definitely pushing his luck.

Shutting up, he lifted his hands and backed out of her office, though not far enough that she could get by without bumping into him. "Tomorrow, then."

She glared, but he could see her mind working. Probably trying to come up with some reason why tomorrow wouldn't work.

After a long pause, she nodded. "Fine."

"No sense coming into the office. You want to come to my apartment?" Tate had been shocked the first time he'd seen Misty in the lobby of his building. All the places in the city she could have moved to, and she'd chosen the same building he had.

"My place," she said. "Tomorrow at eight, if you manage to roll yourself out of bed that early."

"Golly, how is it a nice girl like you isn't married?"

She moved toward him, and he managed to step out of the way an instant before she rammed into him.

Well, this should be fun.

CHAPTER THREE

Somehow, Misty had managed to get a couple hours of sleep, despite poring over case files—and seething with anger—all evening. She'd awakened before dawn with one thought on her mind.

She owed Tate an apology.

It wasn't his fault Leland had assigned him to help her. It certainly wasn't Tate's fault that she'd fallen behind.

She hated to admit it, even to herself, but being kidnapped—again—had rattled her.

It shouldn't have happened. If she'd been wiser, it wouldn't have. When Summer realized that the man who'd kidnapped them in Mexico seven years earlier was in Boston—and had Summer in his sights—she'd offered to send Misty bodyguards, but Misty had refused them, thinking her overly protective older sister was only being paranoid. She'd told Leland what was going on. He'd assigned a couple of cops to escort her from the office to court and home—essentially, to be with her whenever she was outside.

If she'd taken the threat seriously, she'd have been safe. But she'd been in a hurry to get to court that Monday, and the guards had taken a break—her fault because she'd neglected to share her schedule. She'd figured she could make it from her office to the courthouse without incident. What could happen in a three-minute walk?

Such arrogant naïveté. Ramón's men must have been watching her, waiting for the opportunity—and she'd handed it to them. She'd been grabbed and shoved into the back of a van.

And then rescued, thank God.

She'd been off her game ever since, second-guessing her decisions, agonizing over every criminal she didn't put behind bars. When they were locked up, they couldn't hurt anybody. When she failed to get them off the streets and they hurt someone else...

That was on her.

Having now been a victim twice, she understood the seriousness of her job more than most prosecutors could. Including Tate, who'd tried to be kind and gracious, even when she'd treated him with contempt.

After reading her Bible, exercising, and dressing for the day, Misty stepped outside her building and breathed in the early morning air. The freshness should have brought calm, not anxiety. She had to get out there, though. Walk. Be independent. Every day, she had to do it, no matter how much it scared her.

She turned toward her favorite coffee shop, forcing her feet to move at a normal pace. No running scared.

The sun was shining, the birds twittering in the trees planted along the sidewalk. It promised to be another perfect summer day. Another day she'd spend inside.

Which, she admitted, was part of the appeal of working so hard. Being away from her home or her office, by herself... It scared her. She knew Ramón and his men couldn't hurt her now, but that didn't keep her from feeling spooked. Looking over her shoulder. Tensing every time a car drove by.

Breathe, Misty. Just breathe. She was safe. God was with her. He'd been with her. He'd sent Grant to save her. And then to save Summer. As amazing as Grant had been—and it'd been a sight to see—it was God who'd saved her from Ramón, not once but twice.

Why did she doubt Him?

She was new to this faith thing. Summer had told her about the Lord not long after they'd both been rescued that summer. Their mother had tried to raise them to believe in God, but it was hard, living in that house with her father.

Now she was coming to understand that God wasn't like the abusive drunk who'd raised her. God was a good, good Father, and He never left her.

She was safe in His arms, even when the world was falling apart around her.

Frustrated as she was with Leland, he wasn't wrong. She'd worked nonstop since the kidnapping and rescue, only taking two days off to go to Coventry when Misty's cousin, Jon, proposed to his girlfriend, movie star Denise Masters. That had been six weeks back.

Autumn was coming. In another week, students would start showing up at campuses all over the city—a hundred and fifty thousand of them. Before she knew it, the leaves would change. And she'd have missed all of it.

She reached the coffee shop and stepped inside, inhaling the scents of fresh brew and yeasty pastries. The place was already busy.

Behind the counter, a seventy-something man lifted his hand in a wave. "Good morning, Miss Lake." His voice held a heavy Farsi accent. "Where's your computer?"

A year before, Farbod Hashemi had been mugged and assaulted on his way to the bank with the day's earnings. She'd been the prosecutor, and the assailant was still in prison. Mr. Hashemi had been trying to give her free coffee ever since.

"Working from home this morning," she said. Often on Saturdays, she worked at the coffee shop, happier to be around people than not.

"The usual?" he asked, despite the queue of people in front of her.

"I'll need two coffees and two cinnamon rolls today."

"Big date?" His eyes sparkled.

"*Work* date," she corrected. "Take your time." She found a table by the window to wait, thinking through the new case files one more time. She needed a plan or else Tate would barrel in and take over—and she couldn't have that. She didn't trust him to handle her cases the way she would.

She'd perused the files the night before. Most were straightforward, and only a couple involved violent crimes. On those, she'd dig in her heels. People who hurt people needed to be behind bars for as long as possible. They could choose what to do with that time—double-down on their criminal ways or seek a better path. But as long as they were in prison, they couldn't harm the innocent.

One case had her scratching her head. The defendant, an employee of a company called Thornebrook Enterprises, was accused of offering a bribe to a city official to speed up the permits for a building project. Misty had checked the address on her laptop the night before and found a corner lot not far from The Fens, the city park where the famous ballpark got its name.

She didn't generally prosecute white-collar crimes, but one of the lawyers in that division had resigned. Until the position was filled, the other ADAs were pitching in to take up the slack.

Why had the employee offered the bribe? Had he been in a

hurry to break ground? Or was there some reason why the permits wouldn't have been issued?

Had the permits been issued?

Had Thornebrook been behind the offered bribe, or had their employee acted alone?

But what really had her wondering was the name of the man's lawyer, a pricey and well-known defense attorney who took on high-profile cases involving big money and famous people.

Not low-level construction contractors.

Misty was missing something.

Her cell rang, and the screen displayed a name she hadn't seen in a couple of years. "Hey, Judi. How are you?"

"I'm glad I caught you." Judi had been one of the other prosecutors Misty had worked with in Middlesex County. "I don't know if you heard, but Freddy Parks was released from prison. His sentence was overturned on appeal."

"How did that happen?" Had Misty screwed up? How had she not heard until now?

"Nothing you did," Judi was quick to say. "The cop who arrested him was fired for corruption. A lot of his cases are getting overturned."

"But Parks confessed. The man he assaulted nearly died."

"He claims the cop coerced a confession. The point is, didn't he threaten you?"

Freddy Parks hadn't been the first defendant to scream threats at her as he was escorted from the courtroom, and he wouldn't be the last. Though, in Parks's case, she'd believed he was deadly serious. The man had been violent. Terrifying.

Then, about a year ago, he'd asked to see her. She'd never actually spoken to him, but apparently it meant something to him that she'd tried because he'd sent her a note thanking her and apologizing for his threats.

Mr. Hashemi called her name, and she waved to indicate she'd heard. To Judi, she said, "I don't think I need to worry about Parks."

"If you say so," Judi said. "But keep your eyes open, anyway. Hey, let's catch up sometime."

"Sure, sure," Misty said, knowing they never would. "Thanks for calling."

She grabbed her order and paid the barista, despite the kind owner's insistence that she didn't owe anything. But a peace offering for Tate that cost her nothing wouldn't be much of a gift. Hopefully, Tate wasn't the type of guy to hold a grudge.

Phone in her pocket and wallet hanging from her wrist, Misty prayed the whole way back to her apartment building. As cavalier as she'd sounded on the phone, the idea of Freddy Parks showing up didn't sit well. As if she didn't have enough anxiety already.

She was also praying for the coming meeting. She would need God's help to get through it. She'd need a little humility to accept the help she wasn't sure she needed. She'd need a lot of humility to offer the apology Tate deserved.

She would arrive at the meeting barely on time, as usual. Tate would be early, as usual.

Not a great way to start.

When the elevator opened on the eighth floor, she stepped out and hurried down the hallway, past her neighbors' closed apartment doors, and around the corner toward hers. No Tate. *Phew.*

For the first time, she'd actually beaten him to a meeting.

She crouched and set the coffees and pastries on the floor so she could unlock her door.

When she stood again, a hand slid around her mouth.

She gasped, but it only clamped harder.

A man whispered in her ear, but the words were drowned

out by panic. She struggled to get free, but he snaked his arm around her middle and yanked her back, away from the safety of her apartment.

She tried to wrench away. If she could only scream... She elbowed him in the ribs.

"Oomph. Quit." The words were whispered but vehement.

It had to be Freddy Parks. He'd made good on his threats. She remembered the pictures she'd seen of the man's victim, bloodied and bruised, clinging to life. Would she be clinging to life when this was over? Could she hope for that after Freddy had vowed to kill her?

He dragged her into the concrete stairway. The heavy fire door slammed behind them, cutting her off from any hope of help.

The man pressed her up against the wall and flipped her around to face him, holding her in place with his body. Never taking his hand off her mouth.

"It's Tate. Listen to me. I'm not going to hurt you. It's Tate, Misty. It's Tate. Please, please, quit fighting me."

His words, and his image, registered.

Tate? What in the—?

"I'm going to let you go. Don't scream. You can't scream, okay? He'll hear you. I'm sure he's armed."

This man had just accosted her, dragged her into a deserted stairwell, and now wanted her to promise she wouldn't scream? What was he talking about?

Was he insane?

"Misty," he said. "You know me. Please, trust me."

She didn't, she couldn't.

But...but she'd known Tate for years. This didn't make sense. But it was Tate.

"Please?" he said again.

She couldn't speak with his palm covering her mouth, so she nodded.

He removed his hand, and she gasped for air, shaking off the terror.

Tate backed to the far wall, arms lifted in surrender. "I'm sorry." He was still whispering. "We have to get out of here."

"What are you—?"

"There's somebody in your apartment." He started to pull her up the stairs.

She yanked away. "I'm not going anywhere with you! Why did you grab me like that? How dare you!"

"I'm sorry. You're right. I panicked." He lifted his hands and moved in close, holding eye contact. "Listen to me." His words were low, fast. "When I got to your floor, I looked through the window in the stairway door"—he nodded behind her—"and saw a man going into your apartment. He had a gun. I thought you were in there. I was about to try to break in when I heard the elevator ding. Thank God you're not... But the thing is, the guy is in there. Right now. Waiting for you. I already called nine-one-one. Until they get here, I want you to be safe. So we're going to my apartment. Okay? Or, if there's somebody else's apartment, not on this floor, we can go there."

She worked to make sense of what he was saying. There was an intruder in her apartment?

"Who was it?"

"How would I know?" Tate took her hand and started up the stairs, tugging her behind him. "Let's go!"

She could either trust him or not.

She would have been alone with him in her home, so why would he lure her to his? Fear and panic pulsed inside her, making her want to run, to scream. But instead, she decided to trust him. She hurried up the stairs.

He followed. "Tenth floor."

Thirty seconds later, they reached his apartment. He pushed her inside. "I'm going back to watch, see if I can get a look at the guy."

"What? No!" She clutched his wrist. "Stay here where it's safe."

"If he gets away, we'll have no idea who—"

"I think I know who it is." She paused to suck in a breath. Terror had her heart pounding, had her breathing as if she'd been running.

"Who?" Tate's tone was demanding, almost angry.

"A guy I put away. His sentence was overturned. I just found out."

His gaze flicked from her to the door and back. Then, he said, "If it's him, I'll be able to confirm it. Do. Not. Leave." He disappeared out the door, slamming it in his wake.

CHAPTER FOUR

Tate rushed back down the stairs and peered through the window in the stairway door. Waiting, waiting for the intruder to give up and come out.

But nothing happened.

Five minutes passed. Ten.

And then a uniformed police officer walked into view and knocked on her door.

Tate pushed into the hallway. "I'm the one who called."

The cop turned to him, one hand on his gun. "What's your name?"

Another cop came from around the corner.

"I'm Tate Steele. The intruder is in there, or was a few minutes ago. The woman who lives there is upstairs in my apartment. I headed her off before she went in."

"So there's no occupant in there? Just the intruder?"

"Right." At least he assumed so. Misty hadn't mentioned a roommate.

The cop toed the bag beside her door. "Those hers?"

"She set them down before I got to her." Tate started toward them, thinking he'd pick them up, but the cop waved him off.

"Leave it." He kept his voice low. "Your apartment number?"

Tate gave it to him.

"Go back up and wait. Someone will be up in a few minutes."

Tate was tempted to argue. He wanted to see how this played out. But it wasn't as if he could help.

He climbed the stairs again, pressed the keypad to unlock his door, and entered his apartment to find Misty pacing in his living room. She froze halfway between his leather sectional and the windows overlooking the city.

"Well?"

"Cops are going in. They said to stay here."

"What did the guy look like?" She crossed the room toward him, lifting her phone. "This is Freddy Parks. Is this who you saw?"

"Freddy...Frederick Parks? Didn't his attorney call you last night? Wasn't that the message—?"

"I didn't call him back yet. I'm guessing this is why he reached out."

Tate glanced at the mugshot on her screen. "I only saw him from the side and the back. He was tall and built."

She took the phone back and scrolled the screen. "Says here Freddy's five-ten. He was one-sixty when he was arrested."

"This guy was bigger than that."

"Taller, or just bigger?"

"He might've been five-ten. But—"

"Freddy's been in prison a few years," Misty said. "He could have bulked up. What do you think? Could it have been him?"

She looked determined to get a definitive answer, and Tate couldn't blame her.

He pulled out a chair. "Why don't you sit? There's nothing we can do until the police come up. Maybe they caught him."

She settled in the chair but seemed too keyed up to relax.

"Have you eaten?" he asked.

"I'm not hungry."

He filled two glasses with water and set them on the table before sitting.

She grabbed one and took a few sips, then a few more. "Thank you."

"Sure."

"I mean for... I'm sorry. I didn't know it was you. I panicked." The admission seemed to pain her.

"You don't owe me an apology." He could still feel her in his arms, fighting. Terrorized. "I'm sorry I scared you. I didn't know what else to do. I didn't want the guy to know you were out there. I didn't want you to make any noise. I thought you'd hear me." He'd said who he was, over and over. She hadn't heard him or hadn't been able to focus on his words. He felt like a jerk, but what could he have done differently?

His apartment was too quiet. If he were alone, he'd have sports playing on the TV, or music coming from his speakers. Instrumentals. A little Vivaldi would settle his nerves, but he didn't know if it would relax Misty or key her up more.

She leaned her forearms against his table. Her hands were visibly shaking.

"You're safe here."

"I know. Thanks to you. You saved my life."

"We don't know what would have happened." But he couldn't imagine a scenario that ended better than her being safely tucked in his apartment.

"How did the intruder not see you?"

"Oh. Well..." He didn't really want to explain that part.

She tilted her head to the side.

"I was early, because...you know."

"You always are."

"If you're not five minutes early, you're ten minutes late. Or so my father always said."

That almost garnered a smile.

"But then I realized maybe showing up before eight o'clock on a Saturday morning wouldn't be polite. I was lurking in the stairwell."

"Lurking?"

He shrugged. "And then I saw that guy. He pressed the code to open your door, and I would have thought he was somebody you knew. Or maintenance. But as he was stepping in, he pulled a ski mask over his head. And I'm pretty sure I caught the outline of a gun stuck in the waistband of his pants at his lower back."

Misty's already fair skin paled further.

"I was stunned. He had the door closed before I processed what I'd seen. I assumed you were in there. I called nine-one-one and I was about to try to break down the door or something. But then the elevator dinged. I ducked around the corner because...I don't know why."

"Could have been an accomplice."

Probably not, but it was nice of her to say so. "Conceivably. But it was you. And...well, you know what happened next."

"You nearly gave me a heart attack."

"Sorry about that."

She unclasped her hands. Slowly, she reached toward him, laid her cool fingers on his forearm. "Truly, Tate. Thank you. After how poorly I treated you yesterday... You were willing to put yourself in danger to protect me."

"Like I was going to hold yesterday against you. If Leland asked *you* to help *me*, I'd have been furious."

"You wouldn't have taken it out on me, though."

Maybe not, but it seemed petty to agree.

"I brought you a peace offering and everything."

"Coffee and donuts?" He smiled, remembering the items outside her door.

"Not donuts," she said, affronted. "Cinnamon rolls."

"Even better."

"I'll have to owe you."

"You owe me nothing. I'm just glad—"

The loud knock made them both jump.

"Police," the man called.

Tate went to the door, praying they'd caught the guy.

CHAPTER FIVE

Misty hopped up from the table and stood beside Tate as he answered the door.

"The apartment was empty." The man stepped in and introduced himself as Officer Gamble. He had close-cropped hair and hard eyes, which he leveled on Tate. "You sure you saw somebody go in?"

Misty swung her gaze to him. Maybe this whole thing had been a mistake.

"Absolutely positive." Tate's words held no hint of doubt. "He wore black jeans, a gray T-shirt, and tennis shoes. If not for the fact that he pulled the ski mask over his face, I might've thought he was a friend. And the gun under his shirt."

"Maybe you were watching the wrong apartment," the cop said.

"I wasn't," Tate said. "And if I was, then there's an armed intruder on the eighth floor terrorizing somebody else."

The cop ignored that. "What were you doing there?"

Tate told the cop the same story he'd told Misty—that he'd arrived early for their meeting and was waiting in the stairwell until eight o'clock so he didn't show up too early.

"Mmm-hmm."

Did Misty hear suspicion in those two syllables? Her nerves were already frayed. She didn't need this cop making things worse.

She wandered to the windows in Tate's living room. Though his apartment had the same floor plan as hers, it felt different. His furnishings were more expensive, his sectional and tables sleeker, more masculine. The biggest difference, though, was the view. From her window, she overlooked the street and the neighboring building. But Tate's apartment was on the opposite side, his windows affording him an expansive view of the city. She gazed over shorter structures to the Charles River in the distance.

Behind her, Gamble said, "Description?"

"I didn't see his face." Tate sounded frustrated. "I'd guess he was my height or a little shorter. Bodybuilder type. I didn't see any hair because of the hat, which turned out to be a ski mask." Misty turned from the view to find Tate giving her an apologetic look. "That's all I know."

"Skin color?" the cop asked.

Tate closed his eyes. "Caucasian, but not pale." They opened again. "So maybe swarthy, or maybe he just had a tan."

"Weight?"

"One-eighty? Big upper body."

"How'd he get in?" the cop asked.

"He had the code. He pressed the keypad."

Officer Gamble swung his gaze to Misty. "Who else has the code to your apartment?"

"Nobody."

Another "Mmm-hmm" had her hackles rising.

"You have a roommate?"

"I live alone."

"Ever had a roommate?"

"Not in this apartment, no."

The cop made a note. "Boyfriends? Exes? Parents? Siblings?"

"The only person who has the code to my apartment is me. Oh, and my sister, Summer, and I promise you—"

"So someone else *does* have the code." The cop's eyebrows rose.

"I'd forgotten about Summer. But it wouldn't be—"

"Where can we find her?"

"She wouldn't have given the code to anybody. She's a personal security agent and the most protective sister in the world. Trust me, she had nothing to do with this."

The cop stared at her, unsmiling, pen poised over his paper.

Misty rattled off Summer's phone number. "Just give me a chance to tell her what happened or she'll freak out."

"Call her as soon as we're done here. Who else?"

"Nobody."

"That's what you said before. Think before you speak this time."

"She's had a fright," Tate said. "Why don't you give her a break?"

The cop ignored him.

Misty had dealt with her share of overly aggressive men. She wouldn't let this one get to her. "There's nobody else. I'm careful about my personal security."

He waited another few moments, then asked, "Enemies?"

"A man was released from prison recently," she said. "Frederick Parks. Before Parks was sent away, he threatened me."

"Why?"

"I'm a prosecutor."

At that, the cop's eyes widened. And maybe his countenance softened the slightest bit.

"He wasn't happy I put him away, as you can imagine,"

Misty said. "He was supposed to be in for ten years, but his case was overturned on appeal."

Gamble wrote the name down, then spoke into the radio on his shoulder. "Possible suspect, Frederick Parks."

A scratchy voice said something in response, but she didn't catch it.

"Anyone else?"

"I can't think of anyone specific."

"She puts bad guys away for a living," Tate said. "Could be anybody she's prosecuted, their families, fellow gang members—"

"But nobody else comes to mind?" Gamble asked her.

"Not that I can think of."

A knock sounded, and a second police officer stepped in. He was pale and freckly-faced with skin that probably burned at the mention of sun. He was so skinny it looked like he had trouble keeping his shirt tucked in. He introduced himself as Officer Murray. "Had a look at the security tapes. A man took the elevator to the eighth floor at seven fifty-five. He walked to your apartment door and let himself in. We got the call at seven fifty-seven. At eight-oh-one, he let himself out of the apartment, walked to the elevator, and took it down. He left the building at eight-oh-three."

"So he left right after I intercepted Misty," Tate said. "When I was getting her up here."

So close. She didn't want to think about how close she'd been to coming face to face with the intruder.

"You get an ID?" Gamble asked his partner.

"Kept his head down." Murray held out a piece of paper. "Had the manager print a still shot. This is the best we could do."

Misty took it and looked at the image. It was clearer than she'd have expected, but that didn't matter. The intruder wore a hat—a rolled-up ski mask, according to Tate—that hid his hair color. The shot had been taken from above, so it was hard to tell his weight. He looked bigger than Freddy Parks, but it'd been years since she'd seen the man.

Tate sidled close and looked. "That's him."

Gamble took the image and studied it. "No gloves. Maybe we'll get—"

"He's wearing them," Officer Murray said. "They're clear, hard to make out in this image, but we could see them in others."

"We'll have the crime lab see if they can find anything." To Misty, he said, "Stay out of there until we do. You'll need to change the code on your door, maybe get an alarm system. We'll find out if Parks was in the city. Otherwise, we don't have a lot to go on."

"That's it?" Tate said. "She's just supposed to—"

"Let's go down and find out what's missing." Gamble acted as if Tate hadn't spoken.

Misty could feel him seething beside her, but there was only so much the police could do. She grabbed her wallet and followed the two police officers out the door, turning to see that Tate was still standing in his kitchen, looking unsure.

"You coming?"

He seemed relieved as he followed her out.

Gamble led the way to the stairwell and down two flights. When he reached the door leading to her hallway, he peered through the window.

Behind her, Tate said, "See her apartment door?"

"This is where you were?" Gamble looked at where Tate stood behind her, a few steps up the half-flight.

"Like I said, I was—"

"Trying not to be rude. I heard you." But Gamble didn't look convinced as he yanked open the heavy door.

She followed to find her apartment wide open. A man was

kneeling at the door, dusting the keypad. Beside him, the two coffee cups and the bag of pastries hadn't been moved. She snatched both.

Her neighbor's door opened, and Ruth stepped out. The woman was in her fifties, broad and a little pudgy in the face, with bottle-red hair and bright red lipstick. "Omigosh, are you all right?"

Misty quelled a sigh. "Someone broke into my apartment."

"Was it that man this morning? With the gray T-shirt?"

Gamble stepped in. "You saw him?"

"Leaving, yeah. I had a peephole put in my door to keep an eye on things. You never can be too careful."

Plus, Ruth was the nosiest person Misty had ever met, and the hole in her door allowed her to watch everything. Maybe that'd be a good thing now.

"What'd he look like?" Gamble asked.

"I just saw him from behind. Gray T-shirt, jeans. He wore one of those skullcap things like gangsters wear." She shifted her attention back to Misty. "Is this related to the kidnapping? I do wish you'd let me tell your story. The listeners would eat it up."

"What listeners?" Gamble asked.

"I'm a journalist." Ruth seemed to grow taller than her five-two frame with the words. "I do some work for the *Herald*, plus I have a true crime podcast. I've been trying to get Misty to be a guest." She gave Misty a wink. "Or at least let me write her story."

Ruth was so persistent that Misty cringed whenever the woman caught her in the hallway. Which was too often.

To Misty, Gamble said, "You were kidnapped?"

"All the people involved in that are in prison or dead."

"You're sure?"

"I'll give you the name of the FBI agent who ran the investigation. You can follow up with him." To Ruth, she said,

"Thanks for checking on me." Before the woman could protest, Misty started to move into her apartment.

"Try not to disturb anything." Gamble stood in the way, keeping her from stepping in. "We'll need to get your fingerprints to rule them out."

"They're probably on file, but I'm happy to give them again."

Gamble didn't move, just looked beyond her to Tate. "And yours."

"Also on file," he said. "And I've never been in her apartment before."

"We're working on a project together," Misty said. "That's why we were meeting this morning."

From near her door, Ruth said, "What kind of project?"

Misty ignored her.

Gamble said, "Ma'am, if you'd go back inside your place, please. I'll send someone in to take your statement."

Misty gave her a kind smile, and she returned to her home. Her door slammed, but that didn't mean Ruth was gone. She'd probably stand at her peephole and watch.

Gamble gave his partner a long look Misty couldn't decipher.

And then Murray turned to Tate. "Let's talk out here."

Tate frowned but stayed where he was.

Finally, Gamble stepped into her apartment, and Misty followed, bracing for what she'd find. "Tate hasn't done anything wrong. He kept me from..." Her voice trailed as she looked around.

She'd expected...something different. That her electronics would be gone. That the living room, which she'd tidied that morning, would be messy. She'd imagined all sorts of scenarios—drawers overturned, cabinet doors opened, her things rifled through.

But the place looked exactly as she'd left it.

She wandered through her living area, noting that the throw pillows were tucked against the corners of the couch just like she'd left them. Magazines fanned out on the coffee table. Her remote controls tucked in a basket. Her TV mounted on the wall.

In the kitchen, the plates, forks, and knives she'd pulled out in anticipation of the meeting with Tate were waiting for the cinnamon rolls. Her laptop was on the counter, closed, beside the leather bag she carried it in. She peeked inside and saw all her case files.

She set the pastries, drink holder, and wallet down and turned to the police officer. "I don't understand. Did you guys tidy up?"

"No." Gamble was watching her. "Anything missing?"

"It doesn't look like anything was even touched."

She peeked in cabinets and drawers, not that she had anything worth stealing in there, not unless the intruder was a huge fan of Crate and Barrel stemware.

She moved into the bedroom. Her bed was made, the books always piled on her bedside table, untouched. Catching sight of the Cloisonné box her mother had given her for her thirteenth birthday, she sucked in a breath. She crossed to it and opened the top, praying, praying...

Thank God. The pearl ring she'd inherited when Mom died was still there. It wasn't the only thing in Misty's apartment worth money, but it was the most valuable thing to her.

"Check the drawers and closets," Gamble said.

She did while he stood in the bedroom doorway, taking up far too much space. Aside from movers and delivery people, no man had ever been in her room. Having a uniformed stranger watching her only added to the panic she'd been fighting since

Tate slid his hand over her mouth. "As far as I can tell, nothing is missing."

He nodded, expression grim, as he turned back into her living area. She followed.

The man looked perpetually angry. She hoped he used a different expression for his wife, or the wedding ring on his finger might not stay there for long.

"I don't understand," she said.

"How well do you know Mr. Steele?"

Her empty stomach roiled. "I've known him for years."

"Irrelevant. Every killer, burglar, thief, and drug dealer has been known by people for years, and a lot of those people have no idea who they're dealing with."

"We went to law school together. He's a prosecutor in my office. He puts bad guys away for a living."

"So you trust him."

"He's the one who kept me from walking in on an intruder this morning. Of course I trust him."

"Or he kept you from discovering who'd broken into your home. It feels very convenient that the intruder left at exactly the moment when you and Mr. Steele weren't there to see."

That hadn't occurred to her. She crossed her arms, feeling suddenly chilled in the AC blowing from the ceiling. "I see what you're getting at, but I trust Tate. Why would somebody come in and not take anything?"

"Could be Mr. Steele warned him you were coming, and the intruder didn't have time."

"According to your partner, he had seven minutes, right? Seven minutes is a long time. If he'd been looking for something specific, things would be in disarray. If he'd wanted to loot the place"—she swept her arm around her tidy living area—"he needs lessons. Which tells me that he was waiting for me."

The words sent acid to her stomach, but it was the only logical conclusion.

She sat in one of the wingback chairs that flanked her sofa. She'd survived two kidnappings. What were the chances she'd survive a third?

Or had Parks just planned to take her out? Kill her in her own apartment. Leave her body for maintenance to find after a couple of days, after the neighbors started complaining about the stench.

Her roiling stomach clenched, and she crossed her arms and leaned over.

Impervious to her obvious distress, Gamble said, "Maybe the intruder did go through your things and was careful to put them all back the way he found them."

Would she notice if things had been moved a half inch, her socks placed back in the drawer differently than she'd arranged them?

No. She wouldn't.

"Maybe your 'friend'"—she heard the air quotes, even if he didn't make them—"stopped you in order to give his accomplice time to escape."

As uncomfortable as the thought was, Misty forced herself to consider it. But it didn't make sense. "I have nothing Tate would want."

The cop didn't seem impressed by the confidence in her voice. Was she being foolish not to listen to the man? Not to suspect her colleague?

"Tate and I had a meeting this morning." She straightened up, unwilling to look like a scared victim. "How could he have known I was going to go out for coffee? He couldn't have. I'm out of my apartment fifty, sixty hours a week. We work together, so he knows that. If he wanted to break in, he could do it—or have his accomplice do it—anytime between about seven in the morning and six at night, Monday through Friday. Why would he do it today when he knew I'd be home?" She shook her head, the truth of her words sinking in as they left her mouth. Her tone sounded stronger, more confident, as she continued. "Tate knew I'd be here. He stopped me from walking in on an intruder, just like he said."

The cop watched her a long moment, then nodded. "Just to be sure, we'll be looking into him."

"While you're at it, figure out how the intruder got into my apartment. Because whoever it was, he didn't get the code from me. Or my sister. I'd start with the office manager. They don't know my code, but they have a way to get into every apartment in the building."

The man's lips quirked like he might smile, but he managed to keep it together. "I've been a cop for seventeen years. Might have thought of that."

He might *not* have, if he kept focusing on Tate.

"Get an alarm system." Gamble walked to the still-open door. "Preferably today."

Before he stepped out, Tate stepped in. "You're not planning to stay here, are you?"

She hadn't thought past the next two minutes. "I don't know."

"You should go somewhere safe until you can figure out what's going on."

"Wouldn't be a bad idea." Officer Murray was standing in the hallway. "Chances are, if that guy comes back, we'll show up after he leaves. Change your door code, if you can. I already talked to building maintenance, and they're going to change the master code."

"Do they have any idea how he got in?" Misty asked.

"They're calling the company that installed the locks. Said they'd get back to us. Until then..." Murray shrugged.

Gamble held out a business card. "You have an emergency, call nine-one-one. But if you think of anything helpful, call me, and I'll get you in touch with the detective assigned to the case."

She took it and slid it into her back pocket. "Thank you."

He nodded once. "Be careful."

"Don't worry." After being kidnapped just a couple of months before, she intended to be very careful. In fact, she feared she'd be so careful that she'd never sleep again.

∽

Misty closed the door behind the police officers and gestured to the kitchen table. "I guess we should just...have our meeting." Strange as it felt, she wasn't sure what else to do. "Feel free to put the coffee in the microwave. The cinnamon rolls too. They're better warm. I need to call my sister."

"I'll wait until you can join me." Tate moved into the kitchen and leaned against the countertop.

"Okay. Make yourself at home." She moved into the bedroom as she dialed.

"Good morning." Summer sounded chipper and relaxed, so different from the intense, serious woman she'd been since the kidnapping seven years before. She was still living in Denise's guesthouse in Coventry. Misty had figured she'd go to work for their cousin, Jon, who'd opened a private investigation company, but apparently, Summer had turned down his job offer. After being a personal security agent for years, she was studying fashion. Coventry was good for her. Grant, her new beau, was very good for her. She seemed happier than Misty could ever remember.

She hated that she was about to ruin her day. "Something happened, and I need your help."

"Wow. This is a first."

Misty didn't laugh. "I already know the answer to this question, but you're going to get a call, so... You didn't give the key code to my apartment to anybody, right?"

"Of course not." The humor in her sister's tone was gone. "What happened?"

Misty explained the events of that morning.

"Hold on, Misty." Summer's voice became distant. "Grant, come here. I need your help." A long pause, and then, "Misty, you're on speaker. Grant's here."

"Hey." Grant's voice was deep and concerned.

"I didn't realize you two were together. I didn't mean to pull you away—"

"It's fine," Summer said. "Explain all that again."

Misty repeated what she'd already told Summer. "The guy left while Tate and I were upstairs and before the police showed up."

"What'd he take?" Grant asked.

"Nothing. That's what's so weird. If Tate hadn't seen him, I wouldn't even know someone had been here. Unless I'd walked in on him, which maybe was the goal."

"Thank God for Tate," Summer said. "He was the one at the hospital, right?"

"Right." Misty had forgotten her sister had met Tate that summer when he'd gone to Maine after her kidnapping. "We're working on a couple of cases together, so we had a meeting set for this morning. He lives in my building. I just...I can't make sense of it. I often take my laptop to the coffee shop on Saturday mornings and work, and maybe the guy knew that. Which means he's been watching me."

"He was waiting for you."

"Except he wasn't. He left before the police got there."

"He probably had somebody watching the door. Maybe they

saw the cops show up." Summer's tone was hard, angry. "Any idea who it was?"

"Maybe a man whose conviction was overturned, guy named Parks. Police are looking into it."

"You need to come up here until they figure it out."

Misty had known her sister would say that. The truth was, she was tempted. She could hang out with Summer, get to know Grant better, spend some time with Jon, her favorite cousin. She could enjoy Coventry, Lake Ayasha, the mountains, the hiking. She longed to get out of the city, to relax and listen to the birds sing.

She could leave the city, the intruder, and the cases demanding her attention behind. She could be safe and protected by her big sister again. Let Summer manage the hard stuff.

Like when they were kids.

It was tempting, too tempting. But she was an adult now, with adult responsibilities. Behind every case file on her desk was an accused and a victim. The victims deserved justice. The accused needed to be cleared, set straight, or punished. She wasn't about to foist her job on other ADAs, especially knowing how busy everybody was.

"I have too much work. I can't leave now."

"Nothing is more important than your safety," Summer said. "You can work from here. If you need to go back to the city, I'll go with you. But in the meantime—"

"I'm not going to Coventry."

"Why not?" Summer's demanding tone raised Misty's defenses.

Her phone dinged with an incoming text.

Grant had been quiet throughout the exchange, but it was his name on her screen.

> If you're in your apartment, you need to leave before you say another word, just in case.

Before she could respond, he said, "Did you get that?"

Summer said, "Reconsider your answer."

"Uh..." Misty scrambled to catch up with Grant's worries as she walked out of her bedroom. "Okay, yeah, Summer. You might be right. Hold on a sec."

Tate straightened. "Everything okay?"

"Can we go back to your place? Being here is creeping me out."

"Sure." He noted that she was still on the phone but didn't ask as he grabbed the coffee and cinnamon rolls. "We need sustenance."

She slipped her laptop into its bag, shoved her wallet in there, and followed him out the door, checking to make sure it locked behind her. When they were in the stairwell, she stopped. "I'm out. What's going on?"

Grant answered. "If they planted listening devices, we don't want them to know we know. And we don't want to give them any information."

She'd suspected he was going to say that. Now she really was creeped out.

Realizing she wasn't following, Tate stopped and turned back, brows lowered over worried eyes.

She shook her head. "You really think he planted a bug?"

Tate's eyebrows rose.

"It's just a hunch," Grant said. "I'm going to get someone out from GBPA to do a sweep. Until we know, I want you to stay out of there. Okay?"

"Yeah, all right."

Tate nodded up the stairwell. "Come on."

"Right. Okay." She followed him up, barely aware of her surroundings. Barely aware of Summer's voice on the phone.

"...refuse to be reasonable," Summer said. "I'm going to have them send you a couple of bodyguards."

"No, I can't afford that."

"I can—"

"And you're not covering the cost for me."

"Don't be stubborn," Summer snapped. "Remember the last time you refused security."

As if she'd ever forget. "The police would have kept me safe. It was my fault I was kidnapped. I was stupid. I won't be stupid this time."

"That'd be a—"

"Misty, hold on a second please." Grant's words were followed by silence. She guessed he'd muted the phone. They were probably having a vehement conversation on the other end of the line.

She and Tate reached his floor, and he opened his door for her.

"Sorry." She attempted an apologetic smile but feared it'd looked more like a grimace. "This won't take much longer. My sister's being her typical overprotective self."

"Don't worry about it." Tate set the coffee and pastries on the kitchen table.

Her emotions had ping-ponged between disturbed and panicked for more than an hour. The thought of eating turned her stomach.

Tate had no such issues. He set both coffee cups in the microwave and turned it on. While they warmed, he pulled two plates out of the cabinet and set a pastry on each.

Finally, Grant unmuted the phone. "It's possible the intruder didn't want you to know he was there, and you just got lucky that somebody saw him go in. My guess is that he was searching for something or planting something. If that's the case, then you're probably not in any physical danger."

"That makes sense." Grant's reasoned tone calmed her a little.

"But we can't assume that." Summer's voice held frustration. "You're supposed to be in a secure building, but obviously..."

"I agree," Grant said. "It's also possible that, if the intruder had the code to get into your apartment, maybe he also had access to the video cameras. If so, he'd have known you were in the building, and possibly he even saw your friend getting you out of there. I don't know what the cameras cover."

Her emotions bounced right back to panicked. "He could have seen Tate."

Tate turned from where he was taking their cups out of the microwave, eyes narrowed.

Before she could explain, Grant said, "Maybe they saw his face, but that wouldn't tell them who he was."

"You keep saying 'they.' There was only one man."

"If they were monitoring video cameras," Grant said, "then there were at least two. I'd assume this wasn't a one-person operation."

"That's comforting. Thanks."

"Just calling it like I see it. I'm also thinking...maybe the guy had a spotter outside who told him you were on your way. When you didn't show up, he realized either you weren't coming or you'd known he was there."

"So he *was* waiting for me."

"Maybe," Grant said. "Any of those scenarios could be right. Or none of them. The point is, we don't have enough information."

"Which is why you need to come to Coventry," Summer added.

"As nice as that would be—going up there, pretending all is well—I have a job here." Which felt tenuous after yesterday's meeting. Her boss already thought she was too delicate, too traumatized from the kidnapping, to do her job. "There are victims counting on me. If a criminal ends up back on the street because I shirked my duty—"

"Other prosecutors can handle your cases," Summer said. "Your safety is more important than anything else."

Right. Prosecutors like Tate, who'd find the fastest solution. Prosecutors who had no interest in justice.

"Is it? Like yours is? I suppose that's why you went into hiding and steered clear of danger when you saw Vasco Ramón."

The words hit their mark. Because Summer had done just the opposite.

"It's not the same," she said. "I'm a bodyguard. I'm trained to take on bad guys."

"And I'm a prosecutor, trained to put them away. I need to find a way to be safe here."

"Fine." Though Summer seemed far from *fine* with it. A few beats passed before she spoke again. "Why don't you stay at my place? We'll install an alarm system today. You should be safe there, as long as you don't tell anyone where you're going. And there will be security, whether you want them or not."

Misty considered her sister's Back Bay apartment. She'd only been there once, the day Summer packed what she could fit into Grant's pickup and relocated to Coventry. And what did that say about Misty's relationship with her older sister? She'd avoided Summer for years, desperate to put her past behind her —their abusive father, then the kidnapping. Summer, with her overprotective nature, had hovered. If it were up to her, Misty would never have left home again.

Misty had needed to get away. But she hadn't needed to cut

Summer out the way she had. Misty had hurt her, the one person who'd put herself in harm's way, again and again, to keep her safe. Now Misty was trying hard to repair that relationship. She, Summer, and Krystal had decided they'd all devote themselves to rekindling the sisterhood they'd had as kids.

Misty could start by taking her sister's advice. "That's a good idea," Misty said, "if you don't mind."

"Mind? If it were up to me, you'd be here, tucked into my bedroom. Hey, I'm getting another call—a Boston number. I'm guessing it's that cop. We have a contract with an alarm company. I'll have one installed by the end of the day. You still have the key?" Summer had given it to her the day she'd moved to Coventry.

"Yeah."

"Make yourself at home. Be safe."

"I promise." Misty said goodbye and ended the call.

"What's going on?" Tate set her warmed coffee on his kitchen table and nodded to an empty chair.

She slid into it, feeling like she'd been standing for hours. Somehow, it wasn't even ten o'clock in the morning. "Summer didn't give my key code to anybody, of course. Grant thinks maybe the guy was planting a listening device. Summer is part-owner of a personal security agency, and—"

"Green Beret Protection. Met some of those guys after you were rescued this summer."

"Right. They're going to send someone over to look for bugs. Regardless of what they find, I'm going to stay at my sister's apartment."

"Good. Good idea."

At the microwave's beep, he pulled the pastries out.

The kitchen was filled with the scents of cinnamon and yeast, and suddenly she was hungry.

He set the rolls on the table and sat across from her. "Crazy morning."

"No joke." She picked up her fork and started to cut off a piece, but he cleared his throat.

"I know it's weird," he said, "and maybe... I just thought... Would you mind if I pray real quick? After everything that happened, I just feel like..."

"Yeah. That's... That'd be great." If a little awkward.

Tate slid his hand over hers. "Thank you for protecting Misty this morning, Father. You know exactly what's going on. Show us what to do to keep her safe and expose...whatever it is that's happening here. In Jesus's name..."

"Amen." She swallowed a lump, unsure how to feel. She'd spent a whole lot of time and energy not liking Tate. But it was hard to dislike someone who prayed for her—and with her.

A man who'd possibly saved her life.

CHAPTER SIX

Tate hadn't planned to spend the day with Misty. He had errands to run—the grocery store, the bank. He'd wanted to hit the gym later. He was even supposed to go out that night with a woman he'd met at a friend's wedding.

This would be their second date, made with the optimistic hope that he'd enjoy her company more than he had during their first. If he was ever going to settle down and have a family, he needed to find somebody.

The woman was pretty. Smiled a lot. Laughed at all his jokes. Exactly the kind of person he should have been attracted to.

Unlike the woman sitting on the other side of his kitchen table, who he was fairly certain had felt nothing but disdain for him before today. And yet, he'd just as soon blow off the errands, the gym, and the exuberantly cheerful dinner date in favor of spending the entire day with Misty. Proving that, deep down, he was a glutton for punishment.

Probably needed therapy.

He'd already finished the cinnamon roll and was eyeing the remains of hers, which she'd picked at for two minutes before pushing it away. She must've seen a greedy expression because she said, "Go ahead. I can't finish it."

He slid the plate closer. "Well, I wouldn't want to hurt your feelings."

Her slight chuckle died fast.

They'd been sitting in relative quiet since she'd hung up with her sister. He assumed she was processing, and he had nothing to add to what she already knew, so he kept quiet.

He'd just finished the remains of Misty's cinnamon roll when her phone rang. She snatched it up. "Hello?" A long pause was followed by, "Two-nine-nine-four-five." Another pause, and then, "Okay, thanks." She ended the call. "One of Summer's guys. He's going in to check for bugs."

"Did you just give him your key code?"

"I'm going to change it anyway. And I trust them. They wouldn't work for Summer and Jon if they weren't trustworthy."

"Jon is your cousin, right?"

"Yeah." She sipped her coffee and set it down. "I've never properly thanked you for being there this summer. Krystal said you were the one getting information from the police and passing it along to her."

Misty's older sister had been frantic with worry for both Misty and Summer when Tate had called her. "When you didn't show up for court, we knew something had happened to you. Leland notified the police and FBI." When Tate had heard the news, he'd found himself unable to concentrate, too worried about Misty. They hadn't been friends exactly, but he'd always admired her. The thought of someone hurting her had made him physically sick.

He never had delved into those feelings. Why had he cared so much? And if the answer was because he felt something for her beyond appropriate workplace friendliness, he needed to cut it out. Those were feelings Misty would never return.

Now, though, she watched him patiently—without the scowl she usually reserved for him.

"Leland asked me to get information from the authorities and pass it along to him," Tate added, "and when you were found, tasked me with making sure you were all right." Probably because Tate had offered, which was why Leland thought they were friends.

"He's a good guy," Misty said. "He cares about the people who work for him. And you...you went above and beyond." Misty looked around at his apartment, shaking her head. "Like you're doing now."

"Glad to help."

She slipped case files out of her bag. "We ought to get moving on these."

"Don't you want to wait until you figure out what they learned?"

She shrugged. "I'd just as soon be doing something. Maybe it'll kill the time."

Or kill the rapport developing between them, but they had to deal with those cases eventually.

She opened the top file. "Breaking and entering, abandoned building. No priors. Eighteen-year-old kid who swears it was a prank."

Tate skimmed the information. "What are you thinking?"

"Two hundred dollars and six months' probation."

He made a note, pleased this was starting so well. "Next."

"Another B and E, only this one with criminal intent. Guy crawled into the open second-story window of a fourteen-year-old girl. The girl heard him and started screaming. The dad came in and detained him until police arrived."

Tate read the file. "Guy swears he thought it was his friend's house."

"But the dad was awake in the living room. The guy never knocked. And he has two prior arrests, both drug charges."

"You're thinking...?"

"Offer five years."

"Five years?" He tempered his surprise. "For misdemeanor breaking and entering?"

"Misdemeanor? He was there to commit a felony."

"Can you prove that in court?"

She shifted. "He was armed."

Armed? Tate scanned the file again. "You mean his Swiss Army knife?"

"Knives kill people."

"According to this, the thing was two inches long. Doubled as a keychain. I don't think he was going to use it to threaten anybody."

"What if he was? What if we let him go, and the next time he breaks into somebody's house, he ends up murdering someone."

"There's no evidence he's a murderer." Tate worked to keep incredulity out of his voice, but it wasn't easy.

"Nobody's a murderer until they've actually killed someone. And then it's too late. We have to—"

Her phone rang. Glaring at him, she snatched it and swiped to connect. "Hello." She listened a sec, and met Tate's eyes. "You mind if he comes up?"

"It's fine."

She gave his apartment number and ended the call.

A few minutes later, a knock sounded on the door. Tate opened it to a man about four inches shorter than himself—five-eight at most—who looked like he could snap Tate in two. Tate stuck out his hand. "Tate Steele. I think we met at the hospital."

"Right. Hughes." They shook hands, and the bodyguard

stepped inside and closed the door. To Misty, he said, "Good to see you again."

"Not thrilled about the circumstances."

"I get that a lot. We found listening devices in the floor lamp in your living room and another one in a lamp on your nightstand. Between the two, they'll pick up anything said in the apartment. We found no cameras."

Her face paled. "I didn't think...I thought Grant was being paranoid."

"The man has freaky instincts," Hughes said. "This is good news, though."

"How so?" Tate couldn't imagine listening devices in his apartment being described as *good news*.

Hughes barely spared Tate a glance. "If the intruder had planned to kill you, there'd be nothing to listen to. If you'd interrupted him, my guess is that he'd have bolted without hurting you."

Tate could see the man's perspective. "What could he possibly hope to hear at your apartment?"

"I have no idea. I never work from home. Unless..." Her eyes widened. "Did you tell anybody we were meeting this morning?"

His gut clenched. He wished he had a different answer. "It's on the calendar."

The office had a shared calendar. Misty was terrible about updating it and, as far as he knew, never checked it. She looked surprised that he utilized the thing, as if following office rules were beneath her.

"Did you say where we were meeting?"

Tate took out his phone and checked. "I said we were meeting at your place, yeah. No address, but—"

"Who has access to that?" Hughes asked.

"Just people in the DA's office," Misty said.

Was what happened this morning Tate's fault? Had he inadvertently put her in danger? "That includes all the ADAs, the support staff, Leland, his secretary."

"And anybody who has access to any of their devices." Hughes nodded at the phone still in Tate's hand. "Obviously, it's not hard to get."

It suddenly became a very big list.

"But how did they know I'd go out this morning?" Misty asked.

"Probably didn't," Hughes said, "just hoped you would. My guess, they were here and ready. If we're right about this, it narrows the suspect list to people who have a vested interest in whatever you two were working on."

Tate hadn't seen most of the files yet but couldn't imagine any of them would be such big cases that they'd warrant this.

"We should let the police know what we found out," Tate said. "They can look into the people who could have accessed the calendar."

"You do that," Hughes said. "Meanwhile, Grant wants me to leave the bugs in place."

"What?" Misty looked shocked. "Why?"

"So the people who planted them won't know we found them. He wants you to go back to your apartment and pack a bag. I'll be there to make sure you're safe, but it would be helpful if Tate here would accompany you, so you two could talk about your plan. A fake plan. Lake suggested you say you're going to stay with her."

"Lake?" Tate asked.

"Summer. My sister." To Hughes, Misty said, "But that would put her in danger."

"I don't think she's concerned, but Grant suggested you say you're going to your dad's."

"Which would put *him* in danger. Can't I say I'm going…I don't know. On a cruise to Mexico?"

"It needs to be believable," Hughes said. "You could make up a destination. Say you're going to visit Marie in…Sturbridge. The point is to throw them off your trail."

"But if Tate's with me, won't that put him at risk?"

"I'm not worried about it," Tate said.

"I don't intend to get out of the frying pan only to boot you into the fire."

Hughes's gaze flicked between them, finally settling on Tate. "You should ask questions about her plans. You know, 'Where you headed?' and 'Will your friend take you in?' That way, the people listening will understand that you don't know anything more about where Misty is going than what she already told you. It would help if you two make like you're not friends or in a relationship or anything."

"That's true, so that won't be a problem," Misty said. "We're just colleagues."

Tate shouldn't mind the casual way she stated that truth.

"After you pack, my team and I will deliver you to Lake's apartment. We're already having the alarm system installed. We'll have two people posted to keep an eye on you until this is resolved."

"I told Summer I don't want that. I don't have the money to pay you."

"We could talk to Leland," Tate suggested, "see if he'll assign guards."

"He already thinks I'm emotionally unstable. The last thing I want is to look like I spook easily."

Tate hated to agree with her, but she wasn't wrong. "I could contribute to the cost of the bodyguards. I feel responsible, since I'm the one who posted about our meeting." Not that he could have known it would lead to this. But he liked the idea of bodyguards keeping Misty safe, and if he had to help cover it, he'd be happy to.

"I'm not taking your money." She turned back to Hughes. "I don't need bodyguards."

Even as she said it, fear flickered in her eyes.

"Sorry, ma'am," Hughes said. "You'll have to take it up with your sister. And Jon. I just do what I'm told. But if it were up to me, you'd have guards."

"You just said the guy wouldn't have hurt me."

"Only because he thought he'd get what he wanted by listening to your conversations. But what happens when he can't get the information he needs?"

Misty closed her mouth, then her eyes. A moment passed while Tate and Hughes watched her silently. Finally, she opened them. "Fine. You're right."

"Let's get this over with," Tate said. "The sooner you're away from here, the better."

With Hughes leading the way and Tate following, Misty returned to her apartment and went directly to her bedroom.

Tate stayed in the living room, his back to her door. Her apartment was cozier than his, the sofa a soft fabric, so unlike his leather. She decorated more like his mother. Her view was lousy, though. "So, where are you gonna go?" He was careful not to talk louder than he normally would and to sound as natural as possible.

"To a friend's house." Misty followed the script.

"How do you know her?"

"We grew up together. She moved away when I was a kid."

"She'll welcome you?"

"Oh, yeah. She's always saying I should come see her. She has a big house with a pool and a view of the mountains. It should be nice this time of year."

She was doing a good job with this fabrication, so good he

found himself wishing he could go with her. He could picture Misty lounging by a pool, sipping iced tea, laughing with her friends.

It was a distracting image. He groped for another question. "Where does she live?"

"In the Berkshires. Thanks for staying with me while I pack. I'd be too scared to do this by myself."

"Happy to help."

"I'm sure you'll be glad to get rid of me. You must've had better plans for the day."

"Different," he said. "Not better."

She exited the bedroom, pulling a suitcase on wheels.

He grabbed the handle. "You have everything you need?"

She slipped her laptop bag over her shoulder. "If I don't, I'll go shopping. I wasn't exactly prepared to take a vacation."

"I'll try to hold down the fort at work. If you need anything, let me know."

"I'll be fine. I'll see you when I get back."

Silently, Hughes gave them a thumbs-up. He opened the door, and they walked out and closed it.

Misty blew out a long breath. "That was weird." She kept her voice low as she crouched down beside her keypad, tapping buttons. "Give me one second to change the code."

Her neighbor came into the hallway. Tate blocked her, hand outstretched. "We didn't meet. I'm Tate."

"Hi, Tate. I'm Ruth." She ducked around him. "Misty, I was just gonna give you my phone number, in case you need anything."

Misty stood beside Tate. "That's kind of you." She took a piece of paper the woman extended to her.

"Would you mind giving me yours? In case you get a package or I see anybody lurking."

Misty pulled a business card from her purse and handed it over. "You can reach me there."

At the DA's office. Smart not to share her cell phone number with this annoying person.

Finally, the three of them walked to the elevator. Hughes mashed the button before speaking to Tate. "Thanks for your help. We'll take it from here."

"Uh..." He turned to Misty. "I just assumed I'd be coming with you. We still have to work on those cases. And if we're right, one of them might be the reason for what happened today."

Before she could respond, Hughes intruded. "Nobody is supposed to know where you're going."

"I already know, though," Tate said. "I could find your sister's address in five minutes."

Misty looked from Tate to Hughes and back.

The elevator dinged, and the two of them stepped on.

Tate followed. She was going to have to send him away if she didn't want him around. If this was about those case files, then it had as much to do with him as with her.

The elevator descended.

"Tate needs to come with me," Misty said.

Hughes didn't smile. If anything, his expression went from concerned to threatening in the space it took for the elevator doors to slide open. He stepped into the opening and turned. He might've had to look up to Tate, but he clearly wasn't a bit intimidated. "Anything happens to her, remember...I know where you live."

"I'm not the enemy here."

"Be sure to keep it that way. You can't tell anybody where she is, or even let on that you know. If anyone sees you near Lake's building, you'd better have a story ready." Hughes spun and stepped out. Two other men and a woman fell into step around Misty, escorting her like a pop star with her posse.

Tate walked behind them, feeling unnecessary but determined. Once she was at her sister's, his protective feelings would wane. They could deal with those cases, and he could get on with his life.

CHAPTER SEVEN

Flanked by bodyguards, Misty climbed the stairs in her sister's apartment building and unlocked the door.

Hughes stepped in first, looked around, and then waved her in. The alarm installer was working at the bay window—on a third-floor apartment? Talk about overkill.

Hughes went to talk to him. Misty headed for the thermostat. Thanks to the July heat, the space was stifling. She turned the air conditioner on, pleased to discover it. Most of these old places, if they had AC at all, settled for window units.

The apartment looked just as it had the last time Misty had been there. Summer was messy but had tidied up when she'd left for Coventry. Her place was cozy with deep-cushioned sofas and chairs that were positioned not toward the small TV pushed against the wall but toward the old-fashioned fireplace. In it were fake logs, and Misty saw the silver key that would turn on the gas. The furniture was weathered, the kind of decor Misty rarely saw outside of home improvement shows. Farmhouse chic or something. Where Misty's apartment was comfortable but contemporary, Summer's was homey.

"Nice place." Tate stepped inside and lifted the suitcase. "You want me to take this to the bedroom?"

"If you don't mind." She nodded toward the short hallway. "It's down there."

"I'll find it."

The alarm guy stood and gathered his things. "All set."

"I'll teach her how to use it," Hughes said. "Standard codes?"

"They should all be changed immediately." He nodded to Misty, said, "Good luck," and headed out.

It shouldn't come down to luck. That was what she had God for, right?

Hughes explained the alarm system and showed her how to code it. She did, choosing the same random numbers she'd just used for the key code at her apartment.

"I'll be in the hall, and we'll have a second person outside." The bodyguard gave her a list of the team members, when they'd be working, and their phone numbers. "Never hesitate to call if you get spooked or if anything unusual happens. If you can, give us notice when you're going out, but if something comes up last minute, we can adjust. If anyone is coming to see you, let us know. Keep your whereabouts secret from as many as you can." His gaze cut to Tate as he returned from dropping her bag, but he didn't voice his opinion on the matter again. "Questions?"

"Can't think of any."

"You have my number. I'll be right outside, but I'd prefer you call or text. Don't step out the door without warning me, okay?"

She'd been putting people behind bars for a long time. Now, she'd willingly stepped into her own prison cell. She thanked Hughes and closed the door behind him.

She was about to walk into the kitchen, where Tate had settled, when she heard a knock. She pulled the door open.

Hughes didn't look happy. "One, never answer the door without asking who's there."

"I knew it was you."

"Two, engage the deadbolt and alarm. Every single time."

She forced a smile. "Sorry. I will." She closed the door, turned the deadbolt, and hit the alarm keypad before joining Tate in the kitchen. She sat at the small café table. "He's a little intense."

"I'm just glad you're safe. You need to call that ex-con's attorney back. Maybe he knows something about this."

"Freddy Parks isn't the listening-devices type."

"Still," Tate said.

She found Jeffrey Cofer's office number and dialed. His service answered, not shocking on a Saturday. Misty left her name and cell number and asked that he call her back.

When she hung up, she pulled her laptop from her bag, but the table was barely large enough to set it down.

"Let's work in the living room." Tate lifted her laptop. "I'll move our stuff while you call Gamble."

"Right." She'd forgotten about him. She dialed the number on the business card the police officer had given her. He answered, put her on hold, and transferred her.

"Detective Reyes," a woman said.

Misty explained who she was and what they'd learned that morning.

"You're saying someone found listening devices?" The detective sounded dubious. "In your apartment?"

"You can contact Green Beret Protection. Ask for Hughes."

"Oh. I'm aware of them. They know what they're doing." The skeptical tone was gone. "Any idea what the intruder was listening for?"

"We assume something to do with the meeting I was scheduled to have with a coworker. We're ADAs working together on some cases. It could have been any of them." Misty explained the shared calendar.

"Send me the case files and the names of everyone who has access to that calendar." She rattled off an email address, and Misty wrote it down.

"Everybody who works at the DA's office has access," Misty said. "I'll see if I can get someone to send the list to you."

"Great. We're buried in work, so any information you can pass along will help."

Like every organization, the police were short-staffed. "We're about to go through the files," Misty said. "If anything jumps out, I'll let you know." She ended the call and joined Tate in the living room, where she settled on the chair catty-corner to Tate on the sofa. "I need to send her a list of the staff at the DA's office. Who should I call?"

"I just texted Sheila. You know her, right?"

"Oh, right." Sheila had handled Misty's paperwork when she'd been hired. "I should have realized..."

"You've had a rough day."

She had, but was that an excuse? She was usually quick-thinking, but Tate seemed to be a step ahead of her, anticipating her needs, reminding her of all the things she needed to do.

"I asked her to send the list to you," Tate said. "You can forward it."

"Seriously, Tate. Thank you for that. For...everything."

"You can thank me by being reasonable." He lifted one of the files. "This is the B and E."

She feared her definition of *reasonable* was very different from his.

She insisted on offering no less than five years to the man who'd crawled into the bedroom of a fourteen-year-old girl.

Tate argued she'd never get a conviction if it went to trial and suggested they offer two.

They were in a new location, but the discussion hadn't changed. Except this time, Misty was looking at the case differently. "You think this has anything to do with this morning?"

Tate looked up from the notes he was making. "The guy isn't connected to anyone important, as far as I can tell. Let's focus on the deals first. If nothing strange jumps out at us, we'll go back through all the files looking for...I don't know. Red flags or whatever."

She agreed with his plan. Though she argued about the plea deal, ultimately, she took Tate's advice. She might be able to convince a jury that the guy'd had criminal intent when he'd crawled into that girl's window. But she might not, and knowing the defense attorney, he'd recommend his client take it to trial. If that happened, and if she lost, then the criminal would be right back on the street. A little time behind bars was better than none. "We'll offer two. They'll negotiate it down to one. The guy'll be wreaking havoc on the community by this time next summer." The thought of it made her sick, but she knew what she could—and couldn't—accomplish.

"It's not our job to singlehandedly eradicate crime in Boston." Tate's words were spoken gently, but she heard the censure in them.

"Not singlehandedly, but we have a part to play."

"Okay." He drew out the word. "But there're police and other prosecutors and judges and social workers. We're two cogs in a very big machine."

"If nobody in that machine feels responsible, then nothing will change. But if everybody were to take their jobs as seriously as I take mine—"

"You really think you can change the world?"

"At least I'm trying."

He wiped his forehead, where sweat glistened. The room was cooling off, but it had to still be near eighty degrees.

Tate stood and marched into the kitchen. "I'm getting a glass of water. You want one?"

"Check the fridge. There might be soda."

He came back with two cans, which he lifted, a question in his expression.

"Sure. I don't need a glass."

He handed her one, walked away again, and returned with a glass filled with clear, bubbly liquid. He sat, took a deep breath, and smiled. "Let's not argue, okay?"

She doubted they'd manage that. "I'll try if you will."

Tate set the B and E file aside. "Maybe he'll rehabilitate in jail. Maybe he'll surprise you."

"People rarely do." She grabbed the next file. They moved through the narcotics cases quickly but got caught up on the first assault case. "You can't seriously want to let this guy walk." She lifted one of the printouts from the current file, which detailed the bar fight that had landed the victim in the hospital.

"You going to charge the other guy?"

"The one at death's door?"

"According to this"—Tate lifted the police report—"the so-called victim started the brawl."

"Our defendant finished it. Would have finished *him* if other people hadn't pulled him away."

"You're not wrong." Tate seemed to be working to keep his voice level. "But if it goes to a jury, he's going to argue exactly what he told the police." He slapped his hand on the file. "He was attacked, he feared for his life, and he was defending himself."

"You believe that?"

Tate blew out an exasperated breath. "It's not our job to

believe or disbelieve. It's our job to figure out what we can prove and fight battles we can win."

"God forbid your perfect record be sullied."

He reared back as if she'd slapped him. "I don't care about that."

"Fine, then. What do you care about?" Her words came out too loud. Her heart was pounding with frustration. "It seems to me your goal is to get the cases off your desk with as little effort as possible."

"Are you calling me lazy?" His voice rose to match hers.

She shrugged. "Your word, not mine."

"Do you even know what your job is?" He stood and paced, pushing his hands through his hair. He stopped near the bay windows on the far side of the small room and leaned back against the sill. "Who do you work for?"

"The people of Suffolk County."

Tate dropped his head back against the wall and took a deep breath. He was angry, and so was she. But that didn't make her blind. The man had a nice chest. Broad shoulders. Trim waist. She didn't mind that he couldn't see her looking.

But his head snapped down, and his eyes narrowed. "What?"

"What what? You asked me a question, and I answered it." Maybe her tone was a little more aggressive than she'd intended, but the last thing she wanted was for him to think she'd been checking him out.

Even if she had been.

"You work for Leland Humphrey, the district attorney. The man who was elected by the people of Suffolk County."

"God forbid we should upset the great Leland Humphrey. I don't live my life trying to please him."

Like you do.

"Maybe you should," Tate said. "He's the one who hired

you. He's the one who gets to decide how his office is run. He has every right to set the parameters of your job and expect you to follow them."

"What about justice? I have to do what I think is right. He hired me because he trusts my judgment and my dedication to doing what's best for the people of the city."

Tate crossed the room and sat on the sofa again, lifting the file. "If Leland were here, what would he say?"

"He's not here. He hired *me* to do this job. I have to do it my way."

"Except he asked *me* to help you. You really think you'd be serving justice to put this guy away for a decade because he defended himself?"

"He almost killed a man!"

"A man who attacked him." Again, Tate took a deep breath. He gathered the file and set it aside. "We'll come back to it."

"No. We need to... The defendant is obviously violent."

"When provoked, he can take care of himself. Guess what? So can I. If someone attacked me and I defended myself, should I go to prison?"

"That's different. You wouldn't send a guy to the hospital."

"Maybe I would. Maybe I would fear for my life. Maybe I would take it too far, even accidentally. Should I go to prison for a decade because somebody provoked me to violence?"

"What if he wasn't really provoked?"

"All the witnesses backed up his claim that the other guy started it."

"What if he does it to someone else? What if the next guy he beats up doesn't survive? If he's on the street and we could have put him away, it'll be on us. On me."

Tate sat back against the cushions and regarded her for a long moment. "Is that what this is? You feel responsible for—?"

"Don't you? When you let someone go, and they commit another crime, do you not feel responsible?"

Tate's gaze didn't waver as he shook his head. "I don't, no. Not if I did my job well. I can't predict the future. I can't know what someone will do next week or next month or next year. What a weight that must put on your shoulders, feeling responsible for the actions of people you have no control over?"

"That's just it. As a prosecutor, I do have control." Some, anyway.

"Huh."

"What?"

"I'm beginning to understand. I always assumed you were trying to prove something, as if you thought working harder than the rest of us would make you look good. I assumed you were...ambitious."

"Well, I'm not." *Ambitious*. As if she cared about moving up, about making a name for herself. All she cared about was justice. Wasn't that why anybody went to work for the DA, earning a meager salary relative to what an attorney could make in the private sector?

Tate's head bobbed slowly. "You think ambition is bad."

"Not bad, just..." She realized her mistake but didn't know how to fix it. "Just different."

"If Leland hadn't been ambitious, he wouldn't be the DA. But maybe, to you, that's a mark against him."

The heat in the apartment was getting to her. She fought the urge to wipe sweat from her upper lip, fearing Tate would read something into the movement.

And for the second time since the day began, she owed Tate Steele an apology. "I'm not ambitious, but there's nothing wrong with people who are. It's just, to me it seems you can either be eager for justice or eager for personal gain. I don't see how a person can be both."

"Whereas, I don't think it's my job to play judge and jury and executioner. Who am I to decide justice?"

Wasn't that their job?

He didn't seem to think so.

"I trust the system," he said. "I also know we have limited resources and limited time. So I do the work I've been given to do. Maybe you work for justice, but I work for the DA, and I do what he asks me to do. Which is why I'm here."

Right.

He was there to help her because Leland didn't think she could hack it.

Fresh shame rolled over her. She sipped her drink, wishing she'd asked for ice. Condensation from the can wet her hands, which she pressed against her neck to cool off.

Tate closed the case file. "Let's come back to that one."

"Fine."

He picked up the next, read it quickly, and then passed it over to her. "Assault."

"I think we can settle our differences without violence."

He laughed, the sound surprising her in the quiet apartment. "You're funny."

"Usually not intentionally." She glanced at the file and remembered the details. This was the case that would either seal her low opinion of him or start repairing it. Because men who preyed on women and children needed to be put away. If only her own mother had had the nerve to tell the truth about her father's abuse. "Why don't you tell me what you think?"

"The guy beat up his girlfriend. Has two prior assault charges. I say we offer fifteen and don't settle for less than ten. If he serves the whole time, he'll be in his thirties by the time he gets out. Maybe by then, he'll have matured a little. Either way, his girlfriend will have moved on."

Though she'd rather put him away for life, there was no way

to accomplish that. Tate's suggestion lined up with what she'd have done on her own. "Okay, I'll give in on that one."

His eyebrows rose. "You're not going to argue for the death penalty?"

"Not this time. Figured you deserved to win one of these arguments."

Smiling, he shook his head as he grabbed the next file. "How kind of you."

They dealt with the two narcotics possessions easily. He took his time reading the last file. "Bribery case."

"What do you think?"

"I think the file is woefully bare. We might want to get a little more information." A look crossed his features—narrowed eyes, tight lips. It passed before she had a chance to analyze it. "Play it right, it could make you look good for that position."

She sat back. "I don't want to move into white-collar. I like the cases I have."

"You like those?" He waved toward the stack they'd completed. "Mucking around with drug dealers and wife beaters?"

"I like feeling like I'm making a difference. Don't you?"

He didn't bother to answer. "We need to make some calls."

"I agree. We need to know why the bribe was offered, if it was accepted. I assume not, since it was reported, but it doesn't explicitly say."

"Also, why the delay? This incident happened almost a year ago. What held it up? And why go forward now?"

"And was the building ever built?" Misty asked.

"And did Thornebrook put the defendant up to it?"

"Exactly." Tate had come up with the same questions she'd asked herself.

"Do you know what Thornebrook is?"

"Construction company," she said. "Did you notice the defense attorney?"

Tate flipped through the pages. His eyebrows hiked. "Whoa. Heavy hitter. How can"—he glanced at the file again—"this Raul Dawson guy afford her?"

"Or is Thornebrook..." Her voice trailed as a thought occurred to her. "This must be it. This is the case, don't you think? The reason for this morning. A real estate deal, a high-powered defense attorney. This must be the one."

Tate sat up straighter. "Maybe. We can't know for sure, but it's possible. We need more information. A lot more."

He was right, but even so, her instincts told her they'd stumbled onto the case her intruder was interested in. So many questions presented themselves. Was this connected to Freddy Parks? Why did this seemingly insignificant bribery charge matter, and to whom? And what did they want?

And what were they willing to do to get it?

CHAPTER EIGHT

Tate rolled over in his bed and glanced at the time.
Only six o'clock, but the sun was already brightening the sky beyond his window. He'd been wrestling wakefulness all night, his mind continually returning to the masked intruder, to Misty's panic, to the way she'd fought him. The way she'd felt in his arms.

That last one was the most disturbing. Because he could admit that he'd really liked the feel of her there.

And their afternoon together had gone surprisingly well. Yes, she'd dug in her heels on a couple of the cases, but they'd come to terms on all but the one assault and the bribery case.

For the first time, he knew why she didn't settle her cases as quickly as everybody else in the office. She felt personally responsible for the behavior of every criminal whose name crossed her desk. He didn't feel that way, never had, but knowing she did helped him understand her. He could see her point of view, even if he didn't share it. He respected her.

But there was more to it than that.

They'd disagreed more than once, but they'd also worked

well together. They'd laughed together. They'd tried to solve this weird little mystery together. After lunch—they'd had sandwiches delivered—she changed out of her blouse and slacks into khaki shorts and a T-shirt and pulled her hair back into a messy ponytail, so unlike the stark bun she wore most days.

He'd found it difficult not to stare. Because professional Misty was attractive. Casual Misty was downright gorgeous.

Tate had hated to leave her the previous afternoon, but they'd done everything they needed to do, and he did have plans.

Thanks to her bodyguards, she hadn't needed him.

As Tate had expected, his date had been a bust. The woman was sweet, beautiful, and a Christian. But she was the human equivalent of an overeager puppy.

Puppies were great, but if he was going to spend the rest of his life with one, it would be the shorter, furrier variety.

He'd been home by ten. In bed by eleven.

And now awake at dawn. He could go to the gym, then hit the early service at church. Run errands and still have hours to kill. He usually loved Sundays—time to relax, clean his apartment, maybe show up at his parents' house in Wellesley right around dinnertime. He didn't want to do any of those things today.

He wanted to figure out why somebody had broken into Misty's apartment and planted listening devices. Until he knew the answer to that, there'd be little rest.

It was a bad habit that he needed to break, but he stayed in bed and scrolled his emails, then the news. Nothing noteworthy.

Had Misty slept at all? Was she the type to silence her notifications, or would he wake her if he reached out?

He shouldn't. Definitely shouldn't. But he found her phone number and tapped out a text.

> You okay this morning?

Three dancing dots told him she was not only awake but also looking at her phone.

> Awake too early, but otherwise fine. You?

> Awake too early but otherwise fine. I was worried about you.

> I was worried about you.

Her response confused him.

> I'm not the one in danger.

This time, it took a lot longer for her to reply.

> When I woke up, it occurred to me that you might be. You know as much about that case as I do. If we're right about everything, then they only targeted me because we were meeting at my apartment. You could be in danger.

Huh. He hadn't thought about that.

> I'm not worried about my safety.

> Maybe you should be. I couldn't go back to sleep thinking about it. I was about to text you.

She was worried about him. That thought warmed him despite the AC.

Perhaps it wasn't the wisest thing in the world to text a woman he found attractive from his bed. He climbed out, pulled on the T-shirt that matched his sleep pants, and headed barefoot to the kitchen to start the coffee.

Once he'd done that, he texted again.

> The sooner we get this figured out, the better. I'm going into the office after church to learn what I can about that case. If you'll be home, I can come by after.

> Where am I going to go? I'm a prisoner here.

> Hardly a prisoner.

Hadn't Hughes told her she could leave anytime she wanted? But if keeping her whereabouts a secret was important, then maybe she'd be safer if she stayed out of sight.

> Let me know if I can bring you anything. Groceries. Clothes. Dinner?

He shouldn't have added the last part. If he took her dinner, would she think it was a date?

Did he want her to?

He didn't know the answer and ignored the way his heart sped up thinking about it. The only thing he was sure of was that he wouldn't be texting Misty again before he'd had at least one cup of coffee.

Her dots danced again. For a long time. A very long time.

Was she assuming he'd asked her to have dinner—romantically? Was she trying to find a way to let him down gently? Or maybe to tell him off? Or accept?

Did he dare hope?

Or maybe she hadn't interpreted his text that way at all.

Still, those dots danced.

He set the phone down and washed his favorite coffee cup,

which he'd left in the sink the morning before. He poured steaming coffee from the pot, then added a splash of French vanilla creamer—he was secure enough in his masculinity to admit he liked the stuff. He sipped, tried to enjoy it. Opened his blinds to stare out over the city. Buildings glowed gold in the morning sun. Between the trees, the Charles River sparkled as it made its way to the harbor.

Finally, his phone dinged.

> Will do.

Will do? He glanced back at what he'd written. He'd asked her to let him know if she needed anything, and that was her answer?

It took her five minutes to compose a six-letter response?

He tapped the text to give it a thumbs-up, ending the conversation.

Texting was stupid. The next time he wanted to talk to her, he'd just call.

∼

Tate went to church and then completed all his weekend chores before heading to the office after lunch. As a rule, he didn't work on Sundays. Unlike Misty, he managed to get his work done during the workweek, and he'd been raised to take a Sabbath rest. But the sooner they solved the mystery of who'd broken into her apartment, the sooner she'd be safe again.

Though it was a beautiful summer day, other prosecutors were hard at work. Tate waved to a couple before he entered his office.

He spent an hour researching the bribery case, printing off everything he learned to share with Misty. He was scanning the cases he'd need to deal with the coming week when another ADA stepped through his open door. "What are you doing here?"

Tate stifled the irritation the man's voice raised. "Working."

Clinton Lowe leaned against the doorjamb and crossed one foot over the other—like he was posing for a portrait. Everybody else who worked on the weekends wore jeans and tees. Not Clinton. He might as well have been on his way to court—dark gray suit, crisp white shirt, red power tie. He was the picture of professional from his slicked-back hair to his two-tone wingtips. "Never known you to come in on a Sunday. What're you working on?"

Tate got along well with everybody in the DA's office. Just about.

"Nothing special."

Clinton crossed the room and snatched the papers Tate had printed to take to Misty. "Thornebrook. Where have I heard of them?"

He started to flip the pages, but Tate grabbed them back. "Isn't there someone else you can annoy?"

Clinton laughed. "Leland was at the house Friday night. He and Dad go way back. They were roomies at Harvard."

"Really," Tate deadpanned. "I had no idea." Clinton had only mentioned that about a thousand times. Which meant, any second, he'd say...

"That's why I chose Harvard." He pronounced it Hah-vahd, affecting an aristocratic accent that didn't carry over into any of the other thousands of words he felt the need to speak every day. "Wanted to go to the old man's alma mater."

"Harvard?" Tate infused his words with a combination of surprise and awe. Sarcasm at its finest. "You never said."

Clinton's smug expression slipped long enough for him to glare.

"Did you need something?" Tate asked. "Because I've got a life I need to get back to."

"Just thought you'd like to know that, while Leland and I were enjoying a brandy, he asked me to work on an embezzlement case with him." The way his eyes gleamed told Tate he'd been looking forward to rubbing it in. "I figure, when I manage this, he'll put me on in that white-collar opening."

"Would it mean you'd be moved to a different floor? Because, gosh, it'd be so sad to see you go."

Clinton's smile always brought to mind a rat eyeing a hunk of cheese. "I'll come back and visit."

"Feel free not to." Tate shoved a couple of case files in his messenger bag, along with the papers for Misty.

But his office phone rang. He glanced at the caller ID and snatched it up. "Leland. Are you in the office?" He enjoyed the thrill of satisfaction when Clinton squinted, his lips turning down at the corners. Petty, but there it was.

"I'm home," the DA said, "but I thought you might be there."

"Hold on a second, sir." Tate flipped his hand toward the hallway. "Close that on your way out. Thanks." He waited until Clinton was gone. Typical, he'd walked out but left the door wide open just to be a jerk. "Sorry about that. There was someone in my office. What's up?"

"Did you and Misty get to work on those cases?"

"Yesterday morning. We came up with plea deals for all but two of them. We're still hammering out the details for one of those. The other, we need more information. I was going to ask you about it, as a matter of fact. It's a bribery case that's been sitting for a year. I wondered why it's up now."

"Which one is that?"

"Raul Dawson. Accused of offering a bribe to get a permit issued."

"Dawson," Leland said. "Never heard of him. Not sure what held it up. Take care of it, would you?"

"The thing is, I'm not sure if Misty called you, but her apartment was broken into yesterday morning." Tate explained the listening devices that had been found, as well as their theory that the intruder had been seeking information on their cases.

"Why do you think that?"

"Quite a coincidence that we would have been discussing them—"

"What else is she working on?" The question must've been rhetorical because how would Tate know? He said nothing. After a moment, Leland said, "I got a call last night about an overturned conviction. Guy named Frederick Parks."

"Yeah, we thought about him. But why would he bug her place?"

"Who knows why anybody does anything," Leland asked. "There's another case she's working on. Spousal abuse. Defendant is connected—Kyle Griffin."

"Never heard of him."

"I wouldn't be surprised if his guys were behind the bugs. He's loaded, money from iffy sources, though nobody's proved anything yet. Get her to wrap that one up, okay?"

Spousal abuse? He doubted she'd compromise on the Griffin case but said, "I'll do what I can."

"Good, good. I'm counting on you. I don't think she's cut out for violent crimes. I'm thinking I should move her."

Into the white-collar opening Tate coveted? She didn't want it, and he did. He'd thought his only real competition in the office was Clinton. But if Misty was a candidate...

The DA sighed. "She's probably spooked. I guess she's going to want protection again."

Did Tate hear mocking in the man's tone, as if she shouldn't be spooked?

"She's fine," Tate said. "She went to stay at her sister's place just in case, but she can handle it." Which was true, though the bodyguards probably didn't hurt. "She's tougher than she looks. And if she is spooked, who can blame her? She was kidnapped just six, eight weeks ago."

"I know. You're right. Anyway, I'm sure things'll calm down once she gets those cases wrapped up. Have them all off her desk by Wednesday."

Offered and accepted in three days? "I'll do my best."

"I knew you were the man for the job. Keep me informed. You're doing great work."

Leland ended the call long before Tate was finished reveling in the compliment. Maybe he hadn't given him an extortion case like he had Clinton, but Leland trusted him. It was just a matter of time before he would be working on white-collar crimes.

He dialed Misty. "I just got off the phone with Leland," Tate said after she answered. "I hope you don't mind, but I told him about your intruder yesterday."

"Oh."

"Uh...I guess you do mind."

"It's just that he already thinks I'm a basket case."

"He does not." Tate hoped, anyway. "He needed to know. He suggested the intruder might be related to"—Tate consulted his notes—"Griffin? Kyle Griffin?"

She groaned. "Figures."

Based on that, he had a bad feeling about her reaction to the rest of his news. "He wants me to assist you—"

"I don't need assistance."

"Okay. Well..." There was no sense having this argument again. "Can I grab the case file while I'm here? Or any others?"

"I have the Griffin case with me. But there's a stack of files on my desk I'd planned to deal with tomorrow. You can grab those."

"I will, and then I'll head over. Do you need anything else?"

She gave him a short list, and he promised to stop at a store on his way.

With all the files stuffed into his messenger bag, Tate left the DA's office and headed for the T station, feeling as puppy-dog eager as his dinner date the night before.

CHAPTER NINE

Misty hated being trapped at her sister's apartment. There was no gym on the first floor, so no workout. She'd decided to kill time by cleaning, but Summer had scrubbed the place thoroughly before relocating to New Hampshire, so that didn't take nearly enough time.

She tried TV, but what was the appeal of watching other people live their lives instead of accomplishing something of her own? She yearned to go for a walk, but the whole point of going to Summer's was to convince whoever'd broken into her place that she was out of town. The likelihood of her being spotted by some dangerous enemy was slim, but it was possible. Between fear of that, her constant anxiety at being out in the open after being snatched off the street less than two months before, and her need to have bodyguards accompany her wherever she went, she chose to stay indoors and out of sight.

She dug into the Dawson/Thornebrook case but didn't find much. Tate would have better luck from the office, where it would be simpler to tap into county resources.

Obviously, Misty had been working too hard if taking a few

hours off on a Sunday was so challenging. Which was why she wasn't sorry when she received a call from Melanie Castellan, the former girlfriend and current stalking victim of Kyle Griffin, a case set to go to trial on Wednesday. Despite the intruder in her apartment, Misty would be there. No other ADA would care as much as she did. She owed it to the abuse victim.

"Tony changed his mind," Melanie said in lieu of hello.

"What? Why?"

"Wouldn't say. He just said he has to focus on his family." Melanie's flat tone worried Misty more than if she'd sounded distraught or angry. She seemed resigned to what was coming.

Until her call, Misty had felt confident in her ability to secure a conviction against Melanie's abusive ex-boyfriend. Tony, Melanie's brother, was the only person who'd witnessed Kyle Griffin abusing Melanie and threatening her children. Without his testimony, the trial would be a case of he said, she said. She'd never spoken with Griffin, but she understood he was charming, whereas Melanie might come off as coarse and defensive. A jury could be swayed by Kyle's lies.

"Tony is scheduled to be deposed tomorrow," Misty said. "You're saying he won't show up?"

"Said he no longer remembers anything."

"You have to change his mind. It's imperative that he testify. I'll issue a subpoena, but he has to show up."

"He said he won't." Melanie's voice pitched higher. "He said...he's not going to do it, Ms. Lake. He's not going to change his mind."

"Why?"

"Kyle must've threatened him. Tony's got kids. He's not gonna put them at risk for me. Why would he?"

Because she was his sister. Because it was the right thing to do.

"I'll call him," Misty said. Maybe she could sway him. If not, her case was rocky at best. Even if she gave in to Tate's suggestion that she offer a plea deal, why would Griffin take it, knowing he had such a good shot at being acquitted?

She ended the call and immediately dialed Tony. He didn't answer—no surprise. "I talked to your sister," she said to his voicemail. "Please, call me back. We need to discuss our options."

Maybe he'd call her back if he thought there was a way to help his sister without putting himself at risk.

There was nothing else Misty could do. She paced and worried and watched the clock, eager for Tate to arrive. It was nearly five o'clock before she heard a knock and then Tate's voice. "It's me."

She disengaged the alarm and deadbolt and opened the door. He stepped in past the guard. "Groceries and dinner." He wore jeans and a T-shirt that hugged his strong biceps as he lifted a couple of paper bags. His hair was artfully messy, his blue eyes warm as he smiled at her. A bit of scruff on his jaw told her he hadn't shaved. Rather than detract from his good looks, the stubble only made him look ruggedly charming.

She took the bags, ignoring a jolt of awareness when their fingers touched, and headed for the kitchen. Summer had remodeled this room, replacing what Misty would guess had been old, drab cabinets with white ones, some of which were glass-fronted and displayed pretty plates and platters and glasses. The countertop was granite in shades of brown and rust, the backsplash white subway tiles. The whole space was fresh and new despite the age of the old brownstone.

"What do I owe you?"

"Grocery receipt's in the bag." He'd slipped off his backpack and dropped it on a chair. At the counter, he pulled food from the sacks, which she stowed in the fridge and cabinets.

He'd brought enough to last a few days. She'd need to place

a delivery order if this situation wasn't cleared up soon. She found the receipt for the groceries, then opened the bag that held Chinese food. "Where's the receipt?"

"Dinner's on me."

She lifted her gaze to meet his eyes, preparing to argue.

"You can buy next time."

"Deal." She pulled plates out of the cabinet. "You hungry?"

"I could eat."

"Are you one of those guys who's perpetually hungry, always eating and never gaining weight?"

He shrugged, digging into a container of beef and broccoli. She'd requested Szechuan shrimp. "I've never had to worry about it. Like you, I think."

Misty and Summer had their mother's body type—tall and slender—while Krystal had taken after Dad. A little shorter, though not short at five-seven, and much stockier. The only time Misty had ever worried about her weight was when she modeled. Back then, no matter what she did, she never felt thin enough. The best thing about quitting modeling was the ability to enjoy food again.

After getting them both drinks, she grabbed some cash out of her wallet and settled at the café table in the kitchen, sliding the bills toward him. "Thanks for doing this."

Tate took the money, then eyed the chopsticks she unwrapped. "Any chance you could spare a fork?"

Laughing, she snatched one from a drawer. "Never mastered chopsticks? I could teach you."

"Others have tried and failed." He stirred his noodles. "I can't understand why anybody would choose to eat with those when forks exist."

She snagged a bite of spicy noodles and shrimp. "I like a challenge."

"That, I don't doubt." He took a forkful of beefy noodles. "I love this restaurant. I've never tried their Szechuan."

"Help yourself." She pushed the box toward him. "I won't eat all that."

He nudged his box toward her. "Only fair."

They each sampled the others' food. She preferred her spicy noodles, even if her choice required her to replenish her water halfway through the meal.

"Are you comfortable here at your sister's?" Tate asked.

"Sure. I have everything I need. Except food, that is. Besides spices and a few odds and ends, her cupboards are bare."

"Is she coming back?"

"She's trying to decide if she should put this place on the market, rent it long-term, or offer it as a vacation spot. I think a lot depends on what happens with her and Grant."

They chatted about nothing important while they ate. Tate finished his meal, then forked a few more bites of hers before carrying both their plates to the sink. She put the leftovers in the fridge. When he'd texted that morning, offering to bring dinner, she'd nearly refused, fearing he'd meant the offer as something romantic.

But of course not. Tate would never want to date her. He was powerful and ambitious. She was a worker bee—head down, feet very much on the ground. They might be employed in the same office, but they were worlds apart. Knowing that had made it easy to accept his offer. They were friends, nothing more. Before Friday, she'd barely considered him that, but the weekend had changed how she felt about him. Maybe he was a little too quick to push cases off his desk, but he was protective and kind and considerate. Though she hated to admit it, when she heard his rationale for the decisions he made at work, she understood, even if she didn't always agree.

Two days before, she'd disdained Tate Steele. Now, she respected him. More than that, she liked him.

"I did some digging." Tate nodded toward the living room, and she led the way and settled in the chair where she'd sat the day before. From his backpack, he pulled out his laptop, a pile of papers, and a couple of files. The files he set aside. The laptop went onto the coffee table, but the pile of papers he handed over. "Everything I could find out about Thornebrook."

She skimmed the paperwork. "So the building was built."

"Completed this summer. It's owned by a company called IAF."

"What is that?"

"No idea. A Google search turned up a bunch of possibilities, but I haven't had time to figure out which one is associated with that building."

"Huh." She made a note to dig into that and then found Raul Dawson's name. He was lead contractor on the project, and remained so even after the bribery charge, which told her the owners of Thornebrook had okayed—maybe even encouraged—Dawson's bribe. She said as much to Tate.

"I agree. The guy who turned him in is on there. Uh, Zachary..."

"Hardy. Got him. I'll call him tomorrow, see what he can tell us."

"Thing is..." Tate sounded pensive when he spoke again. "I can't imagine why anybody involved in this case would care enough to bug your apartment. It's a simple case, and the bribe wasn't accepted. The accused will probably claim he was kidding or would never have gone through with it." He shook his head, his lips twisting into a frustrated smirk. "I can't figure out why it hasn't been dealt with already."

"Which tells me it's not simple," she said. "There must be a reason."

"If there is, I don't know what." Tate sat back against the cushions. Though it wasn't a small couch, it seemed dwarfed by his broad shoulders. "We'll know more after you talk to Hardy. Meanwhile, we need to settle on a plea deal for that assault."

Misty lifted the file in question, skimmed the facts again. The accused had no priors. He was married with three kids and gainfully employed. But he'd also been drinking in a bar, without his wife. A blood test confirmed he'd been inebriated at the time of the assault.

A violent drunk.

Or so she assumed. But all accounts said the so-called victim had attacked when the accused had stood up for a woman the victim was bothering.

So, maybe not a violent drunk. Maybe a noble...drunk. Who, as Tate had suggested, could take care of himself.

Tate didn't speak while she contemplated the case.

She wasn't wrong. The accused *could* be violent, *could* hurt somebody again.

But Tate wasn't wrong either. All the witnesses confirmed that the man had been defending someone else, and then defending himself. Had he gone too far? No question. But should he lose everything because he'd been standing up for a woman?

Probably not.

"What do you recommend?" she asked.

"Nothing would have happened if the guy hadn't been attacked."

She nodded, saying nothing.

Tate seemed to brace himself before he answered. "I recommend you knock it down to misdemeanor assault, one year suspended and a five-hundred-dollar fine."

She made a note. "I concur."

His eyes popped wide. "You do?"

"I think I was wrong about you." He said nothing, just waited with that same look of shock on his face. "You're not always wrong about everything."

He laughed and sat back. "High praise. I'm honored."

She joined his amusement and tossed the file aside. "That just leaves the bribery charge."

"We could drop the charges completely," Tate said. "Maybe that'll make your intruder go away."

"Do you think that'll happen?"

He looked away. A moment passed before he met her eyes again. "Unfortunately, I don't. I don't know if it's related to Thornebrook or something else, but people don't go to that much trouble without a good reason."

"The question is, what are they after?"

"That's one question. The other is, should we dig into it, or should we let it go, let the police handle it? What would get you out of danger?"

"Not that I want to be in danger, but if it's an issue of justice, then I'm willing to endure a little danger to reach it. So... I'm not ready to drop that charge yet. Let me talk to Zachary Hardy first, learn what I can, and we'll go from there."

His pressed lips said he wanted to argue, but he didn't. "One more thing. Leland thinks your intruder might be related to the Kyle Griffin case. He wants us to get that settled ASAP."

Misty sat back, frustration mixing with the Chinese food in her stomach. "The man is dangerous, and he needs to be behind bars." Not that he would be if she didn't change Tony Castellan's mind.

"Okay." Tate's tone was too calm, like he was trying to rein her in. She resented it. "Tell me about it."

"Griffin and the victim were dating. When he got abusive, she called the police. He was arrested for assault. But the charges against him were dropped."

"Why?"

She shrugged, the movement probably not hiding her anger. "He's connected. The prosecutor decided not to pursue it."

"Who was it?"

"Clinton. Apparently, they didn't teach him how to grow a backbone at Hah-vahd." She drew out the word like their smarmy fellow prosecutor.

"Did you know his father and Leland—?"

"Were roommates?" She laughed. "I think the kid at the newsstand knows. And the lady in the coffee shop."

"Gladys," Tate said.

Misty's laugh faded. "You know her name?"

"She supplies my coffee and never fails to have my favorite creamer. Of course I know her name."

Huh. The woman supplied Misty's coffee, too, but Misty had never bothered to ask.

"Anyway," she said, "he's been stalking the victim since then. Melanie has two kids, and he's even taken to following them. He approached her daughter once after school, grabbed her arm hard enough to leave a mark, and made some threatening remarks about the victim. The kid's only seven. Melanie is convinced he's eventually going to hurt her—or kill her. She's desperate to see him behind bars."

Tate nodded, though the movement was more contemplative than agreement. "It's hard to send people to prison for stalking."

"Melanie's brother was picking the kids up that day, and he witnessed how Kyle grabbed his niece. And apparently had witnessed Griffin's abuse before."

"So you have a solid witness."

Had a solid witness. If she admitted to Tate that Tony was backing out, he'd press her to offer a plea—or drop the case altogether.

"Melanie's kept great records," Misty said. "She has a Harassment Protection Order against him, and she's gotten photographs a number of times when he's violated it." Albeit some of those photos had been taken from behind as he'd walked away, but Misty thought they could be enough of a likeness to prove Melanie's point. She wasn't malicious, just trying to protect her family. Unfortunately, the jury might not realize that.

"Maybe we can find a compromise," Tate said.

"I offered five years. He refused. I'm not offering less."

"Five years? For stalking?"

"For hurting a child and threatening the child's mother because she ended their relationship. And even that made me sick to my stomach."

"Their counter-offer?"

"Two years suspended."

"So you go back with three, and then—"

"They'll refuse, counter, and we'll go back and forth until he gets off scot-free. They think I won't take it to court, that they can just keep holding off and holding off until I fold. Well, I'm not going to fold. I owe it to my client—"

"Your 'client' is Suffolk County."

"Not the county. The human beings who *live* in the county. In the city of Boston. In the Commonwealth of Massachusetts." She worked hard to temper the anger in her voice but knew she failed by the matching frustration in his expression. "It doesn't serve the commonwealth for this thug to be on the street. I'll take my chances in court."

"Leland wants it settled."

"He didn't tell *me* that. If he does, I'll make my case. Anyway, it goes to court Wednesday." And she would win, too. As long as the victim's brother made the right decision and testified against Griffin.

By the look on Tate's face, that wasn't the answer he was hoping for. But she'd done as much compromising as she intended to do. Some cases were worth fighting for, whether they put her in danger or not.

CHAPTER TEN

Tate had already known Misty could be as tenacious as a terrier, so he wasn't shocked when she dug her heels in about the Griffin case.

He *was* shocked at how her passion affected him. How long had it been since he'd cared as deeply as she did about the victims he was supposed to be protecting? He was focused on doing his job efficiently, but should that be his highest goal? It was his job to do the work Leland tasked him with—and to do it the way Leland wanted it done. But it was also his job to protect the people of Suffolk County.

Somehow, in his desire to move up in the DA's office, his true purpose had gotten lost. For him, but not for Misty, who was still glaring in his direction. Even wearing that furious expression, she was beautiful. Fierce and determined to do what was right, no matter what the cost.

He couldn't have stopped the wave of attraction any more than he could pause the surf. The only shock was that he hadn't seen it before—how attractive she was, not just in face and figure. She was a fighter, maybe not like her sister, who'd carried a gun for a living, but in her heart and spirit. Misty was brave and tough.

She was amazing.

And this was bad. Very bad. Because the last thing he needed was for this sudden desire to get in the way of their budding friendship. She needed an ally who wasn't drooling over her.

He'd keep the drooling to a minimum.

"What?" Her single word sounded defensive.

He shook himself out of his stupor and attempted the smile that worked on most women. "I admire your passion."

She stood, snatching her water glass, and headed for the kitchen. "Sure you do." She tossed the words over her shoulder.

He followed with his own empty glass. "I'm serious. Let me know if I can help you with the Griffin case. Gather information or—"

"I've got it under control." Though the words were still clipped, she turned at the counter and met his eyes. "But thanks for the offer. Are we done for the day?"

"Have the police located Frederick Parks?"

"Not yet. Talked to Reyes earlier, and she assured me they were searching, but there's been no sign of him."

"Okay, then. I brought his file, thought we could skim it, see if we can figure out where he might go."

With fresh glasses of water, they returned to the living room, where he found the information they had on Parks. "I haven't had a chance to look through it."

Misty settled on the couch beside him. She leaned close to read the file he'd opened on his lap. Much as he liked her being close, he slid it to the table so she'd shift away—allowing him to concentrate.

"Parks's victim, Ernie Phillips, was hospitalized. He barely survived." She flipped through the file until she reached photographs. They were clearly taken in a hospital room. Tate leaned in to get a better look at the man's face. Eyes swollen shut. Broken jaw. Cast on one arm from shoulder to fingertips.

The thought that the man who did that might be after Misty raised bile in his throat.

Swallowing, Tate flipped back to the first page and skimmed. "Motive?"

"We never knew. Parks was in a gang, but the victim didn't seem to be connected to any illegal activities. He wasn't in law enforcement. He worked for the state, if I remember correctly." She scanned that page, then flipped through the file and tapped the paper. "Right here. He was a building inspector."

"Huh." Tate grabbed the Thornebrook file and flipped through it. "That's a coincidence. Wasn't the guy Dawson bribed also a building inspector?"

"I don't think so. Zachary Hardy worked for..." She leaned closer to read the information, her arm brushing his. The scent of her, floral and sweet, filled his mind with images that shouldn't be there. This was far too close for colleagues. But jerking away would only make an already awkward position worse.

She tapped where she saw the information she'd sought. "Planning and Development."

Tate turned toward her, their faces just inches apart. "What do they do exactly?"

She scooted back on the sofa and turned his direction, putting distance between them. But the sudden tension stretched across the space. Did she feel it?

Or was it all coming from his side of the sofa?

"They oversee zoning and permits in the city," she said.

"Not the same thing." Not that there was any reason to believe Thornebrook and Parks were related. He tossed the

Thornebrook file back on her coffee table. "So you don't think the Parks assault was related to the victim's work?"

"I didn't at the time," Misty said. "But it was irrelevant because there were enough witnesses to put Parks away without knowing the motive. The victim claimed he had no idea why he was targeted. Parks approached the guy in broad daylight right outside his house, yanked him out of his car, and started beating him. Bystanders filmed it, and his face was clear on the video."

"Wait. They filmed it, but nobody tried to stop it?"

"It happened after school. All the witnesses were women and kids, so it's good none of them tried to get involved. They'd have just gotten hurt. Someone did call the police, but they didn't show up in time. When Freddy was done, he ran to his car and drove to Boston. The police found him there on"—she consulted the file—"Aldus Street."

Tate located the police report and noted the address where Parks had been arrested. "Home of a friend?"

She grabbed her laptop and typed in the address, then shifted the screen so he could see. She'd put it on satellite mode, which showed nothing but an empty lot surrounded by brownstones.

"That's weird. Why would he go there?"

"It's possible something's been constructed there since this image was taken. I didn't look into it at the time because it didn't matter to the case."

He searched the police report again. "The attack happened in Billerica? That's a pretty nice town, right?"

"Certainly not a hotbed of gang violence."

He continued to peruse the file, and she read beside him silently.

"I assume they looked for him at his mother's house," Tate said. Parks had been living with his mom and younger sister when he'd been arrested.

"That's probably the first place Reyes went."

"It would've been nice if you'd had a heads-up about him getting out of prison. Cofer should have called you before he was released, not after. He had to have known it was happening. Why wouldn't he warn you?"

"I'll ask him if he ever calls me back. Hopefully, Reyes will find Parks and bring him in. Find out what's going on. Assuming he's the one who bugged my apartment, I want to know why."

Though Misty's words were all business, a look flitted across her expression. More than worry. Fear.

Considering what Parks had done to his last victim, Tate didn't want the man anywhere near Misty.

CHAPTER ELEVEN

Misty hated working from home.
She'd never been very good at making friends but at least in the office there was the illusion of companionship. There was activity, a change in scenery, people to smile at as if she belonged.

Working from home had made her low-grade loneliness acute. Nobody had been happier when employees had been cleared to work in the office after the pandemic.

Now she was alone again, and this time, she didn't have the comfort of her own apartment as she settled at Summer's small kitchen table on Monday morning. Her first call was to Tony Castellan. No answer, again. She left another message, praying he'd call her back.

Her second call was to Jeffrey Cofer, Freddy Parks's lawyer.

"He's not in." The woman who answered the phone sounded harried and impatient.

"This is Misty Lake, ADA. I'm returning his call from Friday night. It's imperative that we talk as soon as possible."

"I'll pass along the message," the woman said. "That's the best I can do."

"Give me his cell number, and I'll call him directly."

"Sorry. I don't do that."

Misty stifled a sigh. "Is he expected in today?"

"He was. I'll tell him you called." She took Misty's cell phone number and hung up.

Frustrated, Misty tried the local zoning office, where Zachary Hardy worked. She learned that he'd been transferred out of permitting, and the person who answered had no idea where to find him. Fortunately, Misty had a contact in the city's human resources department, who was able to find where Hardy was currently employed. Misty called, but he wasn't available. She left a message for him to call her back as soon as possible.

So far, she was oh-for-three. Maybe that meant things could only get better.

With the stack of files from Friday night, Misty started making calls to defense attorneys and offering deals. She hated to admit it, but having Tate talk through the cases had helped her move more quickly than she would have otherwise. Ever since the kidnapping, she'd been second-guessing her decisions, worried she'd screw up and let the wrong guy back on the street. She'd been struggling to see her cases objectively.

But with Tate's help, she'd made decisions on six out of seven cases in the course of a weekend. And she felt good about all the plea deals.

Based on the reactions she got from defense attorneys, they felt good about them too. A couple dickered on some of the details, but by lunchtime, she'd managed to settle all six.

Just like that.

She finished a salad loaded with grilled chicken. Tired of the café table-turned-workspace, she needed to get out of the apartment.

Checking the guards' schedule, she saw that Hughes was on duty again today. She sent him a text.

> Can you check the roof, see if there's any place up there to sit?

His answer came immediately.

> There is.

Huh. Thorough, these guards.

> I'd like to work up there this afternoon.

> Give us a few minutes to make sure it's clear.

∽

Fifteen minutes later, Misty pushed out of the dark stairwell into the sunny August day and breathed in fresh air. Leaving Hughes by the door, she crossed the rooftop to the little patio area, set her laptop and files on a table, and brushed dust off a wicker chair.

It was hot in the sun but comfortable in the shade beneath the awning. Even better, since she was five stories off the ground, many of the typical scents of the city—exhaust and garbage—didn't reach her, and even the sounds were muted up here.

She was still breathing in the fresh air when her phone rang. "Misty Lake."

"Uh, hi. This is Zack Hardy. I got a message to call you?"

"Hi, Mr. Hardy." Misty opened the Thornebrook file. "I'm a prosecutor with the Suffolk County DA's office, and I wanted to talk to you about the bribe offered by Raul Dawson."

The pause that followed her words was unnaturally long. "What do you want to know?" He sounded wary.

"What can you tell me?"

"Not much to tell. I refused to issue the permits. Dawson offered me a bribe."

"How much?"

"Ten grand."

She whistled. "That's a lot of money to turn down."

"I believed in what I was doing."

Believed. Past tense.

"Where was the bribe offered?" she asked. "Were you at the property?"

"Nah. I didn't need to leave the office to do my job. Dawson found me on my way to my car."

"Did he threaten you?"

"Not in so many words, but I got the sense he was serious about getting the permits."

"And you turned it down because...?"

"There are rules in place for a reason," Hardy said, "and those rules shouldn't be overlooked because somebody's connected."

She'd been about to ask a follow-up question when that last word snagged. "You think Dawson was connected?"

"Somebody was, no question."

"To...?"

"I don't know, but after I refused the bribe and turned him in, I was transferred out of that department and given a lousy job with less responsibility. I'd quit and find something else, but I'm counting down to retirement."

"Before that happened, were you pressured to issue the permits?"

"Nope. My boss seemed impressed I'd turned the money

down, even recommended me for a promotion. He was as confused as me when I was transferred."

So maybe Dawson was connected. Or, if not Dawson, then somebody at Thornebrook. "Tell me why you didn't issue the permits."

"The property wasn't zoned for what they planned to build. There're plenty of business districts in Boston, but that was a residential area. Look, I could get into all the specifics, send you the zones and stuff. The point is, that building should never have been built on that spot."

"Would you please send me that information?"

He sighed. "Sure. Why not."

She gave him her email address. "So he offered you a bribe..." she prompted, hoping he'd elaborate.

"Which was stupid. Even if I was dumb enough to take his money, once the building was built, it would be easy to see it didn't belong there. There's not enough parking. Not enough frontage area for an office building that size, and it's surrounded by converted brownstones. If anybody had a gripe about it, they'd easily see I'd issued the permit. I could've gotten fired. Or so I thought."

Another loaded remark. "Explain."

"Well, the guy who replaced me issued the permits. I assume his bank account reflects it. And the building is there, and nobody seems to care. Makes me feel like an idiot. I turned down the money and lost my job. He took the money and, last I heard, is managing the department. Like I said...somebody over at Thornebrook was connected."

"You don't think it was Dawson?"

"He was a cog, low man on the pole. Kind of a rough guy, construction worker, you know? Just doing what they told him."

"Who is 'they'?"

"That's the question, isn't it?"

Indeed it was. "Thanks for your help. Send over that information as soon as you can." She ended the call and made notes.

Somebody higher up in state government had transferred Hardy and moved a more willing person into his position. Was that person connected to somebody at Thornebrook? Or was it somebody from IAF, the company that had the property built, who had connections with state officials?

She made a note to dig into IAF, but first, Thornebrook.

She found a number for the construction company and dialed. A woman with a perfect receptionist's voice answered. "Thornebrook Construction. How may I help you?"

"Hi there!" Misty made her tone as friendly as possible. "This is Misty Lake, ADA. Can I speak with Raul Dawson?"

"Mr. Dawson is off the property at the moment. Can I take a message?"

"Any chance his boss is available? I'd like to speak with someone familiar with the IAF project."

"One moment please."

Misty waited five minutes, six, before an older-sounding man answered the phone with a gruff, "Bob Begley."

"Hi, Mr. Begley. This is Misty Lake with the DA's office. I'm just trying to clear up a few facts about the Raul Dawson case. Are you familiar with it?"

"You'll need to talk to Mr. Dawson's attorney."

"Of course, I understand. I was more curious about the building project itself. It was completed, is that correct?"

"Yeah," he said. "Not sure why that yahoo at Planning and Development tried to hold up the permits, but they were all issued, no problem."

"My understanding is that the property didn't align with the codes. Were adjustments made, or exceptions sought, to get the building built?"

His voice took on a patronizing note. "We aligned with all the codes, ma'am. You ought to drive by it, see for yourself. It's a beaut. We just completed another property for IAF at Hearts and Homes—a rec center. They're having a big grand opening on Sunday. All sorts of bigwigs are coming. The attorney general's gonna be there. Even a representative from the governor's office. Maybe the governor himself. I could probably get you an invite."

Quite a who's who list.

Hearts and Homes. That sounded familiar, but she couldn't figure out why. "Where is that property?"

"Hopkinton."

A town west of Boston in Middlesex County.

"You're saying IAF is connected to Hearts and Homes?"

"International...Aid something, I think," he said. "IAF owns it. They got some kind of housing out there."

"That's very helpful. Thank you."

"You want that invite? We got more tickets than we can use."

She started to reject his offer but thought better of it. "Maybe. Let me get back to you."

Misty ended the call and Googled Hearts and Homes. When the first page loaded, she remembered why she'd heard of it before. Hearts and Homes was a community for displaced refugees. It had first opened years prior, hailed as a place where people who'd gone through the worst tragedies imaginable could find rest and peace. As far as she knew, the place offered just that. But a few years back, there'd been a problem with a furnace, a carbon monoxide leak. The alarms had sounded, but one deaf woman, Jemilla Amin, hadn't heard them. She'd died in her sleep.

The tragedy made the local newspapers. Misty figured there'd been an investigation but couldn't remember how it turned out, assuming she'd ever known. She made a note to look into it.

Maybe none of what she'd learned from Hardy and the guy at Thornebrook mattered. But something told her there was a lot more going on beneath the surface that she hadn't uncovered. Until she knew what it was, she wasn't ready to drop this so-called *simple* bribery case.

CHAPTER TWELVE

Tate spent the morning and early afternoon focusing on his own cases, though he found his mind as much on Misty and her dilemma as on the files he needed to close out before the end of the week.

He was just hanging up the phone when Clinton stepped into his office. "I need to tell you—"

"Your father roomed with Leland at Harvard." Tate pushed back his chair and stood. He'd been in a decent mood. A neutral mood, at least, but the sight of his nemesis made his blood heat. "You went golfing with the boss over the weekend. Or was it lunching or country-clubbing? Whatever it was, you already told me."

Clinton's perfectly shaped eyebrows rose on his forehead. "Someone steal your lunch money?"

"Tell me about Kyle Griffin."

He blinked, and those brows lowered. "Who?"

"He beat up his girlfriend, and she wanted to press charges, but you dropped them."

"I don't remember that case."

"Look it up. He's gone from abuser to abusive stalker, which wouldn't have happened if he'd been behind bars."

Clinton nodded, though the movement was slow and deliberate. "Your case?"

"Misty's. She's taking it to court Wednesday. But she wouldn't have to if you were competent, Hah-vahd notwithstanding."

"Tell you what, Steele. You take care of your cases, and I'll take care of mine." He swiveled and walked away.

Jerk.

Tate settled back in his chair and tried to resume his work, but he found it difficult to concentrate. Thirty minutes later, his desk phone rang.

"Steele here."

"Why aren't you in my office?" Leland didn't sound happy.

"Uh...did we have a meeting, sir?"

"I told Clinton to send you up almost an hour ago."

"He didn't tell me." Tate stood, fresh irritation making his words clipped. "I'm on my way."

After climbing the stairs and getting a go-on-in nod from the DA's assistant, Tate knocked on his door and stepped inside. "Sorry about that."

"Have a seat."

Tate settled into one of the two chairs on the opposite side of Leland's wide desk. "What's up?"

"How're your cases going?"

"No problems." He updated his boss on the work he'd done that morning, though the DA rarely got that involved in day-to-day operations.

"And Misty's cases?"

"She was planning to offer plea bargains on all but one of them today."

"Which one?"

"The Dawson case. Bribery charge."

Leland leaned against his high-backed leather chair. "I thought I told you to take care of that."

"It's her case." Defensiveness rose, and Tate worked to tamp it down. "She feels like she needs more information."

Leland rolled his eyes. "Give me the facts."

Tate did, which didn't take long, considering how little they knew.

"That's it?" he said when Tate was through. "She ought to drop the charges."

Tate agreed, but it seemed disloyal to Misty to say so. "I'm sure she'll reach the right conclusion. She's thorough."

"Which is why I wanted you to help her." He blew out a breath. "Look, Steele. I think you've got what it takes to move up here. Smart, well-educated, ambitious. I know you're ready for a new challenge."

Forcing himself not to look too eager, Tate simply nodded. "I am, absolutely. Not that I haven't enjoyed—"

"White-collar crimes aren't what you're used to. Not that they're victimless, but we're not talking about murderers and rapists here. We're usually talking about embezzlers and"—he gestured toward Tate as if his empty hands held stacks of files—"bribery. I need to know you're the kind of guy who can handle that. The case we're talking about… It doesn't matter if there's more to it or not. It doesn't matter if…what was his name?"

"Dawson."

"If Dawson was acting on someone else's behalf or working alone. For your purposes, it only matters if he did the crime, if a jury can be convinced he did the crime, and if he should do time or pay a fine for the crime. Right?"

"Yes, but—"

"So why hasn't that case been closed?"

"Because it's Misty's case, not mine."

"You'd have closed it?"

"Absolutely." Even if there was more to it, Tate would have dropped the charges and moved on. He'd never have bothered to figure out if there was a conspiracy. Which, sitting across from Leland, seemed like the right decision. But when he was with Misty, he understood her need to understand the big picture.

"And she's not even here." Leland shook his head.

"Because of the intruder in her apartment and her concern for her personal safety, she's working from home."

"She should have decided to do what was asked of her." He exhaled a long breath. "Sorry, that was... It's not your problem. Ever since the kidnapping, she's been off her game."

"She just needs time."

"Maybe." By the firm press of Leland's lips, he didn't look convinced. "I'm just not sure she has what it takes to do this job. I was thinking of moving her into white-collar, but maybe she won't be able to manage that either."

Misty in white-collar crimes. Not Tate, but Misty? She didn't want the position, but if Leland wanted to move her, he would.

Leland seemed to be waiting for him to speak. Tate cleared his throat. Sick to his stomach. Tried to think of what to say. Before he had time to, Leland continued.

"The way her cases piled up...she isn't handling them. You've worked with her. What do you think?"

"Oh, uh..." Tate's stomach churned. With the right response, he could nudge Misty out of his way.

She didn't even want to work in white-collar. But Leland didn't think she could hack the ones she was prosecuting. So maybe it wasn't a matter of Misty staying where she was or moving to white-collar crimes. Maybe it was a matter of Misty moving...or finding a new job.

Was that Tate's problem?

Leland was watching him through squinted eyes, perhaps aware of the very difficult position he'd put him in.

Tate needed to answer honestly, no matter what it meant for him. He spoke with confidence. "Misty is competent and capable, and having worked with her this weekend, I find myself admiring her passion. I think she'll be an asset wherever you put her."

Even though he'd probably put himself further from his goal, and even though his stomach churned with emptiness and nausea, he'd have felt much, much worse if he hadn't spoken the truth.

Leland's expression didn't shift for a long moment. And then he smiled. Was that admiration Tate saw there? Had it been a test?

"All right, then. It's good to know where you stand." Leland stood and held out his hand. "I'm serious about that bribery case. Use your influence with her to get her to drop it. She has too many other cases that need to be dealt with."

"I'll do what I can."

Tate was halfway out the door when Leland added, "Oh, what about Griffin? Did she offer a plea?"

Rather than tell the boss what he obviously didn't want to hear, Tate said, "You should talk to her about that. I'm not sure where it stands."

Which was technically true because something could have changed that day.

But mostly, Tate didn't want to bear any more responsibility for Misty's bad decisions.

CHAPTER THIRTEEN

Misty had been about to finish up for the day when her cell rang. Probably her sister. Summer had called to check on her multiple times a day, despite Misty's assurances that she was safe. Honestly, she was surprised Summer hadn't shown up to babysit her.

But it wasn't Summer on the line.

Recognizing the number as one Misty had dialed that morning, she snatched it up. "Misty Lake."

"It's Tony Castellan." Melanie's brother. His voice was high for a man's, though perhaps only because he was nervous. "I know what you're going to say, but I can't testify."

"You'd sacrifice your sister's safety and that of her children? Why?"

"I have a family too."

"Have you been threatened?" Threatening a witness was a felony. They could put Griffin away for that—if they could get Tony to testify.

"Kyle was my best friend."

"Even after he beat up your sister?" Misty didn't temper her accusing tone. "Started following them around? Injured your niece? Are you really still loyal—?"

"No." By the anger in his voice, Misty was getting to him. "I'm just saying—"

"His friendship is more important than your sister's safety?"

"Of course not."

"Then what is?"

"I can't testify!" He was breathing hard.

"You *can* testify, and I'll be issuing a subpoena to ensure you do."

"I won't show up."

"Tell me what's going on."

In the long pause that followed her demand, she let herself hope he might be swayed.

"I didn't see anything," Tony finally said. "I don't know anything, and if you call me to testify, that's what I'll say. But I do have something I think'll help."

Frustration hummed in her veins. She groped for some way to change his mind, but she'd worked with enough spooked witnesses to know he wasn't waffling. "What is it?"

"I started to suspect he was hurting my sister. Once when I showed up at her house, she had a black eye and a bruise on her arm. She denied it, but I knew. Kyle is..." He heaved a breath. "I'll never forgive myself for hanging out with him, bringing him into our lives, into Melanie's life. It's my fault she got involved with him. He had money, and after that loser boyfriend of hers left her with the kids and Kyle started showering her with presents... I tried to warn her off him, but... The point is, it's my fault, so when I saw the bruises, I knew he was hurting her. I needed to find a way to bring him down."

"You can bring him down by testifying."

Tony continued as if she hadn't spoken. "I set up a camera

at her house, thinking she could use the recording to get him to back off."

Hope and fury mingled in a strange cocktail. "Why didn't you tell me this before?"

"Because...because I have a family too. I didn't realize how he was before. I swear, I didn't know what kind of man he is. We grew up together, me and Kyle. I thought we were friends. I didn't want him hanging out with Melanie because he's..." Another deep breath. "The point is, I got scared, okay? He'd have known either Melanie set up the video camera or I did. He'd have made both of us pay."

"Your sister's been paying all along."

"I know, I know." Again, his voice pitched high. "I'm trying to figure out how to put him away without putting anybody else I love in danger."

"What about justice? What about doing the right thing?"

Tony laughed, the sound humorless. "Tell me you're joking. You work in the DA's office. You know justice doesn't exist."

She knew no such thing. But...

But how often did victims get justice?

Not very.

She thought of all the deals she'd made that morning. Had she been an agent of justice—or expediency? The question didn't settle well.

But she'd done what she could. That was the problem. She could do so little.

"I need that recording." She wouldn't try to talk him into testifying again right now. She'd let the subpoena do the work for her. "Can you bring it by the DA's office?"

"No! I can't go anywhere near there. Or near Melanie. I told Kyle she and I aren't speaking. He's got people watching her all the time. They're watching me too. Kyle's got eyes everywhere."

Was Kyle Griffin really that powerful, or had Tony descended into paranoia? "What do you suggest, then?"

"You gotta meet me somewhere he won't see us. Not at my work, definitely not at yours. Maybe I could leave it for you in the park, and you could pick it up after, like a dead drop, like they do in spy movies?"

She wasn't about to play 007. "A friend of mine owns a coffee shop. I'll get in touch with him and make arrangements for us to meet there. I'll go in through the back door, and you can go in the front and order something. You can pass the recording to the owner, and he can give it to me. Does that work?"

Tony considered that a long moment before he said, "Where is it?"

She gave him the address. "I'll set it up for this evening, okay? Try the cinnamon rolls. They're outstanding."

∼

Unlike the charming storefront of Farbod Hashemi's coffee shop, with its pretty green-and-white awning and wrought-iron café tables on the sidewalk, the back door was dingy and unremarkable, situated between a dumpster and the white van Mr. Hashemi used to deliver catering orders. The dingy alleyway between the old brick building and the one on the opposite side was wide enough for two sedans, but certainly not two SUVs like the one the bodyguard had escorted her to when they'd left Summer's apartment.

Ian was a blond-haired, blue-eyed kid who, aside from the rippling muscles, looked about as dangerous as a golden retriever. He'd backed down the alley—maybe anticipating the need for a quick escape—and parked behind the van.

Misty pulled the handle, but the door didn't open.

"Sit tight, ma'am," Greta said. "Let us check it out first."

The female bodyguard was older and seemed to be in charge. She hopped out of the passenger seat and knocked on the coffee shop door. It swung open, and the woman stepped inside.

Misty and Ian waited in silence for less than a minute before Greta returned to the alley, head swiveling to survey one end to the other.

Ian stepped out and opened Misty's door. "Straight inside, please."

Misty walked between the two armed bodyguards, feeling like the Queen of Sheba.

Or just feeling like an idiot. All this because somebody had broken into her apartment. But she'd rather be paranoid and silly than cavalier and kidnapped—or killed—any day of the week.

She'd only been in the kitchen of Mr. Hashemi's shop once, back when she'd interviewed him about the man who'd assaulted him. The place hadn't changed—the gleaming surfaces, the scents of yeast and cinnamon and coffee, the stacks of industrial-sized food containers.

Mr. Hashemi greeted her without his customary smile. "You are all right?" He licked his lips, his gaze flicking from one bodyguard to the other. She knew the horror he'd escaped in his own country, understood his well-earned fear of men with guns.

She stepped forward, resisting the urge to reach out, to squeeze his arm in reassurance. She didn't know him well enough to touch him. "I'm safe. Thank you for letting us do this."

"I'm happy to have a way to help you, even if it is only this small thing."

"It's no small thing. Has he come yet?"

"Not yet." He nodded to a small room off the kitchen.

Through the open door, she saw a desk covered with stacks of envelopes and scattered papers. Against the wall, a metal shelving unit held baking pans, bottles of various oils, and huge plastic containers of spices. "Please, make yourselves comfortable."

"That's okay. He should be here any minute."

Mr. Hashemi nodded, bending at the waist the slightest bit, and headed through the curtain to the front. Aside from a kid washing dishes and Misty and her bodyguards, the back room was empty.

Misty leaned against the wall near the door. "Thanks for doing this."

"Happy to, ma'am." Ian stood on one side of her. "It's our job."

On her opposite side, Greta said nothing.

They didn't have to wait long before Mr. Hashemi pushed through the curtain again. He approached and held out a flash drive. "He slipped this to me with the money to pay for his cinnamon roll."

"Excellent." She took the flash drive and shoved it in her pocket. "Is he gone?"

"Yes. Left as soon as he got his food."

That was good. The man was probably being paranoid, but if people were following him, they'd be gone by the time Misty and her guards left.

"You will be in tomorrow?" Mr. Hashemi asked.

"Probably not for a few days. I've been missing your coffee."

The old man didn't ask where she was staying or why she'd changed her routine.

Ian stepped outside, then returned a moment later. "Straight to the car."

She followed him into the alley, Greta behind.

Ian was halfway to the car door when a gunshot reverberated off the brick walls.

Ian gasped, went down. "I'm hit!"

Greta pushed Misty forward, around Ian, who was struggling to get up. Misty couldn't leave him.

"Get in!" Greta shouted. "Get..."

Her words were lost in the sound of more gunshots. Masked men were coming from both ends of the alley.

Greta yanked her down, covering her with her body.

More gunshots sounded. Then a man shouted. "Misty Lake! We need to—"

Another gunshot.

In Misty's ear, Greta said, "We'll provide cover. You run back to the coffee shop." Before Misty could respond, Greta rolled off of her, firing.

Misty bolted to the back door. It was locked. She banged on it.

It whipped open, and she was pulled inside.

Mr. Hashemi slammed the door behind her, eyes wide and terrified. "What is happening?"

"I don't know. Call nine-one-one."

"I did. Where are your people?"

Still out there. Ian and Greta, maybe shot. Maybe dying.

Why? Who would be shooting at them?

She didn't know. She only knew she needed to get out of that store, now, before anybody else got hurt. "Wait for the police," she said. "If my guards try to get in, let them. Otherwise, lock the doors and don't open them until you see a badge."

"I have customers."

"Lock them in or kick them out. Just...be safe." She bolted through the kitchen and into the café filled with diners. They were standing, staring at her wide-eyed. The sound of gunshots was muffled but clear enough.

More people who could be harmed because of her. She couldn't have it. She wouldn't.

She ran outside into the warm evening, not stopping to see if anybody followed. She heard footsteps, shouts, though whether they came from friends or enemies or just surprised bystanders, she didn't know.

She ran, flat out, away from the coffee shop and her bodyguards and safety, until she reached a T station. She rushed down the concrete steps, dodging commuters and tourists, and then hopped over the turnstile. Not that she had time to stop and pay the fare, but even if she did, she didn't have her purse or her wallet. She had nothing but her phone and that little flash drive.

She ran again and turned a corner toward the train platform, looking behind her.

At the top of the stairs, a man wearing all black met her eyes. He ran down the stairs, pushing people out of his way.

A train screeched into the station. She jumped on, watching through the window as the man got closer, closer.

He shouted, "I just want to—!"

But the doors closed.

The train pulled away.

Misty collapsed into a seat, heart thumping, lungs burning, staring at the furious man on the platform.

What had just happened?

CHAPTER FOURTEEN

"Are you out of your mind?"

Tate's raised voice had Misty's already racing heart picking up speed. "Don't yell at me." She clicked on the seatbelt and collapsed. She didn't have the energy to talk, much less argue.

"I'm not..." He took a deep breath and shifted the car into drive.

Not until after she'd gotten on the train had she looked to see where she was headed. She'd taken the Red Line to Park Street, then hopped off, walked the underground corridor to Downtown Crossing, and gotten onto the outbound Orange Line train, hoping to throw off the person—or people—following her.

And then she'd called Tate and asked him to meet her at Wellington, a commuter stop almost at the end of the line, not explaining how she'd ended up alone and on the T when she was supposed to be safely tucked in at Summer's apartment.

"Nice car." It wasn't really. An old, dingy Honda Accord. She'd have pegged him as someone who drove a luxury car.

Come to think of it, that summer at the hospital in Maine, she'd seen him climbing into a BMW.

"Not mine," he said. "I was still at the office when you called, and my car's in the apartment garage. I borrowed this." He signaled and turned toward the city. "What happened?"

As she explained, his gaze kept darting toward her, disbelief in his expression. When she was finished, he said, "Do you think this witness...Tony Castellan, did you say? Do you think he set you up?"

She tapped the pocket where she'd left the flash drive. "I don't know. Why would anybody shoot at me?" She could still hear the sound of her name echoing off the alley's brick walls.

She could still hear the gunshots.

And see Ian on the ground.

And hear Greta telling her to run.

At the thought of the people who'd tried to guard her, her stomach roiled. Were they all right?

She needed to find out. Her phone had been buzzing, buzzing, buzzing for half an hour, but she hadn't wanted to answer it until she was safe.

Now she was. She hoped, anyway. She needed to find out if the bodyguards were all right. If anybody else had been hurt.

This was a nightmare.

"It must've been Castellan," Tate said. "Which tells me all this is about the Griffin case, not Dawson and the bribery. Not Parks."

"Yeah. Maybe." His logic probably tracked, but she couldn't think.

"Maybe? Somebody just—"

"I know what happened," she snapped. She took a breath. "Sorry. I'm just..." Her whole body trembled. Being shot at, running. Not until she'd been on the Orange Line, not until she'd started to think she'd actually escaped that guy who'd been following her, did the enormity of what happened start to sink in. Even now, she couldn't seem to get her mind to comprehend it. Rather than explain any of that, she simply said, "Thank you for picking me up."

He nodded but didn't respond.

In the silence, her phone buzzed again.

"Answer that," he said.

She pulled it from her pocket and looked at the screen. Summer. Of course. She connected the call. "Hey."

"Thank God, thank God you're all right."

The simple words had a profound effect, pulling Misty out of her stupor. A sob climbed up her throat, and she doubled over, holding her stomach. She couldn't speak for the emotion clogging her voice.

"Misty?" Summer said. "*Are* you all right? Were you hurt? Ian said—"

"He's okay?"

"Yeah. The bullet hit him in the thigh. He said by the time he figured out what'd happened, you were gone."

"Greta?"

"She wasn't hurt. She laid down cover fire until you got inside. When you did, the shooters took off. She said she expected to find you waiting for her, but you'd taken off. Where are you?"

"I had to get out of there. There were innocent people. Mr. Hashemi, his customers. What if those guys had come in?"

"Greta and Ian would have protected you." Summer sounded like she was fighting anger. "They sent you inside to keep you safe. You're supposed to do what they say."

"For all I knew, they were dead." Misty hadn't meant to shout.

Tate reached across the console and laid his hand over hers, squeezing it in a warm, supportive grip. That simple touch calmed her.

He would want to hear Summer's end of the conversation. She could either put the phone on speaker or repeat what her sister said when Tate questioned her.

She put it on speaker.

Tate shot her a grateful smile.

Gently, Summer said, "Fear can make us do crazy things."

Had Misty been propelled out of the coffee shop by fear? She'd thought she was protecting innocent people. But maybe she should have stayed and waited for the bodyguards. At the time, she hadn't thought they'd be able to get to safety. She'd feared their deaths.

And her own.

"Next time," Summer said, "please stay put at least long enough to find out if your bodyguards are all right."

"I didn't mean for them to get hurt. It's not that I didn't care. I was trying to keep everybody safe."

"I understand. I don't mean it that way, as if it was your job to check on them. I just mean that, if they're able, they'll find a way to protect you. If you'd waited a minute or two, Greta and Ian would have secured your safety. But if you take off on your own, anything can happen. They've been frantic to find you. Not just them but the whole team. Now, can you please tell me where you are?"

"I got on the T, changed trains. I had my friend Tate pick me up at Wellington."

"Okay. So you're with him, in a car, not on the street?"

"Yeah, we're safe."

"Next time, call me, and I'll send a car."

"You keep saying 'next time.' Is there going to be—?"

"I just mean, if something else happens..." Summer's voice

was calm, almost placating. "You need to stay with the people trying to protect you."

Misty swiped at her tears and sat back. She was safe. It was over, for now. "I want to go home or...back to your place, I guess." Change into her pajamas, drink a cup of hot tea, and curl up under a blanket.

Tate cleared his throat. "We need to go to the police."

She didn't want to do that, not even a little.

Summer said, "Your friend's right. Greta's there now. I'm going to send you the address of the precinct. Go straight there. I'll let Greta know you're on your way."

It was the last thing Misty wanted to do, but someone had been shot. And it wasn't as if she'd been making the best decisions in the last hour, running on fear and adrenaline. Fine, then. She'd do what Tate and Summer said. "We're on our way."

CHAPTER FIFTEEN

Tate followed Misty into the detectives' bullpen, a giant room filled with desks—mostly empty at nine o'clock at night—at the Boston PD headquarters. He'd expected to find Misty dressed in her usual work attire when he picked her up—business suit, high heels, hair in a bun. But she wore jeans, a pretty floral blouse, and slip-on sneakers.

Good thing. He couldn't imagine her running through Boston in the heels she wore to work.

Detective Reyes, a middle-aged woman with dyed-red hair, graying roots, and skin so pale it was almost pasty, led them to a desk not far from the elevator. "Have a seat."

Misty did, and Tate pulled a chair from an adjacent desk and settled in beside her. She'd been calm, then crying, then angry. He couldn't imagine what she'd endured, not just the bullets aimed at her, but the fact that one of her bodyguards had been shot.

Tate couldn't do much, but maybe his presence helped.

Misty had called him, after all. When she'd thought her life was in danger, she hadn't called her sister or the police or even an Uber for a ride. She'd called him.

And thank God she had.

It was astounding how important she'd become to Tate in just a couple of days. Maybe because of all the time they'd spent together, perhaps because she'd now been threatened twice—and needed him both times. That was probably all it was, these feelings rising up in him, and they'd be carried away when the autumn breeze blew in.

But he didn't think so.

"Where's Greta?" Misty asked. "How's Ian?" She'd already posed those questions once, the moment Detective Reyes had introduced herself. But the detective hadn't responded, just led them here. "Do you know if Ian's all right? Is he in the hospital? Did he—?"

Opening a notebook, Reyes said, "Your bodyguards already told me their version of events."

"Did you see them? Did you go to the hospital?"

"They came here."

"But Ian—"

"The bullet just grazed his thigh."

"But he fell!" Misty's voice was too loud, and a cop seated a few tables away turned their direction. "It must've been worse than that."

Tate was tempted to take Misty's hand again but feared she wouldn't appreciate the gesture at that moment.

Reyes's expression shifted to a soft smile. "He got down to return fire. He didn't fall."

"But that... Oh." Misty closed her eyes, shook her head. "I thought... He said he was hit."

"He was," Detective Reyes said. "I'm sure it was painful and shocking. It just wasn't that serious."

"That's good." She took a breath. "Thank God."

"Can you tell me what happened?"

Misty recounted the events for the detective, adding a few

details Tate had missed when she'd told him. Like how closely the man following her had gotten in the train station. She'd barely outrun a gunman. Thank God he hadn't fired at her in the station. Thank God the train came when it did.

"You got a good look at him?" Reyes asked.

"Yes. I was on the T, and he was on the platform. He looked right at me."

"It wasn't..." She consulted her notebook. "Frederick Parks, the man you told me about on Saturday."

"No." Misty shook her head. "Definitely not. This guy was older than Freddy, and taller."

"Okay," Reyes said. "Can you describe him?"

Misty closed her eyes. "I'd guess he was in his forties. Taller than I am, but only a little. Maybe six feet. Broad shoulders. Broad all the way down. Like he worked out, and if he quit, he'd be chubby. Thick neck. Big head. Square face. Strong jaw. Really short brown hair. It stuck up on top. It was shorter on the sides. Some gray at the temples. No beard or mustache, but he needed a shave." She opened her eyes. "Does that help?"

"Yes, a lot." Reyes flew over her laptop keys.

"Have you ever seen Kyle Griffin?" Tate asked.

Misty turned to him. "I've never met him in person."

To Reyes, Tate said, "That's where I'd start. Today's meeting was about him."

"He's a defendant in one of my cases," Misty added. "Were Greta or Ian able to identify anybody?"

"There were two shooters, but they both wore masks," Reyes said. "You're the only one who saw a face. Tell me why you were there."

Tate listened while Misty explained the meeting she'd set up with Tony Castellan.

"You have that flash drive?" Reyes asked. After Misty

handed it over, Reyes slipped it into the port on her laptop. She clicked the mouse, then spun the screen so they could see.

It was a video of one person grabbing another person and shoving her—Tate guessed it was a *her*—to the floor. But she fell out of view of the camera. The video had been taken in a living room, but it was grainy, hard to make out.

Worse than that, neither of the people's faces were visible on the screen.

"Is there sound?"

Reyes tapped her volume button, but nothing changed. "Doesn't look like it."

Misty sighed and sat back. "That's useless. What does Tony think I can do with that?"

Tate suspected the man knew the video wouldn't help Misty's case. There was only one reason he'd go to the trouble to get it to her. "Castellan set you up."

"Maybe." Misty looked from him to the detective. "Maybe he's trying to help. He thought Griffin's men were following him. Maybe they followed him there and..."

"And saw you go in through the back?" Tate's frustration rose. Obviously, this Tony Castellan guy didn't care about his sister. "And they just happened to be prepared to ambush you? How long were you in the coffee shop?"

She shrugged. "Fifteen, twenty minutes."

Reyes flipped through her notebook. "Twenty-two, according to Greta."

"Not long enough for Griffin to set up an ambush, right?" Tate looked from Misty to Reyes and back. "Do you disagree?"

"I just hate to think..." Misty rubbed her temples. "The victims are his sister and niece. What kind of person would betray his own sister? Griffin must've threatened Tony's family."

"Okay." Reyes made a note. "We'll bring him in and question him. Meanwhile, you have someplace to stay?"

"I've been staying at my sister's since the break-in on Saturday."

"You're keeping that quiet?"

"Trying to." Misty turned toward Tate, looking like she was ready to collapse.

"We were hoping to throw the intruders off. Remember, they planted a bug, right?" Reyes nodded, and he continued. "We went into the apartment and talked about how Misty was going to go stay with a friend in the Berkshires."

"But they know now that I'm in town. Griffin does, anyway." Misty sounded as tired as she looked. "I never should have taken that meeting. It was stupid. I thought that could help"—she gestured toward the laptop—"but it's useless."

"Griffin and his people don't know where you're staying, right?" Reyes asked.

"Right," Misty said.

"But why would Griffin bug your apartment?" Tate asked. "What did he hope to gain?"

"I guess he wanted to know what kind of plea deal I was planning to offer. Or maybe if I was going to take it to court. Don't you think?"

"Why, though? It's not like it's top secret. You'd offer the plea to his lawyer, his lawyer would tell him. Or you wouldn't, which would show you were going to take it to court. What's the big secret?"

"I don't know."

Across the desk, Reyes was watching, listening.

"What do you think?" Tate asked.

"I think we need to bring him in and ask him." She stood, and Misty and Tate did the same. "Meanwhile, go home or... wherever you're staying, keep your bodyguards close. I'll call you when I put together a lineup." When Reyes stuck out her hand, Misty shook it, and then Tate did the same.

"I need that flash drive back."

Reyes's gaze flicked to the computer. "Sorry. It's evidence."

Misty seemed ready to argue, but then her shoulders drooped. "Not that it matters. It's useless."

"Maybe the case will be irrelevant," Reyes said. "If we can prove Griffin and his men ambushed you, we'll put him away for that."

Eventually. But meanwhile, the man would be free to terrorize his former girlfriend and her children unless Misty could stop him.

And he'd be a threat to Misty.

And that assumed they could prove Griffin had been behind today's attack.

Tate walked beside Misty out of the bullpen. As soon as they left the large room, two men moved to walk beside her, shifting Tate out of the way.

He recognized Hughes. The other bodyguard was new, taller and larger than his partner. Seemed they'd brought in the big guns now. Neither man looked happy as they escorted her out of the building, effectively ignoring Tate as he trailed them.

They got to the ground floor and were about to step outside when Misty stopped and turned to him. "I guess I'll call you tomorrow."

"Tonight. When you're home safely. So I won't worry."

Her lips tipped up on one side, almost a smile. "Okay." She reached out, laid her long, slender hand on his wrist. Her skin was pale and clear, so different from his tanned forearm. She squeezed gently. "Thank you for coming for me today." Dark circles rimmed her light blue irises. The whites of her eyes were bloodshot, evidence of her fatigue and tears. "And for staying with me. It's good to have a friend."

"Anytime."

Her hand slid away, and Hughes and his partner ushered her out the door to the waiting SUV.

Tate watched until they'd driven out of sight, thinking of her last words.

She'd called him friend. A week before, she wouldn't have named him even that, nor he her.

But now, he was thinking of her as much more than a friend. He hoped, eventually, she'd see him as more too.

Of course, nothing could happen between them until this was over and she was safe. Assuming she ever was.

CHAPTER SIXTEEN

On the way back to the police station the following morning, Misty asked her latest bodyguards the questions that had plagued her all night.

"Ian's all right? You're sure?"

The one in the driver's seat ignored her, but the other one said, "He's fine, ma'am." The guard had introduced himself as Marcus. "The bullet just grazed him."

"But he yelled that he was hit."

"He *was* hit. I'm sure it hurt like...a lot." Marcus shifted tack, though she could guess the word he'd been about to use. "When it was over, he was more worried about you than his injury." The guard turned and met her eyes with an intense look. "Anything like that happens again, you stay with us. Don't run away again."

"Greta told me to go inside."

"Did she tell you to take off?"

Misty didn't bother to answer that. "Summer already lectured me."

The man nodded and faced forward again.

"But did they tell you what happened?" Misty pressed.

"From their perspective? Because it all went down so fast, and I think maybe I saw it differently than they did."

She should have asked Hughes the night before, but he'd been all business—and she'd been so tired—that she hadn't bothered trying to get any information out of him.

"We don't think they were shooting to kill," Marcus said. "They were trying to keep you pinned down, shooting at the SUV or over your heads. One of the bullets ricocheted off the ground and hit Ian."

"If they weren't trying to kill us, then...to what end?"

"Greta said one of them called your name. Do you remember that?"

As if she'd ever forget. "I do."

"Her theory is that the person just wanted to tell you something—and obviously to scare you. But then Ian was hit, and our guys returned fire, and you ran. It didn't go down the way they planned it. He never got to deliver his message."

Misty wished he had. It would be very helpful to know what Griffin—or whoever it had been—wanted from her.

At the police station, Misty was shown a number of photographs, one at a time, and asked if any of them looked like the person who'd followed her into the T station.

The first few photos, though they matched the general description she'd given Reyes, were definitely not the guy. But the fifth man...

"That's him."

"How sure are you?" Reyes asked.

She stared at the image on the table. He was younger in the photo, not quite as thick all around as the man who'd glared at her through the train window, but there was no question it was the same person. "I'm positive."

"Okay, good."

"Was that the guy?"

Reyes smiled. "I think you know I can't say."

Right. It was very different, being the victim instead of the prosecutor. She'd played the role more than once in her life, and she didn't like it.

"I should have more information for you soon." Reyes walked her back to the lobby.

"Do you have someone in custody?"

"We'll do interviews today. I'll let you know what I learn. Meanwhile"—the detective quirked an eyebrow, a jaunty, lighthearted look that surprised Misty—"stay out of trouble."

Misty's bark of laughter wasn't amused. "Would you believe me if I said I'm trying?"

Reyes was chuckling as she walked away.

Back at Summer's apartment, Misty settled at the kitchen table to work. She'd already been behind, and everything that'd happened since Saturday had only distracted her from her caseload.

The video that had caused so much trouble wouldn't help her put Griffin away. Without Tony's testimony, Misty saw no avenue to conviction.

Which meant, unless Reyes could prove Griffin had been behind the ambush the night before, he was probably going to go free.

Melanie would still be in danger.

Griffin would win.

She wasn't ready to concede that, not yet. She called Tate.

"Everything okay?"

She'd let him know the night before that she was home safely, but they hadn't talked for long.

"I made an ID this morning. Don't know who the guy was, and I've been resisting the urge to look up Kyle Griffin's photograph. I'm trusting Reyes will figure it out."

"You slept all right?"

"If you consider tossing and turning and churning over all the stupid decisions I made *all right,* then yeah."

"You didn't do anything stupid." Tate's tone was kind. "You were scared, and you ran. Scared people run."

"I could have gotten myself killed." The words sent a fresh wave of fear over her, and she suppressed a shudder.

"You were trying very hard not to get anybody else killed. That's noble."

"Noble...stupid. Apparently, it's a fine line. I read the whole situation wrong. Ian was hit, but he wasn't badly hurt. They said he was shooting back. I didn't even see that. I thought he was dead or dying." She hadn't noticed the lack of blood. Panic had blinded her. "Anyway, I need to get a continuance on the Griffin case. Would you mind filing it for me? I don't have it in me to go to the courthouse today."

"Sure."

"I'm hoping, considering the defendant may have tried to threaten me—not to mention ambushing me and my bodyguards—the judge will agree that delaying the trial is not only acceptable but necessary."

"The police need time to investigate. But if it wasn't Griffin—"

"My gut tells me it was." Not that her gut could be trusted, not after her foolish choices the night before.

"We need to know for sure before it goes to trial. The only thing is..."

"Don't tell me Leland wants me to offer a plea. Or drop the charges altogether. Or...gosh, why don't we just make the guy immune from all prosecution for all time. In fact, let's do that with all the criminals. That'll clear out the courts and the jails. We can all stand around in a circle, prosecutors, defense attorneys, victims, and criminals. Hold hands and sing 'Kumbaya.'"

There was a long pause after her diatribe. "Are you finished?"

By Tate's tone, he was amused. She should really learn to keep her frustrations to herself. "Sorry."

"I was going to say that Leland wants the guy taken off the streets, sooner rather than later."

"Oh."

"You should have heard him this morning when I told him what happened. I've never seen him so livid. His face got all red. He called Reyes himself, demanding to be kept informed. So, no, he doesn't want you to offer a plea deal. He wants you safe. He was going into a meeting, but I wouldn't be surprised if he calls you himself."

"Huh." Okay, so Leland wasn't a jerk. He cared about his prosecutors. Maybe he even cared about justice.

"I'll draw up this motion and run by the courthouse now," Tate said. "I've got a crazy day today and a late court appearance. But assuming we get a continuance on the Griffin case... dinner tomorrow? I'll pick something up."

"I'd like that." She was sorry she wouldn't see him until then. Silly, considering this would be the first day she hadn't seen him since this whole thing began.

Even sillier when she realized that, actually, she'd seen Tate every weekday for months at work. And she'd hardly given him a second thought, unless it was about what a lousy prosecutor he was.

She wasn't used to getting so many things wrong.

When she hung up, she felt considerably lighter. Her boss knew what'd happened and wanted to protect her. That thought encouraged her, no question.

But it was the prospect of dinner with Tate that warmed her heart. Because they'd dispensed with most of the cases they'd been tasked to do together, but their friendship continued.

Maybe, maybe it could be more than friendship.

Did she want that? She'd been alone for a long time. Like her older sister, she'd eschewed relationships with men. Their father had shown her how dangerous men could be. Misty'd never met one she cared enough about to get past the first few dates. She'd never met one she'd considered worth the risk.

She didn't want to be alone forever.

Summer had Grant now. Misty's tough-as-nails sister had finally opened her heart. If Summer could do it, Misty could too.

But could Tate really be trusted?

Maybe, eventually. Right now, she needed to focus on making sure Griffin landed behind bars. And figure out why he had bugged her apartment. Or, if he hadn't, figure out who had.

∼

Misty worked to get caught up on her cases the rest of the day Tuesday and all day Wednesday. Fortunately, after Reyes confirmed that the man who'd followed her into the T station was indeed Kyle Griffin, the judge had agreed that the ambush at the coffee shop needed to be fully investigated before the Griffin case could go to trial. God willing, between the stalking accusation and evidence that he'd attacked her and her bodyguards, the man would end up behind bars.

It was after two on Wednesday when Tate buzzed the apartment. She clicked the button to allow him access to the building, then at his knock, opened the door to see him wearing a sheepish smile.

"Sorry about this."

Misty had been looking forward to their dinner. She hadn't expected to have Tate's assistance on any more of her cases. Unfortunately, Leland had called her and "offered" to lend

Tate's help once again. She'd tried to argue that she didn't need it, but Leland hadn't been swayed.

"Between the kidnapping, the break-in, and what happened at the coffee shop," Leland had said, "you've got enough on your plate. Just let him help you clear some of it off."

At least it was an excuse to spend more time with Tate.

"Come on in." She moved aside, and Tate stepped into the living room, then set his laptop bag on the coffee table.

"When I offered to bring dinner, I didn't know Leland would have us working together again."

"It's fine."

At least Leland had called her himself to find out how she was and see what he could do to help. And Tate was easy to spend time with, even when they were arguing. Misty didn't feel the defensiveness or irritation this time. Tate was good at closing cases.

As long as Misty ensured that the victims received justice, she'd be happy for the help.

She heard her thoughts and chuckled to herself as she headed for the kitchen.

Look at her, growing as a person. Accepting help like a mature adult. Summer would be proud.

"Something to drink?" she asked.

"A soda, if you have one."

She returned a few moments later, an open can for her, a glass with ice filled with soda for him, and settled on the couch.

"Any updates from Reyes?" he asked.

"Not since she confirmed that Griffin was the guy who followed me into the T station. She promised to call me 'soon,'" —she made air quotes around the word—"though I think her definition of that might be different from mine."

Tate had chosen one of the chairs rather than the sofa this time. He was already leaning over his laptop. "You know victims think the same thing about us. They can't imagine that we have other things to do besides keeping them informed."

Misty set the drinks down and sat on the sofa. "I guess I should cut her some slack."

He looked up and smiled. "Rarely a bad idea." He nodded to the stack of files she'd set on the coffee table earlier. "Ready to get started?"

They discussed, argued, discussed, and ultimately agreed on a few more of her cases, cases she'd been wrestling with. Not because they were complex but because the accused were violent and needed to be taken off the streets for as long as possible.

Tate helped her walk through the evidence, figure out what she'd be able to prove and what she wouldn't, and come up with plea deals.

After a couple of hours of work, she sat back and glared at the files they'd set aside. "They're not getting what they deserve."

Tate, who'd been responding to an email, looked up at that. "You can only do what you can do. Besides, aren't you glad you don't always get what you deserve?"

"That's the thing I'm learning right now about God, I guess. That He doesn't give us what we deserve. He's merciful." She sighed. "Mercy is not my strong suit."

Tate's smile spread slowly. "As a prosecutor, mercy isn't your job. We're not paid to be merciful. We're paid to seek justice."

"Exactly. That, I'm well suited to."

"Yes, and that's a gift, your desire for justice. It's just, for me, when I'm offering deals, I like to think there's a little mercy there, a little, 'let's see if you can do better next time' encouragement. Maybe it makes me feel better about not always pushing for maximum sentences."

"Do you think it works? Do you think people do better?" Because in Misty's experience, people didn't change, or if they did, they descended into worse versions of themselves rather than rising to better versions.

That wasn't fair, though. There were plenty of criminals who'd gotten in trouble, gotten caught, and then straightened up.

Tate stared at the wall above Summer's small television set for a long, stretched-out moment. She saw something on his face she hadn't seen before. Uncertainty? "I guess...I guess it's up to them what they do with it." The worry faded, and that little smile returned. "Maybe that's what God thinks too. He gives us mercy, knowing most of the time we're going to screw up again." He smiled and shook his head. "Not that I'm comparing myself to God."

In college and law school, and now at the DA's office, Misty had been surrounded by atheists and agnostics, people who were pretty sure they were the smartest beings in the universe. She'd felt the same at one time, but life had proved to her, over and over, that she wasn't the smartest, and she certainly wasn't the most powerful. She'd come to realize that there was a God, and she was definitely not Him.

"Are you a Christian?" she asked. "I mean, I know you prayed last week, but lots of people pray."

"I am," he said. "Have been since I was a kid. My faith has wavered a couple times over the years, but I've always known who I am. My dad used to say we're just sinners saved by grace. I'm learning to see myself not as a sinner but as a saint who sometimes sins. I think that's how God sees us, anyway."

"Is it?" she asked. "I'm new to it. My mom was a Christian, but it was hard to follow in her faith."

Tate closed his laptop and slid it away. "Why?"

Misty rarely talked about her parents, about the house she'd grown up in. But she wanted to tell Tate. She wanted him to know her. Maybe, if she learned to trust him, and he her, there could be something between them.

"My father was an alcoholic," she said. "A nasty drunk. He used to...he was abusive to Mom. And my oldest sister, Krystal. The one time he hurt Summer, she told my uncle, who called the police. Summer's always been tough, never one to take anything from anyone. Dad left her alone, and most of our childhood, she managed to protect me as well."

Most of it. But Summer couldn't be there all the time.

Tate leaned toward her. "I can't imagine growing up surrounded by that kind of violence."

"It wasn't always bad. There were moments of..." She'd almost said peace, but that wasn't the right word. It wasn't peace if you knew war could break out at any moment. Those moments were just brief and fragile cease-fires. "The point is, it was hard to follow in Mom's footsteps of faith when she was the victim of Dad's rage all the time. And she did nothing to stop it. To protect herself...or us." She heard the bitterness in her voice and worked to hide it. "She always took us to church—Dad never went. One Sunday, the pastor was talking about marriage, how it was sacred. He talked about how marriage was a representation of Christ and the church. And I remember thinking, this is why she won't leave, because God doesn't want her to. If there really is a God, why would He want her to suffer?"

"He didn't." Tate reached out, settled his hand on Misty's.

The gesture was warm and gentle and so different from what she expected from any man. It felt awkward, allowing a coworker to hold her hand. Even a friend. Yet she didn't pull away.

"You know that, right?" Tate asked. "He wouldn't have expected or wanted your mother to stay in that situation."

"I know. But what was the right thing to do? Should she

have left him? Sent him to prison? What does the Bible say about all that?"

"I'm no biblical scholar. I can't give you a definitive answer." He squeezed her hand and then let go, leaving her feeling... unmoored, somehow. "I do know that God didn't want you to live like that. Have you ever asked your mom why she didn't leave?"

Misty settled back on the couch, wishing she could move closer to Tate. His presence was calming. At that moment he'd touched her, he'd felt like...home. Now, she felt chilly in the air conditioning. Alone. "Mom died when I was in high school. Technically, cancer killed her. But I always blamed Dad. She had nothing to live for."

"She had you and your sisters."

That was true. But Mom hadn't fought for them. She'd loved them, and she'd loved their dad. She was good at love.

Assuming love was weak.

But was it?

Misty stood, uncomfortable with the question she'd posed. How could she doubt her mother's love?

But, how could she not?

"Sorry." She looked down at Tate, who was watching her with that intense expression he used when he was trying to figure something out. "That conversation turned ugly fast. I didn't mean..." She grabbed their empty drinks and headed for the kitchen.

She heard Tate behind her but didn't turn to look at him. She needed to shake off the pitiful memories.

"Your childhood, your dad's abuse. It explains your desire to see violent people put away."

She rinsed her can and tossed it in the recycle bin, then rinsed his glass. "More soda?"

"I don't need anything."

She fixed herself a glass of water, mostly to give herself someplace else to focus. Why had she told him all that? She felt raw and exposed, embarrassed.

"It's noble, your desire to protect the weak." He leaned a shoulder against the doorjamb. "Somebody should have protected you."

"Mom never told anybody what was happening. That was on her."

"Definitely not what God would have wanted. He desires truth, even if it's painful and hard."

Misty turned to him. She wasn't sure what to say about that.

"Maybe your mom didn't understand that. Or maybe she was just scared. Of your father. Or maybe of trying to make it on her own. Or maybe..." He shrugged. "I can't begin to understand. I'm just saying, you can't blame God for her decisions any more than you can blame Him for mine, or yours, or anybody else's. Even those of us who love God and want to please Him mess up sometimes. We misunderstand. We make assumptions that aren't true. We just...don't get it right."

"Which brings us back to mercy."

Tate smiled. "I love it when a conversation comes full circle. Like there was a plan we didn't know we were following."

Misty turned away, surprised by the tears stinging her eyes. Because she'd never understood how Mom could have loved the Lord and gotten it all so wrong. Or why God hadn't protected them.

But Mom, Dad, Misty and her sisters... They were all just people. And even when they followed God, even when they tried really hard to do the right thing, people messed up.

Tate had put into words something she'd been wrestling with. Misty might never figure out what had motivated her mother to stay with Dad. Was it fear? Was it devotion or loyalty or love?

She'd never be able to ask, not in this life, anyway. But in heaven, perhaps she'd understand.

Maybe that could be enough for now.

When she turned around again, Tate had gone back to the living room. Had he seen the emotion on her face, known she needed a moment to pull herself together?

She swiped her tears with a paper towel, took a steadying breath, and joined him.

He looked up from the file he was skimming. "It's nearly five o'clock. Should we call it a day, order some dinner?"

Though Misty almost never quit working before five thirty or six, she was ready to be finished. "What'd you have in mind?"

CHAPTER SEVENTEEN

Tate tapped their dinner order in at the restaurant's website, still processing all Misty had told him.

No wonder she was adamant about sending violent criminals to jail. It sounded like her dad belonged there, but how could justice be done when the victims didn't tell the truth?

He'd never understand why a woman would cover for a man who hurt her. In his job, he'd seen it over and over. Misty's mother, whatever her motivations, should have protected her daughters. She should have told the truth about their dad. Maybe he could have gotten help. Gone to rehab. Quit drinking. Learned to manage his anger.

By doing nothing, Misty's mother had only allowed the problem to persist. She hadn't done herself, her daughters, or even her husband any good.

But it was easy for Tate to judge, sitting on the outside. It wasn't his family. It wasn't his life. It wasn't his pain.

He scrolled down the online menu. "Fries or tater tots?" He'd suggested they order sushi, figuring she'd appreciate a fancy meal, even though he wasn't a huge fan. But she'd requested burgers.

He'd never turn down a good cheeseburger.

"Tater tots." A woman after his own heart.

In more ways than one.

"I'm buying." She held out her credit card.

He laughed. "Not a chance. I invited you to dinner."

"We agreed I'd get the next one."

"The next time we have lunch, you can buy."

"Tate, just take—"

Misty's phone rang.

She dropped her credit card beside his laptop and snatched her cell. "Misty Lake." She listened, then said, "One moment, detective. I'm going to put you on speaker." She did, setting the phone on the table. "I'm here with Tate."

Detective Reyes said, "We located Griffin and brought him in for questioning. He admitted having seen you at the T station and trying to talk to you, but he denied having anything to do with the shooting at the coffee shop."

"He's obviously lying," Tate said.

Misty gave him a look—brows lifted, chin lowered—which he read as *stop talking*.

"Sorry," he whispered.

She smiled, clearly not holding a grudge, and returned her focus to the phone. "How does he explain that, considering we've never met in person."

"Said he'd seen your photo somewhere." Reyes's voice was clipped, all business. "Your friend's right, he was lying. As soon as we locate the shooters, we'll bring them in and, hopefully, get them to finger Griffin as the one who put them up to it."

"Are you close to finding them?" Misty asked.

"One witness got a license plate number for the car they were driving. We just have to locate its owner. He's slippery, but we'll get him. I've got guys with connections down there—"

"Where is down there?" Tate asked, shooting a look at

Misty, worried she'd be annoyed again. But her focus was on the phone.

"The owner of the car lives in Quincy. And Griffin does too."

"Quite a coincidence."

"Hardly." Reyes said. "Griffin was behind the ambush at the coffee shop. We just gotta prove it."

"Meanwhile, has he been charged?" Misty asked.

"Not until we have hard evidence. About the break-in at your place..."

"I assume he denied that too," Misty said.

"He did. The thing is, as much as I knew he was lying when he said he didn't plan the ambush, when he denied knowledge about the break-in, I think he was telling the truth. He said he had nothing to do with it, that he hadn't known anybody had broken into your place. He seemed genuinely shocked."

"Of course he wouldn't want to admit it." Misty pushed to her feet. "Of course he'd say that."

Tate looked from her to the phone. "Why do you believe him, detective?"

"It's my job to read people. We were in that interview a long time. He told me the truth about a bunch of things—like having seen you, Misty, in the T station. He lied about other things—like the ambush. I can read tones, body language. I'm telling you, he didn't break into your apartment."

Misty sat again, looking defeated.

Reyes continued. "Also, he doesn't match the person in the video on the elevator. Griffin is taller and broader than the person who broke into your place."

"It could have been someone working for him."

"Could have been, but it wasn't."

Tate admired the detective's confidence in her skills. He just didn't know if that confidence was warranted.

"But if it wasn't him," Misty asked, "then who was it?"

"My money's on Frederick Parks," Reyes said. "We still haven't been able to locate him, despite having reached out to his family and known associates. The guy's avoiding us, and there must be a reason. I'm guessing—"

"But why would he bug my apartment? It doesn't make sense."

"I'll ask him when I find him."

"*If* you find him," Misty muttered.

He didn't blame her for feeling discouraged. "Detective, what did you learn about the security system at our building? And the fact that the intruder had her code."

"Nothing," Reyes said. "We still have no idea how he got into your apartment."

"That's comforting," Tate said.

Misty shot him a sardonic smile, leaning closer to the phone. "Is there anything else you can tell us at this point?"

"I don't think so. When we get Parks in custody, I'll let you know. Meanwhile, keep out of trouble."

"I always do," Misty said.

Reyes was laughing when she hung up, though Tate didn't think any of it was funny.

He leaned back in his chair, frustrated. "Basically, we don't know anything more than we did before her call."

"We know where the investigation stands. These things are never as simple as they look on TV." Misty nodded to his laptop. "Did you get our dinner ordered?"

He pulled his laptop onto his lap, did one final check of the order, and submitted it. "It'll be delivered in thirty minutes." He held out her credit card. "And it's on me. I don't let my dates pay."

"This is a date then?"

He held her eye contact, not surprised by the question.

They had eaten together before, as colleagues. Rather than slither out of it or blow it off, he said, "That was my plan when I asked you, yes." He waited for her to tell him she didn't date colleagues or didn't think he was her type or she'd prefer to spend the rest of her life surrounded by cats, thank you very much.

"Okay, then." She slid her credit card back into her wallet and returned to the kitchen.

He followed, watching as she took out plates. She was headed for the table when he stepped in the way and held out his hand. "Let me help."

She started to, then pulled them back. "Actually, do you want to eat on the roof? There's a nice little area up there, and I'm going stir-crazy stuck in this apartment."

He agreed. She told the guard they'd be on the roof and that dinner was being delivered. A few minutes later, they settled on wicker furniture beneath an awning that shielded them from the early evening sun. The still air was warm—upper eighties, he guessed—but much of the morning's humidity had burned off. A few potted trees were scattered around the area, one of which gave off an unexpectedly sweet scent in the middle of the city.

Even on the top of the building, the view didn't compare to his, but it was nice enough, overlooking the pretty Back Bay neighborhood. "This is pleasant."

"This is the first time I've been out since I got back from the police station yesterday. It's one thing to be trapped in your own apartment, but being trapped in someone else's is the pits."

"I can imagine."

"If Reyes is right and Griffin didn't break into my apartment, then who did?"

"You don't think it was Parks?"

"I don't. Parks had no reason to listen in on my conversations. I still think it must have something to do with the cases I was assigned last week."

"If not for the listening device," Tate said, "I'd agree with Reyes about Parks, but from what I've read about him, he's a low-level thug. Where would he get listening devices or learn how to plant them? And why? If he was out to get you, that's not how he would do it."

She tilted her head to the side. "You researched him?"

"Sure. I mean, the guy might be after you. I wanted to learn everything I could."

Though Misty didn't say anything, her expression softened to one of...was that affection?

She sat back, crossing her ankles, a picture of calm that belied their conversation. "Freddy threatened me after he was convicted, but last year, he asked me to come visit him, said he needed to tell me something. When I got time to go out to Walpole, he refused to see me. The guards couldn't explain it. They did tell me that he'd become a model prisoner, docile even.

"A few weeks later, he sent me a note thanking me for coming and apologizing for his threats and for refusing my visit. He didn't explain it, but he seemed sincere. So...yeah, the timing looks bad, him getting out of prison right before my place was broken into. But I don't think the break-in has anything to do with Parks."

It was possible the guy had become angry again. Maybe he had mental health problems, swinging from docility to anger and back.

But that still didn't explain the listening device.

"I wish it was Parks," Tate said. "It would be easier to fight a single person, even a really scary one like Freddy Parks, than an unknown entity—a person, many people, who knows? At least Freddy is a known quantity."

Their dinners were delivered by the grumpy-looking guard, and they dug in, eating directly out of the Styrofoam boxes.

Warm, salty goodness. His kind of grub. They ate for a few minutes in silence, but the mystery wouldn't leave him alone. "If not Parks, then who?"

"I've been digging into the Thornebrook case." Misty wiped her fingers on a napkin and set it aside. Even eating a messy burger covered in barbecue sauce, she managed to be tidy and put-together. "I called Zachary Hardy a couple of days ago." She explained that the permit office employee, after reporting the attempted bribe, had been transferred out of his department into a job he hated. His replacement had issued the permits, and the building had been built.

"He thinks someone—Dawson, Thornebrook, or the company that built the building—is connected to someone high up in city or county government."

"Except, if that were the case... if it's Dawson, anyway, wouldn't the bribery charges already have been dropped?"

She shrugged. "You'd think so. Maybe the connection doesn't know or care about Dawson. Maybe the...connection doesn't want to get involved. Dawson seems like a pretty small cog."

"A small cog with a big-time lawyer."

"There's that." Misty dipped a tater tot in ranch dressing and popped it in her mouth.

"The building is owned by who again?"

"IAF, International Aid Foundation. They own that and another property out in Hopkinton. Hearts and Homes, a community for refugees."

"Where that woman died." He remembered a story he'd read about the carbon monoxide leak. What good was an alarm to a profoundly deaf person? "All that family did to escape war, all they had to endure to get here, and then she was killed by an odorless gas. Tragic."

"Yeah. It's the Boston property that Hardy was talking about, though. He suggested that anybody driving by would understand that it shouldn't be there."

"Why?"

Misty swallowed a bite of burger, shrugging. "He didn't say, just said it would be obvious."

"Maybe we need to take a field trip. You think your security guards would mind?"

Smiling, she glanced at the scowling man who had his back to the metal door. "They said I could go anywhere I wanted, as long as they stayed with me. Let's do it."

CHAPTER EIGHTEEN

Misty settled beside Tate in the backseat of the bodyguards' SUV and watched the city roll by. The sun was sinking, the evening air cooling. Twilight had always been her favorite time of day, when the world was tucking in for the night. Children climbing down from their tree houses and running home, preparing for baths and bed. Couples walking hand-in-hand, dogs testing the limits of their leashes. Back in the little town where she'd grown up, fireflies would be flashing in the bushes. The scent of grilling meat would compete with those of lilies and freshly mown grass.

Twilight in Boston was very different. There were few children around, and the adults on the sidewalks weren't out for leisurely strolls but rushing, rushing, always rushing.

Sometimes, despite how difficult her childhood had been, Misty missed the quieter suburban life.

Her sister must have, too, though Coventry was too far away from any city to be considered a suburb. Before long, Summer would be countrified. She'd probably start churning her own butter and spinning her own yarn.

"Something funny?" Tate asked.

She didn't bother to hide her smile. "Just thinking about my sister living in the country."

"You prefer the city, I guess."

"I thought I would. I liked living in New York with Summer. And in Boston before that. But, honestly, Coventry's a beautiful little town. I mean, everywhere you look is like a postcard. And the people all know each other—and like each other and help each other out. It's so different from here, where you can walk by the same people day after day and never know their names."

"You can know their names if you ask," Tate said.

What did it say about her that it had never occurred to her to try? "I think you're better at that than I am. Better at making friends. Better at...being a friend. When I was a kid, we learned to keep to ourselves, to hide the truth. I felt like I couldn't get close to anybody because something might slip. I might accidentally say too much about my father, about our home. There was always this...this fear of being known, of being found out." Talk about over-sharing. She looked away. "I always say too much when I'm with you. Why is that?"

She'd meant the question to be rhetorical, but Tate *hmm'd*. "Maybe because you know you can trust me." He took her hand and tugged until she faced him again. "I hope that's why, anyway, because you can."

She wasn't sure what to say to that, so she just settled in for the ride.

After a few moments, Tate chuckled. "Riding in the backseat reminds me of being a kid." He slouched down, taking up far more space than necessary. "Come on, let's be kids for a minute. You gotta make yourself comfortable. You know how kids are, flopping all over the place. Not uptight and focused like adults, totally relaxed."

"But we are adults." Misty tried to sound stern, but she didn't quite manage it.

"Didn't you ever play make-believe? Come on, play with me."

She slouched, stretching her long legs until they bumped against the seat in front of her. The bodyguard didn't react, though he had to have felt it.

She whispered to Tate, "You're weird."

"Maybe." His voice was tinged with humor as he slouched closer, his arm resting against hers.

They stayed like that, skin touching skin. Innocent, but his body heat warmed her, along with his playfulness, his joy.

"Or," he said, "maybe it was all a ploy to get you closer."

"Diabolical."

"Mwa-ha-ha." He made the laugh sound evil.

Giggling, she turned toward him, finding him already facing her way. His breath brushed across her cheek, tickled the hair at her temple. Something decidedly not funny—or childish—washed over her.

He shifted, leaned in. Any second, he was going to kiss her. She wanted him to. She didn't care about the bodyguards in the front seat or the fact that he was her coworker or any of it. All she cared about in that moment was how much she wanted to feel his lips against hers.

But the SUV came to a stop. "This is the place," the bodyguard said.

She started to shift away, but Tate gripped her arm, leaned in, whispered, "We'll finish this later." And then, he slid away and pulled the handle.

So cool, so confident.

She cracked up when his door wouldn't open. "Just like when you were a kid, you have to wait for the grown-ups to let you out."

He scowled, but she saw the humor in the dim overhead light. "Laugh it up."

"Oh, I am. Trust me."

The guards took their time checking the area before opening their doors. Flanked by bodyguards, she stepped out of the SUV.

Tate joined her on the sidewalk, studying the structure in front of them. "Nice."

All glass and sleek dark wood, the building on the corner lot was the picture of modern sophistication. She counted the layers of windows. Seven stories high, much narrower than it was tall. A dim light shone inside, where a security guard sat at a raised desk in the two-story foyer, which was decked with gleaming marble floors and stacked-stone walls.

The words *International Aid Foundation* were etched on the fancy granite sign between the sidewalk and the entry.

Misty backed up and peered down the street in both directions, taking in the neighborhood as a whole.

And understood what Zachary Hardy had meant about the building not belonging there.

The rest of the street was lined with brownstones similar to the one where Summer lived. Aged brick, ivy climbing the sides, old trees in small square lots. The four-story buildings, each nestled against its neighbor, had no doubt been converted to apartments, but they were still homes.

Not that there was anything wrong with sharing a block with an office building. But the IAF property wasn't the proverbial tulip in the onion patch. It was more like a tulip in a rose garden. Because the brownstones were beautiful in their own way, aged and classic.

The office building was beautiful too. It just didn't belong.

Surely that wouldn't be enough to deny the permits, though. That was one of her favorite things about Boston, the way that old and the new existed side by side. The John Hancock buildings were the perfect example of that. The old one had a beacon that lit up different colors, sometimes even flashing, displaying the weather forecast. She forgot what all the different colors meant, but she knew that in winter, flashing red meant snow. During baseball season, it meant the Red Sox game was canceled.

Because Bostonians had their priorities.

That old John Hancock building could be seen in the reflection of the new one, a sixty-something-story mirrored structure that was one of the defining towers in the Boston skyline.

Old and new mixed easily in Boston. But both of those John Hancock buildings were in business centers. Not on residential streets.

She'd skimmed the information Hardy had sent her about the zoning, all the ways this property didn't fit. She'd thought it was strange he'd commented on parking. Boston wasn't exactly a driver's city—most buildings didn't offer parking, at least not without a cost. But now she realized the problem. The road was lined with signs on both sides warning drivers that the parking was for residents only. She searched on her phone and found there was no public parking within five blocks in any direction. Not a problem for city residents, most of whom relied on the T and buses to get around, but would the people visiting the *International* Aid Foundation be residents?

Doubtful. But not a deal-breaker. If refugees needed to come here, they could learn to use public transportation. Still...

Hardy had mentioned other zoning issues, but the point was, the building didn't belong. And yet, here it was. Why? Why here and not in a more appropriate location? Why had the permits been issued?

This hadn't happened by accident. Somebody somewhere had wanted this building in this spot.

But why?

Tate stood beside her, saying nothing, while the bodyguards hovered nearby. There were four of them, the two who'd been in her car and two who'd driven a second SUV. She'd call it overkill if she hadn't been shot at two days before.

"Let's walk a minute," she said.

Tate slipped his hand in hers, and they meandered down the sidewalk, past the well-kept brownstones with their fancy brick-and-stone etchings, their wrought iron stair rails, their front yards smaller than a midsize sedan. It was a peaceful evening, very little traffic on the narrow city street. Aside from her, Tate, and the bodyguards, there were very few people around.

"What do you think?" she asked.

"It's a strange place for an office building."

Ahead, a man and woman stepped outside one of the brownstones, descended the stairs, and hit the sidewalk, heading toward them.

As they approached, Misty smiled and said to her bodyguard, "Can you step aside? I'd like to talk to those people."

The two men in front of her hurried to put more space between them. As soon as the couple skirted around the bodyguards, Misty said, "Pardon me. Can I ask you a question?"

They stopped, eyeing the guards behind Misty and Tate before settling their gaze on her. They gave her cautious smiles. "You lost?" the man asked.

"Just curious. That office building." Misty gestured to the corner. "What do you think about it?"

The man looked at the woman, who tilted her head to one side. "It's pretty. It's a lot better than that ugly trailer." She turned to the man. "Remember that? It was there for years. If not for the construction company sign promising something was going to be built, I'd have worried it was there to stay."

"Do you remember the name of the construction company?" Tate asked.

"Read it every day, so I should. Tanglewood?" She glanced at the man. "Right?"

"That's that music venue," he said. "Out in the Berkshires."

"Oh, right. It started with a T, though. And I know there were two O's—they kind of linked them on the sign. Bad graphics—I'm a designer. Thornewood?"

"Thornebrook?" Tate suggested.

The woman's eyes lit. "Yes. That was it. They had a trailer there for years, just sitting on the empty lot. I never complained about it because who has time? But I heard others on the block did, more than once. We were so happy when they finally started construction."

"Do people come in and out of the place a lot?" Misty asked.

The couple looked at each other before she shrugged. "Every day, I guess."

"Business people, or are there families? IAF runs a refugee home in Hopkinton. I'm just trying to figure out what they do in the city."

"I've never seen families there," the woman said. "Suits, briefcases, that sort of thing."

"That's very helpful," Misty said. "Thanks so much."

The couple moved past them along the sidewalk.

The neighborhood felt peaceful, homey. A group of teens congregated on the steps of one of the buildings. Misty smiled at a girl who looked about thirteen, and she smiled back. Seemed like a nice area. Probably, in another couple of weeks when school started, it'd be more crowded. The proximity to a few of the many colleges in the city would make this a great place for students to live.

Maybe that was the reason IAF wanted to be located here. Maybe they worked with university students. Maybe the woman just wasn't around when young people came and went.

But didn't the organization focus on refugees? "I need to dig into IAF."

"Let's talk through it," Tate said. "What do we know?"

"Raul Dawson attempted to bribe a city official to issue the permits and was arrested. For some reason, though the charges weren't dropped, the case languished for almost a year before it landed on my desk."

"And now Dawson has a high-priced lawyer," Tate added.

"Right. Hired by somebody. Dawson, Thornebrook?"

"IAF?" They walked in silence a few paces before Tate continued. "I looked up the building. They started building it a year ago, but according to that woman, Thornebrook had a trailer here for years."

"Right."

"So first," Tate said, "why a big-time lawyer for a small-time case, and who's paying her?"

"Not that we'll get the answer to that second part. And then there's Hardy, who reported Dawson's attempted bribery and was transferred out of the department. His replacement issued the permits, and the building was built."

"In a place where it probably shouldn't have been."

"Which begs the question, why here? And who works in this building?"

"I was wondering that myself." At the end of the block, they crossed the street and turned back the way they'd come.

They were missing something.

As they approached the end of the block, she glanced up, looking for a crosswalk button. The names of the roads snagged her attention.

She stepped back and stared. Aldus Street and Buttrick Road.

"What's wrong?" Tate asked.

"The streets."

He looked at the two signs. "What about them?"

The IAF building was on Buttrick Road, so that one didn't surprise her, but... "Aldus Street." She'd heard that name. She closed her eyes. Thought back. She'd been in her apartment. Tate had been there. They'd been talking about... "Isn't that where Freddy Parks was arrested? On Aldus Street?"

Tate's eyes widened. "I think so."

"We looked it up, remember? It was a corner lot, an empty lot, surrounded by brownstones."

He looked around, taking in the area. "He was arrested *here*?"

"Maybe, or near here." She nodded across the street at the place that, at the time of Parks's arrest, would have been an empty lot. An empty lot with a Thornebrook trailer on it. She paced down the sidewalk, trying to put the pieces together. "Maybe somebody Parks knew worked for Thornebrook?"

"We need to find out who owned the property at that time," Tate said. "I'm guessing it was IAF."

"Even so, IAF wasn't here. Thornebrook was." She stopped to face him. "Why would Parks come here?"

"I don't know. But it can't be a coincidence." The concern on Tate's face was clear in the glow of the streetlight. "Somehow, Freddy Parks is involved with this property. Maybe with Dawson and...all of it."

"Except he was in prison when Dawson offered that bribe. How could he be involved with that?"

"Maybe Dawson recruited Parks to help with...whatever they're doing. Intimidating you and...there's got to be more to it than that."

"So, what if the break-in at my apartment *is* related to Dawson—"

"*And* Freddy Parks?" Tate finished. "Did you ever get in touch with his attorney?"

She shook her head, thankful for the bodyguards all around her. Something strange was going on, and the more information they got, the more confused she felt. "Cofer never returned my calls. I think I'll pay him a visit tomorrow. Maybe he can tell me what's going on."

"Tell *us*," Tate said. "You won't be going alone."

Not that her bodyguards would allow that, but if Tate wanted to join her, she certainly wasn't going to turn him down. Having Tate with her made her feel safe, or at least safer as she struggled to solve this mystery.

∼

They were nearly back to Summer's apartment when a call came in on Misty's cell phone.

"Ms. Lake," a man said after she answered, "my name is Detective Klein with the Boston PD. I need to see you. Are you available?"

"Now?" She glanced at Tate, who was watching through squinted eyes. "It's nearly nine o'clock."

"It's important." The man's voice was low and smooth as maple syrup. "I went to your apartment, but your building manager told me you are staying elsewhere for a few days. Are you in the city?"

"I'm keeping my whereabouts quiet."

"Okay." She waited for him to ask why, but he didn't. After a moment, he said, "I'd like you to come into police headquarters, or could we meet somewhere else. If you're nearby, that is."

She had no desire to go back to police headquarters, that giant, sterile building. "Hold on, detective." She muted her phone and gave Tate an update.

"Let's meet him at my apartment," Tate said, "assuming he's still there."

"Good idea." She unmuted the phone. "Detective Klein, are you still at my building?"

"Close enough."

"Okay, my friend lives there as well. We'll be there soon."

A couple of minutes later, as the bodyguards pulled the two SUVs over in front of her apartment building, a man in a suit pushed off from the stair rail leading to the front door.

One of the bodyguards—Marcus—approached him. After a short chat and a long look at the detective's badge, he opened her door. "Straight inside, ma'am."

With Tate holding her hand, they entered the building.

Ruth was standing near the mailboxes. "I thought that was you." She eyed the crowd that'd walked in with her. "How are you? Everything okay?"

"Yes, thanks for asking."

"Are you back, then? I haven't seen you at your apartment. Or anybody else, if that makes you feel better. Whoever they were, they haven't returned."

Misty smiled at her nosy neighbor. "Thanks for watching out for me."

"I've been checking for packages every day too. Nothing's come for you. Do you need anything? Can I do anything for you? Water your plants while you're gone or—?"

"I think I've got it under control, but thanks." Misty gave the woman's elbow a quick squeeze and smiled as they walked by. She, Tate, the detective who'd yet to introduce himself, and two bodyguards piled into the elevator and rode silently to the tenth floor.

"This is cozy," Tate whispered, though everybody had to have heard.

She managed to stifle a nervous laugh.

Finally, he unlocked his door, and they stepped into his apartment.

It looked different with the night sky on the far side of the window, the city twinkling below. Sophisticated. Tate flipped on the overhead lights.

"I'm Detective Klein." The man was older than Misty's father and had dark skin and black hair. His pale blue eyes were kind.

She shook his hand. "Misty Lake. And this is my friend, Tate Steele."

The men greeted each other. "I'm sorry to interrupt your evening," Klein said.

"It's not a problem." Tate moved into the living room and clicked on lamps, gesturing for her and the detective to follow.

She sat on Tate's leather sectional, and Tate chose the spot next to her.

As soon as Klein was settled catty-corner to them, he said, "When was the last time you spoke to Jeffrey Cofer?"

The question took her aback. "He's a defense attorney, and I'm a prosecutor. We faced each other in court a couple of times, but it's been years. He works out of Lowell. I've been trying to reach him the last few days. I've left him a couple of messages, but he hasn't returned my calls. What's going on?"

Klein's head bobbed slowly, those unusual blue eyes focused on her. Though his expression was mild, she had a feeling he missed nothing. "Why were you trying to reach him?"

"He left me a message last Friday night. I returned his call Saturday and spoke with his service, and then earlier this week I left another one with his assistant."

"Do you know why he was calling you?"

"I used to work in Middlesex County. A man I put away up there, Frederick Parks, was released from prison on a technicality. Mr. Cofer's message said his call referred to Parks, so I assume he was calling to tell me Parks was free."

"And that mattered to you because...?"

"Parks threatened me, back when he was convicted."

"I see." Klein looked at Tate, but she didn't follow his gaze. "Are you worried Frederick Parks might make good on his threat?"

"I'm not sure what to think." She explained about how he'd reached out to her and then sent her the note apologizing for his threats. And then she told Klein about the break-in at her apartment and the listening devices. "The detective working the case seems to think Parks is involved."

"Do you agree?"

She shared a look with Tate, then shrugged. "We aren't sure what to think. I don't know why Parks would want to listen in on anything I have to say. Tate and I had scheduled a meeting that morning to discuss some of my cases. I think the break-in was related to one of those."

"Who knew about that meeting?"

"We sent a list to the detective working the case. She's been working through it, but it's a big list. As far as I know, she hasn't zeroed in on anybody."

"Which detective?"

"Reyes."

"Good. She's good."

"The thing is," Misty said, "we think it's possible that they're all related. A defendant in a bribery case I'm prosecuting, one Tate and I would have discussed in that meeting, may have known Parks. Or...somebody at his company knew him, we think." She explained how he'd been arrested at the property Dawson had bribed the city official to sign off on.

The detective's eyes narrowed to slits. "Wait...you're saying the guy who was released last week from prison is associated with one of your current cases?"

"Maybe. Or it's just a strange coincidence."

"Hmm. Strange indeed." He stared beyond her a long moment, probably trying to fit the pieces together. At this point, the pieces didn't even seem to belong to the same puzzle.

"Did something happen to Mr. Cofer?"

One of Klein's shoulders lifted and fell. "He hasn't been to work since last Friday and hasn't called his assistant. He's divorced and lives alone, so nobody reported him missing. When his assistant couldn't reach him, she called the police. A couple of uniforms checked his house and found it empty."

Tate leaned forward. "Any sign of forced entry, a scuffle?"

"No. He's just not there. His mail hasn't been picked up in a few days. His neighbors haven't seen him. Nobody seems to know where he is."

Misty asked, "And you reached out to me because...?"

"As far as anybody can tell, his call to you last week was the last one he made. Nobody's heard from him since."

"Oh." She sat back, not sure what to think about that. "Have you looked for Parks?"

"Cofer's assistant told us about him, so he's on our list. After this conversation, he'll be rising to the top." Klein turned his gaze on Tate. "Anything to add?"

"I've never met Cofer or Freddy Parks." Tate glanced at her, almost as if asking permission. She gave him a go-ahead nod. "We've been digging around about a case involving a construction company called Thornebrook, a nonprofit called IAF, and a man named Raul Dawson. He's the defendant Misty mentioned. Maybe Dawson and Parks knew each other? Maybe Dawson recruited Parks to help him break into her apartment. Though even then...why? To what end?"

"Huh." Klein seemed to contemplate that. "Okay. Well, we

don't have enough information to answer any of your questions." He pushed to his feet. "If you learn anything you think might help me find Mr. Cofer, would you let me know?" He held out a business card.

Misty stood and took it. "Of course. Will you let me know when you find him?"

"I'll ask him to reach out." Klein shook their hands again. "Thanks for seeing me. Enjoy the rest of your evening."

After he left, she stared at the closed door. The bodyguard had walked out with the detective, leaving her and Tate alone. "Something very odd is going on."

"I don't like it." The stormy look in Tate's eyes told her he was thinking the same. "I definitely don't like that you're in the middle of it."

"No kidding. Especially considering I don't even know what *it* is."

CHAPTER NINETEEN

The next morning, Tate hurried beneath his umbrella through the steady rain to the metal door leading into a low-income apartment building and scanned the names beside the buzzer buttons for the residents. There it was. W. Parks—the W stood for Winnie, far too cheerful a name for this rundown complex.

Tate had driven the thirty miles north to Lowell that morning, thankful to be going the opposite direction of the traffic. He knew both detectives Reyes and Klein were looking for Freddy Parks, so this was probably a waste of time, but he'd learned early on that some folks didn't trust the police. In the past, Tate had occasionally been able to coax information out of witnesses that the police hadn't been able to get. One of his fellow ADAs had suggested it was because Tate had an "easy face." Easy to trust. Easy on the eyes.

He hadn't known what to think about the compliment when it came from a sixty-something gray-haired grandpa-type. Maybe his looks and—he hated to think of it as charm, but the word probably fit—would make a difference.

He was about to push the button and try to press his case for entry over the speaker when someone else climbed the couple of steps and yanked the door open.

Broken lock. Great security.

He followed the slouchy teenage boy into the building, shook out his umbrella, and folded it. The kid went straight down the dark hallway to the stairwell, but Tate stopped at the elevator, preferring not to work up a sweat in his suit and tie.

He pressed the button. No light came on, but maybe it was blown out. He pressed it again.

Nothing happened.

A man and two little kids hurried out of an apartment farther down the hall. He froze when he saw Tate. Even in the dimness, Tate saw worry and suspicion cross the man's face.

Tate smiled to put the guy at ease and indicated the elevator. "Let me guess. Broken?"

"Like everything else in this building."

"Thanks." He gave the kids a wave and headed for the staircase, where he climbed to the fourth floor. It was even darker up there. He guessed the paint on the walls had once been white. Was *dreary* a color?

He knocked on the apartment that'd been Freddy's home before prison.

The woman who opened the door was the definition of bedraggled. Skinny, she had dark smudges beneath her brown eyes. Her skin had a reddish hue as if she'd spent the afternoon in the sunshine—or maybe she suffered from rosacea. If this was the woman he'd come to see, she should be in her midforties, but she looked twenty years older. She wore a stained T-shirt and cut-off sweatpants that showed off legs that had probably been nice once upon a time but now looked as wrinkly as the rest of her. In her arms, she held a toddler. Unlike the woman, the little girl looked shiny and new, wearing bright, clean clothes that seemed to glow in the surrounding gloom. She had dark brown wavy hair and big brown eyes. She peeked at him shyly, the hint of a smile in her gaze, like she was waiting to see if he was worth the trouble.

"I don't need any," the woman said.

"Good thing, because I'm not selling any." Tate flashed his most effective grin. "I'm Tate Steele. Are you Winnie Parks?"

She squinted wary eyes. "Yeah."

"I work for the Suffolk County DA's office. Can I come in?"

"Why?"

During the drive, he'd considered how to best present himself to get the answers he needed. If he said he was looking for her son, she'd probably tell him she didn't know where Freddy was—and then slam the door in his face.

"I wanted to talk to you about a case I'm helping with. It concerns a man named Raul Dawson." Knowing that after Freddy had assaulted the man in Billerica, he'd run to the empty lot where Thornebrook had a trailer, Tate guessed he was at least acquainted with Raul Dawson. Maybe Mrs. Parks wouldn't be, though. This was a long shot.

The red on her cheeks faded, and her lips hardened at the corners. "Unless you got good news, don't you say that man's name in my presence."

"You and I are on the same side, Mrs. Parks." Tate did his best to hide his surprise. "Do you mind if I come in?"

"It's Miss," she said. "None of that 'miz' business, either. I've never been married, and I've got nothing to hide." Leaving the door open, she spun and carried the child into a small living area.

Tate stepped inside. As rundown as the building was, Winnie Parks's apartment was sparkly clean. A child's sippy cup sat on the kitchen table beside a plastic plate bearing the image of a Disney princess and a few leftover crumbs from breakfast. Otherwise, the room was spotless. The faded linoleum beneath his feet gleamed.

The living room floor was covered with kids' brightly-covered foam tile...things. A worn sofa separated the living room from the kitchen, and a matching loveseat was pushed against the wall. A plastic chest sat in one corner, the top open and toys spilling out. The little girl chose one and settled on the foam floor to play.

"Who's this?" Tate asked.

"Tell him your name, sweetheart." Miss Parks's tone, brusque with him, was gentle as she spoke to the girl.

The child smiled at him. "I'm Mia."

"Hi, Mia. I'm Tate."

Unimpressed, she went back to her toy. He usually had better luck with creatures of the female persuasion.

Against the wall, the TV was playing a morning news program, but it was muted, the closed captioning showing on the screen.

"I don't like her to hear the news." Miss Parks perched on the edge of the couch. "She'll learn what a crappy world this is soon enough. Sit."

Tate settled on the loveseat.

"What you want to know about Raul?" she asked.

"Can you tell me how you know him?"

"He ruined our lives, that's how." The woman's color returned in a rush. She sat forward and glared at Tate as if it were his fault. "Him and my son were best friends all through school. Raul got Freddy mixed up with a gang, landed him in jail."

"I'm aware of your son's legal issues," Tate said. "I didn't realize Raul was involved in that assault."

"That's why he did it, isn't it? Because Raul told him to. Promised him a big payoff."

"Do you know why Raul wanted that man assaulted?"

"Something to do with the people he worked for. Freddy didn't know much about it 'cept he stood to get paid. I was still using back then, and my boy was trying to take care of us. My fault, that was. Much as I wish I could blame Raul, if I'da been a better mother, he wouldn'ta done it."

"You're sober now?"

She nodded, sat up a tiny bit straighter. "Over a year ago, in March. Ever since my Lela was killed."

"Your daughter?" Tate asked.

"She got beat up. Raul did it. Can't prove it, but I know it. Freddy does too."

"Why would Raul come after your daughter?"

"To get back at Freddy. He was gonna tell some lawyer lady the truth about what he done."

"What truth? What was he going to tell her?"

"He didn't tell me, just that he needed to tell the truth. That people got hurt because of him."

"Who, though?" Tate couldn't keep the frustration out of his voice. This was new information, but so vague...

"How should I know? All I know's that he told Raul to warn him, thinking he could distance himself from the people in charge, stay outta jail. But Raul told him to keep his mouth shut or else. Freddy only told me to warn me. Wanted me to watch my back." Miss Parks was warming to her subject. "The 'or else' was supposed to be a warning shot, least that's what Freddy thinks. Raul couldn't get to him, him being in jail, so he went after Lela. She got jumped on the street on her way to pick up the baby at daycare. She was a good girl, my Lela." The woman swallowed. Shook her head. No tears filled her eyes, but the emotion was there, just below the surface. "She worked hard, helped with the rent, tried to get me..." The woman's lips pinched closed. She looked away.

Tate said nothing, just allowed her the time she needed to pull her emotions back in. She didn't seem the type to show them, certainly not to strangers.

"Shouldn't have been fatal." Miss Parks turned back to him. "She shoulda woke up. They say it was a heart defect that killed her. But it wasn't. It was that piece of garbage."

"Was Raul charged?" Tate asked.

"Isn't that why you're here, to charge him? Isn't that what this is about?"

"I'm afraid I didn't know anything about that. We have reason to believe he was involved in another crime."

"You gonna put him away?"

"I hope so, ma'am." Tate gazed back at the little girl playing happily on the floor. "Your granddaughter?"

"Lela's girl. She don't have nobody else. Freddy said he'll help me when he can."

"Freddy is your firstborn, right?" He knew the answer. He also knew it was smart to ask easy questions. She nodded. "You know where he is?"

"No idea. A couple cops called looking for him, but I haven't seen him since he got out of jail." The woman's eyes narrowed to slits. "You looking for him too?"

"I need more information about Raul, and I had a hunch you could help me. I was hoping Freddy could help too."

Which was true. Maybe not the whole truth, but true.

"I don't know where Raul is. Freddy's laying low, staying away from me. Said he don't want to put us in danger."

"How would he?"

"You think he tells me anything? I'm just praying he stays out of trouble. We could sure use another income around here."

Tate nodded to the child. "Her father help?"

She looked at the little girl and lowered her voice. "Her father's as useful as wet dryer lint. He don't care she exists."

Tate leaned forward, also lowering his voice. "You care, obviously. Enough to get sober and offer Mia a clean, safe place to live. I'm sure Lela would be proud of you if she could see the home you've created for her daughter."

The woman looked away again, but not before Tate saw the sheen of tears. "Least I can do after I screwed up with my own kids."

"Not everybody gets offered a second chance in life. You're doing a good thing with yours."

When she turned to him again, her tiny smile belied the red eyes. "With God's help. Can't do nothing by myself."

"None of us can. You and God, though. I have a feeling that's a strong combination."

"That is the truth." Her expression hardened again. "You're not gonna go after Raul for killing my girl?"

"I'm with the Suffolk County DA. Unless it happened in Boston—"

"Pfft. Shoulda known you wouldn't help."

"If Raul Dawson is up to no good, I promise you, I'll do everything in my power to put him away. And if I get any evidence that proves what you said about him attacking your daughter, I'll pass it along to the Middlesex County DA. Maybe they'll bring a case."

"They won't." Miss Parks looked at her granddaughter. "They don't care about little people like us."

"With all due respect, ma'am, there's no such thing as little people and big people. All people are infinitely valuable, and that includes you and Mia and Freddy and Lela. If I can help put away the man who hurt your family, I'll do it."

CHAPTER TWENTY

That morning, Misty had searched for more information about IAF's Boston property. Real estate records revealed that the nonprofit owned the land outright. A perusal of the nonprofit's website told her the lot had been donated by a corporation called Redstone.

A quick Google search had returned nothing of value on Redstone, and fishing around on the county's records gave her zero information.

She didn't know what was going on with Dawson and Parks, but everything seemed to lead back to the IAF property. She'd cared before—bribery was a big deal, and people who offered bribes needed to be punished. If prosecutors adopted a no-big-deal attitude about bribery, it wouldn't be long before America turned into the type of country where slipping cash to the powers-that-be became the modus operandi.

But there was much more than bribery going on here. Jeffrey Cofer was missing, and the police were convinced it was related to Freddy Parks. Assuming Parks had harmed him, why would he do that?

She pondered the question as she and her bodyguards exited the SUV and crossed at the crosswalk before heading down a narrow walkway to a state office building.

Had Parks hurt Cofer to keep him from talking? Why would he, when attorney-client privilege applied? Cofer enjoyed a successful career as a defense attorney. He wasn't about to risk that by divulging confidential information.

Maybe Parks didn't understand that. Or wasn't willing to take the chance.

She and Tate had uncovered a few more puzzle pieces, but she still couldn't get a handle on the big picture.

Her feet and the hem of her slacks were wet by the time they stepped inside the state office building.

Nancy was waiting for them and hurried forward. She was in her early fifties, though the gray hair made her look older. She was comfortably overweight, the kind of woman who chose cheesecake and wasn't ashamed of it. Her access to business records had proved valuable to Misty. "I'm glad you called."

"I'm sorry I interrupted your work."

"After what you did for my family," Nancy said, "you're never an interruption."

Nancy's son had been an addict and a low-level drug dealer. When he was arrested a year earlier, Misty had worked with the court to give him the option of going to rehab instead of jail. Even though it was business-as-usual for Misty, Nancy had been incredibly thankful, offering her assistance if Misty ever needed it.

"How's Connor doing?"

"Still clean, thank God. And thanks to you for getting him into rehab."

"All I did was dangle the carrot. Connor did the hard work. And you and your husband paid for it."

"None of it would've happened if not for you." Nancy glanced at the bodyguards. "You all right?"

"Had a little trouble with a defendant. I hoped you could look up a business for me."

"Come on back."

They snaked past cubicles to Nancy's office, where she sat behind her desk. Misty settled in one of the chairs on the opposite side.

She didn't know Nancy's title, but the woman had enough pull to be able to access multiple state systems. "The company is called Redstone."

Nancy tapped on her keyboard. "There's a restaurant that goes by that name."

"Is there another company—?"

"I'm seeing it, but..." More tapping. "Hmm. It's a corporation owned by a corporation owned by... It's a mess." She looked past her screen. "It might take me a while to dig through this. Is it urgent?"

"I'd like it by the end of the week, if you can."

"No problem. I'll call you when I have the information."

Misty stood. "There's one more thing. Could you get me everything you can learn about a nonprofit called International Aid Foundation?"

"I'm on it." Nancy made a note and then glanced at her watch. "You have time for lunch?"

Lunch? She and Nancy weren't friends, not really. But Misty wouldn't mind if they were.

Behind her, Marcus cleared his throat. His voice was low when he said, "Maybe you could order in?"

"I'd love to have lunch with you," Misty said, "but I'm behind on my work. Can we do it another time?"

Nancy's smile was the kind that lit a whole room. "I'd like that."

Feeling like she'd accomplished something, Misty made her way back to the door. Maybe she'd made a new friend? She could always use more of those.

CHAPTER TWENTY-ONE

Tate was eager to get to Misty's, to tell her everything he'd learned. But he had to stop by the office first. After looking up and printing out all the information he could find on Raul Dawson and Lela Parks, Tate scrambled to get caught up on his own work.

"You mind if I sit?"

Leland filled his office doorway, and Tate stood so fast that his chair banged against the wall behind him. "Sure. Come on in."

Never, in the three years Tate had worked for the DA, had Leland come to his office.

His boss settled in the small chair in front of Tate's desk. Tate felt uncomfortable as he sat in his cushy seat.

"I wanted to find out how Misty's doing."

"Really good." Tate didn't know why the DA asked him and not her, but he updated Leland on all the work they'd done together. "I'm sure she spent her morning hammering out details of the plea deals."

"Glad to hear it." Despite his words, Leland didn't look glad. "What about Griffin?"

"Nothing new on that, as far as I know."

"You'd know, wouldn't you? Weren't you with her last night?"

Tate thought of their dinner on the roof, their walk in the neighborhood where the IAF building was located, their conversation in his apartment with Detective Klein. He thought of how he'd almost kissed her in the SUV, how he'd wished they could get back to that playful, romantic mood at the end of their night so he could make good on his promise. But news of the missing attorney had done nothing to encourage romance.

How could the DA know about any of that?

But of course he meant that Tate had left the office early to go over the new batch of cases with her. "Far as I know, she hasn't heard anything else from Detective Reyes about the ambush."

Leland consulted a piece of paper in his hand and rattled off some of the cases Misty had been assigned. As he did, Tate reported where they stood with each.

"And Dawson? She got that one off her desk yet?"

"It's more complicated than it looks on the surface."

Leland shifted forward on the too-small chair. "How so?"

Tate explained everything they'd learned the night before and what he'd learned that morning. As he talked, Leland's expression shifted from curious to annoyed to aggravated. By the time Tate was finished, he'd leaned back, lips pressed together tightly.

"We talked about this," Leland said, "about how it's irrelevant whether there's some big conspiracy going on."

"I remember, but—"

"I made a promise in my campaign to return this office to swift justice, and that case has been clogging up the pipes for a year. What's the holdup?"

"If that case is related to her intruder—"

"I thought we agreed that it was Griffin's people who broke into her apartment."

"The police don't think so. They think her intruder was the convict who was released last week, Freddy Parks. This morning, I confirmed that Parks and Raul Dawson are connected."

Leland said nothing for a long moment. Outside Tate's open door, the other ADAs and support staff continued their work.

Clinton walked by, glanced in, and frowned at the back of Leland's head. If he'd overheard the conversation, he'd be grinning.

Finally, Leland spoke. "It seems you're just as distractible as she is. The question Misty—and you—have to ask is simple: Did Dawson offer a bribe, and can you prove it?" Leland blew out a long, irritated breath. "I wanted you to exert your influence over her, and instead you've gotten pulled into her craziness."

Her *craziness*?

Tate worked to temper his reaction. *You're her boss,* he wanted to say. *Why don't you exert your influence?* Why was this Tate's problem?

More importantly, did Leland really expect Misty to overlook everything they'd learned for the sake of expediency?

The thought brought Tate up short, not because it was outlandish but because, had the Dawson case been assigned to him, he'd have closed it already. He'd have uncovered none of what they'd learned because Misty had kept asking questions.

But it wasn't Misty's job to sort out this mess, and it wasn't Tate's job either. That was what law enforcement was for.

"Look, Steele. I'm trying to give you the chance to stand out. You're smart and quick-thinking, and I can see you rising in the ranks here, getting into white-collar, maybe higher-profile cases. I'm trying to prepare you for that, to help you gain the skills you'll need to do the work. Part of that is learning to deal with difficult attorneys—even the ones on your side. Even the beautiful ones."

"That has nothing—"

"Misty's not like you." Leland held up a staying hand, and Tate clamped his lips shut. "She's never going to amount to anything more than a junior prosecutor in this office, not because she's not smart and talented but because she can't keep her eye on the ball. You're better than that, at least you were before I teamed you two up. You get your focus back, and you'll have a great future."

Tate couldn't think what to say. Half of him wanted to defend Misty, but the other half—the louder half, apparently—silenced that instinct. "Thank you, sir."

"Help Misty understand what her job is—and what it isn't. If she can't learn to let the irrelevant things go, then..." He shook his head. "I just don't know that she belongs here." He pushed to his feet. "Let me know when that case is settled. And when you hear anything else about Griffin."

Tate stood as well. "I will, sir."

After Leland left, Tate collapsed in his chair.

What was going on here? Why was Leland grilling Tate about Misty's cases, pushing him to accomplish what was her job?

Was Leland really thinking of letting Misty go? After everything she'd gone through that summer—after everything she was still going through—would he fire her?

And why did Tate have to know that? Why was Tate involved at all? How could he remain loyal to Misty and to his boss? To his dreams and goals and plans? To the job he'd worked so hard at?

What am I supposed to do here, Lord?

He sat in his office a long time, trying to hear the answer to his prayer. When none came, he shut his door and called his father.

"Everything okay, son?" Despite Dad's thriving law firm, he always had time to take Tate's calls.

"I need some advice," Tate said. "You have a minute?"

"For you, always."

Tate laid out everything that'd happened from the moment he'd been asked to help Misty the previous Friday to the conversation he'd just had with his boss. "I'm trapped. How can I do right by both Misty and my job? I have to choose one or the other."

"If that's the case, then what's the problem?" Dad's tone was matter-of-fact. "Not that this other lawyer isn't important, but it sounds like she's not cut out for the job."

"She cares about justice more than pleasing Leland."

"But pleasing Leland is the job, right? Doing what your boss says? Look, I have nothing against ideology, and obviously, justice is important, but what have I always told you about work? Who do you work for?"

"I work for Leland."

"Before that, Tate. Who do you really work for?"

Tate knew the answer his father wanted. "I work for myself."

"Exactly. You work for you, always. Those other things—pleasing Leland, putting bad guys away—those things are very important. They're critical. What you do matters. But at the end of the day, you work for you. Someday, you'll work for your family."

"You're saying I should look out for number one." Tate kept his tone level, but the words tasted sour in his mouth.

"It's not as mercenary as that. The more power you have, the more power you'll have to affect change in the world. God needs people like you in positions of power. You can't sacrifice that because you're trying to help one woman—a woman who, it seems, doesn't know how to do her job. You need to do what your boss is asking and let the chips fall where they may. This Misty person isn't your responsibility."

Would Dad say that if he knew how Tate felt about Misty? The words settled on the tip of his tongue, but he didn't speak them. Now wasn't the time.

If anything came of their relationship, he didn't want his father's first impression of her to be that she wasn't competent to do her job.

Tate ended the call. His dad wasn't wrong. Tate had always believed it was his responsibility to do what his boss told him. When he did, then someday, he'd be the boss. Then, he could accomplish great things.

In order to achieve his dreams, he needed to meet powerful people—business leaders, policy-makers, wealth-builders. He'd been stuck in the muck at the DA's office too long already. Three years, and he was still dealing with low-level drug dealers and minor assault cases. He needed to move into white-collar crimes.

There were other options, but he had no desire to go into private practice or end up at a law firm where he'd spend his days making the partners rich. Even if he eventually became a partner, money wasn't his goal.

Any decent lawyer could make partner at a law firm. Tate had higher aspirations than that. Goals that felt more out of reach every day.

He needed to stay focused.

Leland had to do what was best for the county and the DA's office.

Misty was so focused on getting justice that she allowed cases to drag on far too long. She was good at what she did, but if she didn't get *faster* at it, she was going to lose her job.

If Tate could get her to drop the charges against Dawson, he could prove to Leland he was ready to move up. He'd also protect her position. She claimed to want to keep working for the DA's office, so closing that case would be good for her as well.

It was just a bribery charge, after all.

The rest of it—the intruder, the mystery surrounding the IAF property, the connection to Parks, even the disappearance of Jeffrey Cofer—none of that had to do with Dawson's attempted bribery. Leland was right. Giant conspiracy or just one man's stupid decision, it didn't matter. What mattered was whether or not Dawson had offered the bribe, whether Misty could prove it in court, and what punishment he deserved.

The second part—the proof part—that was where the case hinged. It would be Dawson's word against Zachary Hardy's. And even if Misty could prove Dawson had done it...to what end? Maybe a short prison term, which would probably be suspended. Maybe a fine.

It was a waste of time. And if Misty didn't drop it, it would be a waste of her career. If she wanted to stay in the DA's office, she was going to have to compromise on this one.

And if Tate didn't want to see all his dreams slip away, he was going to have to convince her to do just that.

CHAPTER TWENTY-TWO

It was after four that afternoon when a knock sounded on Misty's door.

Her heart flip-flopped. Ridiculous how much she'd been looking forward to seeing Tate. She hurried and flung it open.

On the far side, Tate smiled.

Next to him, Hughes scowled. "What did I tell you about not answering the door until you know who it is?"

"I knew who it was. And besides, you're here."

"He didn't buzz you, just waltzed in as if he belonged."

How did Hughes know he hadn't buzzed? Could he hear? Or...more likely the guard outside had told him.

"Someone was coming out when I got here," Tate said. "I thought it would be okay if I just came up."

Hughes ignored him, intense gaze on Misty. "I could be dead. He could be a murderer." The man's serious expression contrasted with the smile Tate was trying to suppress.

"Sorry," Misty said. "I'll do better next time."

After Tate stepped in and closed the door, Misty whispered, "The guy's as serious as terminal cancer."

Tate let his smile bloom. He was gorgeous already, but that

smile made him nearly irresistible. "He's just trying to keep you safe."

"I know." Their date the night before, walking hand-in-hand, almost kissing, settled between them awkwardly, like an invisible band stretching the tension.

Until Tate leaned in and kissed her on the cheek, sending a pleasant flush to her face. Such a simple gesture, that kiss, but the band snapped.

"Sorry I'm late." He'd said he'd be there by midafternoon, and it was nearly five.

"I got a lot of work done." She turned and headed for the kitchen. "Come on in."

He followed her, pausing at the threshold. "What's that smell?"

She'd started the meat cooking that morning. "Since it's chilly and rainy, I decided a warm dinner was in order. It's pot roast."

He went to the slow cooker and lifted the lid, inhaling the scent of roasting beef. "Please tell me I'm invited to stay."

"I'll be offended if you don't."

He set the lid back down. "If you insist." He added a wink, then tipped his head to the pile of mail on the counter. "Shouldn't you open that?"

She'd picked it up the night before after they'd talked to Klein, but she hadn't looked through it yet. "I'll deal with it later. It's just going to be bills and junk."

"I have to open my mail immediately. Always the hope there'll be a million-dollar check made out to me."

She chuckled. "Let me know if that ever happens."

Heading toward the cabinets, he said, "Do you mind if I—?"

"Help yourself." She loved watching him move around her space as if he belonged. Well, it was her sister's space, but the point remained. She liked the idea of him belonging where she was. Belonging in her life.

Okay, they weren't there yet. She needed to tap the brakes on her imagination. Maybe she'd struggled to keep her mind off him all day, but that didn't mean he felt the same way.

Tate poured soda over ice in his glass, then leaned against the counter. "Have you learned anything else about IAF?"

"That land on Altus Street was donated."

"Ah. That's why they built there. By whom?"

"Company called Redstone. Ever heard of it?" When he shook his head, she explained how she was having somebody look into it for her. "What've you been up to?"

His grin was wide, his eyes sparkling. "You'll never guess."

They sat while he explained his visit to Freddy Parks's mother and what he'd learned.

She interrupted to make sure she understood. "You're saying Raul Dawson and Freddy Parks were school friends? Freddy's mom thinks Raul got him into the gang."

"Which might be true, might not," Tate said. "Moms always blame the other kid."

"True. But according to her, Freddy attacked his victim"—she thought back, remembered the man's name—"Ernie Phillips—"

"A building inspector," Tate reminded her.

"Right. You're saying he attacked a building inspector because Dawson paid him to. We already know that when Parks did it, he drove to the property at the corner of Aldus and Buttrick, which at the time had a Thornebrook trailer on it. And that's where the police caught up with him."

"Exactly. And Dawson works for Thornebrook," Tate said, "so that tracks. Maybe Dawson was there, or Parks thought he would be. Parks went there to see him, maybe to collect his money. Maybe because he knew he was about to get arrested and wanted a lawyer."

"Jeffrey Cofer," she said.

"Whose fees, I'm sure, Dawson or his people paid. Freddy's mom wouldn't have had the money. But here's the thing. Apparently, last year Freddy was feeling guilty about something he'd done. He said people got hurt because of him, and he was going to tell, in her words, a lawyer lady."

"Oh." Misty pushed back from the table and paced to the far wall, putting it together. "When Freddy asked me to go see him, he must've planned to tell me."

Tate stood as well. "That's what I was thinking. But he told Dawson what he was going to do—Miss Parks thinks he wanted his friend to distance himself or something—and Dawson warned him to keep his mouth shut. When did you go to see Parks in Walpole?"

She returned to the table and leaned over her laptop, searching the previous year's calendar. "March twenty-second."

"And that was how long after he contacted you?"

"Probably two weeks," she said. "I don't remember exactly."

Tate slid a piece of paper from his bag and set it on the table, face down. "Miss Parks said that Raul threatened him to keep him quiet. I don't know if Freddy refused to be quieted or what, but his sister, Lela, was attacked on March twentieth."

Misty sat again. "Is she all right?"

Tate's lips angled downward at the corners. "Apparently, the attack shouldn't have been deadly, but she had a heart condition they didn't know about. Between that and the assault, it killed her. But if not for the assault—"

"She'd still be alive."

Tate flipped the paper, and Misty read the police report. "I should have gotten out to Walpole sooner."

"You think it would have changed anything? Dawson—if it

was Dawson—attacked Lela to warn Freddy off. Don't you think a revenge attack would have been worse?"

"I don't know. Maybe he'd have been arrested. What was he going to tell me?"

Tate shrugged. "Miss Parks didn't know."

"Or wouldn't say."

"I don't think so. Lela had a little girl. Miss Parks is raising her. She wants Dawson to pay for what he did."

"Was he questioned? Charged?"

Tate tapped the police report between them. "There's no evidence. Nobody was ever arrested. Lela never regained consciousness, so she couldn't say who'd attacked her."

Misty settled against the chair back and stared out the window at the falling rain. "So...Freddy Parks and Raul Dawson used to be friends. But they wouldn't be now, not after Dawson killed Freddy's sister. Meaning they're not working together. So...what's going on? Where is Freddy?"

"His mother said he's lying low."

"Avoiding Dawson, or trying to find him, maybe." She shook her head. "It's all so convoluted."

"And you're in the middle of it. Which is exactly where I don't want you to be."

She didn't want to be there either. Afraid to stay in her own apartment. Afraid to leave the house without guards. But she and Tate were closing in on it. It was just a matter of time before she figured out what was going on and got the people responsible thrown in jail. And then she'd be safe again.

∼

Misty swirled the last bit of her roll in the dark gravy and ate it, considering how to answer Tate's latest question. The roast was delicious, but she'd been enjoying their conversation even more.

"By your long pause, I'd say there's a story with your sisters."

He'd asked if they were close—a simple question with a complex answer.

"I was never that close with Krystal. She's four years older than I am, but that's not the reason. She was always by Mom's side, like she was trying to support her or protect her or something. Even when Dad would go into his rages, Krystal would stay until Mom or Dad forced her to leave. But Summer would grab me at the first sign of his temper, and we'd run or hide. In fact, that's my earliest memory. They were fighting. There were all these scary noises coming from the living room, bangs and screaming. And Dad yelling. And then Summer picked me up out of my booster seat."

"Whoa, you were that young?"

"Four. I think I remember it because I was scared. Summer was only six or seven. She got me out of there."

"So she's always been protective."

"As long as I can remember. I wasn't at all surprised when she became a bodyguard. It seemed a natural fit for her. What I'm learning—what she's learning, too, I think—is that her protectiveness was a defense mechanism. She's good at it because she'd had so much practice, but she became protective because Dad was abusive. I think she's trying to figure out who she is now that she doesn't have to always watch her back. She's trying to learn what she's gifted at. Who she might've been if not for our father."

Tate gazed past Misty toward the window. Outside, the clouds were breaking up, allowing the setting sun to bathe the world in gold. "We have these natural...bents, I guess." Tate drew his attention back to her. "Everybody has talents, abilities, gifts, and I think part of the key to life is figuring out what ours are and finding out how to use them. How God wants us to use them."

"Exactly." Misty leaned toward him. "I think of the difference between me and my sisters and you and your siblings. You grew up in a happy home, a fairly...normal home, right?"

Tate had been telling her about his family earlier in the meal. "I'd say so. Not perfect, but we loved each other."

"I assume you were encouraged to explore who you were and what you loved. You weren't expected to fit into a certain mold. You were given the freedom to be who God created you to be."

Tate nodded, though the action was so slow she wasn't sure if he agreed or was simply contemplating what she'd said. Finally, he nodded slowly. "Yes."

The word was tentative enough that she put her point aside. "Yes...but?"

"We were a happy family, all encouraged to find out what we loved and what we were naturally good at. Our parents encouraged us to seek God and follow His leading."

That sounded pretty perfect to Misty, but she could tell there was more to the story.

"That worked for three of us. But my older sister, Hannah has a learning disability. She was held back in school, so she and I were in the same grade. In high school, I took AP classes while Hannah struggled in the mainstream classes. I realize now how that probably made her feel—underachieving compared to her younger brother. At the time..." He shrugged. "I'm ashamed to say I liked it. I was always competitive, and I was winning. Since I could never beat Derrick, it was nice to beat Hannah."

"But it wasn't a competition."

"Right. It shouldn't have been. But that's what I see in retrospect that I didn't see at the time. My father, he wanted us to all work hard. He always talked about how difficult the world was, how we'd have to fight for what we wanted. He always compared us to each other."

"You were smart," Misty said, "a high achiever. You probably came out pretty well in those comparisons."

He shrugged. "Hannah never won. Mom and Dad hired private tutors for her, got her into programs to help her overcome her disabilities. They did everything in their power to ensure Hannah would be successful."

Except make sure she understood she was good enough, Misty guessed. Good enough just like she was.

"Was she?" Misty asked.

"In high school, she started dating an older guy who got her into drugs. She quit school just a few months shy of graduation, moved out of the house and in with her boyfriend. The day she told our parents her plan, Mom begged her to reconsider."

"What'd your dad say?"

"'You want to ruin your life, that's your choice. But when it all falls apart, don't come running to me.'"

"Oh, no."

"I've never seen my mother so distraught or my father so angry. I was furious with all of them. I don't think I spoke to my dad for weeks afterward. Not that I didn't understand. Hannah's choices crushed him. I was furious with her too."

"Where is she now?"

"Her boyfriend dumped her a couple years later. She'd called Mom a few times over the years, but when the loser kicked her out, she was afraid to go home. She ended up in a homeless shelter. The thing is, Mom was always reaching out to her, trying to make sure she was all right. And she always paid for Hannah's phone. Mom called her one day, found out where she was, picked her up, and took her to rehab."

"What'd your dad think about that?"

"I honestly thought their marriage was going to end that weekend. I was home from college, but I think they forgot I was there. I heard the whole argument. Dad said he wasn't paying for rehab, that Hannah deserved what she got. Mom said he was paying for it one way or another. He could write the check now, or it would come out of their divorce settlement."

"Whoa."

Tate laughed, though there was little humor in it. "My mom is the sweetest woman in the world, but she's fierce when it comes to her kids. They paid for Hannah's rehab, and she got clean. She's a hairdresser, and she's really good at it. I think that's the thing. She didn't need to make good grades to be successful in a career. But Dad didn't see it that way. To him, bad grades meant underachievement. And underachieving was unacceptable."

"But we're not all book smart. There are other ways of measuring intelligence."

"Exactly. Hannah figured that out. She's dating one of her customers. I think they might get married."

"She and your dad are okay?"

"You know how families are. The history doesn't go away, but we have to learn to look past it, right? To love each other despite our flaws and failures."

"You've forgiven them both?"

"Oh, yeah. Dad shouldn't have done what he did, but I can understand his frustration. He tried so hard to help Hannah, and she defied everything he believed in. I think he thought if he gave her an ultimatum, she'd give in to his demands. She'd finish school and get her act together. Dad was trying to do the right thing by her."

"But she was stubborn."

"And so was he," Tate said.

"Huh." Misty considered all he'd said alongside what she knew about Tate. "Is that why you're so ambitious, a desire to please your father?"

His head tilted to one side. He seemed about to speak but

caught the words before they left his mouth. After a moment, he exhaled. "I was going to say no, but... Maybe. Ambition is such a part of me, it never occurred to me to attribute it to my dad."

"But it tracks," she said. "Your father values achievement, and you crave your father's approval."

He averted his gaze. Thinking about what she'd said? Or had she annoyed him with the observation? Would he be angry that she'd seen that in him? Maybe storm out or deny it, even when it was so obvious?

She waited for an irrational response, certain she'd pushed a button she shouldn't have pushed. At least she didn't have to worry he'd fly off the handle like her father would have, had anybody dared to analyze his behavior to his face.

Tate's eyes narrowed. His lips pressed into a line. He focused on something beyond her, or perhaps on something not in the room at all.

Then his face cleared. He set the glass down and leaned toward her. "I think you might be on the money. I've always wanted to achieve something big, something impressive. It felt like...like that's what Steeles should do. Dad is the founding partner in one of the most successful law firms in New England. Derrick, my oldest brother, is moving up in rank in the Navy. Caroline is one of the highest earning brokers at her firm—and she's only twenty-six."

"And then there's Hannah," Misty said.

"Right. The only underachiever in the family, and Dad barely spoke to her for years." Tate seemed to contemplate that for a few moments. Misty stayed quiet, giving him the space to think it through. Finally, he met her eyes and smiled. "Obviously, ours wasn't the perfect family. But my parents weathered it. Hannah's okay. Mom and Dad did their best, which I guess is all we can ask. And if I'm a little too focused on achievement... maybe I need to spend some time with the Lord on that." He forked a bite of mashed potatoes. "We were talking about you, though."

Just like that, Tate was past it. Not defensive. Not annoyed. Just thinking it through.

She liked that. She liked that she could trust his rationality to hold, even when he was pressed.

"My family was different from yours," she said. "It wasn't... safe. I think we all—my sisters and my mom—felt like we had to be quiet, to blend into the walls. The last thing any of us wanted was to set Dad off. It wasn't that we couldn't explore what we loved, but we couldn't express it. We couldn't get excited about anything because Dad always took it personally. I guess he felt like a failure, and anybody's success made it worse. So we all just...hid. I don't even know if that makes sense."

Tate nodded. "You're all successful now, though, right? I got to know Krystal this summer. She seems happily married, has good kids. I'd guess she loves her life."

"I think Krystal set out to create a family completely different from ours." Misty sipped her water, contemplated what she'd said. "Except, not completely different. Mom was amazing. She loved us so much. If Summer were here, she'd say Mom didn't love us enough to protect us, but I don't think that's accurate. I think Mom loved Dad just as much as she loved us. She felt trapped, like she couldn't love us all at the same time. For years, I blamed the church for Mom's staying with Dad, but I think she didn't leave him because she didn't want to. She loved him. Why, I have no idea. Krystal, I think, has dedicated her life to being like Mom in all the good ways."

"Your mom was a Christian, right?" At her nod, he said, "I bet she prayed for you three every day of her life. Maybe that contributed to your success in life. I know Mom prayed for Hannah constantly after she moved out, and she attributes the fact that Hannah came home and got clean to God's work.

Maybe you and your sisters are bearing the fruit of your mother's prayers."

Oh. Misty'd never considered that, but it made sense. Mom might've died young, but her prayers wouldn't have died with her. Mom's prayers were probably still affecting their lives today.

Mom had always seemed so powerless, and yet, if Tate was right, maybe she was the most powerful person in their household. It was a little mind-blowing to consider.

"But you and your sisters aren't close." Tate brought them back around to the question that'd begun the discussion.

"That's my fault. After the kidnapping, I wanted to put all my past behind me. My dad, which makes sense. But also my sisters. Summer and I stayed with him for a while, and being in his house again reminded me of all the ugly things. Even though he was different, he'd quit drinking, he'd been trying—he's still trying, I think—to get his anger under control. Still, I just...I couldn't stand it. So, I moved out. I decided I wanted to be a lawyer, and I worked hard for it. And along the way, I sacrificed my relationships with them."

"Why?" The question held no censure or rebuke, just simple curiosity.

She sighed, hating the answer but choosing to be honest—like Tate had been honest. "I blamed Summer for the kidnapping, which was irrational. But she'd always been my protector, and when I was in danger, I felt like she'd failed. I knew intellectually that was wrong. I was being unfair. But emotionally, I guess I'd attached my safety to my sister, as if it was her job. It took me years to get past that. And when I did..." Misty sighed, not wanting to go on. "My behavior is so stupid, it's embarrassing."

Tate smiled. "You seem so perfect."

"Ha. We both know that's not true."

He shrugged, his lips tipping up. "You seem pretty perfect to me. You had an irrational reaction to a bizarre and terrifying situation—that just makes you human."

Misty was plenty human. "It was years before I realized what a jerk I'd been. I needed to apologize, ask her to forgive me for being an idiot."

"Did you?"

"When I spotted Summer on a dinghy, motoring to that evil man's yacht, I thought I'd never see her again. I thought I'd missed my opportunity." She was glad Tate knew enough about her latest kidnapping that she didn't have to explain herself. "I was sitting on a rocky piece of land, so cold I thought I'd freeze to death, and all I could think was how I'd screwed up the most important relationship of my life, and I'd never be able to fix it. I hardly knew anything about God, but I've never prayed so much..." She pressed to the back of her mind the memory of the cold, terrifying time.

"A few weeks after we were rescued," she said, "Jon asked Denise to marry him, and we were all invited to watch. They had a big party afterward. When it was winding down, I took Summer and Krystal aside and asked them both to forgive me for cutting them out. And they did, just like that. And Krystal and Summer had some stuff to deal with from our childhood, and they both apologized." Misty remembered the scene so well, she and her sisters sitting at the picnic table in the park on the shore of Lake Ayasha. The scents of grilling meat, the people talking and laughing, and the three of them, bent close, pouring their hearts out. Hugging, weeping. "It was a big cry-fest." Even now, just thinking about it, Misty's eyes filled. She laughed and swiped away the tears with a napkin. "Sorry. It's good to have them back."

"Sounds like God was in that whole situation." He ate

another bite of roast. "Maybe I should do that with Hannah. Apologize to her for always..."

"Winning?"

He laughed. "Yeah, how would that go?"

"Maybe you can find a better way to phrase it."

"Let's hope." Tate pushed his plate away. "I have to stop eating, but it was delicious."

"Thanks." She stood and reached for his plate. "Let me just get these rinsed."

She cleared the table and put away the leftovers, not bothering to waste time washing the dishes.

When she joined Tate in the living room, he turned from the gas fireplace. "I hope it's okay." He'd lit the flames and lowered the lights in the room.

"Of course." Better than okay.

She sat on the sofa, and he settled on the space beside her.

But he didn't stay there long, instead pushing up and angling to face her. "I need to say something. And maybe it's..." He shook his head, offered her a self-conscious smile. "This is going to sound...I don't know. I just wanted to say that I like you."

Oh. Her heart fluttered. She couldn't seem to think how to respond.

"Wow. I sound like a junior high school kid." His face turned an adorable shade of pink. "Anyway, obviously you knew that. We've been eating dinner together, and held hands, and"—he gestured to the fire—"this isn't exactly a work environment. But since we also work together, I thought I should make it clear. I've always had great respect for you. You're smart and capable and passionate. It's so strange to think, all these years we've known each other, I've never seen you as anything except a rival and colleague. I mean, obviously, you're attractive, so that's not entirely accurate."

He paused again, smiled, glanced at the flames. "Anyway, now that I know you, I really like you. I feel like...like you could matter to me. To my life. Like maybe this could turn into something."

While he gazed at her, his expression serious, maybe a little worried, she turned over everything he'd said, taking a moment to gather her thoughts. He'd always seemed blindly ambitious. Now, she understood his ambition—the family he'd come from and the pressure he must feel to succeed. He was efficient at work in an effort to please his boss, not to be a suck-up but to be a superior employee. There was humility in that.

Tate laughed, the sound low and nervous. "It would really help if you'd say something."

"I like you too. A lot."

He smiled, his white teeth gleaming in the firelight. "Well, that's good. If you didn't, the whole working together thing was about to get really awkward."

She took his hand, which felt forward—and then felt so right as he closed his long fingers around hers.

"It's funny," she said. "Having my house broken into, almost walking in on an intruder, all the fear and confusion and mystery we've dealt with... It's funny that something so scary could lead to this."

He leaned in closer. "I think that's how God works. He uses the hard things to open our eyes to His blessings. He allows the hard things because He doesn't want us to miss what matters."

Like Tate. Like the thing brewing between them. Could it matter to God? Could it be His plan for her?

Maybe. She was only just learning about Him, but maybe what they said at church was true. God loved her and had good plans for her.

Plans that might include Tate.

He brushed her hair back, then slid his fingers against her

scalp, raising goose bumps on her skin and desire much deeper. He closed the distance between them.

The instant their lips touched, her body responded with a flush of heat and pleasure. She let go of his hand and wrapped her arms around him.

Never letting their lips separate, he shifted her legs until they draped over his, moving her into his embrace. He deepened the kiss, and she lost herself in it. Lost herself in him.

How could this man she'd barely tolerated a week before have such an effect on her? How could he awaken her to yearnings she'd hardly known she had? But as their lips moved together, as the heat of his body raised hers, she found herself imagining more of this, more of him.

When, too soon, he ended the kiss, she wasn't ready to pull away. She gripped the shirt at his back and pressed her cheek against his chest, his heart racing beneath her ear.

She had no idea how it happened, but Tate...Tate was exactly what she wanted. And what she wanted wasn't out of reach. It wasn't some big *out there* desire, like truth and justice.

No, Tate was real, here. Holding her close.

For the first time in her life, Misty wanted something, someone, who wanted her back.

CHAPTER TWENTY-THREE

Tate fell asleep with a smile.

And woke up with a sense of dread churning in his stomach, much heavier than the pot roast he'd eaten too much of the night before.

He shouldn't have done it. It'd been stupid and selfish, and he shouldn't have done it.

Not that he could make himself regret confessing his feelings to Misty. He did like her, a lot. He'd been looking for a woman to spend his life with for years, never realizing the woman he was seeking was working in an office down the hall.

Before now, the timing hadn't been right. She hadn't been a believer until recently, and they'd both been focused on their careers. Now, it felt perfect.

Almost perfect, anyway.

But confessing his feelings and kissing her... Those should have waited until after he'd talked to her about the bribery case.

He spent more time in prayer that morning than usual, begging the Lord for guidance. There was no clear *do this and it'll all work out* answer. One thing he knew was that he needed to see Misty immediately—before work—and tell her what he should have told her the night before.

She'd be angry—justifiably so. But how angry, and would she forgive him?

He skipped his workout and took the T to Kenmore Square, then walked a few blocks to the apartment building. Like the evening before, somebody was coming out as he approached. Unlike the evening before, though, Misty wasn't expecting him. He pressed the button.

"Yes?" Misty said a moment later through the speaker.

"It's Tate."

The door clicked, and he let himself in and climbed to her floor. He nodded to her bodyguard, who looked Tate up and down like he'd study a serial killer.

"We met a couple nights ago."

The man said nothing, just shifted away from her door so Tate could knock.

This time, she said, "Who is it?"

"It's me."

She pulled the door open. "Hey." Wearing jeans and a short-sleeved shirt, no shoes on her feet, she flashed a wide, happy smile. He'd known she was beautiful, but when she looked at him like that, like he'd made her day just by showing up... Wow.

"What are you doing here?"

He stepped inside and closed the door on the grumpy guard. "I need to talk to you."

"Okay." Her eyes gleamed as if she were in on the joke. He wished he could return the expression. He wished he were there to pick up where they'd left off the night before. There'd been a lot of kissing, laughing, chatting, and more kissing. He'd forced himself to leave when he started considering other options. The cold shower when he got home had helped.

Now, all he wanted was to take her in his arms. Once he said what he needed to say, she might never allow him to again.

"You want some coffee?"

"I can't stay. There's something I should've talked to you about last night."

"Get distracted, did you?"

"You have that effect." He took her hand and led her to the couch, then changed his mind about sitting beside her. He settled in the chair.

The gleam in her eyes dimmed. "Something wrong?"

He took a deep breath. "Don't be mad at me, okay? I'm just the messenger."

She sat up straight. The flirty attitude slipped off, and suddenly she was all prosecutor. "Whose message?"

"Leland's."

"What?"

"He wants you to get the Dawson case taken care of immediately."

"Huh." She pushed to her feet and paced. "Why doesn't he talk to me himself?"

"I don't know. Probably because you and I have been working together. And I'm at the office and you're not."

"I can fix that." She started toward the hallway that led to her bedroom.

Tate propelled to his feet and grabbed her hand. "Let's just talk."

She turned and pulled away, but she didn't continue down the hall. "I'm not dropping that case, Tate. I can't believe you'd suggest it after everything we've learned."

"I'm not saying we drop the whole thing. But the bribery is a separate issue. Whether Dawson attacked Lela Parks, whatever is going on between Parks and Dawson and Thornebrook—all that is separate from the bribery."

"Is it? You're the one who made the connection between Parks's assault victim and Dawson. The victim was a building inspector. The assault had to be related to Thornebrook—maybe even paid for by them. I'm hoping to track down Phillips, the victim, today, see if he knows why Parks attacked him."

"I'm not saying there's no connection. Obviously, there's more going on here. I'm saying if there is a larger conspiracy or something, it's unrelated to the bribery charge."

"But it's not. Or at least, it might not be."

"Maybe. But that case is separate. The questions are, did Dawson offer Zachary Hardy a bribe, and can you prove it?"

"So that's it. Back to dropping cases we can't win—or offering pleas to get them off the desk. No sense of justice or rightness? Expediency wins at all costs? I thought you were past that."

"Past doing my job well? You thought wrong." He took a breath to temper his frustration. "This isn't about me. Leland's your boss. Your job is to do what he wants, and he wants it dropped."

"Even if he's wrong."

"Yes, even if he's wrong."

"Do you think anything is worth fighting for, or do you always cave?"

He took a step back, surprised. Hurt. "I've been on your side through all of this. I'm still on your side. I've been fighting this battle for days."

Her eyes hardened. Her mouth opened, then snapped shut. She swiveled and started down the hallway.

"What are you doing?" he called.

"I can fight my own battles. I'll see you at the office." She disappeared into her room and slammed the door.

"Don't..." But she wouldn't hear him now. He leaned against the doorjamb and waited.

Fifteen minutes later, she stepped out. She'd put on makeup and twisted her hair into a bun. She wore a white blouse under a navy business suit, a pair of stilettos dangling from one hand. She froze when she saw him. "Why are you still here?"

"You're working from home because somebody at the office leaked information about our meeting to the intruder. Somebody with access to the office calendar is working against you, which means it's not safe. I think you should continue to work from home."

"I'll be fine."

"If you believed that, you'd have been there all week."

She passed him on her way to the kitchen. "My bodyguards can keep me safe. I've stayed home because...because I was nervous. But I need to quit allowing my irrational fears to keep me imprisoned."

"Your fears aren't irrational, Misty." Tate followed, stopping at the threshold.

She shut off the coffee maker and slid a container of milk into the refrigerator.

"Someone shot at you the other day," he said. "Somebody broke into your apartment."

"Griffin knows better than to try that again." She moved to the sink. "It's just a matter of time before Reyes and the police find the shooters and bring them all into custody."

"There's still Dawson and Parks."

She straightened from putting a dish in the dishwasher. "Which you want me to drop."

"Leland wants you to drop the bribery case. And yeah, honestly, I do too. I want you to turn over everything you know to the police and let them handle it."

"They won't do anything."

"You don't know that. They're equipped for this sort of thing. Much better equipped than you and I are."

The chill in Misty's glare felt frostier because of the heat they'd generated the night before. "We don't even know what crimes were committed," she said. "What are we going to tell them?"

"Exactly. We have no idea what's going on. So we turn over what we do know and then step away. If you do that, you'll be safe."

"Will I?"

Tate cut off the assurances he was about to utter. Would she be safe? She'd started on this quest *because* she'd been threatened. The threat had come first. "I don't know. I think so."

"Well, for sure let's risk that."

"I'm not saying get rid of your bodyguards. I'm saying drop the case, turn over everything you know, and move on. Get back to your normal life as much as you can. Maybe...probably, whoever broke into your apartment will just—"

"Get away with it."

She wasn't wrong. But neither was he. They weren't cops. They weren't in the business of hunting bad guys. "Hopefully, they'll go away. I'm not saying you go back to business-as-usual. Obviously, you'll need to keep being cautious. But maybe it'll blow over."

"So you think I should let it all go," Misty said, "just to please my boss, a man who doesn't know the half of what's going on?"

"Not to please him." But Tate's argument sounded feeble.

Though Leland hadn't told Tate to keep their conversation between them, confidentiality was implied. But Misty needed to understand the other issue at play here. "Leland might have suggested that if you can't let that bribery case go, it means you're not cut out for the job. I'm trying to help you here."

Her skin paled. She moved to the table and dropped into a chair. "He's going to fire me?"

"I hope not." Tate pulled out the one beside her and sat. "I just think, for the sake of our careers, you should do what he says."

Her eyes popped wide. "What do you mean, *our careers?*"

"Your career... And, he wants me to get you to do it, so—"

"So if I don't sacrifice my beliefs—"

"Don't be melodramatic."

"Is that what I am? Fighting for justice makes me melodramatic?"

"This isn't a capital murder case, Misty. If you don't want to drop the charges, then don't. Offer a plea. If you took it to court, you'd just as likely lose as win. It's one person's word against the other. It's not that big of a deal."

"It's a big deal to Freddy's mother. If Dawson killed her daughter—"

"Then the Middlesex County DA should bring charges. Getting him on a small-time bribery charge isn't going to achieve justice for murder."

"But that's not what you care about. All you care about is your career. You want me to drop the charges so it'll make you look good to the boss."

"That's not what this is about."

"Right."

"Let's not make this about you and me."

"You made it about you and me when you told me that you like me. And we"—she gestured to the living room, where they'd discovered how well they fit together the night before—"got too close."

Her words sent his heart racing. "What happened last night has nothing to do with this."

"Of course it does. Because you know if you'd told me this before, then *that*"— again, she waved toward the couch—"would never have happened. Interesting timing."

"You want me to admit that I confessed my feelings before this conversation on purpose? Fine. I admit it. I was afraid that, if I encouraged you to drop the charges, you'd get angry and push me away."

"So it didn't mean anything. You're just trying to manipulate me—"

"No!" His shout reverberated as he pushed back in his chair and stood. "Is that what you think? That I'd...I'd use you like that?"

"How would I know?"

Tate squeezed his hands into fists, trying to let out some of the tension building inside. He closed his eyes. Took a breath. Blew it out and opened them again.

Misty was watching him closely. If he didn't know better, he'd swear he saw fear in her expression.

He settled back on the chair, laid his hands flat on the table. "I'm sorry I yelled."

She blinked. "It's fine."

"If I made you nervous, then it's not fine. I hope you know, no matter what you said or did, I would never hurt you. That's not the kind of man I am."

Her head bobbed, a series of short nods that said she wasn't sure but didn't dare disagree.

Inching his hand forward, he flipped it palm-up. "These are two different things. There's work, and there's you and me. Everything I said last night is true. I wanted to say it before we talked about Dawson because I wanted you to know how I feel. Okay?"

Her gaze flicked to his palm. Then, she slid hers against it. Her hand was cold, and he covered it with his other. "Let's not make this bigger than it should be. I want what's best for you. Not just that you'll be safe, but that you won't lose your job."

"And you want what's best for you." Her words were flat.

Though she was letting him hold her hand, she wouldn't look at him.

He angled into her line of vision. "Is that bad? Is it bad I'm trying to protect my career too?"

She swallowed. "No."

"I didn't ask for this, you know. I didn't ask Leland to assign me to help you. I'm glad he did, don't get me wrong, because it's given us an opportunity to get to know each other. But he hasn't been happy with either one of us this week."

"He should direct his displeasure *with* me *toward* me."

Not that Tate minded taking some of the heat off her. It might end up being bad for his career, but...but Misty was worth it. "He's the boss, so we can't exactly tell him that."

She bit her lip, an unconscious gesture that had his pulse racing for a different reason. Everything about her drew him to her. How had he missed it for so long?

"Will you please stay home one more day," he asked. "I know you'll probably be safe at the office. It's the getting to and coming from that makes me nervous. You'd be back in an old routine, which anybody could learn and use against you."

"I went out yesterday. It was fine."

"But nobody knew you were going. Look, you know Leland's not in the office most Fridays anyway. I heard him talking about some big event this weekend he's getting ready for, so he's probably not going to be there today. Maybe we can figure this out by Monday. If nothing else, we'll have had a couple more days to think it through." When she said nothing, he leaned in. "Please?"

Her eyes narrowed like she was annoyed, but he caught a hint of amusement at his begging. "Fine."

He allowed a moment of relief. He had until Monday to talk her into dropping the charges against Dawson and turning all the information they'd dug up over to the police. Maybe, if he used his charm, he could convince her. He could protect her and protect both of their careers.

Either that, or Misty would prove to be as stubborn as he'd always suspected.

CHAPTER TWENTY-FOUR

That morning, Misty focused on her other cases, but she couldn't stop thinking about Tate.

It wasn't fair to be angry with him for passing along Leland's message. It also wasn't fair to expect him to sacrifice his career and ambitions because she was too stubborn to drop—or at least settle—a simple bribery charge.

Misty had spent enough time in counseling to understand that her emotions didn't always track with what was fair or true or right. She was trying to be reasonable, to trust that Tate had been honest with her about his feelings, not manipulating her into doing his bidding.

She was trying, but it wasn't easy.

She'd thrown herself wholeheartedly into those kisses. And she and Tate had talked for hours. She'd shared things with him that she didn't share with anybody.

Tate had listened, asking questions every so often to be sure he understood. He'd been tender and gentle and...

If it was all an act, what a fool that would make her.

She could imagine him laughing all the way home, congratulating himself on getting her right where he wanted her.

But no. No. That wasn't who Tate was, and she refused to let her anxieties screw this up. She hadn't asked for his help, but she was learning how to accept it, something she'd never been good at. She didn't want to go back to doing everything by herself. She hadn't realized how lonely she was until...Tate.

So she and Tate didn't agree on everything. So what? There'd probably be a lot of that in their future if they stayed together. They approached their jobs very differently. But if they wanted to have a real and growing relationship, if it had any chance of blooming into something bigger, then they would have to learn to leave work at work.

After contemplating everything Tate had said, she knew he was right. Whether she dropped or settled the bribery case wouldn't matter to the other things she was learning. And as much as she didn't want to lose her job, she really didn't want Leland to take out his displeasure with her on Tate.

She dialed Dawson's lawyer, who of course wasn't available.

"Ask her to call me on my cell." Misty left the number. "It's regarding the Raul Dawson case."

She hung up frustrated, but at least she'd started the process.

Next, Misty found a home phone number for Ernie Phillips, the building inspector Parks had assaulted. She called, but nobody answered the phone.

That was the kind of day she was having. She left a message for Ernie Phillips to call her back.

She started a plate of leftover roast beef warming in the microwave and picked up the week's worth of mail she'd been avoiding.

The bills went in a pile, the fliers offering everything from faster Internet to lower insurance straight into the garbage.

One piece stood out. It was a business-sized envelope with

her address handwritten in a messy scrawl. There was no return address.

She opened the flap and pulled out a white, unlined piece of paper.

A short note was written in the same handwriting.

They're watching you. Be careful. There's more going on than you know.

Her stomach swooshed as the microwave dinged for a meal she wouldn't be able to eat.

Who'd sent this?

Who was watching her? Who were *they*?

Her heart raced, and she fought a sudden need to run. Masked men haunted her memories, hovering at the edge of her vision as if, should she turn too fast, she might catch a glimpse. Those masked men seemed to be closing in.

She closed her eyes, tried to focus on what was real. She was safe in Summer's kitchen. Nobody was coming for her. And if they did, the bodyguards would protect her.

She breathed in and blew out, praying for peace and waiting until God answered. Amazingly, He did, and her heart rate slowed.

Still, she held the letter in shaking hands.

Her anxiety might have been overblown, but the letter was real, not memory or hallucination. Someone had written it, stamped it, mailed it. She needed to think logically. What was *true* about it?

It had been mailed to her apartment, and she hadn't been there in days.

And she'd already known *they*—whoever *they* were—wanted to watch her. Or, more accurately, listen to her, since they'd planted bugs in her apartment.

The note said there was more going on than she knew. Obviously. Were she and Tate on the right track? Maybe, maybe not.

Scary as the note was, it contained no new information.

Except that somebody had tried to warn her.

Who?

Jeffrey Cofer? It would make sense that Freddy Parks's attorney might want to reach out to her anonymously. Maybe, constrained by attorney-client privilege, he felt compelled to try to warn her about an attack from Parks. She checked the postmark. The letter had been mailed from Boston on Monday, three days after Cofer had tried to reach her. So maybe he'd decided he couldn't risk a call and instead mailed a note.

Or maybe the note wasn't from Cofer. Or maybe Cofer had sent it knowing Dawson might be after her.

But how would Cofer know that?

And why would Dawson have anything against Misty? Sure, she was the prosecutor assigned to his case, but threatening her could only hurt him—and over a small-time bribery charge?

Maybe Dawson knew she and Tate were digging into the whole Thornebrook/IAF business. But if that were the case, then Tate would be in danger too. Was he? Should he be watching his back?

Or maybe this note was from somebody associated with Kyle Griffin.

She could still see the man's face on the far side of the train window the other day. He'd looked furious.

The memory dripped a chill down her spine.

She dialed the police station. "Detective Reyes please. It's Misty Lake."

A moment later, the detective came on the line. "You all right?"

She explained the letter. "I'm thinking maybe it came from Jeffrey Cofer."

"Can you see the postmark without touching it?"

"Already looked," Misty said. "It was mailed Monday in Boston."

"Don't touch the letter or the envelope again. I'll get a uniform over there to pick them up."

"Okay." By the detective's tone, Misty had the strong impression there was more going on than she understood. She snapped a photo of the note and the envelope, knowing she'd soon lose possession of both. "Did something happen?"

"I'll be in touch. Stay out of trouble." The call ended.

Strange.

The stupid microwave had continued to ding every thirty seconds, reminding her of her lunch. Misty took the plate out and put it straight into the refrigerator. Her stomach definitely couldn't handle meat and gravy now. She grabbed a handful of crackers and returned to work, though it was harder to concentrate than it'd been before. She wasn't sorry for the interruption when her phone rang.

"Misty Lake."

"It's Nancy. I got most of the information you wanted. I'm still digging, but I thought I'd share what I know."

"I appreciate that." Misty sat in front of her notebook and pen. "Shoot."

"Redstone is a real estate development company. It's a division of a larger corporation called HMI—Hawthmarks, Inc."

Nancy spelled it, and Misty wrote it down. "That's a weird name. Is that a thing—Hawthmarks?"

"Not as far as I know. Redstone is just one of its subsidiaries. I got the board members." She read off a list of names, and Misty wrote them down. None of them sounded familiar. "I'm still working on getting an employee list. I did learn something else about IAF. Did you know they were awarded a federal grant for the resettlement of refugees? I can send you the details."

"That makes sense. That's what IAF does."

"Yeah, but the grant is supposed to be used for housing."

"IAF has a refugee property in Hopkinton."

"Hearts and Homes. I know, but the thing is, this grant was awarded last year. Their Hopkinton property was completed a few years ago, right?"

"Maybe they used the grant money for improvements, or to add apartments."

"The paperwork I'm looking at indicates that they used the bulk of the funds on the building in the city, the property on the corner of Aldus and Buttrick. The one you said was donated by Redstone."

"But that's an office building, isn't it?"

"According to the information I have," Nancy said. "Which is why I'm confused. The paperwork could be wrong. Maybe it's housing. The area is zoned for residential."

The building Misty had taken to be IAF's headquarters certainly looked like an office building on the outside. Could it be a home for refugees?

If so, it was an extravagant one, with marble floors and stacked-stone walls in the lobby. And a twenty-four-hour guard.

Had IAF used grant money intended to house refugees to build themselves a cushy office building?

If so, what would it mean for IAF? Had Redstone donated the property in good faith, assuming it would go to people fleeing oppression and war? Did they know it hadn't been used in the way they'd intended?

More puzzle pieces, but for the first time, Misty felt like she was starting to get a sense—broken and confusing as it felt—of what the big picture was going to look like.

"Thank you so much for this, Nancy."

"Anytime. I'll keep digging into Redstone and Hawthmarks and let you know what I learn."

Misty was making notes about what Nancy had told her when her buzzer sounded. She hurried to the intercom, hoping maybe Tate had returned.

But the voice on the other side belonged to Detective Reyes. "Mind if I come up?"

She pressed the button to unlock the outside door and opened hers just as the detective reached the top of the stairs.

Ignoring the scowling guard, she said, "I thought you were going to send somebody."

"Decided I needed to talk to you in person."

Misty stepped back to let her in. "The letter's on my kitchen counter."

Reyes closed the door on the bodyguard and went into the kitchen, slipping on gloves. She put the letter and the envelope in a plastic bag she'd pulled from her back pocket. "We'll look for fingerprints, but I'm guessing we'll only find yours."

"Worth a shot though."

"Can we sit down for a minute?"

The kitchen table was covered with papers and files and Misty's laptop, so she led the way into the living room and settled on the sofa. "What's up?"

Reyes took the chair. "I know you talked to Detective Klein about Jeffrey Cofer."

"Yeah, a couple nights ago. Did you guys find him?"

"I'm afraid so. He's dead."

Misty gasped, her hands flying to her mouth. "Oh, my gosh. What happened?"

"According to the coroner, he was beaten to death, his body tossed into a dumpster. He had no ID on him, which is why it took all week to identify him."

"His poor family. Do you have any idea who did it?"

"Cofer defended a lot of rough guys, but we can't find anybody who'd have a reason to kill him. The only one who's off the radar is Parks."

"Why would he kill his attorney? The guy who got him out of prison early?"

"We'll ask him when we find him."

Misty let the new information settle, trying to fit the pieces into the puzzle. "Tate and I uncovered a few things you might be interested to learn."

"Tell me." She pulled a little notebook from her pocket, all business.

"Tate talked to Freddy's mother yesterday morning."

Reyes straightened, and by the look on her face, she wasn't happy, but all she said was, "At her apartment?"

"In Lowell, yeah. She said she doesn't know where Freddy is."

"That's what she told us Saturday."

Misty filled Reyes in on everything she and Tate had learned about Freddy and Dawson in the last couple of days.

Reyes's pen flew across her paper. "So Parks and Dawson used to be friends, but Parks thinks Dawson killed his sister?"

"According to his mom, yeah." Misty went to the kitchen and found the police report Tate had brought the night before. Reyes snatched it from her outstretched hand. "She never regained consciousness," Misty said, "so she couldn't say who'd attacked her, but Miss Parks believes—and says Freddy also believes—that Dawson did it."

Reyes scanned the paper. "This is irrelevant. Maybe Parks

is after Dawson, but he's also after you. Revenge for putting him away. Maybe he wanted to punish his attorney too."

Misty considered that, but it didn't make sense. "There's more going on here than vengeance. I think maybe we've got this all wrong. I don't think Freddy Parks is after me. And Dawson has no reason to come after me, none that I'm aware of. Not unless they know Tate and I are looking into these old real estate deals. How would they know that?"

"Who else knows what you're up to?"

"Nobody, as far as I know. Well, our boss."

"You and Tate are digging into...what, though? A bribery?"

"And trying to figure out why Parks assaulted that guy in Billerica. And the connection between Thornebrook, the construction company, and IAF, if there is one. And Redstone and Hawthmarks."

"Which is all"—Reyes waved the words away—"way above my pay grade. But if there's something illegal going on there, it'd be a good reason for someone to come after you."

"Except we knew nothing about any of it until after somebody tried to bug my apartment. If not for that, we wouldn't be looking into any of this."

"Not all criminals are masterminds." Reyes sat back and pressed her lips together, staring at the far wall. "Maybe the bug isn't about that case."

But if not, then Misty had no idea what it was about. Griffin? But why?

Truth was, none of her cases was important enough to risk planting a bug. Her defendants weren't rich or powerful or connected. They were wife-beaters and small-time drug dealers and low-level thugs.

Griffin was the exception. Though the man had never been convicted of any crimes, he'd been connected to quite a few, not the least of which was the ambush behind Mr. Hashemi's coffee shop the other day. What could Griffin possibly learn by listening to her meeting with Tate? Or by listening to anything Misty said in her apartment?

It didn't make sense.

Reyes set the paperwork on top of the evidence bag on the coffee table. "You say Tate talked to Miss Parks yesterday?" At Misty's nod, Reyes's lips slipped into a frown. "Did he say anything about her planning to take a trip?"

"Not to me. Why?"

"We stopped by there this afternoon. Miss Parks and her granddaughter are gone, along with most of their belongings. It seems Freddy and his family have skipped town."

"Oh. Oh!" Misty fought to bring all the pieces flying around in her brain together. "So maybe... I told you Parks reached out to me when he was still in prison, right? And then when I went to Walpole—"

"He refused to see you. What about it?"

"Assuming his mother is right and he didn't see me because he didn't want his mom and niece to suffer the same fate as his sister, maybe he took them somewhere safe so he can tell me—or someone—whatever it was he was going to tell me when he summoned me to the prison."

"No idea what it is?"

"Not a clue."

Reyes nodded slowly. After a minute, she said, "Nice theory, but I wouldn't count on it. Considering the violent way Cofer was beaten—which is very similar to the way Parks's first victim was beaten—I'd say Parks murdered Cofer. No idea why he'd ask you to visit the prison, but I'm guessing it wasn't for any good reason. Which tracks, considering the guy's been off the grid since he got released. No, Parks is our killer, I'm convinced." She stood and headed for the door. "Glad you've got protection. Stay with them until we have him in custody."

"What about Griffin?"

"Yeah, him too." She managed a slight smile. "You're a magnet for trouble, aren't you?"

Kidnapped twice, and now two bad guys after her? It sure felt that way.

CHAPTER TWENTY-FIVE

The rain had tapered off, but thick clouds hung low overhead, making the late afternoon as dark as dusk. It was a little after four, and Tate was approaching Misty's apartment building when Detective Reyes pushed out the door. A police cruiser was double-parked on the street, a uniformed cop in the driver's seat.

Tate quickened his pace. "Detective!" She turned, and he called, "Everything okay?"

"You're here to see Ms. Lake?"

"Yeah." Worry pounded a drum beat in his chest. "Is she all right? Did something happen?"

"She'll fill you in." Reyes gestured for him to follow her back into the building and let the door close. They stood in the lobby between the stairwell and a closed apartment door. "I understand you went to see Winnie Parks?"

"Yesterday, yeah."

"When you were there, did you get any sense that they were moving?"

"The place was tidy. There were no boxes or luggage. Why?"

"And she didn't mention that they were taking a trip?"

"No."

"What'd she say about Freddy?"

"That he was lying low and staying away from her. Did Misty tell you she and Freddy think Dawson killed Lela Parks? Freddy's sister?"

"She did." Reyes tilted her chin and raised her eyebrows, gaze boring into his. "You should have told me. That's information I need."

"You're right. It's been busy."

The detective didn't shift her stare. "What you had to do was more important?"

"No, of course not. If I learn anything else I think you need to know—"

"If you learn anything else, whether you think I should know it or not..."

"Right. I'll let you know."

"You do that." Finally, she broke eye contact and pulled open the door.

He took it and held it for her. "Detective." When she turned, he said, "Why are you here?"

"Ask your girlfriend. I'm sure she'll fill you in." She descended the steps and climbed into the cruiser.

Tate ran up the stairs to the third floor, where Hughes was standing guard.

"Everything okay?" Tate asked.

He shrugged and knocked on the door himself, calling, "Steele's here."

It swung open. The smile Misty had greeted him with that morning was gone. "Come in."

He did, closing the door, then pulled her into a hug. Only when she was pressed against him, her arms circling his back, her cheek resting on his chest, did he relax.

"I ran into Reyes outside. She told me you were all right, but I needed to see for myself."

She didn't let up her grip on him. She was trembling. No. Sobbing.

"Sweetheart, what happened?"

She sniffed and stepped away to wipe her eyes on the sleeve of her sweatshirt. "I'm sorry. It's just..." But she didn't seem to know how to finish the sentence.

He took her hand, leading her to the couch. After he slid off his trench coat and draped it over a chair, he sat beside her. "Tell me what happened."

"Jeffrey Cofer is dead. He was beaten to death. Reyes thinks Freddy Parks did it."

"For what reason?"

"That's what I asked. Maybe he's lost his mind. Maybe he's psychotic. Or maybe he thought Cofer knew too much."

"About what?"

Misty shrugged. "I don't know. There's so much we still don't understand. Just when I think I'm getting a handle on the big picture, someone comes in and...rips the puzzle pieces apart."

"This is why I hate puzzles."

She smiled, though it didn't hold, and squeezed his hand. "I'm glad you're here. I wasn't sure if you'd come by tonight or not."

"I wanted to see you before... I actually have plans, but I can cancel—"

"No, don't do that. I'm fine." She sat up straight, shook her head like she was trying to shake off ugly images. "Really. It was just a shock, that's all. Hot date?"

He sat back. Her question had been a joke, but maybe there was more to what she was asking. The two of them had spent a lot of time together, but they'd only been on two dates, and they barely counted since they hadn't gone out anywhere. It wasn't like they were exclusive. But he wouldn't mind if they were. "If I'd had a date planned for tonight, I'd cancel it to spend the evening with you. You're the only woman I want to date right now."

"Oh." This time, the grin spreading across Misty's face looked genuine. "Okay then. I feel the same way. Well, except for the 'woman' part."

Did his heart do a little flip at her words? Maybe. Did that make them...exclusive? He wasn't sure what it made them, but it seemed they'd taken a step, albeit a tentative one, toward a real relationship.

"What are you up to tonight?"

"I hang out with friends from my undergrad days once a month. Tonight's the night, but I can cancel if you want me to stay."

"It's fine. I'll watch a movie and go to bed early."

Her phone rang, and she reached for it. "I think I know who this is." She answered with, "Misty Lake." A pause, then, "Hold on one second, okay?" Standing, she muted the phone and headed for the kitchen. "It's Ernie Phillips, the building inspector who was Parks's assault victim."

"Oh, great."

"I'm going to put him on speaker so you can hear." She returned, carrying a notebook and pen. "But I don't want him to get spooked."

"I'll be quiet."

She tapped the phone screen. "Sorry about that. I'm a prosecutor in Suffolk County, but I used to work in Middlesex. You probably don't remember my name, but I was—"

"I know who you are. You got the guy who jumped me thrown in jail, right?"

"That's right."

"And now he's out."

"Unfortunately, yes."

"Could you have prevented that?"

She pressed her lips closed, lifted her shoulders and dropped them. "If I'd known the cop who arrested Parks was dirty, I might have done things differently. But I didn't know. Most cops are trustworthy."

"It just ticks me off, you know?" Ernie Phillips sounded not so much angry as resigned.

"I called because I need to ask you about the assault," Misty said. "Do you know why Parks targeted you?"

"Yeah, of course. His people tried to get me to overlook some problems I found in a building I'd inspected, and I refused. They warned me I'd be sorry, and they were right. Did you know the department let me go? I can't move like I used to. My knees have never been the same. And I get these headaches. I drive for ride-sharing apps, but lemme tell you, the money is nothing compared to what I used to make. My wife had to go to work because we couldn't afford health insurance."

"I'm so sorry to hear that. How frustrating for you."

"Yeah, considering after I was targeted, the building passed inspection."

"The building you'd...failed? Is that the right term?"

"It's not a test you pass or fail. I found some flaws that needed to be fixed. But before I turned in my report, Parks came after me. At my house. My wife and kid were inside. My son was watching through the windows until Marianne pulled him away."

"I'm sure that was traumatic for all of you." Misty managed to sound both businesslike and compassionate. Tate had never quite managed the combination, but she made it look easy.

"My son didn't sleep for weeks. Imagine that, seeing your

old man getting the tar beat out of him. My wife probably would have run out there if she wasn't trying to keep him safe."

"Thank God she didn't. Sounds like she did the right thing, keeping your son safe. So, on the building, you wanted some improvements made—?"

"The construction was shoddy. I wouldn't let my dog live there. But when I was in the hospital, the department sent over a young guy, and he found no problems."

Again, Misty took notes. "Maybe they fixed everything?"

"Obviously not, considering a woman died."

Whoa.

She met Tate's eyes, hers wide with surprise. "Who died? What happened"

"Out at that Hearts and Homes place," Phillips said. "That refugee lady who was deaf and didn't hear the alarm? The carbon monoxide leak was the result of faulty installation of the furnace. Which was on my list of things they needed to fix."

Tate closed his eyes, trying to fit all the pieces together. Hearts and Homes was an IAF project. Had it been built by Thornebrook?

Had Dawson been involved back then?

He felt like they were finally closing in on what was going on.

"Did you report that?" Misty asked.

"It was months before I even remembered all that stuff. When I did, I called my old boss and told him what I just told you. He thanked me for the information and hung up."

"Do you know if he did anything about it?"

"You'd have to ask him, but I'd guess not."

"And you didn't feel the need to report any of this to the authorities?"

Tate didn't miss the censure in Misty's tone and figured Mr. Phillips didn't either.

"Why would I?" the man asked. "I went up against those people once and almost died. That guy ruined my life. You know how much I make now? Not enough to keep my house, that's for sure. We lost everything. You really think I was gonna open myself up to that again?"

Misty scowled at the phone, but Tate understood where the man was coming from. Aside from the pain and the loss of income, the humiliation must've been awful. Why risk it again? Mr. Phillips had tried to do the right thing, and he'd been punished in the worst way.

No. Not the worst way. Parks had to live with his sister's death—and the belief that he was responsible. Assuming Miss Parks had been telling the truth.

"Now I told you all that stuff," Phillips said, "but you gotta keep my name out of whatever you're doing. I don't have much left, but I sure as heck don't wanna lose it. My wife's busting her butt to take care of our family, and neither one of us needs any more trouble."

"You've been very helpful."

"Maybe you think so. Or maybe I just put a target on your back. Freddy Parks is psycho. The last thing you want is to be on the wrong side of his fists. Watch yourself."

"I'll do my best."

Misty ended the call and bent over her notebook, scratching notes.

Tate closed his eyes and thought about what they'd learned, trying to make the pieces fit.

"It's all connected." Misty pushed to her feet, tossing her notebook on the coffee table. "Hearts and Homes is an IAF property. Parks took Ernie Phillips out of the picture. Maybe somebody—Thornebrook, IAF, Dawson or someone else—intimidated the replacement inspector, and he overlooked the problems to avoid Ernie's fate."

"Or maybe he was incompetent," Tate suggested.

She threw up a hand, accepting that. "Either way, the building passed, refugees moved in, and then... When was the carbon monoxide leak?"

Tate pulled his laptop from his bag and searched. He found an article about it. "Last..." He looked at her as the date of the woman's death fit into the calendar in his head. "February."

Misty's eyes widened. "Late in the month?"

"She died on February twenty-seventh."

"Freddy reached out to me about then. So..." Misty paced to the bay window and back. "So maybe Freddy realized that by taking Ernie Phillips off the board, he'd enabled that building to pass. Maybe he was feeling guilty for that woman's death."

"Which was what he wanted to confess," Tate said.

"But Dawson warned him off. For whatever reason—maybe Parks refused to budge or just to give Parks a taste of what would happen if he defied them—Dawson attacked Lela Parks."

"And she died," Tate said. "Probably not Dawson's plan, but still, murder is murder. Parks got nervous. He couldn't protect his mother and niece from prison, so he refused to see you."

"But that doesn't mean he got over it." Misty froze in the middle of the room. "He was supposed to stay in prison another five years. But suddenly, he got out. Thanks to Cofer." Her voice lowered, trailed at the end. She took a breath and resumed pacing. "Which is why I don't think Parks killed Cofer. Doesn't make sense. The guy got him out of prison years early. As far as I know, he's not suspected of being involved in any other crimes."

"He is," Tate clarified. "He's suspected of killing Cofer and breaking into your apartment. But nothing before his release."

"Right," Misty said. "So why would he kill his lawyer, his advocate?"

Tate didn't have any answers, and her silence told him she didn't either.

She sat beside him. "It goes back to IAF and Thornebrook."

"And maybe Redstone," Tate said. "What have you learned about that?"

"Redstone's a real estate developer owned by a corporation called Hawthmarks. Ever heard of it?"

"Nope." Tate glanced at his watch. It was after five.

"You need to go?" Misty asked.

"I don't want to leave you, but..." If he wanted to be on time to meet his friends, he should have left already.

"Go." She pushed to her feet. "Seriously, I'll be fine. I have leftover pot roast and Netflix. I need to get my mind off all this stuff for the night. A distraction."

He stood and took her hand. "I can think of a few ways to distract you." He waggled his eyebrows, and she smiled.

"That might be more fun than watching a movie."

"Might?" He took her in his arms and pulled her close, gazing at her upturned face, those wide, beautiful eyes, those very kissable lips. He bent to taste them, then dove in for more.

Misty snaked her arms around his neck, her fingers tickling the hair at the back of his neck and sending desire through his body. He held her closer, deepening the kiss. His mind wandered to all the ways they could spend the evening.

Which had him loosening his hold and ending the kiss.

"I'm almost convinced," she said.

He chuckled. "Maybe I should stay."

"No." She stepped away, leaving him chilly and wanting more. "You have plans. If you're not busy, maybe you could come over tomorrow."

"Of course." It hadn't occurred to him that he wouldn't. There was the mystery they were trying to solve, but it was more than that. The idea of going an entire day without seeing her...

That was why he needed to go. One night apart wasn't going to hurt them. They'd spent so much time together, maybe they both needed a little distance to figure out how they felt.

He did, for sure. Because his feelings were going very deep, very fast. He couldn't tell if that was because Misty was the perfect woman for him or if he was confusing his concern for her well-being for something it wasn't.

Maybe he could fall in love with her. Maybe she could fall in love with him. Or maybe circumstances had thrust them together and danger had acted as glue.

He needed to know, now, before either one of them got hurt.

"I'll go under one condition," Tate said.

Her eyebrows hiked. "What's that?"

"If anything happens, you call me. Okay? With Cofer dead, this whole thing seems more dangerous than it did before. I won't be able to relax with my friends, or sleep tonight, unless I know you'll call if you need me."

She moved closer and wrapped her arms around him. "You do the same, all right? If this is about all the stuff we're learning, you could be in just as much danger as I am."

CHAPTER TWENTY-SIX

A distant shout pulled Misty from sleep. Past the blinds, she saw only darkness. Street noises rarely reached to her eighth-floor apartment but had little trouble seeping through Summer's third-floor windows.

Misty turned over to go back to sleep.

Something pounded.

Not coming from outside.

She swung her feet over the side of the bed.

The pounding came again. "Ms. Lake. It's Hughes. Open up."

Heart racing, she snatched her bathrobe, slipping it on as she ran down the hall. She bolted through the living room to the door. "What's going on?"

"Open up. Now."

Definitely Hughes.

She yanked the door open.

"Let's go."

"What? What's—?"

"Now, Misty." His use of her first name snapped her out of her stupor. He gripped her upper arm and pulled.

She had no idea what was going on, but Summer trusted Hughes, and Misty trusted Summer. She followed him outside the apartment and closed the door.

He manhandled her not toward the staircase going down but toward the other end of the hall, where it led up. "Hurry."

Something popped. Was that a *gunshot*?

Below, a door banged open.

Hughes turned and held a finger over his lips.

She pressed her mouth closed and nodded.

They climbed, silently.

Tension in her chest squeezed, squeezed until she wanted to scream. But she knew when it was time to scream and when it was time to hide. This was definitely time to hide.

They continued past the fourth floor up to the door to the roof. Hughes unlocked it and pushed it open.

After she stepped onto the roof, he closed the door quietly and pulled her around to the back of the little building that housed the stairwell, putting himself between her and the door.

She barely registered the rain and chilly wind, just watching him as his gaze scanned the rooftop.

He said nothing, and she couldn't seem to make words form.

After a few long seconds, he said, "Go hide behind those boxes." He pointed, and she saw what he meant. They were some kind of electrical...things. They were small, though. Too small to hide her.

"Maybe I could hide behind the couch." The outdoor furniture would be big enough.

"Hopefully, the cops'll get up here before he does. But if not, that's the first place he'll look." Hughes gripped Misty's upper arms and leaned down to meet her eyes. "Trust me. Do as I say. Do not move until I tell you to. Got it?"

She nodded, and he practically pushed her toward the small boxes. She ran across the roof and crouched behind them. Her bare knees hit cold, wet tile. She bent low, trying to get her terrycloth bathrobe to cover more skin. Trying to make her too-tall body smaller.

She wanted to peek, to see what was happening. But she didn't. Instead, she closed her eyes, fighting panic.

Memories of her childhood assailed her. All those nights hiding while her father shouted curses. The slap of flesh, the thud of fists. Screaming. Begging. Crying.

This wasn't that. Mom was gone. Krystal and Summer were safe. Dad was alone in his house, suffering the consequences of a lifetime of poor choices.

Crouched on the wet roof, Misty felt like that scared little girl, hiding behind her big sister—a sister who, like the electrical boxes, hadn't been big enough.

Please, keep me safe. Keep my guards safe.

Far away, a siren sounded.

Closer, a door creaked.

Footsteps ran.

Misty covered her head with her arms as if thin flesh and bone could protect her.

"Oomph." The sound was muffled, then more grunts. Who was fighting? Who was winning?

She wanted to look, but Hughes had told her to stay hidden, to trust him.

She opened her eyes and kept watch on the tiny bit of floor in front of her. What would she do if someone came? He'd be too close to run away from. She'd be trapped. Again. Maybe this time, she wouldn't survive.

"Clear!" A man's voice... Could it have been...?

"Clear!" another man shouted.

A third voice cursed a blue streak.

"Shut up or we'll do it for you." That was definitely Hughes. "Ms. Lake, it's safe now."

She stood from behind the boxes.

Hughes and... Oh, it was Ian, the one who'd been shot. She hadn't seen him since the coffee shop. He'd apparently recovered because he crouched over a man who was facedown. He looked at her and grinned. "You all right?"

Was she? Her stomach was churning, and she feared she might be sick. She swallowed, swallowed again.

Ian's smile faded.

She forced words past her lips. "I'm okay."

Hughes hadn't lost that intense look he always seemed to wear. "Come on, before you freeze."

She hurried across the roof, and he slipped off his jacket and draped it over her shoulders. "Let's get you inside." To Ian, he said, "You good here?"

Ian was sitting on the guy's legs. He'd already secured the intruder's hands behind his back with zip-tie cuffs and was doing the same with his feet. "He's not going anywhere."

From the open doorway, the pounding of footsteps reached her. She backed away, ready to run.

"It's the police. You're safe." Hughes gripped Misty's arm, but she shrugged away to get a look at the intruder's face, believing she was about to come face-to-face with Parks for the first time since he'd threatened her in the courtroom. But it wasn't Parks. Or Griffin. A stranger looked back at her.

She let Hughes lead her through the door and into the stairwell. They'd just reached the landing between the roof and the fourth floor when uniformed police officers running up the stairs met them.

"He's on the roof," Hughes said. "We'll be in Ms. Lake's apartment. Three-B."

"Got it." The cops continued past.

"Did somebody get shot?" Misty asked. "I heard... Did I hear gunshots?"

"Ian was trying to slow them down. He saw them approach the building and start working the lock. He told me and then called nine-one-one."

They reached Summer's apartment. The door was wide open. It looked like it'd been kicked in.

She'd have to deal with that. Eventually. She stepped inside and stopped in the entry, unsure what to do next.

"Did anybody get hurt?" she asked

"Not as far as I know." With a hand on her arm, Hughes led her to the couch and gently urged her down. "Blankets?"

"Um..." She couldn't think, but he found a throw in a basket by the fireplace and tossed it over her. "You probably should change into something dry."

She would, in a minute. She pulled her legs up to her chest and huddled beneath the blanket, only this moment feeling the chill. Her teeth chattered.

"Who was that guy?"

"The cops'll figure it out." Hughes checked the windows. She wasn't sure if he was worried or just expending nervous energy. He returned from the kitchen and stood opposite the coffee table. "You really should get dressed. The police will want to question you. I assume you'll want to be wearing something...else."

Right. She was in pajamas and a bathrobe. She needed socks. A sweatshirt. Pants.

She stood, wrapping the blanket around her shoulders, and shuffled to the bedroom.

After she closed the door, she stood there, stupidly, for a long time.

She might have thought it was a bad dream if not for the damp clothes. Someone had come after her. It was real and altogether too familiar. Memories played like a slideshow in the back of her mind—the kidnapping. The other kidnapping. All the fears and worries, all the terror of those events, seemed to crowd into the too-small bedroom, settling like uninvited guests.

Her stomach roiled, churned. She swallowed, but this time, the nausea wouldn't be denied.

She bolted out of the room and into the bathroom, barely making it to the toilet before she threw up.

When she was finished, she washed her hands and brushed her teeth and stared at her image. "You're okay."

The woman in the mirror didn't look convinced.

Voices came from down the hall. She needed to dress and go out there and talk to the police. She needed to find out who that guy was. And why he'd come after her.

Back in her bedroom, she slipped into a pair of jeans and the sweatshirt she'd worn earlier. She added socks and sneakers, since her feet were freezing. Then she grabbed her phone and checked the time.

Two thirty-seven a.m.

She'd missed a message from Tate. He'd texted at ten thirty, but she'd been sleeping.

> I hope you had a good night. I missed you. Talk to you tomorrow.

Sweet of him to check in. She hated that she hadn't texted back. But seeing his name reminded her that she'd promised to call if anything happened.

Getting yanked from her bed and hiding from a...a bad guy —a gunman?—on the roof definitely qualified. It could wait until morning. It wasn't as if Tate could protect her from an event that had already occurred.

But she wanted to talk to him. She needed to tell somebody.

What if Tate hadn't really wanted her to call. What if he'd just wanted to *seem* like he cared?

She took a steadying breath, though it came out shaky. If

that was the case, better she knew now that the man couldn't be counted on. She lifted her phone and dialed.

He answered on the second ring, voice groggy with sleep. "Misty? You all right?"

Suddenly, emotion clogged her throat. "Yeah." The word came out high-pitched.

"What happened?"

"I'm not sure yet. Somebody tried to get to me, I think. I have to go out and talk to the police, but you asked—"

"You're at home or...Summer's?"

"Uh-huh."

"Are you hurt?"

"No, just..." Again, she fought tears trying to seep into her voice. "I'm all right."

"Someone's with you?"

"Hughes and Ian and the police."

"I'm on my way. Call if you need me. Okay?"

She couldn't speak. Her words were clogged. Her eyes leaking tears. Her throat swollen and aching.

"Misty."

"Okay." The squeaky word was barely audible, but he must've heard it.

"I'll be right there." She could tell by the noises coming through the phone that he was already up and moving. "You'll be okay until I get there?"

"Yeah." She swallowed. Cleared her throat. "Yeah. I'll go out and talk to them."

"Good. Tell them I'm coming."

She ended the call, shoved her cell in her pocket, and opened her door. It was time to figure out what was going on.

CHAPTER TWENTY-SEVEN

Tate left his car in an almost-legal spot near the police cruisers lining the street.

It was no longer raining, but the air was cool and thick with moisture as he jogged to Summer's building. A cop was standing on the stoop. Tate started up the stairs.

"You live here?" the officer asked.

"I'm here to see Misty Lake. I'm a friend."

"Name?"

"Tate Steele."

"Hang tight." He spoke into the little radio on his collar. "Steele's here."

There was no answer, at least not one Tate heard. "Can I go up now?"

"Someone will come down."

He was itching to get inside. He'd been sound asleep when she called, but the tone of her voice, the tears and fear he heard, had hit him like a bucket of ice water. He'd been dressed and out of his apartment in minutes. Now, he paced in front of the building, getting more worried by the minute.

Finally, the door opened, and Detective Reyes came out and joined him on the sidewalk. "What are you doing here?"

"Misty called me. What happened?"

"Come on in."

Thank God. He followed her into the building. But she didn't start up the stairs. "What do you know about what happened here tonight?"

"Misty said someone tried to get to her, but that she was okay. Her bodyguards protected her, right? She's not hurt?"

"According to Misty, you were the only person who knew where she was staying."

Tate opened his mouth to respond, then snapped it shut. The scene reframed itself in his mind. Someone had attacked Misty, and Reyes suspected him—of what exactly, he wasn't sure. Surely, she didn't think he'd try to hurt Misty.

But it was her job to suspect everybody.

More to the point, as far as Tate knew, he had been the only person who knew where Misty was staying. Yet, someone had found her. How?

Tate hadn't done anything criminal, but maybe he'd done something stupid and led her enemies here. That remained to be seen. Either way, he needed to tread carefully.

"Did you have a question for me, detective?"

"Who did you tell?"

He thought back to the conversations he'd had that week. The only person he'd talked to about Misty was Leland. Had he mentioned where she was?

Maybe.

"I might have told Leland Humphreys, the DA. My boss. *Our* boss. He was worried about her safety after the intruder, and I told him she wasn't staying at home. I might've told him she was staying at her sister's place. I don't remember the conversation word for word."

"You were asked not to share her location, and yet you did."

"With her boss, who's a high-ranking law-enforcement official and who understood she was keeping her whereabouts quiet. It's not like I posted it on social media."

"Who else did you tell?"

"Nobody."

"You're certain about that."

"Absolutely."

She watched him for a long moment, maybe waiting for him to confess his crimes and beg for mercy.

"Okay," she said. "Who knew you and Misty are dating?"

"We weren't... I mean, we are dating now, but we weren't last weekend. That's a new development. But I haven't told anybody."

He thought about all the stupid things suspects did and said, things that were used to put them away. Most suspects' biggest problem was their inability to shut up. So, he'd answer the questions she posed and hope she figured out the right ones to ask.

She huffed a breath. "Before the new development...developed, did you tell anyone you and she were spending time together?"

"Leland knows we're working closely together because he asked me to assist her on some cases."

"Besides the DA. For instance, maybe you told Winnie Parks."

"Not that I can recall."

"That's a very well-crafted answer. Short and to the point."

"I'm a prosecutor, detective. I know what you're doing."

"What am I doing?"

He didn't answer.

"Do you want to help me or not?"

"I do, absolutely. But I don't want you to waste time on me. I would never willingly, knowingly put Misty in danger."

"Is it possible you *un*willingly, *un*knowingly put her in danger?"

Though he hated to admit it, he nodded. "Though I haven't told anybody at the office I'm working with Misty, it's possible somebody guessed."

"How would that have happened?"

"By following the clues. For instance, when we got that list of people who had access to the calendar for you?" He waited until Reyes nodded before continuing. "I'm the one who called HR and asked them to send it to Misty. Also, I've accessed some of her files for her. I've been in her office a couple of times this week to grab things for her. It's possible somebody saw me doing those things and guessed I was working with her."

Reyes reached toward him, curled her hand into a fist, and pulled it back. Like she was trying to pull words out of him. "Keep going, Steele."

"If somebody figured out I was working with her, or even overheard me talking to Leland yesterday in the office, they could have followed me here."

Reyes dropped her arm. "Seems plausible."

"Which makes this my fault." The truth of it settled like a barbell on his throat. His carelessness could have gotten her killed.

"Anybody come to mind?" Reyes asked.

"What do you mean?"

"At the office. Did you see anybody watching you? Or hanging around when you were talking to Leland?"

He squeezed his eyes closed. He'd seen a few people walk by his open office door, but only one who'd peeked in.

"I can tell by the look on your face you have a name for me."

He opened his eyes. "This guy and I are rivals. I mean, I'm going to be really honest here. He's the only person I work with who I don't like. So if you talk to him, he's going to tell you that —and it's going to be true."

"What's his name?"

"Clinton Lowe." *Boot-licker-in-chief.*

She wrote it down, then looked up again. "Why don't you like him?"

"He's an arrogant, weaselly, name-dropping jerk."

"Is that all?" For the first time during their conversation, Reyes's expression softened.

"I'm sure I could think of a few more adjectives, but you'll come up with your own when you meet him. Oh." Something else occurred to him.

"What?"

"Kyle Griffin was arrested for beating up his girlfriend a while back. Lowe was the DA on the case. He dropped the charges."

"Why?"

"You'll have to ask him. When I confronted him, he didn't say. Come to think of it, I told him Misty was the prosecutor of the stalking case."

"So you might have been the one to put Griffin on her in the first place."

"No, I confronted him after the ambush. The point is, he knew Griffin, and he knew, or at least could have guessed, Misty and I were working together. I'm just saying, maybe there's something there."

She flipped the notebook closed. "All right. That's helpful. You're off the hook for now. But let's don't take any trips until this is cleared up."

"Don't worry. I'm not going anywhere. Except upstairs, if that's all right."

She stepped out of the way, and he took the stairs two at a time to the third floor.

A bodyguard he hadn't met before was standing outside. "I'm Tate Steele."

The man knocked, and the door swung open. Tate looked past all the men in the room to Misty.

She stood and crossed the room toward him. Her hair was disheveled, her skin pale with dark smudges beneath her eyes. But she was alive and well and, as far as he could tell, uninjured.

Right in front of everyone, she fell into his arms.

"Thank God," he said. "Thank God you're okay."

CHAPTER TWENTY-EIGHT

All Misty wanted was to stay wrapped in Tate's arms until this was all over. Instead, she took his hand and led him to the couch.

"Sorry it took me so long." They settled on the sofa. "Detective Reyes wanted to talk to me before I came up."

"About?"

Hughes came from behind the couch. "Ms. Lake, can we talk for a second?"

The apartment was filled with bodies—police officers, lab techs, bodyguards, and now Reyes was back too.

"Sure."

His eyes flicked to Tate. "Privately, if you don't mind."

Leaving the comfort of Tate's side, she followed Hughes out the apartment door onto the landing. She figured the people in the other units were cursing her and all the commotion in the middle of the night.

Hughes walked to the end of the hallway and turned. "How well do you know Steele?"

The question startled her. "I've known him for years. We went to law school together."

"So you trust him?"

"Should I not?"

"Did anyone else know where you were staying?"

Besides Summer, only Tate knew. And Reyes, but she figured the detective didn't count.

"It's possible he let your location slip," Hughes said. "Reyes thinks somebody followed him here. I'm not convinced. You and he are getting closer. I got the impression you weren't particularly close last weekend. True?"

"Yes, but—"

"You sure he's not playing you?"

She was. Of course she was. Wasn't she?

"I'm not convinced he can be trusted. Are you?" His dark eyes held a challenge, daring her not to take his question seriously.

Tate had done nothing but help her all week. He'd worked with her on the cases. He'd gone with her to see the IAF property. He'd even gone to visit Freddy Parks's mother. Surely he wasn't working against her.

"Is it possible," Hughes asked, "that Tate has been sticking so close because he wants to know what you're up to?"

"No." Right? "I don't think so. I mean, it was Leland who assigned him to help me. Leland's idea."

"You're sure?"

When Leland had asked Tate to help, he'd seemed surprised. But that could've been an act. Maybe he'd offered to help, and Leland had taken him up on that offer. Maybe he'd insinuated himself in her cases for a reason.

But if that was true...

Then none of it was real. Not the kisses. Not the affection he'd claimed.

But he was here. She'd called him in the middle of the night, and he'd rushed over. He could have not answered his phone, pretended it hadn't rung or he'd had it on silent or it'd died. Not that his being here was proof of anything. If he was trying to fool her into thinking he cared—and keep tabs on her—what better way than to show up in the middle of the night?

What would Tate have to gain by spying on her? Did she really think he was working against her?

If so, then he was working with her enemies. Who? Griffin?

Tate wouldn't be involved with a guy like that.

Or Parks and Dawson and whatever was going on there. A man had been murdered this week, and she could have been as well. Did she really suspect Tate of colluding with murderers?

No. Everything in her told her Tate was trustworthy.

"I trust him," she said.

Hughes's lips slipped into a smirk. "That's your prerogative. I don't. I'm not comfortable leaving you alone with him."

"Good thing for me you don't get to decide who I spend time with."

"I recommend you rethink your opinion, or at least entertain the notion that I might be right."

"He's an assistant district attorney. He works *against* criminals, not with them. If he were working with Griffin or Parks or Dawson, that would make his entire life a lie. No, that's not who he is."

"If you say so." Hughes nodded toward the door, and she spun and marched back in.

She refused to let herself doubt Tate. He was the only friend she had in this mess, and she wasn't going to let Hughes's paranoia—or anybody's—take that away from her.

~

Misty was seated on the couch beside Tate, holding his hand. She'd spent twenty minutes talking Summer out of rushing to the city to be with her. Hughes and the rest of the guys were bad enough. The last thing Misty needed was her big sister hovering, telling her where she could go and what she could do.

It'd be like childhood all over again.

After she'd finally ended the call with Summer, Misty snuggled up beside Tate on the couch, where they waited while police and lab techs moved around the apartment as if they belonged.

She wished she could say she'd put that conversation behind her, but Hughes's words echoed in her mind. Of course Tate could be trusted. Hughes didn't even know him, so it made sense he'd be suspicious.

If nothing else good came out of this week, being isolated from work convinced her she needed to quit trying to live her life alone. Summer had been saying as much to her for a month. Her recent scare with Ramón had convinced her she needed people in her life—so much so that she'd picked up everything and moved to New Hampshire.

Krystal, their oldest sister, had been saying the same thing for years—to both Summer and Misty. That they needed friends, community. And each other.

Misty understood now what she'd been missing. If not for Tate's frequent visits, she couldn't imagine how isolated she'd feel. He'd been kind to her. Not only that, but he felt something for her. He liked her.

And she liked him.

She refused to let Hughes's paranoia destroy their budding relationship.

But what if it's not real? What if he's lying about everything?

She shook her head to rid it of the unwelcome thoughts and focused on the activity around her. Almost an hour had passed since Tate's arrival. A lab tech had dusted the doorknob for fingerprints and then moved out of her line of sight.

Reyes had stepped out a few minutes before. Now, she returned, said something to one of the cops, and then circled the chair nearest Misty to sit. Finally. "How you doing?"

"I'd like to know what's going on."

"There were two men. Your second bodyguard was in a car down the street, watching the door. We understand from Mr. Hughes that sometimes, the second guard stands on the stoop, so maybe the intruders thought he wasn't there. One of them crouched to pick the lock, and"—she consulted her notes—"Mr. O'Brien—"

"Ian?" Misty guessed.

"Right. He notified his partner, called the police, and then crept up and engaged them in a fight. While he was fighting one of them, the other one got inside the building."

"I heard a gunshot."

"The guy O'Brien was fighting discharged his weapon, but it missed its mark."

"Who were they?" Tate asked.

"We're still working on that. They've been taken to the station, where they'll be questioned."

"Nobody got shot, though, right?" The last thing Misty wanted was for someone to be harmed. And Ian had already taken a bullet once that week.

"Nobody got shot," Reyes confirmed. "While O'Brien and the first intruder were fighting, the second intruder came in the building. He got to your apartment and kicked the door in."

Misty glanced that way. Someone from Summer's agency was crouched beside it, repairing the damage.

Reyes continued. "We think he searched pretty quickly, based on the timeline. Then he went up to the roof, where Mr. Hughes took him down."

"I helped."

The words came from behind Misty, and she turned to see Ian standing there, beaming.

On the opposite wall near the door, Hughes scowled.

Reyes glanced at the younger bodyguard. "Mr. O'Brien cuffed the guy outside to the railing and joined the fight on the roof. And then we showed up, late to the party. I think you know the rest."

"Any idea how they found me?"

Reyes's gaze flicked to Tate. "It's possible somebody followed Mr. Steele when he came to see you."

"I've been thinking about that." Tate sat up straighter beside Misty. "If that's true, they'd know the building, but how would they know which apartment?"

By the lack of surprise in Reyes's expression, she'd considered that already. "Miss Lake, your sister owns this unit?"

"She bought it a couple of years ago."

"So somebody could have looked up real estate records and found that your sister lived in the building. That would tell him which apartment was hers."

Tate settled against the cushions again. By the rounded shoulders and downturned lips, he was blaming himself.

Misty squeezed his hand. "It wasn't your fault."

"This is what we get for trusting our coworkers," he said.

"What do you mean?"

"Who else would have known you and I were working together?" Tate asked.

"Oh." That made sense.

"Unless you told somebody?" Reyes directed the question to Misty.

"Only people at the office. I had one of the interns look up a few files and print them to give to Tate. So she could have guessed."

"I'll need names," Reyes said. "When you get a minute, you

two think about everybody who might've known or guessed you were working together."

For the next few minutes, Misty and Tate compiled the list. By the time the police gathered their things to leave, Misty was able to give it to Reyes.

"Thanks for this. We've already started looking into your coworkers. We'll be able to cross-reference this with the ones already on our radar."

It was a chilling thought, that somebody at the DA's office might be working with criminals.

She and Tate waited until, finally, everybody headed for the door. The bodyguard who'd replaced Hughes, Smitty—she thought that was his name—closed the door after them but stayed inside. He stood with his back to the repaired door as if he intended to stand right there, all night.

"You can go into the hall."

"Hughes asked me to remain in here as long as you're not alone." This guard was shorter than Misty by an inch or two and thinner than many of the guards she'd seen. But he seemed strong enough, and confident in his role.

"Tell Hughes I appreciate his concern, but I'll be fine."

The man squinted. She didn't miss the way his eyes flicked to Tate.

Beside her, Tate tensed.

This was ridiculous, considering she'd been alone with him countless times prior to tonight.

"Step outside, please," she said.

"You let me know if you need me." Smitty glared at Tate for a long moment. "I have a key. I can be inside in a second."

She waited until he stepped into the hall and closed the door, then exhaled and collapsed against the sofa cushions. She rolled her head to face Tate. "Sorry about that."

"I don't blame them for suspecting me. I can't believe I was so careless."

"We don't know what happened. Let's not jump to conclusions."

"Reyes seemed pretty confident."

She smiled. "My cousin Jon always says it's important to be confident, especially when you have no idea what you're doing."

That made Tate grin.

"You need anything?" she asked.

"I'm fine."

She settled against him, allowing herself to relax for the first time since Hughes had woken her. She yawned. "You don't have to stay. I'll be fine by myself."

Tate shifted away. "Do you want me to go? Are you mad at me for leading them here?"

"It wasn't your fault." She angled to face him. "I don't want you to go, but I understand if you want to."

"I don't think I can leave you alone tonight. If it's okay, I'll just stay here, on the couch."

"It's okay." She snuggled beside him, thankful for his warmth and the comforting arm wrapped around her.

"You must've been so scared."

She nodded against his shoulder.

"Especially so soon after what happened this summer. I can't imagine."

"It's funny, though. I wasn't thinking about the kidnapping. Maybe because I was hiding—and sure I'd be found. The thing Hughes had me hiding behind was too small, but I guess he figured the darkness would cover me. Anyway, it reminded me of being a kid, when my dad was on a tear. I used to hide behind my sister as if she could protect me. But she was little, too, you know? She couldn't shield me from everything."

"Let's get comfortable." Tate shifted, stretching his long legs out on the couch. She followed suit, settling her back against his chest. He pulled a blanket up to cover them. "So, you were thinking about your father?"

Should she tell him more about her life and her family? It wasn't exactly a happy story, but if there was going to be anything between them, she wanted him to know her, the real her, even the ugliest parts of her past. And the memories were so close, they felt like a presence in the room.

Suspicion was still buzzing like a fly inside her, but she needed to silence it. She could trust Tate. She could.

Right?

She closed her eyes, breathed in his presence, but focused on the Lord. *Should I trust him?*

There was no answer. There was also no anxiety or fear. Maybe she was crazy or tired or stupid. Or maybe Tate really could be trusted.

She decided to believe in him.

"Summer always tried to protect me. But there was this one time when she went to a friend's house after school. Her friend's parents were supposed to bring her home before dinner. She was always careful to be there before Dad got home from work, just in case. But I think their car broke down or something, so she was late. Krystal wasn't home either. It was just me and Mom and Dad. He got home early from work that day and started drinking." She'd always thought it apropos when people called liquor *spirits*. When Dad drank them, he became possessed. "By dinnertime, he was raging."

Misty could picture the scene so easily. Their kitchen was decorated in pale yellow and bright red, but the cheerful decor had no effect. The room was a place of fear. The whole house was.

Mom had fried haddock, and the scent of it hung heavily in the air. Misty'd never been a fan of fish, and that night her stomach was roiling with fear and nervousness. She kept her head down and picked at the meal.

Dad was on his second helping when he caught sight of her plate. "Finish your dinner!"

His shout had startled her, causing her to drop her fork. It clattered to the floor.

"Pick that up! What is wrong with you?"

"Sorry, Daddy." She'd scrambled down to grab it, then tossed it in the sink before pulling another from the drawer and returning to her seat.

"What are you doing?" he barked. "Clean the floor. You can't just leave fish guts there."

Mom pushed back from her seat. "I'll take care—"

"Let her do it. Spoiled little brat thinks she can do whatever she pleases."

Fighting tears, Misty grabbed a sponge from the sink and crouched to wipe the floor, making sure to clean all around where the utensil had hit, just in case.

Back in her chair and holding her breath to keep from smelling the fish, she shoveled the gross stuff into her mouth.

"Is that how we eat? What are you, a dog? Slow down."

Daddy hadn't always been nice to her, but he'd never been so mean. She'd heard him talk like that to Krystal and Summer, even to Mommy sometimes. But she'd thought he liked her. She'd thought she was special.

She started crying but kept her head low so Daddy wouldn't see. She was careful to eat more slowly, trying not to gag.

Finally, she finished and gulped her water.

"Well, get up and clear the table," Dad barked.

"Yes, sir." She took her plate and Mom's to the counter, then returned to get Dad's. She reached for it, but he grabbed her arm and gripped hard.

It hurt, but she didn't say anything. She didn't move or even try to get away. She thought about the neighbors' scary dog, how, if you didn't look it straight in the face, it would leave you alone. So she kept her eyes on her feet and her mouth clamped shut.

"What do you think you're doing?"

Clearing the table, like he'd asked, but she didn't say that. That was the wrong answer.

"Answer me!"

Before she could form words, he stood, lifted her, and flung her across the room.

She whacked into the wall, banging her head.

"Stupid girl."

Mom ran to help. She bent close and whispered, "Go to your room and don't come out."

Misty didn't need to be told twice. She ran, trying not to hear the shouting and fighting behind her.

Somehow, the words, the memories, spilled out of her mouth now.

Even though years had passed, tears dripped down her cheeks.

Tate didn't say anything for a long time.

When he did, his voice was low. "How old were you?"

"Seven."

He sucked in air through his teeth, tightening his arms around her. She was facing away from him, so she couldn't see his face, but she heard—or maybe felt—a growl low in his throat. "Your dad still like that?"

"He quit drinking. With Mom gone and us not living there, he doesn't have anybody to take his anger out on anymore. And I think he's softened a little over the years. After Summer and I were kidnapped, he asked us to come home. He wanted to take care of us. We could tell he was trying to make us feel safe there. But how could he, after everything he'd done? Did he really think a month of good behavior would make up for an entire childhood of abuse? We left as soon as we could. And now Dad's alone. I think he'd like us to come around more, but he's dealing with the consequences of his choices."

"Serves him right." Tate kissed the top of her head. "That's not very charitable of me, but I sort of want to kill him for what he did to you. And your sisters."

She didn't mind knowing Tate would stand up for her, that he wanted to protect her.

"I can't imagine such a horrible childhood."

"It wasn't always horrible. I got the best of it, honestly. Summer protected me most of the time. And Krystal...looking back, I realize she allowed herself to take the brunt of Dad's anger. She never fought back like Summer. I think she was trying to keep him away from us."

Her sisters had tried so hard to protect her. It was one of the reasons she tried to protect others by putting bad guys away. It felt like the least she could do.

"When my parents fought, we'd all pile onto Krystal's bed, and she'd read us *The Boxcar Children*. We had the whole set, but I always liked the first one the best."

"I don't know that book."

"Four orphan siblings run away and make a home for themselves in an abandoned boxcar. I remember dreaming of running away. I thought we could have a happy home, my sisters and I. That was always my dream." She chuckled, almost didn't want to admit the rest. But she wanted Tate to know her, even the weird things. "To this day, when I feel sad or lonely, I pull out my copy and read it. Silly, huh?"

"Not silly. Sweet. Innocent. And isn't that what you've done? You've created a life for yourself, a home."

"Yeah, I guess. But it's not what I imagined. What was beautiful about the story was the way the siblings worked together. It wasn't just that they were safe. They were a family."

He held her a little closer. "You're not alone, Misty."

Because he was there. Gratitude bubbled up inside her, threatened to escape in the tears stinging her eyes. She settled in, thankful for the arms holding her, the man who'd rushed over in the middle of the night to be with her.

"Can I ask you a question?" Tate's voice was tentative in the quiet.

"I guess."

"Why did tonight remind you of your father?"

"Oh." She considered her answer, wondering about it herself. "I think maybe the helplessness—and hopelessness—of the situation. Knowing there was absolutely nothing I could do to protect myself. If Hughes and Ian had lost the battle and the bad guys had won, whatever their goal was—to hurt me or take me or kill me—they'd have done it. I was utterly defenseless. I didn't even have on shoes." Her voice broke in a laugh—or maybe a sob. "And maybe that too. Being in my pajamas, being pulled from my bed. All of it reminded me of my childhood, listening to my parents fight through the door."

"Helpless," Tate said. "And hopeless. Those are two of the worst feelings in the world. But, as a child of God, you're never either one of those. You know that, right?"

"I was praying God would help, and He did."

"Even if He hadn't intervened, He would have been with you. Ultimately, your help comes from Him, and your hope is in Him."

"It's hard to feel that in the moment."

"There's a difference between what we feel and what we know is true."

She'd been fighting the battle of her feelings for years, so she knew Tate was right.

He traced circles on her shoulder with his fingertips, the feeling comforting and relaxing.

She yawned, and he did, too, then chuckled.

"You can sleep, sweetheart. I'm not going anywhere."

It should feel strange to sleep in Tate's arms, but it didn't. There was nothing inappropriate about their position, or her feelings, or his behavior. He was simply making her feel safe and protected.

She let her eyes drift shut. Maybe she'd just rest for a few minutes. She really ought to get up and go to bed—and let him go home. But she feared being alone, dealing with the memories of all that had happened that night—and in her past.

So she closed her eyes and let go of it all, reveling in the safety of Tate's arms.

∼

Misty hurried to the door around nine the next morning to press the intercom. "Yes?"

"I'm back."

She buzzed Tate in, tamping down her eagerness to see him. It was silly, really, considering he'd only been gone an hour.

They'd slept all night on the couch, cuddled up together. She'd never spent an entire night with a man. She'd never trusted any man enough to be that vulnerable with him. But Tate made her feel safe. Not once from the time he'd walked in until he'd kissed her goodbye that morning—a quick peck on her cheek—had he given her the impression he wanted anything from her. All night in his arms, and his hands had never strayed anywhere they shouldn't.

There was something incredibly attractive about a man who wasn't all about a physical relationship. And his early morning look hadn't hurt. Crumpled clothes, messy hair, unshaven cheeks. For a moment, she'd allowed herself to imagine waking up beside him every morning for the rest of her life.

Now, she pulled her door open and stood aside for Tate to enter.

Rather than taking the time while he was gone to shower, she'd slipped into yoga pants and a T-shirt and used the solitude to read her Bible and pray. Despite the crazy events of the night before, she felt calm. Knowing how she'd reacted to being kidnapped both times, she could only attribute her peacefulness to God.

Tate sniffed, his eyebrows lifting. "Do I smell bacon?"

"I promised you breakfast, didn't I?"

He headed into the kitchen, where she'd pulled bacon out of the oven to cool a few minutes earlier.

"Eggs or pancakes?" she asked.

"I should say eggs, but..."

"Pancakes it is." She started to pass him, but he grabbed her hand and kissed her. A quick *happy to be back* sort of kiss that morphed into something more.

She certainly wasn't complaining.

He ended it but didn't let her go. Brushing hair back from her neck—sending shivers over her skin—he said, "I've been dying to do that since I woke up, but I decided I'd better brush my teeth first."

She laughed. She'd been thinking the same thing.

While she cooked, he set the table and found butter and syrup, then moved the bacon from the rack to a plate.

They were a good team, not just in making breakfast but in all the things they'd accomplished that week. They did things differently—even thought differently—but they complemented each other.

She'd finally learned to accept help, and for the first time, she understood what she'd been missing. She really didn't have to do everything alone.

When the food was on the table and they were seated, Tate took her hand. "Mind if I pray?"

"Please."

He did, asking for a blessing on the food and praying for her safety. "Lead the police to whoever was behind last night's attack, and help Misty and me understand what's going on with Parks and Dawson and that whole situation. Lord, nothing is hidden from You. Reveal the truth to us."

More than anything else he'd said or done, that prayer told her Tate was on her side.

When he finished, she held his hand a second longer. "Thank you for that. And for being here."

He kissed her knuckles. "There's nowhere I'd rather be."

They ate their breakfast and talked about nothing important. She was enjoying just being with him, seeing him smile, watching him enjoy the food she'd cooked.

She'd almost forgotten Hughes's suspicions.

Almost, but every few minutes, a little voice inside her head wondered if Tate's feelings were sincere.

It's just an act, the voice said. *He's using you to get information.*

She wanted to curse Hughes for planting those thoughts. There was zero reason not to believe Tate. He'd done nothing wrong. And he would never work with criminals. Even if not for her, he had ambitions. Why would he risk the future he craved for the sake of money? He wouldn't. Nor would he risk his reputation.

No, there was no reason for Misty to suspect him. Once again, her feelings were steering her wrong.

Thanks to the focus they'd given Dawson, Parks, and the IAF property that week, they were both behind at work. After breakfast, he set his laptop up in the living room while she settled at the kitchen table and read over new case files. After the shocking events of the night before and the short night of sleep, she found it difficult to focus and wasn't sorry when the phone rang around eleven, giving her an excuse to step away from her computer for a little while.

She stood and grabbed it from the counter. "Misty Lake."

"Hey, it's Nancy. Sorry I didn't get back to you last night."

"No problem. Hold on a sec." She covered the mouthpiece with her hand. "Tate, it's my friend at the secretary of state's office."

He hurried into the kitchen. "Can I hear?"

"Nancy, I'm going to put you on speaker. My friend Tate is here. He works with me at the DA's office, and he's been helping me figure all this stuff out."

"That's fine."

Misty tapped the speaker button and grabbed her notebook. "You're on with Tate."

"Great. So, here's what I learned. Remember Hawthmarks?"

For Tate's benefit, Misty said, "The parent company that owns Redstone."

"Exactly. They also own Thornebrook, the construction company."

"Ah. That makes sense. When Redstone donated the land to IAF, Thornebrook set up a trailer on it. I guess IAF allowed them to keep the trailer there because they were going to do the construction."

"Right," Nancy said. "A couple of Hawthmarks execs are on the board of IAF."

"Oh." Misty tried to work that all out in her head.

Tate said, "Wait a minute. You're saying Redstone donated

land to IAF, and Redstone is owned by Hawthmarks, and Hawthmarks has people on the IAF board. Yes?"

"There's nothing wrong with that," Nancy said. "Lots of business execs donate their time to nonprofits."

So Hawthmarks owned Redstone and Thornebrook and had at least some affiliation with IAF. The pieces were coming together in Misty's mind. "And the construction was paid for by a federal grant awarded to IAF—"

"What's that?" Tate straightened. "What grant?"

"I guess I didn't tell you." Misty caught him up on the grant Nancy had discovered the day before—and how it was used.

"You're saying you believe IAF misused grant money?" Tate clarified.

"We think so." Misty explained how the money had been awarded for housing but had been used to construct the office building.

"The rest might be innocuous," Tate said, "but that's got to be a crime, to misuse federal funds."

"I haven't had the opportunity to look into it," Misty said, "but I'm sure you're right. Hawthmarks, via Redstone, donated land to IAF, who then hired another division of Hawthmarks, Thornebrook, to build a fancy office building, improperly using federal funds intended to house refugees. Have I got it right?"

"That sums it up," Nancy said.

"We need names." Tate's tone was low and angry. He snatched a pen and pulled Misty's notebook close. "Who owns Hawthmarks?"

"The name 'Hawthmarks,' is a mash-up of last names," Nancy said. "I can't figure out how the first one fits. But the second two are family names, Thorne and Marks. My guess, doing some research, is they're the maiden names of the founder's mother and grandmother. I just can't figure out where the 'Haw' came from."

Tate's pen tapped an impatient beat on the notebook. "Who is it? Who's the founder?"

"Henry Humphrey."

Humphrey?

Wait...

Tate straightened. "Say that again?"

"You heard me right," Nancy said. "Henry Humphrey started Hawthmarks, Inc. He's deceased, and his brother runs the company now. Clark Humphrey. I bet you can guess who's on the board."

Tate stepped back from the counter. "Damien Humphrey?"

"Keep going."

"I don't believe it." Tate's gaze flicked from Misty to the phone, his eyes wide.

Misty vocalized what she knew he was thinking. "Not Leland."

"Afraid so." Nancy's voice was solemn. The woman took no joy in exposing this. "From what I can tell, the DA isn't personally involved in the running of the company, but Damien is. And he's the president of IAF."

Whoa.

Misty stared at Tate, but he didn't meet her eyes. His lips pressed into a thin white line. Emotions flitted across his face. Worry. Anger. Fear.

She focused on the phone again. "Nancy, can you send me everything you've dug up?"

"I've already got it in an email, and I'm pressing 'send' now."

"Thank you for doing this."

"Listen, I don't know what's going on here, but this is a powerful family. The fact that one of the members is the DA doesn't make them good. It makes them all the more dangerous. Be careful."

Nancy wasn't wrong.

A man had been murdered. A young woman too.

If Leland Humphrey was behind any of the events, then this...

Conspiracy. There was no other word for it.

It was more insidious than she'd ever imagined.

CHAPTER TWENTY-NINE

Tate continued to stare at the phone long after Misty ended the call. It couldn't be. Surely Leland Humphrey wasn't involved in this whole mess. But the company, Hawthmarks, seemed to be. By the surprised, almost eager expression on Misty's face, she was convinced they had uncovered some diabolical plan.

"This is it," she said. "This is what links them all. And I know you didn't mean to, but you told Leland where I was, right?"

"Let's not jump to any conclusions."

Misty's expression shuttered. "Jump? I don't have to *jump* anywhere. It's obvious. What are you saying?"

Tate had worked for Leland Humphrey for years. The man had never been anything but straightforward and above-board. Tate trusted his boss. He believed in him.

Had Tate judged him wrong? Maybe. But he wasn't sure.

"Damien is up to something," Tate said, "but that doesn't mean Leland is part of it. Can you really see him doing any of this stuff? He's the district attorney. His job is to put bad guys away. You really think—"

"Yeah, I really think. You're so bent on impressing him and ingratiating yourself with him—"

"That's not fair." Tate's anger bubbled up. "He's my boss. Of course I'm trying to impress him. You should be too."

"You're too close to it." Misty's tone didn't soften the slightest. "You can't see what he's doing."

"What is he doing? Even your friend said he's not involved with running any of the companies. He probably has nothing to do with anything."

"If he wasn't involved before, he obviously is now. When he found out the Dawson case had been assigned to me, he asked you to assist. When have you ever been asked to help me—or any of the ADAs—on anything?"

"You were falling behind."

"A *little*. But not so much I needed you to ride in on your white horse and rescue me."

"I didn't ask for—"

"This whole idea about him firing me? That doesn't fly either." Misty'd latched onto this idea like a train, and it was racing out of the station. "I do my job and I do it well. I'm conscientious and consistent and capable. My last review, I was given high marks. Leland has always been happy with my work. Yeah, since I was kidnapped, it's taken me a little while to get my feet back under me. But nobody's been hounding me to close my cases faster. Until last Friday, my pace wasn't a problem for anyone but me. All of a sudden, after I was assigned the Dawson case, Leland decided I needed help. And he chose you. Why do you think that is?"

"He told us why." Tate worked very hard to keep his tone even. "He thought we were friends because I'm the one who notified your sister that you'd been kidnapped. I'm the one who picked her up and drove her to Maine and stayed with her until we knew you were safe. You know why I did that?"

"Because he asked you to."

"No. I offered. I *insisted*. Because, even though you've never liked me—you could barely stand me before this week—I always respected you. I always wanted to be your friend. And when I found out you'd been kidnapped..." Tate swallowed the anger dying to claw its way out of his mouth. "I cared about you—as a friend. And now, it's..." He let his voice trail, not sure how to define their relationship, which he could feel unraveling. "Leland wanted me to help you because, as far as anybody could tell, I was your only friend at the DA's office."

She blinked.

He didn't miss the wounded expression that crossed her features. Regret rose, a drop of cold water, sizzled by flames of frustration and fury.

"Leland knew you'd talk me into dropping the Dawson case so we wouldn't learn any of this stuff."

Tate took a breath, praying for patience and understanding. "I'm not saying you're wrong. But your evidence is circumstantial." She started to argue, but he spoke over her. "You might be right. But you might not. I've always liked and respected Leland, the same way I've always liked and respected you."

Her mouth opened, but he lifted a *give-me-a-second* hand.

She did, thank God. He needed to tread carefully. He cared about Leland, and he cared about his job, but Misty'd somehow jumped ahead of both of those. He had to watch his words, his actions. He had to be careful not to say or do anything that would cause a rift between them.

His father and his sister, though always polite to one another, treated each other like one might a spooked animal. Gentle, but never familiar. From them, Tate had learned that some actions, even if forgiven, would never be forgotten. They were father and daughter, and their relationship had never recovered from Hannah's decision to quit school and move out—and Dad's cruel words when she did.

That knowledge, coupled with his growing feelings for Misty, were cold water on the blaze inside him.

Misty studied him, curiosity and wariness in her expression.

He smiled at her and saw her shoulders relax. "If somebody came to me with circumstantial evidence pointing to you being a criminal, I'd be just as reluctant to accept it because you're my friend. Leland has been my boss since I graduated from law school. He's never given me any reason to distrust him."

She tilted her head to the side. "You really don't think this is a reason?"

"I know you're convinced, but I'm not." He stepped toward her and reached out. "I don't want to fight with you. Can you and I still be together, even if we don't agree on everything? Because if we can't, then we probably ought to end this right now."

She looked at his hand, then at his face. Finally, she closed the space between them and slid her palm against his. "Whatever Leland's motive, I'm glad he assigned us to work together. I'm glad we've gotten to know each other. And this summer…it meant something to me when you drove Krystal to Maine and stayed there with us for so long. Knowing you did it because you wanted to be there… It means something."

He brushed a strand of Misty's hair behind her shoulder, then shifted closer. When she didn't balk or push him away, he pulled her against his chest, thankful for the connection.

Misty hugged him back. "I think…" She stepped away. "I think Leland telling you my job—and your career—are on the line, proves he understood at least that the Dawson case was related to his family's company."

Tate considered it, conceded she was probably right.

"Maybe Leland doesn't realize there's more to it than simple bribery. Maybe he's doing Damien a favor."

Misty's eyes brightened. "His brother. Damien. Don't you remember? They were on the phone when we went to the conference room last Friday. What did Leland say? Something about, 'My brother always has something going on.' They were talking about some event." She gasped. "I know exactly what it is too!"

She grabbed her notebook and flipped back a couple of pages. "Yes, right here." She jabbed the paper with a fingertip. "The IAF property out in Hopkinton—Hearts and Homes—they're having a grand opening for their new rec center, which Thornebrook built. The guy from the construction company told me that they were having an event out there, they had constructed another building for them. This must be the event Leland was talking about."

"Knowing about a grand opening event and knowing what you and I have uncovered are two very different things, Misty. There's nothing wrong with him supporting his brother. It doesn't mean he knows anything about the crimes."

"I can't believe you're being so stubborn about this. You're blinded by ambition."

He was not. Was he?

Tate hadn't remembered that Leland had been on the phone with Damien when they'd walked into the conference room because he had been so excited to be called in to see the boss. Between hoping to impress Leland—and hoping to impress Misty at the same time—he hadn't been paying any attention to what Leland was saying.

Maybe Leland was involved. Maybe Tate's ambition and loyalty were keeping him from seeing the truth. If Leland was crooked, if he'd sent those men after Misty the night before...

The thought of it burned in his chest.

"Look." Misty laid her warm hand against his forearm. "This obviously makes you very uncomfortable. I'm going to settle the Dawson case as soon as his lawyer gets back to me. That's what Leland asked you to do. Maybe you should go, let me take it from here."

"What? No." He studied her face, tried to figure out what she was thinking. He saw indecision there. This was typical Misty behavior—not trusting anybody to help. Thinking that only she could do it right—whatever *it* happened to be. "I thought we were past this. Do you want me to go?"

"Do you want to?"

It was a fair question. He wasn't exactly eager to dig up dirt on his boss. But Misty was in danger. He needed to stay with her. He needed to know she was safe.

She was watching him closely. "I don't want to pull you into this if you're not on board."

"I'm on board with finding the truth. I'm just not sure we know all of it yet. But I want to stay with you, I want us to do this together." He raked his hands through his hair. "Don't mistake caution for fear. You might be right about all of it. I don't know. Let's just think about it, pray about it, and consider what we should do from here. Together. Okay?"

He'd hoped to see relief in her expression, but she was still torn. She wanted his help. But she also wanted to do everything her way.

The problem was, her way wasn't going to work.

They had no evidence that Dawson had beaten up Lela Parks, and they had no evidence that Dawson or Parks had been involved in the listening device planted in Misty's apartment. Reyes still hadn't gotten back to them about the men who'd attacked the night before. Who knew if they could be linked to this whole mess.

There were still too many puzzle pieces missing to make out

the whole picture. So, though Misty was acting like they'd blown some big conspiracy wide open, Tate wasn't convinced. And it wasn't just his worry for his job or hers.

It was entirely possible that Damien Humphrey was doing something illegal, and Leland had no idea.

Tate needed to figure that out—before Misty went and lost them both their jobs.

∽

Tate led Misty to the living room, where they asked God for wisdom to know how to proceed. The more he prayed, the more convinced he was that he needed to reach out to Leland directly and talk about some of the more innocuous things they'd learned. He thought he'd be able to gauge Leland's guilt or innocence by the way he reacted. He was trying to figure out how to explain his plan to Misty when the buzzer sounded.

She hopped up and pressed the intercom. "Yes?"

"It's Detective Reyes."

She pressed the button, turning to Tate with wide eyes. "Maybe this is it. Maybe she'll have information to tie the whole thing together."

Misty seemed eager to prove their boss was crooked.

The idea that Leland could be involved in all this—not just IAF's misuse of federal funds, but two murders—made Tate physically sick.

She swung the door open, and the detective moved past the guard into the apartment. Like every other time he'd seen her, she wore a business suit that looked too warm for the summer day. She nodded to Tate but focused on Misty. "How you doing?"

"Ready to hear what you've learned."

"Let's sit." She settled in the chair, and Tate and Misty took the sofa.

"We ID'd the two men." Reyes rattled off names Tate had never heard before. "It didn't take long to get them to admit they work for Griffin."

Misty stiffened. "Kyle Griffin?"

"Right." The detective looked confused by her question. "Does that surprise you?"

"No." But the word sounded tentative. Clearly, Misty'd been sure Dawson, or maybe even Leland Humphreys, had been behind the attack.

"What was their plan?" Tate asked.

Reyes kept her focus on Misty. "Griffin paid them to break in and intimidate you in order to get you to drop the case against him. They swear they weren't going to hurt you."

"But they were going to have to get past the guards," she said.

"They thought they could dispatch one pretty easily. They weren't going to kill him, just 'incapacitate' him—who knows how. They hadn't counted on the second guard."

"Was it the same guys who shot at her at the coffee shop?" At Reyes's nod, Tate asked, "Was that the plan then?"

"That's what they claim." Reyes still spoke to Misty. "They said they were going to pin you and your guards down, at which point Griffin was going to yell at you to drop the case or the next time would be worse. They swear they weren't trying to shoot anybody. Which tracks with what our experts tell us."

Misty was nodding silently. Tate couldn't tell if the news had upset her or just surprised her. Either way, she seemed to need a minute to pull herself together. "They underestimated the guards," he said.

"Twice." Reyes's lips twitched as if she might smile. "Griffin is arrogant. His punks are just stupid."

"Stupid but dangerous," Tate said.

"Mm-hmm. This is good news, Ms. Lake. The thugs are being charged. Griffin's in custody. I can't see a judge offering him bail after this. You might not be able to get him on the stalking charge, but conspiring to have your home invaded and intimidate you should get him put away for a while."

"Did you uncover any connection between Griffin and Raul Dawson?"

"Uh...no. Should I have?"

"What about Freddy Parks. Are they connected in any way?" At Reyes's head-shake, she said, "Damien Humphrey?"

Reyes's curious gaze flicked to Tate. He wasn't sure what to say.

Misty was so intent on proving her theories about the Humphrey family, her vision was distorted. She was seeing conspiracy everywhere.

"As far as we can tell," Reyes said, "the two cases aren't connected."

"But you still consider them two cases," Misty clarified. "The two attempts to intimidate me aren't connected to the intruder at my apartment."

"Correct. We still have no leads on that."

Misty frowned.

Tate was almost afraid of the answer, but he asked the question that'd been humming in the back of his mind anyway. "Do you know how they figured out she's staying here?"

"You were very helpful on that front," Reyes said. "I talked to your friend Clinton Lowe this morning. He admitted that Griffin paid him a visit Friday morning." To Misty, she said, "He asked him where you'd been. Apparently, someone had been watching the DA's office, waiting for you to show yourself, but you never did. Lowe told him he had no idea. But he said Griffin made him 'feel unsafe.'" The detective's rolling eyes accompanied the air quotes. "And so he mentioned that he didn't know where you were staying, but Tate might."

"I didn't tell Lowe that." Tate turned to Misty. "Have you talked to him?"

"Never, if I can help it."

"He overheard it," Reyes said. "He claimed he happened to be walking by when you and Leland were talking Thursday. I suspect he was eavesdropping, like you said."

"Then they followed me after work yesterday," Tate said, "And I led them right here." Like an idiot.

"Inadvertently." Reyes's eyes were kind. "One of the guys told me Griffin was the one who figured out which apartment to look in."

"What about Jeffrey Cofer?" Misty asked.

"I'm not the lead on that investigation, but Klein hasn't made any arrests. We're still looking for Parks, but wherever he is, he's hiding well."

"You still think it was him?" Tate asked.

"I do. Last I heard, Klein did too." The detective pushed to her feet. "At least we got those three bad guys off the street. Of course, two of them will probably cut a deal for cooperating."

"As long as Griffin gets put away." Misty's voice brightened just a little. "I'll let Melanie know that she and her kids don't have to worry about him anymore."

"It's a step in the right direction," Reyes said. "But with Freddy Parks still out there, I recommend you keep your bodyguards."

"I will," Misty said. "Don't worry."

And Tate would be sticking close. He and Misty might not agree on everything, but that didn't change how he felt about her. If he had to risk his job to make sure she was safe, he'd do it.

One thing was clear to Tate—Misty wasn't thinking clearly.

"This doesn't change anything." She paced across the small living room. "So what if Leland didn't send those guys last night? Jeffrey Cofer's dead. Maybe we should just go public with everything we know."

"And throw mud at a bunch of people who may or may not be guilty?" At the flash of irritation in her eyes, he lifted a hand. "We might have to go that direction. Right now, we don't have enough information."

"Your loyalty to Leland is blinding you." She paced to the far side of the room and turned to face him.

He stood. "Your obsession with destroying your boss—"

"This has nothing to do with that! If Leland is guilty, then I'm going to prove it."

"What if he's not? What if you go public with all this information, smear him and his family, lose him his job—what if you do all that and he's not guilty?"

"He'll have a chance to prove his innocence."

"He shouldn't have to *prove* his innocence, Misty. We should consider him innocent until proven guilty."

She brushed off his words with a wave of her hand. "You know what I mean. If he didn't do anything wrong, then going public with all of this won't hurt him."

"That's not true. *If* any of this goes to court, maybe he'll be found not guilty. But meanwhile, what'll that do to his reputation? Are you so certain you're right that you're willing to destroy a man's life?"

"A murderer."

"Oh, come on." Tate couldn't help the derision in his voice. "Do you really believe Leland Humphrey had Jeffrey Cofer murdered?"

"We don't know what—"

"Exactly," Tate said. "We don't know. So let's just settle down and think."

If looks were claws, he'd be bleeding.

"I'm not saying we drop it," Tate said. "I'm saying we keep investigating until we have *evidence* we can use. If that evidence leads us to Leland"—he lifted his hand to stop the interruption he could see forming on her lips—"beyond guilt by association and the fact that he assigned me to help you, then I'll help you bring him down. Okay?"

"Except you don't think he's guilty."

"I haven't made up my mind because I don't have enough information."

She tapped her foot on the floor. "Fine. We'll keep digging. But where?"

That was the question. They needed to stop repeating the same argument and think.

"We're both behind on our other cases," he said. "Let's work on those, put this on the back burner for the day. Maybe an idea will present itself. Talking the thing to death isn't helping."

Slowly, she nodded. "I'm not dropping it."

"I never thought you would."

He added a smile, but she didn't return it, just went back to the kitchen and settled in behind her laptop.

Tate did the same in the living room. He needed to think.

They couldn't get access to Hawthmarks's books, but all nonprofits' financial statements were available to the public. He navigated to the IRS website and managed to find the International Aid Foundation's information. He perused the form.

As executive director, Damien Humphrey was earning... Yikes. Over four hundred grand a year. Other employees had six-figure salaries, though none nearly as high as Leland's brother.

Tate was no expert in analyzing these kinds of documents, but from what he could tell, a lot of money was coming into IAF, and less than a quarter of it was being used to support refugees.

Maybe those salaries were necessary, though. Maybe the IAF employees were specialists who could earn even more in the private sector.

Tate needed help from somebody who knew more about nonprofits.

He snatched his phone and dialed. Dad answered right away. "How you doing?"

"I need your help."

"Anything," Dad said. "You know that."

"Is there anybody at your firm who can analyze a Form 990 for me? It's the IRS's nonprofit—"

"I know what it is. What are you looking for?"

"Any red flags. Anything that looks off. I think this nonprofit might have misused federal grant money, so evidence of that, or proof I'm wrong. I'm concerned about the employees' salaries too."

"When do you need it?"

"As soon as possible. I know it's Saturday, but—"

"No problem." Dad had always been eager to help his kids. What would it be like to have a father like Misty's, one who squashed their dreams—and their security? He couldn't imagine. Dad had not only always been eager to help, but when he had a problem, he wasn't afraid to ask for it. Tate had seen that modeled his whole life.

Misty, meanwhile, had learned early on that most people couldn't be trusted. Especially men.

"I'll find somebody to look into it," Dad said.

"It's important this stay quiet."

"Then you owe me a dollar, and my firm is representing you."

"I'll mail you a check."

Dad chuckled. "Send the information over. We'll get back to you today."

When Tate hung up, Misty was standing in the doorway.

"I'm having someone at Dad's firm look into IAF's financials."

She squinted in that suspicious way of hers. Was she really worried his father couldn't be trusted? But then, her expression shifted to a smile. "Good idea."

Tate forwarded the form to his father's email address.

"I thought we were taking a break from thinking about it."

"You're right." He closed the laptop. "I just thought of that and decided to get it done."

"I should have thought to look up that information earlier." Her gaze flicked to the hallway. "I'm having trouble keeping my eyes open."

"You going to take a nap?"

"A shower should wake me."

"Is it all right if I stay?"

"Of course." She wandered down the hall. A few minutes later, the water turned on.

Tate tried to turn his attention to his other cases but found he couldn't focus on them. The question of Leland's guilt or innocence kept nagging at him.

Had Leland really assigned Tate to assist Misty because of the Dawson case? And if so, how much did he know about Raul Dawson? Or, for that matter, IAF and what they were up to?

How could Tate find out for sure what Leland knew?

He considered the question, but the only answer was obvious. Tate needed to talk to him. If he was careful with how much he shared, and how he shared it, maybe he'd be able to gauge the DA's involvement.

If Leland was innocent, then Tate would try to convince Misty to tell him everything they knew. They could ask Leland for access to Hawthmarks's books and find proof that IAF had misused the grant money. They might even get information that could prove the company was associated with Dawson and Freddy Parks.

Once they had proof, Misty, Tate, and Leland could go to the authorities together. That might protect Leland's position as DA—though ultimately that would be up to the people of Suffolk County.

Tate wanted to bring down the bad guys, and he wouldn't mind coming out of this situation with him and Misty looking like heroes.

On the other hand, if after talking to Leland, Tate suspected the DA was involved, then the question would be, to what extent? Had he hired people to break into her apartment and bug it? Had he been involved in the Lela Parks assault?

In Jeffrey Cofer's murder?

If so, then Tate would bring him down.

CHAPTER THIRTY

Misty dried off after her shower and dressed. Lack of sleep and the heavy breakfast had weighed her down, but the shower had revived her.

She brushed her hair and towel-dried it, not in any rush. Taking a little time away from her laptop helped her understand Tate's point of view. She'd accused him of blind ambition, but that wasn't fair. There was nothing wrong with wanting to be successful, and maybe he was right to take a more cautious approach. Though she was convinced Leland had asked Tate to assist her because he wanted the Dawson case settled quickly, it was possible the DA didn't know anything about the rest of the stuff they'd uncovered. Sure, it would be wrong for him to try to influence a case in which his family's corporation played a part, but he wouldn't be the first DA or prosecutor to overlook a crime for personal reasons. It was wrong, but not villainous.

They needed someone on the inside at Thornebrook—and IAF, if possible—who could share internal records, someone who could gain access to information she and Tate couldn't get.

They needed a whistleblower.

Which meant they needed to get to know people within

both organizations. It could be a long process, but in this kind of game, there were no points awarded for speed. If it took weeks, even months, as long as they got to the truth in the end, it would be well worth the wait.

She couldn't keep hiding out. Fortunately, since Griffin was in custody, now was the perfect time to return to work. If she was right and her intruder had hoped to get information about the Dawson case, and if she settled it, everything could go back to business-as-usual. She wasn't sure what to do about the bodyguards. She'd have to pray about that, maybe talk it through with Tate and Summer.

Meanwhile, she and Tate would have to use their spare time finding people on the inside to get them the information they needed to prove what they'd learned. Or keep digging themselves.

It wasn't a perfect plan. It was barely a plan. But like a seed that wouldn't grow unless planted, her plan wouldn't take shape until she put it into motion.

And she knew exactly how to start.

She crossed the hallway into the bedroom and dialed, hoping someone would answer on Saturday.

The line connected a few moments later. She recognized the gruff voice.

"Mr. Begley, it's Misty Lake. We spoke the other day. I've been doing a lot of research on Hearts and Homes, and I'd like to know more. You mentioned some kind of grand opening...?"

"Tomorrow night. You want I should get you an invite?"

"I'd love that, if it's not any trouble. Two invites, if you can swing it."

"No prob. They gave us a whole bunch. I'll email 'em to you."

"That'd be great." She gave the man her email address. "I guess I'll meet you tomorrow."

After she hung up, she hurried down the hall to tell Tate. By the sound of it, he was on the phone. She approached quietly so as not to interrupt.

"Not at the office," Tate said. "Somewhere private. What about that place where we celebrated Barnard's retirement?"

Who was he talking to? Someone from work, obviously.

"Soon." A pause and then, "Wow. No, that's great. You should call Misty and tell her yourself. She'll be glad..."

She started to step into the room to get his attention. She wasn't in the habit of eavesdropping.

"It's about one of the cases you asked me to look at," Tate said.

She froze. He was talking to Leland?

"It's got to be in person." Tate leaned over the coffee table and jotted a note. "Listen, don't tell anybody we're meeting, okay?"

Tate ended the call, then looked up.

When he saw her standing there, his face paled.

And she knew. She *knew*.

"Get out."

"It's not what you think. I was going to tell you."

She stepped closer. "So that wasn't Leland?"

"It was, but I was going to—"

"What? Lie to me about it? Come up with some reason why you had to run out, and then meet with Leland so you could tell him everything?"

He stood and scooted out from behind the coffee table. Where his skin had paled a few moments before, now his cheeks turned red. "I'm trying to help."

"Better take a bottle of water so your mouth doesn't get too dry, all that boot-licking."

He took a step back. His jaw worked like he was trying to

grind out the anger. "No matter what I do, you're never going to trust me."

"Why would I trust you? This"—she gestured to his cell phone—"this is what I get for trusting you."

"I just want to gauge what he knows. That's all."

"Right. By warning him so he can protect himself and his family. Ought to be great for your career."

Tate's mouth opened, then snapped shut. "That's what you think of me?"

"What else could I think?"

"You could try assuming the best about a person, not the worst."

"I did that, and look where it got me. Betrayed."

"I didn't—"

"Get out."

He stepped toward her. "Don't do this. Just let me—"

"I want you out!" She said the words loudly enough for the bodyguard to hear.

A moment later, the door swung open, and Jones stepped inside. "You need help, Ms. Lake?"

Tate looked between the hulking man in the door and her. "If you'd let me explain—"

"I understand where your priorities lie." This was what she got for accepting help. This was what she got for trusting anybody. "If it was me against bad guys, maybe you'd be on my side. But me against the boss—you'll choose your career every single time."

"That's not what's happening here."

"Right."

"Let's go." The bodyguard stepped toward Tate, who backed away, lifting his hand.

"Let me get my things." He sat on the couch and snapped his laptop closed. Sliding it into his bag, he looked up at her. "If

I were trying to hide something from you, do you really think I'd have made that call sitting in your living room?"

"You didn't talk to me before you called him because...?"

He gathered his papers, shoved them in the bag, and stood. "Because I knew you'd be against it. But that doesn't mean it's the wrong play."

"Go then. Have a nice little chat. Just don't come back."

"I'm on your side here."

She crossed her arms. There was nothing else to say.

The bodyguard said, "Come on. Let's go."

Tate gave her a long look. She would swear she saw sadness in his gaze, but what was he sad about? Her catching his betrayal? Probably.

He grabbed the handle of his bag and headed for the door. He turned at the threshold. "I would never betray you, Misty. I hope, someday, you understand that. This thing"—he gestured between them—"could be something amazing. Or at least..." He blew out a long breath and stepped away, muttering as he walked out.

Misty stared at the closed door a long time, Tate's last words resonating in her heart.

It could have been.

CHAPTER THIRTY-ONE

Walking—maybe stomping was the right word—down the Back Bay sidewalk, Tate tried to figure out what in the world had just happened.

He'd planned to tell Misty about the meeting. That she thought he hadn't—that she'd gone so quickly to believing he'd betrayed her—said more about her than it did about him.

Maybe he should have told her before he called Leland. Fine. Maybe.

But she should have let him explain. Not kicked him out of her apartment, out of her *life,* without a second thought.

He had half a mind to forget the whole thing. Why should he stick his neck out to get more information? Why risk his job for her? He should cancel the meeting with Leland, go home, have a nice, normal weekend. He could go back to work Monday as if he'd never learned any of this stuff.

But of course he wouldn't.

He wiped sweat from his brow. The midafternoon sun wasn't that hot, but the humidity was killing him. He probably should've taken the T. Anger was clouding his judgment.

Leland had been at the office when Tate called. He'd

suggested they meet at a restaurant close by, but Tate hadn't wanted their conversation to be seen or overheard. They settled on a place near Faneuil Hall.

It took Tate nearly a half hour to walk there. By the time he reached the historical marketplace teeming with tourists, sweat was dripping down his back.

Great way to impress the boss.

But that wasn't his goal, not this time.

He was early, but Leland was already there, seated in a booth on the far side of the packed seafood restaurant. The diners were loud enough to nearly drown out the music playing overhead. The scents—grilled, fried, and raw fish—didn't mix well with the frustration churning in Tate's gut. It was too warm in the old brick building, though most of the diners didn't seem to mind.

Tate slid into the booth, and Leland nodded to a beer on the table, moisture dripping down the glass and pooling on the cardboard coaster. "Wasn't sure if I should order you one."

"Not today." Tate wasn't much of a drinker, and certainly not in the middle of the afternoon when he was working. And ticked off.

A server approached, and Tate ordered a glass of water.

"What're your specials?" Leland smiled at the college-aged woman, relaxed as could be.

She rattled off a few options, none of which appealed to Tate.

"You know what you want?" Leland asked.

He glanced at the menu, picked the first thing that caught his eye. "Lobster roll and french fries."

"Baked haddock," Leland said.

The woman took their menus and left.

"First," Tate said, "thanks again for dealing with Clinton." On the phone, Leland had said he'd fired the other

ADA after learning he'd told Griffin how to find Misty. "It means a lot."

"His dad and I go way back." Leland's jovial expression shifted into a frown. "But we need to know we can trust each other. What kind of guy rolls over on his coworker like that? Where's his loyalty?"

Loyalty. Tate had always prided himself on loyalty. But how could he be loyal to both Misty and Leland? To both his job and his values?

"Have you told Misty yet?" Tate asked.

"I called, but she didn't answer."

He stamped out the twinge of worry. Misty had probably just avoided talking to the man she was convinced was corrupt.

"Let's get to it," Leland said. "What's so important we had to talk today—and so secret that it had to be here? Not that I'm complaining. Cecelia's visiting the grandkids, so I was on my own for lunch anyway."

"I need to ask you about a case."

Leland gave him a go-ahead nod. Tate should have used the half-hour walk to pray about this meeting rather than stewing about the argument with Misty.

The server dropped off a basket of rolls and Tate's glass of water, and he took a long sip, using it to cool off and get his head in the game.

He set the glass down. "The Dawson case."

Leland spread his napkin on his lap. "Has she closed that yet?"

"She's waiting for a call back from opposing counsel."

"So what's the problem?"

"Did you know Raul Dawson works for Thornebrook Construction?"

Though Leland's eyes gave nothing away, the skin around his lips tightened.

"If I'm not mistaken," Tate said, "Thornebrook is a subsidiary of your family's corporation."

No surprise on Leland's face. If anything, he seemed to relax. He leaned forward. "This is why I stepped away from the business when I ran for DA. Not that they're doing anything illegal, of course, but people are always quick to accuse. I'm trying to avoid even the appearance of impropriety." He tipped his beer toward Tate. "And this conversation is why I know you'll be great in the white-collar division. Digging deep like that, looking for connections... Your skills are wasted where you are."

Tate's heartbeat thumped, and not because the promotion he craved felt within reach.

The misdirection—focusing on Tate's career rather than the underlying question.

Leland said, "Misty isn't great at differentiating between what's important and what's not. I don't care if the guy is prosecuted, but I'd rather it not go to trial. It would be embarrassing if the press got ahold of the information."

"Is that why you asked me to help her, because you wanted me to encourage her to settle it?"

"She needs to work with somebody like you, somebody who can teach her how to prioritize."

Tate did his best to keep his expression neutral. Misty was right about some of it. But was she right about the rest of it?

"I appreciate your discretion. It shows maturity and wisdom."

"Thank you, sir." There was that boot-licking tone Misty must hate. Leland, however, visibly relaxed. "Can I ask something else?"

"I have nothing to hide."

"Did your brother ask you to intervene?"

Now, a wrinkle appeared between Leland's eyebrows. He set down his roll. "Why do you ask?"

"According to Zachary Hardy, the guy Dawson attempted to bribe, the property in question is owned by IAF. Damien's on their board, right? I just wondered if maybe he was worried about blowback."

Leland's eyebrows lifted. An invitation to say more?

Or maybe a dare?

Tate had never been one to back down from a dare. "According to Hardy, he was transferred out of that job, and his replacement issued all the permits. The office building was constructed. It is an office building, right?"

"It is." Leland's voice was flat.

"I went by there the other night."

Leland straightened the tiniest bit. "What night?"

That wasn't the question Tate had expected. "Wednesday."

"What time?"

"I guess it was maybe eight or eight thirty. Dusk. Why?"

"Place was broken into that night. Did you see anything unusual?"

"I'd never been there before, but everything looked fine to me."

"What were you doing there?"

That was the question he'd anticipated. "Hardy told us the building didn't belong there. I guess he was defending his decision to deny the permits. I wanted to have a look myself." He figured it wasn't a good idea to bring Misty into this.

"What'd you think?"

Tate shrugged. "It's impressive."

"I'm glad it finally got built." Leland took a bite of his roll.

"Hardy seemed to think the building didn't meet the neighborhood's codes, and he was transferred for not issuing the permits. True or not, the accusation is out there. I've been wondering if maybe Damien..." Tate shrugged, acted like he wasn't sure how to finish the sentence.

This was where it got interesting.

If Leland seemed confused or gave the impression he'd look into Hardy's claims—and Tate believed he was sincere—then he'd conclude Leland was probably innocent.

But if he didn't...

Tate prayed for discernment. He prayed the Spirit would help him judge truth from lies.

Leland sipped his beer, studying Tate over the top of the glass.

Despite the festive mood, tension stretched between them.

"Are you accusing me of something? Or my brother?"

"It's just curious, that's all. I mean, I talked Misty into letting it go because there's nothing there, certainly nothing criminal."

"Right," Leland said. "I'm thinking...Hardy? Was that his name?"

"Zachary Hardy."

"He must not have been very good at his job, which was why he was replaced. And why the permits were ultimately issued—without the need for any money to change hands."

"So Damien didn't have anything to do with Hardy being punished for reporting—"

"Who said he was punished?"

"Well"—Tate lifted a shoulder and let it drop—"Hardy did. But if he wasn't good at his job, then it makes sense he was transferred."

"Exactly." Leland added a nod to the word as if to punctuate it, effectively ending the discussion.

Their meals were served, and Leland thanked the server and waited until she'd walked away. He snatched the salt and sprinkled it over his meal. "I appreciate that you came straight to me with your questions. You know how these things can morph into something they're not." He aimed the shaker at Tate. "I appreciate how thorough you are."

Tate figured Leland at least suspected it had been Misty's thoroughness, not Tate's, that'd uncovered the connection to Leland and his family.

Leland cut a bite of flaky fish. "You can put this issue to bed now. Misty'll plead the case out on Monday, and then you won't have to work with her anymore."

Rather than show his disappointment in both Leland and Misty, Tate ate a bite of his lobster roll. It melted in his mouth, but he barely tasted it. "I haven't minded working with her."

"I bet." Leland winked, then dug into his baked potato. "Even still, come Monday, you're going to be busy getting up to speed on your new job. You'll do great in white-collar crimes."

"Thank you, sir." His smile felt as brittle as clay, the words like sand in his mouth.

That job had been Tate's goal since he'd started at the DA's office—which Leland well knew. So, was the promotion a reward for a job well done?

Or payment to keep his mouth shut?

～

The rest of lunch was torturous. Tate and Leland talked shop, Leland sharing some things Tate would need to know once he moved into prosecuting white-collar crimes. Tate tried to take in everything hoping, when this was all over, he'd need the information. Hoping that what happened next wouldn't destroy his career.

All the while trying to figure out how much Leland knew.

Maybe he didn't know everything about Thornebrook and

IAF. Even so, he was obviously willing to use his position to protect his brother, IAF, and Thornebrook.

Willing to use his influence to protect the corporation that had made his family rich.

It didn't necessarily make him guilty of conspiring to commit assault—or murder.

But he wasn't innocent either.

When they finished their meals, Tate pulled out his wallet, but Leland waved him off. "It's on me, a celebration lunch for your new job."

"Thank you, sir. And thanks for the opportunity." The words came naturally and, he hoped, hid the suspicion buzzing in his brain.

Tate left Leland and went straight to the T station. He was still irritated enough with Misty that he considered keeping what he'd learned to himself. But he'd had lunch with Leland to find out what he knew so he could share the information with her.

Maybe, once he did, she'd realize she was wrong about him.

And then what? They'd pick up where they'd left off?

Not a chance. He'd liked her, had even thought she might be the woman he would spend his life with. But after she'd turned on him that morning, assuming the worst about him?

He'd rather be alone, thank you very much, than live his life with someone like that.

His phone dinged with an incoming text. Dad.

> Just sent you an email. IAF salaries are suspicious, considering the lack of experience, especially the execs. Grant money was probably misused, but more investigation needed.

Before Tate finished tapping out his reply, another text came in.

> The Exec Director is Damien Humphrey.

Three dots signaled his father wasn't finished.

> I hope you know what you're doing.

Tate stared at that last one a long time.

He knew exactly what he was doing. Risking his career in order to bring down his boss.

Was he nuts?

Maybe.

But some things were more important than achieving success. If Leland Humphrey's family was guilty of everything Misty suspected, their sins needed to be exposed.

His phone dinged again.

> ???

He replied.

> Pray for me. I'm gonna need it.

He exited the T at Kenmore Square and walked to Misty's sister's building. No bodyguard stood on the stoop, but sometimes, they watched the door from a nearby car. Tate climbed the front steps and jabbed the apartment number.

No reply.

Which might make sense, if Misty knew it was him. But the building's security hadn't been upgraded to include cameras.

He hit the button again.

Someone stepped outside, and he grabbed the door and let himself in. Maybe she was napping, or maybe she was avoiding everybody, not just Tate. He climbed to the third floor and rounded the corner to her apartment.

Jones wasn't there. Nobody stood guard.

His heartbeat raced. He banged on the door. "Misty?"

Nothing.

He pressed his ear against the wood and listened, but no sounds came from within.

Another door on the floor opened up, and a young mom stepped out, followed by a couple of school-aged kids. They bolted past her and ran down the stairs. She called after them, "Do not go outside until I get there!"

"We know!" one of them yelled back.

The woman locked her door, then turned to him. "If you're looking for the blonde, she took off."

"Any idea where she went?"

The woman shrugged. "She was pulling a suitcase, so I guess she's gone for good. A day too late, if you ask me." She started down the stairs. "My kids were up half the night with all that commotion."

Misty was gone?

Tate wasn't sure if he should be hurt or angry. Both, he decided. He pulled out his phone and texted her.

> Where are you?

He sent it, waited for a response.

But the phone never showed it as delivered. He sent another text, but the same thing happened.

He dialed her number.

The call went straight to voice mail. Which meant either her phone was off, or...

She'd blocked him.

She'd *blocked* him.

Fury coursed through his veins. What did Misty think, that he was going to lead her enemies to her doorstep? Did she really believe he'd put her in danger for the sake of his career?

He was proud of himself for not voicing the words screaming in his brain.

Fine, then. He'd go home, go through the information himself. Try to reach her via email.

He was just as invested in getting to the bottom of this mystery as she was. The sooner they did, the sooner he could get on with his life and career, whatever was left of it.

Without Misty Lake.

CHAPTER THIRTY-TWO

It'd been hard enough making herself at home at Summer's apartment. This was going to be so much worse.

Not the place. The place was amazing. At least it seemed so, though Misty hadn't gotten past the expansive foyer with the stairway that led up multiple flights of stairs. She set her laptop bag on her suitcase. "I didn't know there were any brownstones left in Boston that hadn't been converted to apartments."

"There aren't many." Jacqui Cote bounced a baby on her hip, a little boy with bright red hair to match his mother's. He looked five or six months old and kept lifting his head from her shoulder to smile at Misty before hiding again. "My family's owned this place since long before I was born."

The child was precious, and the hidden place in Misty's heart, the place she always tried to pretend wasn't there, melted.

Would she ever have a husband, a family? Would she ever find a man she could trust?

Jacqui led her past a dining room on one side, a living room on the other. Both were decorated as old and expensive places often were, as if the furnishings were as much a part of the space as the walls and fancy moldings. The tables and chairs seemed somehow both antique and unpretentious. Shelves overflowed with books. Magazines had been tossed haphazardly on the coffee table. The only thing that didn't seem to belong was the flatscreen TV.

Jacqui gestured to a door beneath the staircase. "That leads to the basement. I converted it to a laboratory when I still lived here full time. The washer and dryer are down there. Help yourself if you need them."

"What kind of lab?"

"I own a medical device development company. Before I met Reid, I was a bit of a workaholic." She continued to the kitchen which, unlike the rest of the first floor, had been fully upgraded. White cabinets, gray-and-white granite countertops, stainless appliances. "The fridge is mostly empty. You might find something in the pantry." She turned back to Misty. "We're not here very much, and when we are, we usually order out. There's a market on the corner, not that they'll let you walk there."

They meaning the bodyguards stationed outside the front and back doors. Summer had secured this place when Misty told her about Tate's betrayal.

She'd called in tears, looking for comfort.

Summer had responded in her typical Summer way. She'd been sympathetic...for a minute. Then jumped into action, making sure Misty would be safe.

As if Tate could be a threat.

He might care more about his job than her, but he'd never hurt her. Since Leland knew where she'd been staying—and Misty was convinced Leland was, if not intimately involved, at least complicit in the crimes of his family's company—it seemed wise to find somewhere else to stay until this mess was cleared up.

"Please," Jacqui said, "help yourself to anything you want."

"Thank you. And for letting me stay here."

"I'm just glad we're in town. Not that you couldn't have come if we weren't. We'll be spending most of the day and tomorrow at the convention, then we'll head back to Coventry. But you're welcome to stay as long as you need to."

Tears filled Misty's eyes. She swiped them quickly.

The shorter woman reached out and took her hand. "I don't know all of what you've gone through, but I'm sure it hasn't been easy. I found my life in danger once, and it was terrifying. I don't know where I'd be if Reid hadn't been there for me. And last winter, your cousin saved Denise's life. Your sister kept our Ella safe from that...that madwoman. I wouldn't presume to know how you feel, but..." Her words trailed.

Was Misty's life in danger? Even if it was, thoughts of people coming after her hadn't sent tears to her eyes. She'd been weepy ever since she'd sent Tate away. She'd never felt so alone.

Now, having this woman and her husband, along with Summer and Grant and Jon, all worried about her safety... She didn't know how to think about it. She was so accustomed to doing everything by herself. She'd finally decided to let someone get close, let someone help her, and look what happened.

Misty had always been okay with the solitude of choosing her own path. But now, away from home, away from the office, with nobody to talk to about all the things she'd learned...

The connection to this redheaded stranger meant something to her. More than she could articulate.

Jacqui squeezed her hand and then let go. "Anyway, make yourself at home. Eat and drink whatever you can find. Read the books—you'll surely find something of interest. I don't have cable, but Reid's configured the TV to pick up local stations and gotten one of those internet-capable devices if you want to watch something. Here's the Wi-Fi code." She tapped a sticky note on the counter, then gestured around the pretty kitchen. "You need anything else?"

"No, thanks."

"Let's head up then."

Misty grabbed her suitcase and bag in the foyer and followed Jacqui and the baby up the stairs. She'd met her and Reid the previous month at Jon and Denise's engagement party. Reid was Denise's ex-husband, Ella's father. Which made them sort of distant family by marriage, or they would be after the wedding.

Jacqui had been quiet at the park that day, more of an observer than a participant. Misty hadn't given her much thought. She certainly never would have guessed the woman owned a house like this. Or a lab. Or a company that developed medical devices.

Just went to show how wrong first impressions could be.

They reached the second floor. It was...different. The hardwood floor, very similar to the stairs, looked newer. The walls were freshly painted. Even the doors didn't match those below.

"We had a fire," Jacqui said. "We could've had everything restored perfectly, but the time and expense seemed needless."

"It's still beautiful."

"They did a good job." She walked down the hall, and Misty peeked into a bedroom and a second room lined with bookshelves—which also looked far newer than the brownstone. The center of the space held a crib and changing table.

Jacqui started up the next flight. "You'll have the third floor to yourself. I apologize for the climb, but you should be comfortable up here. Your own room, plus there's a little sitting room and a bath. It's meant to be a guest suite."

The baby was one of the quietest Misty'd ever seen. His eyes were bright, taking everything in. Sort of how Jacqui seemed, silent and observant. Obviously, mother and son had more than just their red hair in common.

"Here we are." Jacqui stepped aside, and Misty entered the bedroom. It was as large as the master bedroom below. She left her small suitcase by the door and her bag on a queen-sized four-poster bed with a pretty yellow quilt. A large high-boy bureau was pushed against one wall. A small writing desk and chair near the bay windows would be a perfect place to work.

"Not a lot of noise on this street," Jacqui said. "And up here, you shouldn't hear much of it. It does tend to get warmer on the third floor. I hope you'll be comfortable."

Misty turned and smiled. "It's lovely. Thank you."

"Do you need anything?"

"Not that I can think of."

"Then this little guy and I will head back to the convention." She squeezed the baby's foot, eliciting a giggle. "We probably won't be home until after eight. There are some frozen things, but with everybody here, I suspect you'll need to call out for dinner."

"Uh...who is 'everybody'?"

Jacqui's light brown eyes rounded. "Didn't they tell you? Clearly not, though I'm surprised by your...surprise. Obviously, Summer, Grant, and Jon are all on their way." She shifted the baby and glanced at her watch. "I bet they'll arrive in the next hour or so. Reiterate my offer for them to stay here, would you? I know Summer has her own place, but I have two bedrooms upstairs, plus a pull-out in the sitting room down the hall. Plenty of space." She looked around at the walls. "It'd be nice to see this place brimming with people. It's been a long time."

"I'll tell them."

"You have my number now," Jacqui said. "Call if you need me."

At Misty's promise to do that, the woman headed back

down the stairs. A few minutes later, the front door opened and closed.

Leaving Misty alone in the giant home, feeling...unsettled.

Slightly nervous.

And, without Tate by her side, incredibly alone.

She unpacked her few belongings, finding empty drawers in the bureau and plenty of hangers in the closet. She put her toiletries in the bathroom, then set up her laptop on the desk.

All the while checking her phone. No messages from Tate, but then she'd blocked his number. Still, every time she saw the blank screen, her heart clenched a little.

She missed him.

When she'd stowed everything, she sat in front of her laptop and pulled up her email.

There were forty-seven new emails, but the one from Tate caught her eye first. She clicked on it.

I have information about IAF and Leland. If you want it, call me.

As if she'd trust anything Tate had to say. It was bad enough he knew everything they'd uncovered so far. She should have sent him away days before. She should have sent him away when she'd first felt him pressuring her to close the Dawson case. For all she knew, he'd been in on this conspiracy with Leland from the beginning.

But she was curious about what Tate would say. More than curious.

She tapped out a reply.

We can communicate through email.

After hitting send, she busied herself with her other messages.

She was halfway through deleting all the junk when his reply came in.

No.

That was it, just *no*.

Jerk.

Fine, then. She didn't care what he had to say. It was probably a lie anyway.

He'd had someone looking into IAF's financial statements, but she could do that herself. She found the proper form on the IRS website and downloaded it.

And groaned.

She stared at the numbers, trying to make sense of them. Lack of sleep and the crazy events of the day—and the night before—had her fighting the pull of the mattress. The figures were starting to dance a little in her vision when the faint ding of a bell gave her a great excuse to step away.

A knock followed it.

She hurried down the two flights to the door. "Who is it?"

"It's the plumber," Summer said. "I've come to fix the sink."

Misty swung open the door to her sister, smiling at the old line they used when they were kids.

Summer stepped through and wrapped Misty in her arms. "Thank God you're okay." After a very brief hug, she stepped back and held her shoulders. "I can't believe you didn't call me after what happened last night. Someone came after you, and I had to hear it from Hughes!"

"Oh. Sorry." Misty hadn't called because she'd known how Summer would react. She should have known Hughes would tell on her.

"You're okay? You're not hurt?"

"I'm fine."

"Good." Summer moved deeper inside, allowing Grant and Jon to enter.

Jon wrapped her in a hug and held on tight. "Glad you're okay."

Grant stepped in behind him and gave her a side-hug. "Good to see you safe and whole."

"And not being held captive by madmen. It's an improvement."

He smiled, looking little like the fierce warrior who'd rescued her that spring.

The two men took up a lot of space in the foyer. "Come on in. This place is amazing." To her sister, she said, "Have you ever been here before?"

"No. I knew Jacqui had a place here, but..." Her words trailed as they walked through the living area and into the kitchen. "Wow."

"Wait till you see the rest of it. Jacqui wanted me to tell you you're welcome to stay." Misty turned at the counter island to include the men in the invite. "All of you. She has plenty of room."

"Grant and Jon are staying at my place," Summer said. "I'll be here with you until I know you're safe. Tell us what happened last night."

After Misty found cans of soda and filled a couple of glasses with water, the four of them sat at the small kitchen table that overlooked a rear courtyard. She told them about Kyle Griffin and the thugs who'd invaded her home, being very careful not to talk about—or even think about—the man who'd rushed to her side and then comforted her all night long.

CHAPTER THIRTY-THREE

Tate had to quit waiting for his phone to ring.
 Obviously, Misty wasn't going to call him. Maybe he should just forward the information and let her run with it. But he needed to tell her about his conversation with Leland because...

Because why? What did it matter what she thought of him?

It didn't.

But...it did. He wanted her to understand why he'd chosen to meet Leland. Tate wanted her to know she was wrong about him. Maybe, deep down, he still hoped there could be something between them.

Idiot that he was.

After an hour in the gym, he showered and then plopped himself in front of the TV. But nothing held his interest. He tried to focus on a basketball game, but it turned into a blowout. He switched to a movie he hadn't liked all that much the first time around.

He wasn't sorry when he checked his fridge and found it empty. He hadn't gone to the grocery store. He'd hardly been at his apartment since he'd saved Misty from walking in on that intruder a week before.

What did she think, that he'd been part of a plot to plant listening devices?

Probably.

Grabbing his keys and phone, he headed for the door. A nice long walk in the summer evening air might help him take his mind off her and her ridiculous accusations. He'd go to his favorite burger joint. It would be packed on a Saturday night. The crowd noise would make him feel less...alone.

The elevator stopped halfway down, and an older couple stepped in. They were probably in their sixties. Gray hair. Wrinkled skin.

Holding hands.

Would he ever be one half of a gray-haired couple, a dad, a grandpa? Would he ever have what his father had?

They reached the lobby, and the happily-marrieds preceded him through the door. Tate paused when the heat of the summer evening hit him, breathing in the familiar sights and sounds and scents. Pretending he wasn't wishing for anything else.

A man bumped into him, and he turned, an automatic smile on his face.

But fingers curled around his biceps and squeezed.

A jab in his side was dull but insistent.

The face, just inches from his, looked menacing.

And familiar.

"Don't say anything." Freddy Parks's voice was low. "Don't scream. Don't try to get help. Just walk with me to that car. I swear I'm not gonna hurt you."

An old Honda idled at the curb. A man sat in the driver's seat.

Tate tamped down a rise of panic. Breathed. Prayed. Hoped like crazy Freddy wasn't lying.

Freddy had a round, unshaven face. He was about five-nine, shorter than Tate, but his barrel chest radiated power. They reached the car. "Climb in and slide to the far side."

Tate did as he was told, and Parks slid in beside him. The compact car's backseat felt extra cramped with the armed man inches away.

As soon as the door closed, the driver hit the gas. He was probably in his midtwenties with curly light brown hair and a long nose. Tate couldn't see his eye color or even the shape of his face from the backseat, but he'd keep watching. He'd need to identify these people later.

Assuming there would be a later.

Freddy blew out a breath. "Thanks for not fighting me."

At the strange remark, Tate looked his way. He wore a dingy white T-shirt that revealed tattooed arms as thick as Tate's calves. In his hand, he held a short piece of pipe, the thing that'd been jabbed into Tate's side.

Not a gun. What a fool Tate was. He should have fought. Or run.

"I'm not gonna hurt you," Freddy said. "But I need to talk to you, and I'm not tryna to go back to prison. I was scared you were gonna raise all sorts of commotion and get the cops after me."

"Kidnapping is a felony whether you use a gun or threats and manipulation," Tate said, "so I'm thinking you *are* trying to go back to prison." Where the calm tone came from, he didn't know. It certainly belied the fear thumping in his chest.

The driver made his way on surface streets toward the North End, winding along the narrow roads seemingly at random.

"Okay, fine." Freddy sounded annoyed. "I'm not going back

to prison *yet*. Okay? I'm not gonna hurt you. I need to talk to Misty Lake, and I know you know where she is."

"I don't. And even if I did, there's no way I'd tell you." Thank God, thank *God,* Misty had left her sister's apartment. No matter what this guy and his thug friend did to him, he wouldn't be able to tell them her location.

If nothing else, at least Misty would be safe.

Freddy didn't look angry at his response. His lips slipped into a smirk. "Yeah, you know."

"Why would I?"

"'Cause you two are together, right? She's tryna find me, and you went up to Ma's on Thursday, and she told you about Lela and what Raul done to her. She remembered your name and told me."

But Tate hadn't mentioned Misty's name to Winnie Parks. "I'm not denying that. And I'm not saying I don't know Misty. We're coworkers, but—"

"Listen, Steele." Freddy's heavy eyebrows lowered and angled together. "I got a lot of patience, but it runs out real quick when people lie to me. I might not look smart, but I'm not dumb."

But how did he know Tate was lying? He swallowed his denial and tried a different tack. "What makes you think Misty and I are together?"

"Saw you two, didn't I? Outside the IAF building. Holding hands."

Leland said the building had been broken into that night. Freddy must've done it. But why?

"I remember her from court," Freddy said. "Didn't know who you were, but then Ma said you went to see her Thursday, and I looked you up. Your picture's on the internet."

"Fine," Tate said. "We were dating. We had a big fight

today, and we're not anymore. I went to where she was staying this afternoon, but she's gone."

"She go home? We been watching the building, waiting for both of you."

Heartwarming, knowing their addresses were so easy to find.

"She's in hiding," Tate said. "From you."

"I'm not gonna hurt her." The ex-con who'd beaten a man nearly to death had the nerve to look insulted.

"What, you're all about flowers and butterflies now?"

"Did I hurt you?"

Tate glared at the short bit of pipe still in the man's hands. "You forced me into your car. I get the distinct impression that you wouldn't like it if I tried to get out."

To his friend, Freddy said, "Pull over."

The driver did, stopping beside one of the many Italian restaurants in this part of town. Pedestrians wandered by, some stopping to read the menu in the window.

"G'head. Get out."

Tate didn't know if this was a trick or what, but he wasn't going to wait to find out. He reached for the handle.

"Thing is," Freddy said, "I think you and I are after the same thing."

Tate pulled the handle. He'd feared maybe there'd be a child safety feature that would keep him trapped inside, but the door unlatched.

Freddy grabbed his arm and held on tight.

Tate barely kept himself from yanking away and diving out the door. Instead, he turned to the man beside him, lifting his eyebrows.

"You gotta listen to me." Parks didn't release him, but he eased his grip.

Tate thought, hoped, he could leave if he wanted to. And if

Freddy fought him, he could shout. There were plenty of people around to hear.

Even still, he gave the hand on his forearm a pointed look.

Freddy let go. "You're tryna bring down the people who had that building built. Thornebrook and IAF, right? 'Cause that's what I'm tryna do too."

"Sure you are." But the disbelief he'd tried to infuse his voice with didn't come. Because he didn't disbelieve.

"They killed my sister," Freddy said. "And not just Lela." His eyes—the terrifying ex-con's eyes—turned red around the edges. And filled with tears. "Mr. Cofer was nothin' but good to me. He got me outta jail even when I had nothing to pay him. And that lady who died..." He swiped a hand down his face. "Listen, man. I'm sorry I scared you. I know the cops think I hurt Mr. Cofer, but I didn't. And I'm not tryna hurt Miss Lake. I just thought, seeing you two at the building, then you goin' up to Ma's house, I thought we could work together. 'Cause I gotta bring them down, but I really don't wanna end up in prison again. Or dead. I need help."

CHAPTER THIRTY-FOUR

Misty pulled another slice of pizza loaded with veggies from the box. Summer and Jon had already made themselves at home at Jacqui's place. Though Misty hadn't known Grant well before tonight, he already felt like family. After she'd concluded the story about Kyle Griffin, the guys had decided they needed sustenance before they could go on.

Summer had rolled her eyes playfully before calling out for three large pizzas.

Misty wasn't sure she'd ever seen her sister do anything *playfully* before in her life.

She liked this new Summer. Without the tough veneer she'd worn for years, she looked not only calmer but more confident. In fact, she looked fabulous.

Misty couldn't help it. She wiped her fingers on her napkin and reached across the table to touch Summer's sweater, which she'd slipped on over her T-shirt after complaining about the air conditioner. "Is that cashmere?"

Summer's eyes sparkled. "You like it?"

"It's gorgeous. The green looks so pretty with your skin tone."

"I'll get you one." She gave Grant a sidelong glance, then bent close like she was about to share a secret. "I'm thinking of starting a boutique."

"A...what?" She couldn't help the shock in her voice.

"I know. Crazy. But now that Grant has settled on the job with the Coventry PD, it looks like we'll be staying there. And there are no good clothing stores within thirty miles." The way she talked about herself and Grant, as if their staying together was a foregone conclusion, took Misty aback. Her sister had completely let her guard down.

Jon cleared his throat. "Besides Hamilton's outlet store," he said. "Which has everything a body could want but is apparently not good enough for Her Majesty."

Summer whacked him, and he feigned injury.

At Grant's chuckle, Summer kissed his cheek.

The love between them made Misty's heart hurt.

"Hamilton's is fine for outdoor wear," Summer said. "And they have great everyday clothes, don't get me wrong. But the town needs high-end shops to appeal to the high-end tourists who come to visit. New resorts are going up by the lake. I think it could do well. Denise thinks so too."

Misty couldn't help it. She laughed. "Because as a movie star, she has a real handle on the life of the everyman."

Jon scowled and plopped down his meat-covered slice of pizza, clearly ready to take up his fiancée's cause.

"She's totally down-to-earth," Summer said, beating him to it.

"Mm-hmm." Misty winked at Jon to show she was teasing. "Does *she* shop at the Hamilton outlet?"

Summer and Jon traded a look. "Well, not unless there's a clothing emergency," Summer said. "But that's the point. She's not the only wealthy person who vacations in Coventry."

Jon cleared his throat. "She *lives* there. Maybe not all the time, but—"

"You know what I mean." Summer's excitement seemed to fade a little. "It's just an idea."

"It's a fantastic idea, sweetheart." Grant bumped her shoulder. "By the time you're done, the whole town'll be decked out in high fashion."

"I agree." Misty was happy for her sister's obvious bliss, despite a petty twinge of jealousy. "Especially if you can get me discounts." She eyed the sweater again, and Summer grinned.

They'd agreed not to talk about anything important during dinner. Misty had plenty of time to tell them all about Hawthmarks and Thornebrook and IAF later. For now, she was content to just be with her family. How had she survived so many years without her sisters in her life?

Thank God they were restoring their relationship now. If not for the danger Misty still found herself in, she'd have invited Krystal to join them.

Of course, Krystal would have spent the entire evening lecturing her to find a less dangerous job. But for ninety-nine percent of the ADAs in the world, the job wasn't dangerous.

Just bad luck that Misty landed in the one percent.

Summer's phone rang, and she stood and grabbed it from her purse on her way out of the room.

Ten seconds later, she returned. All amusement had faded from her expression. Her spine was straight, her eyes focused. The bodyguard was back as she held the phone out to Misty. "It's for you. I think you'd better put it on speaker."

What? Who would be calling her on Summer's phone?

She did and set it on the kitchen table. "Misty Lake."

"It's Tate. We need to talk."

"How did you...? Why are you calling me? Can't you take a hint?"

"I'm here with Freddy Parks. He needs to see you. Tonight."

~

Thirty minutes later, Misty followed her sister down a long hallway at the Green Beret Protection Service office, the company partly owned by Summer and Jon. Despite the bodyguards surrounding her, she had to fight the urge to flee.

Freddy Parks was in the building. Freddy, who'd threatened to kill her, and who was wanted for murder. He was here—with Tate. How did they know each other? How long had they been working together? And why had they insisted that they needed to see her?

Tate hadn't been willing to explain on the phone.

She'd refused until Summer and Jon's partner had come on the line and encouraged her to hear them out. Apparently, he'd been alone at the office when Tate and Freddy had shown up and demanded he contact Misty via Summer. Summer and Jon trusted Bartlett, so Misty should too. But she'd never have agreed if not for the bevy of bodyguards.

She followed her sister into a brightly lit conference room.

The room was empty except for Tate, who looked up from a bundle of papers he'd been studying. He barely spared her a glance as he stood and held out his hand to her sister. "Good to see you again."

Summer reintroduced him to Grant and Jon, whom he'd met in Maine after the kidnapping. He knew Hughes and Ian, of course.

Misty sat on the far side of the table from Tate, not right across from him but close enough that she could watch him. She didn't trust him. At all.

The fact that he'd been working with an ex-con suspected of murder certainly didn't raise her opinion.

Where was Freddy?

Summer sat next to her. Beneath the table, she reached over to squeeze Misty's hand.

Jon and Grant stood behind them. Hughes and Ian positioned themselves on the far side, behind Tate. Armed sentries there to protect her.

Tate returned his attention to the stack of papers in front of him.

Aside from the occasional scratching of his pen on paper, the room was quiet. The silence stretched like a tension line.

Finally, an older man entered. "Freddy wanted to get cleaned up a little." He glanced around the table until his gaze landed on Misty, then he crossed the room to her. "I'm Bartlett."

She stood and shook his hand. "Sorry about this."

"Not a problem." He returned to the door and poked his head out. "Well, come in. This is your party, after all."

Freddy stepped across the threshold.

Misty's stomach plunged at the sight of him. He wasn't particularly tall, but he'd bulked up in prison. All muscle and hate. Except...

He smiled. "Thanks for coming. I shoulda just wrote everything in the letter."

"You sent that warning?" she asked.

He shrugged. "I didn't figure you'd believe me if you knew it was from me. Not that you should. And I'm not so good at explaining stuff on paper."

Bartlett pulled out the chair across from her. "Have a seat."

After Freddy did, Bartlett sat at the end of the conference table.

"Go ahead." Bartlett spoke to Tate, who slid his papers aside.

"I think Freddy should start." Tate angled his chair slightly and gave the man beside him a go-ahead nod.

Freddy's Adam's apple bobbed. His gaze flicked above her head, presumably to Jon and Grant, who were probably glaring at him.

He averted his eyes fast—to Bartlett at the end of the table. To Summer. He swallowed again.

Tate gripped the man's shoulder. "Ignore everybody else. Just tell Ms. Lake what you told me."

"Okay." He turned back to her.

Misty had never looked this closely at him before. When she'd prosecuted his case, she hadn't cared what he looked like, only concerned about putting him away. When he'd screamed his threats at her, she'd just walked out of the courtroom as if he didn't matter.

She looked now. He was big and built, but not scary, not the way he was looking at her. His hair was combed. His cheeks looked freshly shaved. He had a round face, and when he gave her a shy smile, dimples.

He was a human being, a person who mattered.

She had no idea what was going on, but if he had information, she wanted it. And he'd done his time. Maybe not as much as he deserved, but she was learning that the last thing anybody wanted was to get what they deserved.

She was the recipient of mercy. She could extend it to this man.

She stood and reached across the table. "We've never been properly introduced. I'm Misty Lake."

He looked at her hand the briefest moment before standing and shaking it. "Ms. Lake. I'm Freddy."

"Call me Misty." She sat again, and he did too. "Tate tells me you wanted to talk to me?"

"You remember when I asked you to come see me?"

"I'm sorry it took me so long to make the time."

"You got better things to do than visit some loser in prison."

"You're not a loser, Freddy. And I didn't have better things to do, just more pressing things. Though, in retrospect, I wish I'd gotten out there sooner."

"So you know what happened, right? Tate an' me been talking, and he says you guys worked it out. See, after that lady out at Hearts and Homes died... That wrecked me, you know? Like, it's one thing to beat up a grown man. I shoulda felt bad about that, but"—he broke eye contact, shrugged—"I didn't feel much of anything back then. But a lady, a mom with kids who'd worked so hard to get here... She died 'cause of what I did." He blinked a couple of times, and his eyes turned red.

Like he was about to cry.

Beside him, Tate said, "You mind if I tell everybody else what you're talking about?"

Freddy gave Tate a grateful look. "G'head."

Tate addressed Summer, Grant, and Jon. Misty figured Bartlett had already heard this story.

"Freddy was paid to intimidate a building inspector into glossing over some issues he found at the Hearts and Homes refugee building in Hopkinton."

Beside Misty, Summer nodded. On the far side of the room, even Hughes seemed to lean in.

"The man refused to budge," Tate said, "so Freddy beat him, badly. He ended up in ICU. After that, another inspector passed the building without a hitch. A year later, a carbon monoxide leak set off the alarms in the house. One woman was deaf."

"Jemilla Amin," Freddy said. "That was her name."

"Right." Tate gave Freddy a kind glance. "Her kids were at a friend's house for the night. She didn't hear the alarm."

"She died." Freddy's voice pitched high. "It was my fault, see. If I hadn't beat that guy up... How hard would it'a been to fix that? The builders were just cheap is all, didn't care about those people. And I helped 'em. They had all those stories about the lady and her family on TV, all the stuff she hadda go through to get her family to the States, and now those kids have no mom, and it's my fault." He banged a fist on the table. "*My* fault. I was so broken up about it, I went to see the prison chaplain, and he told me I could be forgiven. I just hadda give my heart to Jesus. So I did, but the guilt didn't go away. I hadda make it right." He closed his mouth, but his lips trembled.

Misty couldn't help the tears that dripped down her cheeks. She swiped them away with her fingertips. "That's when you reached out to me."

"An' Raul. He was my best friend. I wanted to warn him I was gonna tell what happened. I told him I wasn't gonna name him but that maybe he oughta get a lawyer or something. I didn't wanna cause him trouble. But he told his boss, and Raul or someone roughed up my sister. And..." Freddy looked at the ceiling, shook his head.

Again, Tate gripped the man's shoulder and spoke to the room. "His sister had an undiagnosed heart condition. The assault probably wasn't meant to kill her, but she didn't survive."

Freddy swiped moisture from his face.

Misty did the same.

"I was scared for my mom and my niece, you know? I shoulda told before, but I couldn't let anything happen to them. Ma refused to hide. I was tryna learn to live with it, and then Mr. Cofer, he said maybe he could get me out. An' he did, and I finally talked Ma into going away. Moved her out of state where Raul and his people can't hurt her. And now I gotta take 'em down. I gotta."

"I understand." Misty worked to get her voice level. She and Tate had been right about everything, including Freddy's innocence. "We're on the same side."

He nodded, glancing at Tate. "Like I said."

"You probably could have started the conversation that way. You know, without kidnapping me."

Kidnapping him? Her gaze snapped to Tate, but he didn't meet her eyes.

"This again?" Freddy sniffed, grinned. "You sure know how to hold a grudge."

"It's been two hours."

Freddy laughed. The banter seemed to relax him a little.

It did the opposite for her. What was Tate doing? Trying to play both sides? Stay in Leland's good graces while keeping one foot in her camp? Hedging his bets?

She'd ask him to leave, but he seemed to have a calming effect on Freddy.

"Why bug my apartment?" She wasn't sure Freddy had, but she wanted to throw him off.

The levity on his face melted away. "That wasn't me." He looked at Tate. "I told you it wasn't me."

"So tell her."

"I don't know who did it for sure, but we were talking, me'n Tate, and we think maybe it was Dawson and his crew. See, they're looking for me. They know I asked to see you before, so maybe they thought I might find you to tell you all this stuff I was gonna tell you last year."

Misty was having a hard time following. "Why would they bug my apartment?"

"We think," Tate said, "maybe they were hoping if you talked to Freddy, you might say where he was, or perhaps where you planned to meet him."

"Yeah, yeah." Freddy nodded. "That makes sense. They wanted to know where I was. Tryna shut me up. Figured they could follow you to get to me."

Summer asked, "So you don't think Misty is in danger from these people. Is that what you're saying?"

"I mean, if she didn't care about any of this stuff, maybe. But she's been digging around, so"—his gaze returned to her—"sorry, but I think you are now."

"It's not your fault." Not if everything he was saying was true. "What about Jeffrey Cofer?"

"That *is* my fault." He swallowed hard. "I never thought they'd go after my lawyer. I don't know for sure, but I think they were trying to get him to tell where I was. Tate here told me he was beaten bad, like Phillips."

"The building inspector," Tate said for the benefit of everyone else in the room.

"Like they wanted people to think I did it," Freddy said. "But I didn't. So maybe they were hoping to figure out where I was. But Cofer didn't know. I didn't tell nobody."

"Where have you been staying?" Misty asked.

"Guy from prison had a place for me. I'm not gonna say where, though. Don't want none of this to blow back on him. And there might be blowback 'cause I gotta bring these people down."

"Would you be willing to testify to all of this?"

He angled away. "Testify? In what, some trial? Like it's ever gonna get to trial. These people are powerful. They got money. They got influence. We gotta force the issue or they're gonna wiggle out of it. Maybe Raul and his crew go down for killing my sister and Cofer. I wanna see that happen. But the guys pulling the strings—ain't no way they're goin' to jail unless we make it all public."

"So what do you propose?" Misty asked.

"There's a thing tomorrow out at Hearts and Homes."

"They're dedicating the rec center," Misty said.

"I figure there'll be all sorts of powerful people there, maybe press an' stuff. I thought I'd just…" He shrugged, glanced at Tate.

"His plan is to interrupt the meeting and tell everybody what happened."

"Not just tell 'em. This is why I gotta have your help. We need proof, laid out all pretty and easy to understand. I'm not good with that kind of thing, but you guys can do it, right? Put together some papers and stuff we can hand out."

Misty tried to understand his plan—if you could call it a plan. "You want us to hijack the dedication and accuse the people there of—"

"Murder," Freddy said. "It's what they did, isn't it? To that refugee lady. Mr. Cofer. Lela. If the press see it, then the cops gotta deal with it. They can't just look the other way."

Misty shifted her gaze to Tate. "What do you think?"

"I think there are better ways to handle it."

Of course he did. Ways that made him and his boss come out looking squeaky clean.

Not that he was wrong, at least about coming up with a better way.

She laid her forearms on the table. "Let's put the information together and present it to the attorney general and the FBI. We can let them take it from there."

He scowled, bringing to mind the terrifying ex-con she'd forgotten to fear. "They won't do nothing."

"It's their job to—"

"But they won't care. Why would they care about a coupla dead women—a refugee and a single mom? Maybe they'd care about Cofer, but we got no way to pin that on 'em. No. I was gonna do it that way before, when I asked you to come see me, but they decided to play dirty. Now that I got my ma and niece out of town, I'm taking them down."

"Okay." Misty worked to keep her tone calm. "But we can always go to the press later, if the authorities—"

"Later, when I'm back in prison for crimes I didn't do?"

"That's not going to happen," Misty said. "You'll just have to tell—"

"Tell who? Your boss? Humphrey? He's in on it, don't you see?"

Misty flicked her gaze to Tate, but he didn't seem alarmed by Freddy's accusation.

Freddy's eyes flashed—fear or fury, she wasn't sure. "The DA's gonna prosecute me for Cofer's murder just to shut me up."

"All right, all right." Misty tried to sound placating. "I see what you're saying." She shifted her attention to Tate. It was possible she was wrong about him. "What do you think?"

"I think charging in and trying to hijack a fancy dinner is a bad idea." He gave Freddy an apologetic look. "There might be some bad guys there, but most of the people will be supporters, good people. We don't want to scare anybody."

"People gotta know the truth. They gotta know who they're giving money to."

"I agree," Tate said. "I think we need to work together to come up with a plan. Maybe a two-pronged approach. We alert the authorities"—he nodded to Misty, agreeing to her point—"and send the press all the same information, simultaneously."

Not a bad idea.

But would Tate whitewash Leland's involvement?

She was about to ask him point blank when Freddy pushed back from the table. "Yeah, okay. Maybe. I gotta...I gotta think about it." He started to walk away, but Hughes shifted to stand in front of the door.

Freddy turned to face her. "Can I go to the bathroom?"

She smiled at him. "Of course. And then we'll come up with a plan together."

CHAPTER THIRTY-FIVE

A grown man asking for permission to use the bathroom. That was what prison did to a person. It was an interesting dichotomy—strength coupled with subservience.

The marriage of determination and fear.

Tate couldn't help admiring the ex-con for his desire to bring to justice the people who'd hurt his sister. But not just his sister. This had all started because he'd cared about a stranger, a refugee whose name most people wouldn't remember. But Freddy remembered.

Proving no heart was too hard for God to soften.

Speaking of hard hearts... Misty regarded him with wariness. She still didn't trust him.

The realization sent fury coursing through Tate's veins. They hadn't worked together for a week before she'd turned on him.

"Would you like to know what I learned from Leland?" he asked her.

She sat back and crossed her arms. "As long as we're here."

He couldn't even look at her. Instead, he shifted his focus

above her head to Jon and Grant. "You two can sit. There are no threats in this room."

Jon said, "I don't think Misty agrees."

Tate tamped down the instinct to defend himself. Ignoring Misty, he spoke to the others in the room. "I made a lunch appointment with Leland." He quickly explained their theory that Leland had assigned him to work with Misty on the Dawson case because he wanted Tate to get her to drop it —or at least plea it out quickly. "Misty was convinced. I wasn't."

"Why not?" Jon asked.

Tate nodded to Bartlett, still seated at the end of the table, then to Grant. "These guys are your friends?"

His eyes narrowed. "Yeah."

"Would you be quick to believe one of them was a criminal?"

"We served together. I trust these men with my life."

"Fair enough," Tate said. "I never went into combat with Leland, but I've worked for him for years. He's never given me a single reason not to trust him. I don't write off people so easily."

He met Misty's eyes, and she flinched.

Good.

He addressed her sister and the men behind her. "I thought I could gauge Leland's guilt or innocence."

"And?" The question came from Grant.

"He knew the Dawson case was connected to his company and admitted he'd asked me to help Misty in hopes I'd get her to close it quickly. He didn't care if it was pled out or dropped, only that it didn't go to trial."

Misty sat up straighter. "He told you that?"

"He also confirmed that the building on Aldus is offices, like we guessed."

"Meaning IAF misused grant money."

"It isn't just housing IAF offices," Tate said. "The corporation, Hawthmarks, has moved their headquarters there."

"How do you know that?"

Because Freddy had broken into the building and gone through the records. He'd even taken pictures of all the name plates on the doors. Damien had an office there. So did his uncle, Clark Humphrey, who ran Hawthmarks.

So did Leland.

"Freddy figured it out." The man had committed a crime, but for a good reason. Tate wasn't going to tell Misty. She'd probably throw the book at him. "When I asked Leland if Damien had pressured him to make sure the Dawson case was dropped, he didn't deny it. He did compliment me on my discretion."

"What are you saying?" Misty asked.

"Leland was using his position as DA to protect his family's company. He offered me the white-collar job."

Misty's eyes rounded. "Just what you wanted."

"Not like this." He pushed back from the table and stood. "Do you think I want a job offered as a quid pro quo?" She started to speak, but he cut her off. "Don't answer that. I know what you think."

Silence settled, broken when Jon spoke. "What is this about grant money?"

Tate handed a stapled packet of papers across the table.

Jon snatched it.

"It's IAF's Form 990." He slid another copy to Summer.

Misty leaned in to look.

"It's a federal form all nonprofits have to file."

"How'd you get it?" Grant looked up from peering at Jon's copy.

"It's public information. Got it off the IRS website. I had an attorney at my father's firm look it over for me." Tate sat again, pulled his laptop from the bag at his feet, and navigated to the email. "There's nothing obviously improper going on, but according to Dad's guy, the board's salaries are suspicious."

"I'd say." Jon slipped into the chair beside Misty. "The executive director is making four hundred grand a year. Who makes that? Oh, I see." He looked up. "This is the Damien you mentioned earlier."

"The DA's brother," Tate said. "The attorney did some digging and discovered that Damien doesn't even have a college degree. He dabbled in drugs when he was young, even got arrested a couple of times, though it looks like his daddy always managed to get the charges dropped." Tate shifted his gaze to Misty. "Their father—his nickname was Hawk. Dad remembered that."

"Hawk," she said. "That's where the H-A-W came from in Hawthmarks."

"Exactly. The point is, though some nonprofit execs *might* be able to justify getting paid that much money, Damien has zero experience working with refugees or foreign governments. He had zero professional experience before he joined IAF's board."

"So IAF is funneling money to Damien." Jon sat back. "I don't understand, though. Why wouldn't Hawthmarks just give him a job?"

Tate shrugged. "Who knows? Maybe his uncle thought he could do good at IAF. Or maybe they put Damien there because they knew he wouldn't balk at bending the rules."

Misty looked up and met Tate's eyes. For the first time since she'd walked in, he remembered why he'd been falling for her. Was that affection in her gaze? Maybe regret?

Too little, too late.

"Do we know if the Aldus Street building was paid for with the grant money?"

"The timing adds up, and the numbers. We'll need to dig into the financials to know for sure."

She closed her eyes. "So let's put it all together. Hawthmarks, owned by the Humphrey family, hired Thornebrook—"

"A subsidiary of Hawthmarks," Tate reminded her.

"Right. They had Thornebrook construct the Hearts and Homes property. Thornebrook did a shoddy job. Ernie Phillips, the first building inspector, said he wouldn't let his dog live there. They had Freddy..." She looked around. "Where is Freddy?"

Bartlett pushed back from the table. "I'll check on him."

Misty continued. "Freddy beat Ernie up, his replacement passed the building, and then that woman died."

"Right," Tate said. "Meanwhile, Redstone, another Hawthmarks subsidiary, donated the property at the corner of Aldus and Buttrick to IAF, where they built an office building."

"Probably using federal grant money intended for refugees," Misty added. "And the building isn't only for IAF. It's for Hawthmarks."

"Damien Humphrey is the executive director of IAF." Jon looked up from the paperwork. "Damien, whose family owns Hawthmarks."

Tate could see the man's wheels turning. Rather than tell him what he believed, he waited to see what conclusion he'd draw.

Jon's brows drew together. "It sounds like Hawthmarks was using the nonprofit to not just funnel money to a family member but to steal federal funds for its own use."

"Exactly." Tate jabbed the paperwork in front of him. "But it all *looks* fine on paper. It all *seems* fine. Sure, there was an investigation into the carbon monoxide leak, but that was blamed on a faulty furnace."

"Phillips says it was the installation," Misty said.

Tate stood, wanting to move around, to think. But Hughes and Ian were standing sentry like Tate might pull out a gun and start shooting. "Do you mind?"

Hughes's gaze flicked to Misty, who said, "It's fine. He's not a threat. You guys can sit."

Ian took the chair next to where Freddy had been seated, but Hughes just shifted to stand near the door.

Tate paced behind the chairs. "But that was all brushed under the rug, despite the woman's death. Because of the DA's connections? Maybe. And then Freddy, from jail, threatened to tell Misty everything he'd learned. They had to shut him up, not just to protect Thornebrook from blowback and the real possibility of lawsuits. They needed to keep anybody from looking too closely into Hawthmarks. So Dawson or someone who worked for him attacked Lela Parks to convince Freddy to keep his mouth shut."

"The bribery charge was small-time," Tate said. "But Leland and Damien couldn't let it go public or somebody might start connecting dots. Leland managed to back it up in the system for a year, but that couldn't go on forever. He figured I'd get you to sweep it under the rug."

"Except exactly the opposite happened," Misty said. "We started digging."

"It's always the cover-up." Summer pushed the forms away, clearly disgusted. "People like this always get themselves into hotter water trying to hide their crimes than they ever would have if they'd just fessed up."

Tate stopped pacing and looked across the table at Jon, Grant, and Summer. He couldn't quite bring himself to look at Misty. "The question is, can we prove it?"

Movement near the door had him turning in that direction.

Bartlett stepped inside. "Actually, the question is, what is Freddy going to do now."

"Where is he?" But Tate already suspected what the man would say.

Holding out a piece of paper, Bartlett said, "He left a note."

Tate grabbed it. The scrawl was barely legible.

Thanks for listening. I'm going to the opening at H&H. I'm bringing them down, one way or another.

Tate handed the note to Misty and closed his eyes. Without help, Freddy would just end up getting himself arrested—if not killed.

The man was risking everything to bring the people who murdered his sister to justice.

And Tate was going to help him.

CHAPTER THIRTY-SIX

"I'm going tomorrow night. I have to try to stop Freddy. He'll only make himself a target."

Misty didn't miss the determination in Tate's voice. She wished they were alone. She needed to apologize, but she didn't want to do it in front of Summer, Grant, and Jon.

Hughes and Ian had walked out of the conference room with Bartlett a few minutes earlier.

Beside her, Summer said, "I'm not sure that's a great idea. You'll be walking into the lion's den."

"Nobody knows what we know." He rubbed his forehead as if staving off a headache. "I'm not sure how I'll get in but—"

"As it happens," Misty said, "I have a couple of tickets."

He narrowed his eyes, not looking at all pleased.

"You need to steer clear of that place," Summer said.

Misty ignored her overprotective sister.

"How'd you do that?" Tate asked.

"Remember, I called Thornebrook last week to ask about the building in Boston. The guy there offered to get me tickets to the opening. I called him back today and took him up on his offer."

"Why?" Tate's single word sounded almost angry.

"I thought we might need to take more of a long-term approach to figuring out what was going on, which meant we'd need to know people at Thornebrook and IAF. I was thinking maybe we could find a whistleblower."

Tate studied her a long moment before conceding, "Not a bad idea."

"Better than charging in with our paltry evidence."

"It's not that paltry." He took a pile of papers out of his bag and slid it across the table. "I procured some of Hawthmarks's records. I haven't gone through everything yet, but these came out of Clark's office."

She slid the pile closer. "How did you get them?"

"I'd rather not say."

"You didn't steal them?" She couldn't help the shock in her voice.

"I did not."

She waited for an explanation, but none came. Meaning somebody *had* stolen them. And she guessed that the *somebody* didn't want to go back to prison.

Jon reached his hand toward the papers. "Do you mind if I…?"

"Help yourself." She was too tired to decipher the information anyway.

"It's mostly tax forms," Tate said. "As far as I can tell, it shows the dates and expenses for the construction of the headquarters, which was built last year, and the IAF rec center, which was completed last month. There is mention of a…I think it says *dormitory* at an address on Buttrick Road, but if you plot that address on a map, you'll see it's the side of the Aldus Street property."

Jon looked up. "There's a dorm attached to the office building?"

"No. They claimed to have built housing but didn't."

"They were hoping nobody would check." Jon's brow furrowed as he studied the paperwork.

"If you look up that address on the internet," Tate said, "your search will lead you to a fancy page about a dormitory for refugees. But the building doesn't exist."

"You're sure?" Grant asked.

"Misty and I were there a few days ago." Again, Tate barely glanced her way.

"We saw nothing resembling housing," she added.

Summer asked, "Is this enough information to take them down?"

"It's enough to force an investigation." Misty leaned in to study the paperwork with Jon, but the words blurred. She yawned, and Tate followed suit. Not shocking, considering neither of them had slept much the night before.

"Why don't we get together tomorrow and make a plan?" Summer suggested.

"Good idea." Grant pulled out her chair for her when she stood. The old Summer might've scowled at him, but this newer, softer version gave him a sweet smile.

Misty tried to meet Tate's eyes, but he was packing up his laptop and paperwork. When he did look up, he focused on Jon. "You can keep that. I have copies." He started for the door.

"Wait." Misty's voice came out too loud, almost desperate.

He looked at her over his shoulder. "What?"

"Can I talk to you for a second?"

He said nothing, just stood there while Summer, Grant, and Jon walked out. Jon closed the door.

Misty walked to the end of the table, then stopped close enough to Tate to touch him.

The look on his face kept her from reaching out.

"I owe you an apology."

He didn't shift or smile or nod. She'd always thought of his hazel eyes as warm. His icy stare was anything but.

"When I heard you on the phone with Leland, I jumped to the wrong conclusions. I should have given you the chance to explain." Still, his expression didn't shift. "Will you forgive me?"

"Done." He reached for the door.

She gripped his arm. "Wait. That's it? You're not... I mean... I'm sorry. I'm trying to make this right."

He glared at her hand until she dropped it, her hopes tumbling alongside.

"I need to be with someone who believes in me," he said. "Someone who trusts me. You don't."

"I do now." She blinked back tears. It wasn't that she loved Tate, but she could. She'd come to rely on him.

She should have trusted him. She should have believed in him.

"Would you really throw this away because of one mistake?"

"There is no *this*." He gestured between them. "And it wasn't a *mistake*. A mistake is forgetting to pick up milk. You made a decision not to believe in me."

"And now you're making a decision not to forgive me."

"I forgive you. I just don't want to be with you."

He yanked the door open and walked out.

She watched the empty doorway a long time, not even trying to quell her tears. Her distrust hadn't just lost her a man she'd come to respect and care for. It'd lost her a friend.

CHAPTER THIRTY-SEVEN

Tate aimed his BMW toward the brownstone where, earlier that day, he and Misty, along with Summer, Grant, and Jon, had dug into all the information they'd collected. As Tate suspected, they had enough to force an investigation, but not enough to bring indictments—especially if they didn't turn over the information in the files Freddy had stolen. Since nobody wanted to explain how they'd come to be in possession of those documents—not even Misty, to Tate's surprise—they hoped an investigation would prove their suspicions.

They'd put all the information on a handful of thumb drives to distribute to the attorney general, the FBI, and the press. Tate had a couple of them with him, just in case he ran into somebody that night who might be able to help their cause.

They'd already placed a call to Summer and Grant's friend at the FBI, Agent Golinski. It was Sunday, so no surprise he hadn't responded yet. Tomorrow, they'd focus on disseminating the information they'd gathered.

He double-parked and texted Misty that he was there. Rude, no question. He might've forgiven her for her lack of faith in him, but he wasn't over it. And he certainly didn't want her to get the wrong idea about tonight. This wasn't a date. There would be no more dates. And though he felt a twinge of guilt whenever he recalled the look of hurt on her face the night before, he tamped it down. It was only fair that she feel a little of what she'd caused him. He had a right to his anger.

Misty stepped onto the landing. She was wearing a shimmery pale blue dress with a high slit that showed off silver stilettos—and shapely legs—as she descended the steps to the sidewalk.

Wow.

He looked forward and told himself—not for the first time—that she wasn't the woman he wanted.

Smart, capable, and beautiful, sure. But suspicious and quick to believe the worst about a person. He wanted to marry someone like his mother. Kind, generous of spirit, always believing the best. Mom was loving. Misty was...not.

Not that anybody'd said anything about marriage.

She settled in the passenger seat and dropped a fancy little bag by her feet. "Nice car."

The bodyguards' SUV was parked behind him, waiting for him to pull into traffic.

"You don't need to go tonight," Tate said. "I can find Freddy by myself."

"We've been over this. I'm going."

"You could be in danger. Even Freddy said so."

"So could you."

But Tate could take care of himself.

"They don't know we've put it all together," Misty said. "Leland knows you figured out why he asked you to help me, but that's all, right?"

"Are you suggesting I lied to you?"

"Oh, for crying out loud." Misty had been overly polite all

day, pretending things were normal between them even if Tate couldn't manage to do the same. Apparently, her patience had run out. "I'm not accusing you of anything. Just clarifying."

"I'm not accusing you of anything, either," he said, not believing her at all. "Just clarifying."

"Drive."

"I don't want you to go. I don't want you with me." There. That was honest. If cruel. But if it got her out of the car, worth it. "Go inside and take off that"—he stifled the word *gorgeous*—"ridiculous dress, and I'll call you when it's over."

She clicked on her seatbelt. "Your problem, Steele, is that you don't have tickets. I do. Drive."

He growled under his breath but hit the gas. The bodyguards followed. They'd stay close until Tate and Misty entered the Hearts and Homes grounds. They hadn't been able to secure tickets for the bodyguards, but they'd stay close. He'd known it was a long shot, getting her to stay. The last thing he wanted was to have to worry about her safety.

No. That wasn't quite right. His worry wasn't the issue. Her safety was. He wanted her to be safe because that was what men did, right? Protected women?

Even irritating, mistrustful women they found annoyingly attractive.

He turned up the music, his favorite classical playlist.

She turned it down. "Summer and the guys left an hour ago to watch the property," she said. "No sign of Freddy yet."

"Okay."

"Maybe you should let me take the information to the attorney general and the FBI tomorrow."

He shot her a look. "Why?"

"There's no reason for both of us to risk our jobs. If I send it—"

"Afraid I won't follow through?"

"What? No."

He angled onto I-90, thankful for the lack of traffic that allowed him to vent his frustration on the gas pedal.

"Tate, I trust you."

"Just not enough to have me pass along the thumb drives."

"I know how important your job is to you. I'm trying to keep you from losing it. Or even losing the promotion."

"You don't care about your job?"

"This is more important."

"You don't think justice is more important to me than my job? That's what you think of me?"

"That's not what I'm... Obviously, you're willing..." She sighed. "Forget it."

Gladly. Tate increased the volume again and enjoyed the music—and her silence. Until she interrupted the tenuous peace.

The music went back down. "I find it interesting that you're willing to risk...maybe not your life, but possibly your career by trying to warn Freddy off. If you're seen trying to help him, or even stop him, as he attacks Leland and the Humphrey family, you could lose everything. Yet you'll do it—all to protect a convicted felon."

"He did his time."

"He got off on a technicality."

Tate changed lanes. "He's trying to do the right thing. He's risking everything for the sake of making his sister's killers pay."

"So he's forgivable. I wonder what I'll have to do to earn forgivability."

Was that even a word? He stuffed the rising fury, forced a deep breath. Reached for the stereo.

"And isn't it ironic how quick you are to think the worst of me."

He dropped his hand. "What are you talking about?"

"I was trying to do something nice just now, to protect your job because I know what it means to you. What we do tonight and tomorrow might be bad for my career, but let's face it, I'm never going to ascend very high at the DA's office, and I'm content with that. If I lose my job..." In the corner of his eye, he saw her shrug. "I was trying to protect yours."

He waited for her to continue her explanation, but she said nothing else.

"I don't see any irony."

"You're so quick to think the worst of me, yet you won't forgive me for thinking the worst of you."

"I told you I forgive you."

"I'll do the same, then."

"You'll forgive *me*? What did I...?" And then he realized what she was saying.

Ever since she'd jumped to the wrong conclusion about him the day before, he'd been furious with her. And yes, maybe that meant he was jumping to wrong conclusions about her. But she'd given him good reason to suspect her motives. "It's different."

"If you say so."

He cranked the music, silently daring her to turn it back down. She didn't, and Vivaldi filled the space between them, not that he could enjoy it.

Twenty minutes later, he exited the interstate and followed his navigation system along narrow roads lined with forest on both sides.

He so rarely got out of the city. Thanks to the recent rain, humidity had hung heavily all day. The temperature was dropping now. A good thing, considering the monkey suit he'd donned for this dinner.

Nothing said fancy like sweating through a tuxedo.

They reached the driveway leading to the property and

turned. The bodyguards sped past while Tate stopped behind a line of cars on the narrow asphalt hemmed in by thick trees on both sides. Grudgingly, he lowered the stereo volume. "They're checking tickets."

She tapped her phone and handed it over silently. He opened his window as he approached a teenager holding a clipboard.

Tate handed him the phone, and the kid made a note on his list before handing it back. "Follow the cars. There's valet parking. When you get out, walk to the right of the main building."

"Thanks." As Tate drove, the woods opened up to a grassy clearing in the center of which stood a four-story building large enough to take up a city block. According to the H&H website, the building held a hundred units.

"We're here for one reason," Tate said. "Find Freddy and stop him from doing anything stupid. If you see him, let me know. If I see him, I'll do the same. I think if we approach him together, we can talk sense into him."

"Okay."

"Don't confront anybody. Don't cause any trouble. Don't do anything to make anybody think you know anything."

"Act dumb. I'm blond. I can do that."

It wasn't funny. Dawson and his crew were probably here. The last thing Tate wanted was for them to come after Misty.

"Can we at least reach a truce?" she asked. "We are supposed to be attending this thing together."

He came up with a flippant response and turned to her with the most natural smile he could conjure.

The expression on her face—hurt mixed with fear—twinged his conscience. His words died on his tongue. "I'm sorry. I'll do my best."

"Good to know it'll be such a chore."

That wasn't what he meant, but they were out of time for

chit-chat. He braked at the curb, and a young man opened her door. "Good evening, ma'am."

She climbed out, and Tate did the same. He slipped the valet a five-dollar bill and walked beside Misty behind another couple toward the edge of the building.

When they turned the corner, he got a sense of the size of the grounds.

A playground sported colorful equipment beside a field that had soccer goals on each end. Beyond those, a white fence enclosed a valley where two chestnut horses grazed near a barn.

It was peaceful, probably a welcome respite for the refugees who lived here. This wasn't meant to be a permanent home but a place for families to regroup, to secure jobs and save money until they could afford to move out.

On the surface, Hearts and Homes was the sanctuary it was meant to be. His research had told him the people who ran it did good work. He hoped and prayed that, in taking down IAF, they wouldn't hurt this place. He didn't want to harm the organization. He wanted to ensure it received all the funding it deserved.

They reached the back of the housing. On the far side of a low brick building—the new rec center?—a white tent had been set up. The fabric sides had all been pulled back and secured to tent poles, allowing the evening air to circulate.

Men and women in tuxes and evening gowns milled near the entrance or stood in clusters inside. Music came from a string quartet playing on a stage on the far end. Behind them, a screen flashed photographs of the new rec center—a basketball court, a workout room, a track—along with residents' smiling faces.

They were beautiful, the residents. They were brown, black, and white, tall and short, young and old. Some wore hijabs or other clothing traditional in their cultures. Others wore jeans and T-shirts.

They were human beings with value, people who'd had jobs and lives in their home countries. Most often, only those with money could afford to leave war-torn nations. By the time they reached safety, though, most had spent—or had stolen from them—everything of value.

In their home countries, they were doctors, lawyers, bankers, and teachers. Here, most would do menial jobs.

They were parents and children and siblings and friends. They'd had everything that mattered stripped away.

They were the reason Tate and Misty had to expose what they'd learned. Because the people running IAF were taking money out of the hands of the poor to shove it in their own bursting pockets.

They needed to be stopped.

"Who are those guys? Guards?"

Misty's question drew Tate's attention back to the surroundings. Stationed at various intervals inside the tent were burly men watching the scene. They wore black slacks and black polos and flat expressions. He scanned their faces but didn't see anybody resembling Raul Dawson.

"Probably."

They stopped at the back of the queue of people entering the tent. Wearing those ridiculous heels, Misty was nearly as tall as he was.

"Try to keep a low profile." As if everybody wouldn't notice her in that dress. "Our names were on a list. They know we're here."

"We expected that."

But seeing those thugs so close, the thought of Misty anywhere near them had his fists clenching.

A judge he'd met a few times caught his eyes, and he smiled, trying to look casual. They reached the front of the line, where they gazed at the seating chart. "We're at table sixteen." He glanced quickly at the other names, a trick Dad had taught him. Events like this were great places to meet people.

"Nathan Tucker is here." He was surprised to see that. "The attorney general."

"Oh." She peered at the seating chart. "It's a who's who."

He pressed a hand to the small of her back to urge her forward, trying to ignore the jolt of awareness touching her brought. They weaved among the round tables toward the far side of the tent. Most of the people had congregated near the bar and the appetizer spread, giving them a little space to talk.

Before they reached their table, he stopped and faced her, keeping his volume low and hoping the music—the quartet was playing "La Vie En Rose"—would keep anyone from overhearing. "I think we should go talk to Tucker," he said. "Introduce ourselves and give him the flash drive. Maybe if we talk to him personally, he'll prioritize it."

She glanced toward the table where Tucker was seated, alone. "You should do it."

He backed up a step. "Alone? Why?"

"One of us needs to be looking for Freddy. You're determined to be a part of this, right?" At his nod, she continued. "You have much bigger career goals than I do. Maybe his knowing who you are can shield you from backlash. It can't hurt."

She was right. But did she really trust him to go without her?

She gripped his forearm, the pressure light and warm. "Go, Tate. If I see Freddy, I'll call you."

"Don't leave the tent."

"Nothing's going to happen. I think we're safe. If we start to get nervous, we can call in the cavalry." Misty dropped her hand from his arm but smiled, the expression open and honest. As unkind as he'd been to her, she was still going out of her way to be nice.

Maybe he could let go of his grudge. Maybe she'd been punished enough.

As she walked away, that last thought swirled in his middle.

Had he been *punishing* her?

More than once he'd told her he forgave her, which obviously wasn't true. Instead, he'd been cruel and distant, distrusting and angry. All in an effort to...

To punish. To hurt.

Making his way toward Tucker's table, he faced the truth. Who did he think he was? What gave him the right to hold a grudge, to punish anybody?

He was behaving just like his father.

Dad hadn't wanted to help Hannah because he thought she deserved whatever she got for her poor choices.

As if Dad had the right to mete out Hannah's punishment.

As if Tate had the right to mete out Misty's.

Just days before, he'd argued in favor of mercy over judgment. Easy to say when he wasn't the wronged party. But when he was, he fell hard on the side of judgment.

What a fool.

First chance he got, he'd apologize.

And then maybe, if she was willing, they could pick up where they'd left off the day before. The thought seemed to fill him like helium. Or maybe it was letting go of his anger that lightened his mood.

Tucker was seated alone at a table near the stage, phone pressed to his ear.

Tate stopped in the attorney general's sightline but far enough away not to eavesdrop on his conversation. He caught Tucker's eye and smiled.

The man nodded. A moment later, he stood and stowed his cell phone. He waved Tate over. "Have we met?"

"No, sir. Tate Steele. I'm a prosecutor in Suffolk." They shook hands.

"Any relation to Theodore Steele?"

"He's my dad."

"I see the resemblance."

Tate had always been happy to be compared to his father. He wanted to be like him—and was in many ways. But he needed to overcome the bad things Dad had passed on and embrace the good.

Tucker motioned to the chair beside his and sat again. "My wife's gone to get us some food. What can I do for you?"

Tate took the chair, pulling a flash drive out of his inside jacket pocket. "I'd like you to take a look at this. I'll be forwarding the information to the FBI and the press first thing in the morning, but I thought you'd want to see it first."

Tucker took it and slipped it in his own pocket. "Go ahead and spoil the surprise."

"It's about Hawthmarks and International Aid Foundation."

The man looked around at the apartment building and the beautiful grounds surrounding them. "You can't tell me you have a problem with this place. It's amazing."

"It is, I agree. But I have reason to believe Hawthmarks has funneled funds away from IAF for its own purposes."

Tucker's eyes narrowed. "Clark Humphrey is an old friend of mine. Are you suggesting he's doing something illegal?"

"I'm suggesting there needs to be an investigation. Maybe Clark isn't aware of what's going on. I hope Leland isn't. He's my boss, and I have great respect for him."

Speaking of... from the corner of his eye, Tate caught sight of Leland Humphrey. He didn't want to have to explain what he was doing talking to the AG, not yet.

The enormity of what he was doing pressed in on him. Tried to steal his breath. His courage.

It was the right thing, even if it terrified him.

He stood. "Just look at the information, sir. The people this place is supposed to help deserve that."

Before Tucker could answer, Tate moved away, careful to keep his back to Leland.

When this was over, whether Leland had seen him or not wouldn't matter. Either way, he'd likely just forfeited his career.

CHAPTER THIRTY-EIGHT

Misty filled a small plate with nibbles, grabbed a glass of water, and headed for their table. It was empty except for a heavyset redheaded woman who seemed to be adjusting her pantyhose.

As Misty got closer, she slowed. Surely, it wasn't...

The woman looked up, and Misty plastered on a smile. "Ruth. How nice to see you."

The woman practically beamed. "I saw your name on the table assignment...thing, and I couldn't believe it! What are the chances we'd both be here and sitting together?"

Of all the bad luck. Except, maybe it wasn't. Ruth was annoying, sure. But she was also a reporter. Ruth had been pestering her to give her a story for months. Now she had one to share.

She settled into the chair beside her neighbor, setting the plate of appetizers between them. "Help yourself. I got more than I can eat."

"Ooh, thanks." She plucked a stuffed mushroom and ate it in one bite. "Yum." What are you doing here?"

"I came to support Hearts and Homes. Same as you, I assume."

"Not me," Ruth said. "The paper sent me. Puff piece, you know, dedicating their new rec center to the woman who died."

"Are they? I hadn't heard."

"The Jemilla Amin Recreational Facility." She grabbed another snack off Misty's plate. "I figure after a while everyone'll just call it the JAR."

"You may be right."

"You here with that hottie from last weekend?"

"Tate's here, but we're not together."

Ruth smirked. "Married, huh? The good ones always are."

"Not married." She didn't feel compelled to explain her relationship with Tate, especially considering she barely knew how to define it herself. "I assumed this table would be for people who worked at the construction company. They gave me the tickets." Misty looked around as if searching for Thornebrook employees. Not that she'd recognize any of them.

Maybe Freddy had changed his mind about showing up tonight. He didn't have a ticket, so he'd need to find a way onto the property without being seen. Summer and the guys were out there, hoping to stop him. But the grounds were huge, and woods beyond the horse paddock and soccer field were thick and deep. He could slip by them.

"Police figure out who broke into your apartment?" Ruth asked

Misty forced her attention back. "They have some theories."

"Yeah? Like?"

"I can't say."

"Related to the kidnapping, though, right? I mean, it has to be."

"No." Ruth's obsession with Misty's kidnapping hadn't

abated. "We think maybe it was related to one of my cases, but like I said, they're just theories right now."

"Which case?" Her bright eyes were eager. "There's a story? I'd love to hear it."

She almost didn't want to reward Ruth's nosiness. "I might have a story for you. It's about this place."

Her eyes widened. "Yeah? What about it?"

"Can I contact you tomorrow?"

"What's wrong with now? I'd much rather report a conspiracy than turn in a dull human-interest piece. What'cha got? Just the high points, give me something to look forward to."

"Tomorrow, I promise." Misty stood, scanning the crowd for Freddy. Still no sign of him.

She did see Tate, halfway across the tent chatting with a woman. A very attractive woman.

Misty quickly looked away. He'd made it clear he wasn't interested in her. It wasn't as if this were a date, though it was supposed to look like one.

She gazed toward the entrance, then the twilight evening beyond the tent. Maybe Freddy was out there, waiting for the dark, watching. Maybe if she made herself evident, he'd find her.

She picked up her bag. "I'm going to find the restroom."

Ruth popped up. "I'll take you. I know where it is."

Of course she did. Misty sent Tate a quick text telling him where she was going, then followed Ruth. He'd told her not to leave the tent, but there were people moving between the tent and the rec center on the path outlined with lights strung from poles. It would be safe.

On her way to the exit, she caught one of the guards watching her walk away.

Ruth might be a little annoying, but Misty was thankful she was there. There was no way Dawson and his men could know what she and Tate had learned. Still, she didn't want to run into any of them alone in the dark.

The sun had sunk below the trees, and it took her eyes a moment to adjust to the lower light after the brightness beneath the tent. A breeze blew across her skin and raised goose bumps. She rubbed her hands on her upper arms to warm them.

"Shouldn't need a jacket in August, but it's gonna get chilly." Ruth's voice was too loud in the night, and a few guests milling on the lawn turned their way.

Misty kept her head down, wishing she'd worn something different. She didn't own much formal attire. She'd bought the shimmery gown for a friend's wedding the summer before. It had seemed perfect for a summer party, but it stood out against all the tuxedos and little black dresses. She felt as flashy as a disco ball.

If nothing else, if Freddy was out there, he'd see her. That was the point of this little jaunt.

Ruth yanked open the door, and they stepped into a brightly lit hallway.

Misty inhaled the scent of new construction—fresh lumber and some rubbery chemical scent. Ahead, a bunch of women stood in line outside the bathroom, their chatter echoing off the walls.

"Well, darn." Ruth grabbed Misty's hand. "There's another one this way." She tugged Misty around a corner and down a long hallway lined with doors on both sides. The lights and sounds of people faded behind them.

"Are you sure we're supposed to be here?" Misty kept her voice low. She'd never been much of a rule-breaker.

"It's not blocked off or anything," Ruth said. As if that was implied permission.

Far away, a door slammed, the sound sending adrenaline to Misty's veins.

"I think I'll go back." She tugged to free her hand from Ruth's grip, but the older woman held firm.

"What are you, spooked?" She laughed. "That kidnapping really did a number on you. I bet you get nervous in all sorts of normal situations. You were snatched right off the street, right? What was it like?"

Resigned to wander the dark building, Misty said, "I'm not going to talk about the kidnapping."

"It'd be a great story."

They entered a large open area lit only by red exit signs over the doors. It was a gym, basketball hoops on each end. On her right, windows showed off an exercise room complete with high-end machines and weight benches. In the darkness, she caught movement and gasped.

But she was only seeing her reflection in the mirrors on the back wall.

"Not a bad life for a refugee, eh?" Ruth said. "They got a better workout setup than we do."

"Considering everything they've endured to get here, I don't begrudge them the space."

Ruth shot her a look. "Oh, me either. I'm just saying." She took a few steps without explaining what exactly she was saying. "I got the full tour earlier, you know—the perks of being with the press. The locker room's right up here. So, what's the scoop on this place? Is it about the people? Lots of Muslims, I hear. I worry they're letting in terrorists or something."

"Nothing like that." The more Ruth talked, the less Misty wanted to give her the story. Surely she could find somebody less offensive to work with.

"Corruption, then? Somebody stealing?"

They angled across the court toward a door on the far end. "I'll send you all the information tomorrow. I don't want anything to slip out tonight."

Ruth came to a quick stop and swiveled to face her. "Why? You scared of something?" She leaned in close. "Or someone? You should tell me, in case they get to you. It's good to have a backup plan."

"Nothing like that." Misty's heart pounded. She hadn't even needed to go to the bathroom. She'd only wanted to show herself to Freddy, give him an opportunity to find her before he did anything stupid.

Tate would be furious if he found out where she was. Nearly all alone in an abandoned gym. She might as well have painted a target on her back.

Despite the anger he'd directed at her during the drive, he seemed to care what happened to her.

"Yeah, you're scared of someone," Ruth said. "You can tell me all about it tomorrow." She continued to the locker-room door, her footsteps thumping—a contrast to the tapping of Misty's stilettos. "If you change your mind and wanna tell someone tonight, I'm your woman." She pulled the door open and stepped aside to let Misty enter.

It was pitch black. Misty groped for a light switch.

A hand snaked around her arm and tugged her inside.

"Well, well, well." The man's voice was too close, low and terrifying. "What have we here?"

Misty gasped.

Behind her, the door slammed closed.

Ruth's footsteps thumped away.

CHAPTER THIRTY-NINE

Tate scanned the lawn between the tent and the rec center where he'd been told the restrooms were.

Surely Misty would return any minute. But there was no sign of her.

If he'd been paying better attention, he'd have noticed when she left. But the wife of one of his father's partners had pulled him into a conversation, and he hadn't felt like he could slip away.

Where was she?

It'd been ten minutes since she'd texted.

Could it really take so long to use the bathroom? Maybe there was a line. He'd seen a lot of women returning, so that seemed like a good guess.

Still.

He'd introduced himself to the people at his table, employees of Thornebrook. Down-to-earth folks who wore ill-fitting suits and sipped from cold bottles of beer, telling jokes and remarking on the open bar as if it were the highlight of their summer.

He'd described Misty when he'd joined them—tall, blond,

and gorgeous in a shimmery blue dress. Though a few of them had noticed her, none had seen her in a while.

He wouldn't relax until he knew she was safe. He excused himself and walked to the tent entrance, where the crowd had thinned, most of the guests already at their tables.

The music faded as he reached the rec center and pulled open the door.

A woman startled on the opposite side. Short, stocky, red hair.

"'Scuse me." She stepped past him.

"Wait. It's Ruth, right?"

"Oh, hi. You're Misty's friend."

He stuck out his hand. "Tate Steele. Have you seen her?"

"She was in the bathroom, but she went back to the party already."

"Are you sure?" He glanced that way, peering toward their table. There was no sign of her.

"I didn't watch her leave or anything." Ruth looked as well. "Isn't that her, on the far side?"

He tried to see what she did, but there was nobody who looked remotely like Misty. "I'll just check inside."

"Suit yourself." Ruth ambled back toward the tent.

Tate stepped into an empty hallway and stood outside the ladies' room, waiting for someone to come out.

A minute or so later, a middle-aged woman did.

"Would you do me a favor?" he asked.

"Depends, I guess."

"See if there's a woman named Misty in there."

"Sorry, hon. The bathroom's empty."

"You sure? Would you mind checking?"

The woman entered the bathroom and called, "Misty?" The single word echoed loudly.

A second later, she returned. "Like I said, empty. She's

probably back at the party. I think they're about to start serving." She headed for the door, leaving him standing in the too bright corridor, alone.

Now what?

He'd texted Misty twice already. Called her a couple of times too. He dialed her number again.

The call rang four times and then went to voicemail. She'd told him she unblocked his number, but maybe she hadn't.

She was probably fine. There was no reason to think she wasn't fine. But his heart was racing as if it knew better.

He dialed a different number, thankful he'd committed it to memory. Summer answered with, "You find Freddy?"

"No. I lost your sister."

"What? How?"

He gave Summer a rundown. "She texted fifteen minutes ago. I'm at the bathroom, but it's empty."

"Okay. Hold on." Her pause lasted thirty interminable seconds. "I got her location. Looks like she's in the rec center."

"So am I. Can you see where?"

"North side—side farthest from the tent. This locator thing isn't a perfect science, so keep your eyes open."

Tate started down a hallway.

"Let me know when you find her," Summer said. "If you need our help, we'll come in. And answer the phone if I call. If you don't, I'll assume something's wrong."

"I will. Thanks."

"Share your location with me, in case we lose you too."

"Will do." Tate ended the call and shared his location with Summer as he walked.

The building was empty, his footsteps echoing against the walls. He strained to hear talking or movement or anything, but there was only silence.

The farther he walked, the darker it got. He turned on his phone's flashlight and followed it into a gym.

"Misty?"

His call seemed to get louder as it echoed.

He could have sworn he heard a door closing far away. But it was impossible to tell where the sound had come from.

He wasn't even sure he'd heard it.

He checked a workout room on his right. Empty. Then a couple of offices beyond that.

Locked, but a glance through the windows in the doors showed them empty as well, unless Misty was hiding behind a desk.

He seriously doubted that.

She had to be here somewhere.

The lockers were on the far end. He knocked on the ladies' locker-room door.

No answer.

He opened it to pitch black. "Misty?"

Silence.

He found a light switch and flipped it on.

On the floor just ahead was Misty's sparkly little bag.

But she wasn't there.

CHAPTER FORTY

The man had taken Misty's bag from her hand and tossed it. She'd heard it crash against something far away.

Then, he'd searched her, his hands sliding against her dress, her skin.

She'd closed her eyes, doing her best not to recoil from his touch.

"You got a wire? Any more phones?"

"No."

He'd held her arms in a tight grip and spoken inches from her face. "You scream, you die. You fight me, you die. You lie to me, you die."

God help her, she believed him.

"Is there any way for anyone to track you?"

"Just the phone. In my bag."

"Guns? Knives?"

"No." Tears filled her eyes, her voice. She was defenseless. Utterly defenseless. Again.

Keeping a grip on her arm, he opened the locker-room door and pulled her out, then dragged her around the corner, not back the way she'd come but in the other direction. Down a narrow hallway, past an indoor pool, and toward a red glowing exit sign.

He'd just pushed open a heavy metal door when she heard Tate call her name.

In the second it took her to inhale enough air to scream, the man had slapped a meaty hand over her mouth. "You try it, you die."

As if she could yell around his strong grip.

As if she could breathe.

And then they were outside.

He propelled her across the grass. A mist had risen in the cooling air, swirling around her legs.

She stumbled, slipped off one shoe.

The grass was chilly and damp against her bare foot. She was cold, but she'd been colder.

Swimming in the Atlantic in May had been colder.

But when Grant had thrown her off the yacht into the water, she'd been on her way to safety. Unlike now.

Now she was on her way to...what? What did this man want with her?

She stumbled again, slipped off the other shoe. Her captor didn't notice.

Paltry breadcrumbs, but maybe somebody would find them.

Though she knew there was a gathering on the far side of the rec center, she couldn't see the tent. She couldn't hear the people. Only the faint strains of the stringed instruments reached her, too low to even recognize the tune.

If she screamed, would anybody hear her?

Would it matter, if she was dead before they found her?

This couldn't be happening again. It couldn't.

All the years Misty had spent in college and law school, learning to put bad guys behind bars, and this would be the result? She should have gone into business with Summer. She should have learned to defend herself.

She'd kill to have Summer's skills right now.

Then at least she'd have a chance to fight this man off.

Did Summer and Grant and Jon see what was happening?

Probably not.

Tate and Misty were supposed to watch the area near the buildings. The bodyguards were patrolling the outside edge of the property, the far side of the forest.

Nobody would see her.

The man moved her toward the woods. In the darkness, the thick tangle of branches and leaves hovered like the edge of the world. The thought of being forced among them raised fresh panic as she imagined limbs grabbing, needles stabbing.

But when the man reached the tree line, he didn't urge her in but crept in the shadow along the boundary.

Toward the horse paddock. Was he taking her to the barn?

It was just a smudge against the backdrop of the forest. No lights shone from within. There weren't that many outbuildings on this property. If they went to the barn, surely somebody would find them.

They reached it but skirted around the back to the far side.

And then, he tugged her toward the woods.

She couldn't go in there. She couldn't. She'd die in there.

She fought, tried to pull away. "No. Please." Her voice was low. She tried to get volume, but terror filled her throat, strangling the sound.

The man towed her forward. "You won't like it if I have to carry you."

Her mind flashed to memories of the kidnappings.

It was a tumbledown shack in Mexico.

It was the bowels of a yacht owned by a killer.

"I can't go in there."

But the man yanked her into the darkness.

Dead leaves and twigs dug into the soles of her feet. They were on a narrow path, heading toward an abyss.

But the darkness she saw ahead morphed and took shape. An old shed.

The man pulled open a door that creaked on ancient hinges and pushed her inside.

She'd expected darkness, but a faint light glowed from a lantern set on a table against the far wall.

Another man moved in the shadows. "Did anybody see you?"

"No, but somebody was calling for her." He shoved her forward.

She stumbled, righted herself, and faced the man in charge.

"Misty Lake, in the flesh." In the dim light, she caught sight of his face. He was not as tall as she, not even as tall as Freddy. Maybe five-seven. Built, but not overly so, with narrow shoulders and a trim waist. Short dark hair, a long nose. His features were delicate, almost feminine.

She'd only seen a photograph of him. But she had a guess. "Raul Dawson. Nice to meet you in person."

He didn't seem surprised at the use of his name. "I'm sure it's the highlight of your night. Have a seat."

The cramped space was filled with rotting lumber and rusty tools.

There was a single chair, and she had the feeling it'd been set there just for her. She sat.

"Tie her hands and feet," Dawson said.

The other man crouched in front of her, then looked up. "What happened to your shoes?"

"I left them inside. They're not exactly easy to walk in."

It was hard to see his face with his back to the light, but maybe she saw worry there. Maybe he realized what she'd done.

Would he tell Dawson? Would Dawson be angry? Or send this man to find them?

She held her breath, but the man said nothing as he wrapped nylon rope around her ankles and tied them together.

She didn't fight him as he moved on to her hands, which he tied in front of her. A small blessing.

He returned to the doorway, and Dawson stepped closer. Standing over her, he tapped the flat of a short dagger against his palm. "I need you to tell me everything you've learned and everyone you've told."

"About what?"

He bent closer. "Tell you what. I'll be straight with you, and you be straight with me, okay?"

He seemed to be waiting for a response, so she nodded.

This man and Freddy Parks had once been best friends. Same age, roughly the same height. But Dawson, though he spoke with a similar accent, didn't use the same speech patterns as Freddy. He spoke like someone educated. She'd expected him to be a low-level thug, but she'd been wrong.

This man came off as smart and capable. It would take maneuvering to outwit Dawson, and she had little time to figure out how to do it.

"I don't like games, Misty. You know what I want to know. Talk."

"All right." She needed to stall. Tate was looking for her. By now, Summer, Jon, and Grant as well. The police were probably on their way. Would they find this little abandoned building in time?

The longer she kept Dawson talking, the better. Tate had told her to play dumb. She could do that. "You offered a bribe to Zachary Hardy in the city permitting office. He didn't accept it and turned you in. You were arrested and charged with bribery. I don't know if your lawyer told you, but I called her on Friday to try to work out a plea deal. She hasn't returned my call. When she does, despite all this"—Misty let her gaze skim the space—"the deal will still be on the table. Three years, suspended sentence, with community service. Of course, she'll negotiate that down. She'll probably ask for one year suspended, no service. I'll agree, and this'll all be over." She extended her hands. "Assuming, of course, you untie me and let me go."

He looked from her face to her hands and back, no amusement in his expression. "Keep going."

"Our boss..." She lowered her hands to her lap. "Leland, the DA, pressured me to drop the case. Because the company you work for, Thornebrook, is a subsidiary of his family's corporation, he was afraid it would blow back on them. But I'm not going to pursue that. I mean, I don't want to lose my job."

"And?"

"It's awful the way people use their positions to garner favors. I never thought Leland would do it. I'm disgusted. But in this case, you're the recipient of the favor. You'll be off the hook. You just have to let me go." Again, she lifted her hands as if he might use the knife to cut her loose.

Praying, praying...

He shifted the blade to his left hand.

And backhanded her.

The pain, sharp and shocking.

She tumbled off the chair and landed on the hard wooden floor, banging her head. Her face stung and she tasted blood.

She spit it on the floor. Evidence for later. Assuming they moved her body after they killed her. Assuming the police wouldn't find it right there beside a pathetic little drop of blood.

"Pick her up."

No, no. She wanted to stay on the floor, curled up. To hide. To close her eyes and pray and sob.

But strong hands lifted her and set her on the chair.

"It didn't have to come to this," Dawson said. "All we wanted was to find Freddy. If you'd stayed in your apartment, eventually, he would have contacted you. You two could have set up a meeting, we'd have been there and taken him out. None of this would have happened."

There was little celebration in knowing their theories had been correct.

"It wasn't you who planted the bug, though. Right?" The man in the video had been larger than Dawson.

"No." He tipped his chin toward the other man. "Mackie did it. He's great with electronics." He turned to the guard. "Wait outside. Let me know if anybody comes."

Mackie nodded and slipped out the door.

"How did you get into my apartment?" Misty asked.

"Oh, that was all me. Made nice with your neighbor. You think she can afford to live in that building on a reporter's salary? Turns out Ruth has a rap sheet. Grand larceny. She claimed her husband was the mastermind. He went to prison, and she got off with a slap on the wrist. I offered her money to get me your key code. All she had to do was watch you use it. Getting her help tonight cost me a lot more, but nobody'll ever know she led you to me."

Betrayed by her neighbor.

"Where is Freddy?"

Who? That would be the play-dumb answer. But the word lodged in her throat, silenced by the pain still throbbing in her head, her cheek. "I don't know."

"But you have seen him?"

Lie or tell the truth? She didn't know what to do. Couldn't think.

Dawson bent close. He pressed the flat of his blade against her burning cheek. The cold metal felt strangely soothing. What would the edge feel like as it sliced into her skin?

"It's a simple question, Misty," Dawson said. "Have you seen Freddy Parks?"

"Yes."

"Where is he?"

"I don't know. We met him last night, but he wouldn't tell us where he was staying."

"Who is 'we'?"

She hadn't meant to say that. "A friend of mine was with me. It doesn't matter."

"Matters to me, very much. Any chance that friend is Tate Steele?"

She couldn't answer. Wouldn't answer. She closed her eyes, waited for retribution.

The knife was lifted off her cheek.

A sudden blow to her stomach. She doubled over.

When she opened her eyes, she expected to see blood gushing from her middle. But he hadn't stabbed her. He'd punched her.

"Look at me." His fingers gripped her chin and lifted it. She had no choice but to stare into his eyes. "Where is Freddy?"

She gasped for breath. It was a moment before she managed, "I don't know."

She cringed, waiting for another blow.

But Dawson stood and paced. He checked his phone. He paced some more. "What do you know, and who have you told?"

"About you?" Her voice rose, pitching high. Her whole body trembled. "Besides the bribery, there's nothing. The charges are going to be dropped."

He waited.

"I learned about Hawthmarks and IAF. But except for the bribery, none of that has anything to do with you."

"Now we're getting somewhere." He smiled, the expression terrible beneath cold, empty eyes.

Misty had no good options. Refusing to tell him everything would invite more pain. But the faster she spilled what she knew, the sooner death would come.

She didn't know much about God. She hadn't spent nearly enough time learning about Him since she'd become a believer. Now, she prayed that everything Summer had told her was true. That the God she'd put her trust in existed. That He was there and saw what was happening. That He could be counted on.

CHAPTER FORTY-ONE

After calling Summer to tell her he'd found Misty's purse and phone in the locker, Tate searched the rec center, opening doors and yelling her name. Frantic.

The building was empty.

He was standing in the middle of the basketball court, trying to figure out what to do next.

Soon, the police would arrive. Summer, Jon, and Grant were already trying to get onto the grounds. They'd alert the security guards. But did the security guards work for Dawson? Would they help? Or warn Dawson? Maybe even do their best to misdirect the searchers?

Alerting the guards felt like the wrong play.

He had to find Misty. Now.

The thought of her in Dawson's hands...

Think, Steele.

Dawson wouldn't take her into the refugee house. Too many people.

Summer had said Grant would watch the driveway. If Dawson tried to leave the grounds with her, surely he'd stop him.

Unless there was another way off the property.

Which there probably was. A back road. A path.

All those woods.

She was back there, somewhere. Had to be.

He bolted down the hallway, past the swimming pool, and outside. He stopped as the door slammed behind him.

Fog had settled over the valley, obscuring the grounds, the woods. Hiding her, but maybe also hiding him.

He walked toward the forest, looking for footprints. Something. But it was dark.

And then, something sparkly caught his eye.

One of Misty's shoes.

He left it, texted Summer.

> Behind the rec center, headed toward the woods and ran across her shoe. On the right track.

He made sure his phone was muted, then stuck it in his pocket. Felt the answering vibration. She'd seen.

Nearly to the forest's edge, he found Misty's other shoe.

He stopped and listened.

Only heard the distant sound of the quartet.

No noises closer. He peered through the trees. No sign of her. Of anything. Had they gone that way?

To the left, the grass stretched for a couple hundred yards.

To the right, the horse paddock and stable.

He took out his phone and started another text.

> Which way should I search?

Summer responded quickly.

> I'm on the west. Jon's coming from the north.
> Go east.

Couldn't she just tell him left or right?

Summer had said the north end of the building was farthest from the party, which meant Jon was coming through the woods in front of him.

He turned to the right.

While he walked, he tapped.

> Going toward the horses.

Misty hadn't left any more signs that she'd been there.

Ahead, he barely made out the fence that surrounded the paddock.

When he reached the barn, he nudged the door to the side and slipped in. Empty. Silent. The scents of hay and horses hit him.

He searched each stall, ignoring the horses' eyes that followed his movements through the darkness.

She wasn't here.

He stifled a curse word, texted,

> Barn's empty.

Got a thumbs-up.

He slipped out the back, doing his best to move quietly. Stood there a long moment, praying, praying. Listening to the night sounds—chirping crickets, buzzing insects, croaking frogs.

And then he heard something else.

Voices?

Or he was hearing things?

He saw a very narrow trail...maybe a trail. Maybe just wishful thinking.

He followed it, moving silently, slowly.

The noises took form. A man's voice.

A woman's voice.

Misty!

He pulled his phone out, tapped the keyboard. *She's in the woods behind...*

A sharp jab to his elbow. The phone flew out of his hand.

An arm snaked around his neck, squeezing.

Tate fought to get free, but the arm wouldn't budge. Stars filled his vision, made him lightheaded.

Nearby, branches rustled, the snapping of twigs. Someone was coming. He prayed it was Jon or Summer or Grant or police or anyone who could help.

A blow to his head killed the hope.

Disoriented, he stopped fighting. He needed to stay conscious—and alive.

The two men dragged him forward. A door creaked.

He was shoved inside.

He lost his balance, landing on his knees on a hard, wooden floor.

"Nice of you to join us, Tate." The man jabbed at Tate's side with his foot. "Sit up."

He did, blinking in the dim light.

A third man stood over him, looking down, a dagger in his hand. He'd seen Dawson's photo enough to know it was him.

Misty was seated, eyes wide and terrified.

Dawson flicked his gaze toward the door. "You got his phone?"

"Powered it down," the thug said.

"Crush it, just in case."

The sound of glass and metal being ground to dust made

Tate sick to his stomach. That was Summer's only way of tracking him. Would she notice the phone was off? How long would it take before she realized he was no longer communicating?

Would they be found in time?

He couldn't tear his gaze away from Misty. A red stain on her chin told him she'd been bleeding. One of her eyes was swelling. This man had harmed her. Hurt her.

Fury and hopelessness rolled over him in bitter waves. He couldn't let them show. Couldn't let them stop him from thinking straight. "It's okay, sweetheart. It's going to be okay."

Tears coursed down her cheeks. "I'm sorry, Tate. I'm so sorry you got dragged into this."

"Touching." Dawson turned his back to Tate as if he barely mattered. A gun stuck out from the waistband of his jeans. Probably not the only gun in the room. "Mackie, tie him up."

One of the thugs yanked his hands at his waist and tied his wrists together. Then moved on to his ankles, pulling the rope so tight he feared he'd lose circulation in his feet.

"Put him on the floor next to his girlfriend."

Mackie did, propping his back against the wall beside Misty's chair.

The other guard said, "I'll be outside." The door closed softly behind him.

"All right," Dawson said. "Misty seemed reluctant to fill me in on everything you two learned about Hawthmarks and IAF."

From his perspective—below and slightly behind her—Tate wouldn't be able to meet her eyes unless she turned toward him. Which she wouldn't, not with Dawson so close.

"We might as well tell them everything," Tate said. "The AG has the information now. By morning, every news outlet in Boston will. And the FBI, of course."

Dawson crouched in front of Tate. "Here's how it's going to

work. You're going to tell me what I want to know. If I think you're lying or being coy, I'm going to hurt her. Let me demonstrate."

"No need for that," Tate said quickly.

Dawson shrugged, his smile cruel as he leaned over Misty. "Let's see. What shall I do?"

"I'll tell you anything you want to know. Just don't hurt her."

"Hmm..." Dawson leaned in close to Misty, inhaling her scent as if anticipating a perfectly cooked steak.

Tate didn't see what he did next, but Misty gasped.

"Leave her alone!"

"I never understood Freddy's penchant for violence. Always sort of looked down on him for that. It was useful, of course, even if a little sick. But then, with Cofer... I have to admit, there's something satisfying about that gasp of pain." Dawson stepped back. "But we made a deal. You talk, and I don't hurt her."

"Whatever you want to know."

"Where's Freddy?"

"Here, I think."

Dawson's eyebrows lifted. "Here as in—?"

"He told us he was coming tonight. His plan is to tell everybody the truth, loudly. We told him we'd take what we learned to the authorities, but he thinks the Humphrey family will wiggle out of charges. Money and power..." Tate took a breath. Slowed down. No need to rush through this. "He thinks, because Leland Humphrey is the DA, he'll find a way to protect his family."

"Almost smart," Dawson said. "Just like Freddy to think things seventy percent through. Because of course, as soon as he starts talking, he's going to get arrested for killing his lawyer."

"That's why Misty and I are here. To stop him."

"I see."

"But when Misty disappeared, I left to find her. Who knows what's happening at the party. For all we know, Freddy's already spilled the beans to everyone."

"Ah," Dawson said. "That would be bad."

"It doesn't matter what he says or if he shows up," Tate said. "We put all the information on flash drives. I gave one to the attorney general tonight. The people we're working with will send them to the FBI tomorrow, and the press."

"What information exactly?"

Tate told him everything they'd uncovered, about the Boston building that was supposed to be housing for refugees but was really a posh office for IAF and Hawthmarks. He told him about the misused grant money, the attempted bribery of Zachary Hardy. The assault on Ernie Phillips, which led to Jemilla Amin's death. He told him about Lela Parks's assault and subsequent heart attack. He told him about Jeffrey Cofer's murder, and how it all tied together.

"You thought Cofer could tell you where Freddy was," Tate said, "but he didn't know. Freddy didn't tell him, just like he wouldn't tell us. You killed a man for no reason."

Dawson shrugged as if the man's life didn't matter at all. "Evidence?"

While Dawson paced, Tate laid out everything they knew and everything they could prove.

"So you see," Tate said, "they already know what you did. If you kill us, you'll just add to the crimes they'll charge you with."

Dawson stopped and looked down at him.

The smile spreading across his face told Tate more than words could. He'd miscalculated. He didn't know how, but he had, and his mistake would cost Misty her life.

"None of your evidence points to me," Dawson said. "Somebody beat up Lela Parks, but it wasn't me. Somebody paid

Freddy to assault Ernie Whatshisname, but it wasn't me. Somebody murdered Jeffrey Cofer." He pressed both hands to his chest. "But it wasn't me."

"They're smarter than you think, Dawson. They'll figure it out."

"Oh, I don't care what they figure out. I care what they can prove. With you two out of the picture, I'll just need to shut Freddy up."

"You'd kill your old friend so easily."

For the first time, real emotion flashed in his eyes. "He betrayed me first. He started it. I'm going to end it."

"Killing his sister wasn't enough?"

"That was an accident. I always liked Lela."

As if this man could feel genuine affection for anyone.

Had he always been a psychopath, or had he simply committed so many crimes, so much evil, that his conscience had been seared beyond repair?

"You won't get away with any of it." Tate was desperate to stretch this out. Someone would come. Someone had to come. "You think the Humphreys won't take you down with them? They will. They'll turn on you and toss you away like trash."

Dawson laughed. "Damien has a wife and kids. He knows what I'm capable of. He'll keep his mouth shut."

Tate shifted his gaze to Mackie, who stood by the door. "You think you're safe? You think, when the authorities come to question Dawson—and they will, mark my words—he won't turn on you? Use your head, Mackie. Freddy Parks was his best friend, and he's planning to kill him. Already killed his sister."

The guard's gaze flicked from Tate to Dawson and back.

"Don't bother. Mackie knows where my loyalties lie."

"With yourself." Tate's voice was cold. "People like you never care about anybody else. You don't care who you destroy."

Dawson started toward him. He braced himself for the coming blow.

But the man stopped in front of Misty. "Looks like you and I are gonna have some fun."

"Leave her alone!" His shout seemed to get absorbed by the ancient wooden walls. But he'd heard their voices from the barn. Maybe somebody else would hear.

God, send help. Please!

Dawson didn't look away from Misty. "Take him into the woods and kill him. When you come back, wait outside."

Mackie pulled a hunting knife from a sheath on his calf and sliced through the rope holding Tate's feet together.

Tate leaned close, lowered his voice. "Don't do this."

But Mackie yanked him up, nearly dislocating his shoulder.

"Dawson." Tate turned to the man holding all the cards. "You don't need to do this. Come on. We can work something out. We can give you time to get away."

Mackie pulled Tate toward the door.

Dawson ignored him, looking at Misty like a tiger its prey.

"Sweetheart, I'm sorry. I love you."

He didn't know where the words came from, only that they were true. What he felt for her could have grown into a forever kind of love.

Instead, it would blow away like the mist in the valley. Here and gone before it made any difference at all.

Hers eyes filled with tears. "I love you."

Three words he'd hold onto until his last breath, no matter how soon it came.

∼

The chill seeped through Tate's tuxedo jacket, but he didn't mind. Didn't mind the smell of the forest as he was pushed through it. Didn't mind the breeze that blew across his skin.

He didn't even mind the sharp jab of the gun pressing against his back.

It was life, to feel.

How had he never noticed the simple blessings of breathing moist air? His heart sped, maybe trying to beat as much as possible before it stopped.

Tate wasn't afraid to die. He wasn't *that* afraid to die, anyway. He knew where he was going.

And Misty knew God. She was His. She'd be with Him in paradise.

But what would she have to endure between now and then? He'd have done anything, said anything, suffered anything to protect her.

He'd failed.

In that, he was glad he was about to breathe his last. He wouldn't be able to live with how thoroughly he'd screwed everything up.

"You don't have to do this," Tate said.

"You heard what he said about Humphrey's family. I got a wife and kids too. I seen what it looks like to be on Raul's dark side."

"So take him down."

Mackie said nothing.

"You really think you're going to wiggle out of this? It's one thing to be his accomplice, but what you're doing right now? First-degree murder. It's a life sentence."

"Better that than my family dead."

They walked twenty feet, thirty, deeper into the woods. Any second Mackie would kill him. Would he shoot him in the head?

Tate dreaded the moment. Hoped the dread was worse than the deed.

He prayed for Misty. Prayed Summer and Jon and Grant and the authorities would accomplish what he'd failed to do.

And then, a soft rustling in the forest.

Mackie turned that direction.

Tate used the distraction. He dropped to the ground, grabbed Mackie's wrist and pulled him down.

The guard tumbled on top of him.

Tate rolled onto the arm holding the gun. He was too close, and with his hands bound, couldn't get much power behind a punch.

Mackie struggled to get free, but Tate was in a fight for his life. And Misty's.

He shifted so his back was pressed against the guard's chest and jabbed his elbow into his face. He felt the blow, heard the satisfying crunch of bone. He jabbed again and again.

Mackie quit fighting and instead tried to protect his face with his free arm.

Snapping branches told Tate somebody was coming.

He twisted, snatched the gun out of Mackie's hand, and whacked him on the head with it.

The man's eyes closed. He slumped against the ground, not unconscious but disoriented.

Tate struggled to his knees, his hands still bound, and aimed at the person fumbling through the woods.

Freddy stepped around a tree, lifting his hands. "Dude. I was tryna rescue you."

Tate lowered the gun, pulling in blessed air. He was alive. Somehow.

He scooted away, still panting for breath. "He's got a knife on his—"

"I know where he keeps it." Freddy bent down and took the

hunting knife out of the sheath attached to Mackie's calf. "How's the family?"

Mackie's stream of obscenities came out nasally, thanks to his broken nose.

Freddy loomed over him. "Stay down or I'll down you permanently. You got it?" Not waiting for an answer, he moved to where Tate was still on his knees and sliced through the ropes.

Tate stretched his hands and stood. "He's got rope in his pocket. Can you tie him up?"

"Sure." Freddy crouched again. He pulled out a cell phone and tossed it to Tate.

Tate's hands were shaking, but he managed to dial Summer. She answered instantly.

"Where are you?"

"Misty's in a shack in the woods behind the horse barn. Dawson's gonna kill her. I'm on my way there." Tate ended the call. "Let's go."

"Almost done." Freddy finished tying the goon and stood. "What kind of a man hurts a defenseless woman?"

"Your former best friend."

Misty was in the hands of a psychopath. Tate had to find a way to save her.

CHAPTER FORTY-TWO

Misty figured Raul Dawson liked to savor his meals. He was certainly savoring this moment. Enjoying her terror.

She had plenty of terror for him to feed on. She was living her greatest fears.

She'd left a dangerous criminal on the streets.

And she'd become a captive again.

Two for two.

With Tate and Misty out of the way, unless Damien Humphrey grew a conscience—and she wasn't holding her breath—then the only person who'd be able to bring Dawson down was Freddy. Assuming Dawson didn't find him and kill him first.

Dawson had murdered Jeffrey Cofer. He'd assaulted Lela Parks, which led to her death. He'd ordered the assault that had kept the inspector from reporting the faulty furnace at Hearts and Homes, which resulted in Jemilla Amin's death. And he'd just ordered Tate's murder.

She couldn't think about that.

And any second, he'd take her life. And there was nothing

she could do to stop him. No way to make sure he paid for his crimes.

But whether he did or didn't wasn't up to her. All these years she'd fought to make sure justice was done, she'd failed to understand one important thing.

God was a God of justice. Nobody cared more about justice than He did. And hadn't she read that vengeance was His?

Misty didn't have to fight the justice battle alone. In fact, she didn't have to fight it at all. God had it under control.

Even if she died right here, God would see. He'd repay Dawson—or have mercy on him. She didn't have to decide. His life didn't belong to her. Dawson, like Misty and Tate and every other human on the planet, had been created by God for His purpose.

God could figure out what to do with him.

Misty let go of her need to see justice done. She opened her hands and felt the burden float away, float to the God who'd been handling justice since the beginning of time.

There was still the matter of her death. Hopelessness darkened the edges of her vision, but she pushed it back. Every moment he didn't kill her took her one moment closer to rescue. She had to believe she'd be rescued.

She had to believe Tate would be rescued.

She should have studied her Bible more, should have learned how to pray better. She didn't know if there were right words to say, couldn't even think of prayers beyond the phrase repeating in her mind.

Deliver us from evil.

Only God could do that.

And He would, one way or another. Either He'd deliver them from death, or He'd deliver them through it. Either way, though she was captive in that moment, freedom awaited her.

Dawson knelt at her feet and ran the knife blade up her calf. Gently. If he drew blood, she didn't feel it. "I like the slit."

She wasn't sure what to say to that. He'd run the knife down her arm, down her neck. But he'd yet to cut her. He held a gun in his other hand, but he hadn't threatened her with it.

"Are you afraid?" His voice was smooth.

Hers was ragged. "Yes."

"It's strange how much I enjoy that. Like I feed off your fear. It makes me stronger."

Stronger? The man was a fool. Nobody got stronger by hurting those weaker. The power he felt was counterfeit. Nothing compared to God's power.

Deliver us from evil.

"What's it feel like," he asked, "knowing you're about to die?"

She swallowed the fear clogging her throat. "You're going to die, too, Raul. How do you feel?"

He sat back on his heels. "Oh, no. I'm not going to die, *sweetheart.*"

Tate's term of affection sounded ugly on his tongue.

Deliver us from evil.

"Eventually, we all die. Maybe I'll meet God tonight. I'm not afraid of that. But you'll meet God someday too."

He chuckled. "There is no God. There's power, and there's weakness. And there's pain."

He stabbed her in the leg.

She gasped.

She heard a faraway, "No!"

The door banged open.

A figure burst into the shed.

Dawson dove behind her chair an instant before Freddy could barrel into him.

Another man came through the door. Tate.

Tate!

He froze.

He lifted his hands. He held a gun in one of them. "Don't."

That was when she felt it, cold steel against the soft skin right beside her eye.

"Your men are down," Tate said. "The police know where we are. There's no way out."

"Sure there is. I'm gonna take her with me. Freddy. Cut the rope at her ankles."

"No." Freddy looked determined to stand up to him. "You're just gonna make it harder on yourself. It's over."

"Cut them. Now." He pressed the gun hard into her skull, and she closed her eyes and waited for death.

"Cut them or I'll kill her."

Freddy knelt, his body heat warm near her cold legs.

"You won't get far," Tate said.

"You better hope I do 'cause if I get caught, she dies."

Freddy's hands shook as he sliced through the binding holding her ankles together. He looked up at her. "I'm sorry. I tried to fix it. I tried."

"It's not your fault." Where the calm tone came from, she couldn't have said. But she felt calm. At peace. Whatever happened, happened.

She'd prayed to be delivered from evil, and she would be. "It's going to be okay." She looked at Tate, saw the horror and regret in his eyes. And maybe something else. Something hopeful she didn't try to analyze. "I'm glad you're alive."

He said nothing, just nodded.

Dawson gripped her upper arm, the gun still pressed to her forehead. "Stand up."

She did.

"Inside, Steele. You and Freddy stand by the wall."

When they did, Dawson backed to the door, giving Misty a

long, last look at the man she'd come to love. She held his eye contact. "It's okay. I'm okay."

Dawson's tone was almost cheerful as he called, "See ya," and pulled her into the quiet night.

"Drop the gun!"

The words came from behind.

And then, a gunshot.

Searing pain.

"No!"

Tate's voice echoed.

She crumpled. Everything went dark.

CHAPTER FORTY-THREE

Tate couldn't think past that horrible moment. The gunshot.

He could still hear it.

Still see Misty fall.

The blood.

The horror.

"Hey, stay with me." Detective Reyes shifted into his line of sight. "Get him a blanket. He's in shock."

"I'm not." He tried to push himself off the gurney.

Strong hands held him in place. "Sit tight, sir." The paramedic had already checked him over. He wasn't injured, but they wouldn't let him go.

He needed to see her.

The police had ushered him away from her, across the misty field and back to the circle drive in front of the refugee house. All he'd wanted was to lie down on the ground and join her, but they wouldn't leave him alone.

He was seated on a gurney behind an ambulance, surrounded by emergency personnel, staring toward the little shack in the woods.

Where was she? Why weren't they coming with her? Surely they wouldn't just leave her there, lying on the cold dirt. He anticipated and dreaded that terrible moment when he'd see them carrying her body, covered with a sheet...

A blanket wrapped around him. He felt like a child. Like a small, small child waiting for the adults to tell him what to do.

Misty.

She'd been shot. In the head.

She'd been shot in the head.

He couldn't wrap his mind around it.

He didn't want to.

Again, the detective stepped into his line of sight. "Tate. Is anybody else out there? I need to know what happened. How many were there? Come on, Steele. Live up to your name. For her sake."

He blinked, and the detective's face came into focus. "I only saw three. Dawson, Mackie's the guy in the woods behind the shack, tied up. And the other guy's near the door."

"And Parks," Reyes said. "We got him in custody."

"What?" Tate shook his head, tried to clear it. "No. Freddy rescued me. He tried to rescue Misty."

Tate could still picture the scene.

He and Freddy had gone back to the shack.

Freddy had crept up behind the other guard and whacked him with a big rock. Knocked him out.

While Freddy secured him, Tate saw flashlights coming through the woods. He'd been quiet, not wanting to alert Dawson that they were there. He'd tried to get Freddy's attention, to show him help was on the way.

But the gasp of pain from inside the cabin...

Tate had felt desperate to get in there but knew the authorities would be better equipped.

But Freddy had charged inside.

"So Freddy was going in there to stop him?" Reyes asked.

"Yes, yes. I told you. He saved me. We tried to save..."

Tate couldn't say her name. He couldn't.

Men and women in tuxes and gowns wearing terrified expressions hurried around the building. Young valets handed back keychains and directed them to their cars, parked in a distant field.

It was chaos.

Residents peered through windows at the commotion.

On the far side of the horse paddock, past the barn, silhouettes moved about, lit by the spinning lights on the police cars. One took shape, running. The man bolted around the short fence, toward where Tate sat in the circle drive.

Was that Grant?

He didn't pause, just kept running, down the driveway and out of sight.

Tate looked back to the silhouettes at the edge of the field.

Two paramedics carried a gurney to an ambulance.

Tate needed to see Misty before they took her away. He started to push to his feet, but the EMT's hand on his shoulder kept him in place. "Just a few more minutes until you get your legs back."

He let them hold him there. Weak, too weak to face her. To face them.

A siren screamed in the night. Lights came on, and the ambulance tore away.

Summer bolted after it.

In the driveway, an incoming car pulled over to let the ambulance pass. It tore out of sight.

But the car came closer and did a U-turn.

Summer climbed in.

Go, Tate thought. He didn't want to face her.

He'd never forgive himself.

He dropped his gaze to the pavement. Tears dripped from his eyes, but he didn't care. Misty was worth his tears.

A hand gripped his shoulder. "She's alive."

His gaze snapped up.

It was Jon. Misty's cousin.

"Don't say that." He couldn't handle it, the hope. Wouldn't survive if it wasn't true.

Jon turned to Reyes. "We'll be at the hospital if you have any more questions." He gripped Tate's arm and tugged. "Come on. They're gonna leave without us if we don't hurry."

He ran beside Jon to the sedan and climbed in the back.

Jon slammed the other door, and Grant hit the gas.

As if time mattered.

As if, maybe, maybe Misty's heart was still beating.

CHAPTER FORTY-FOUR

Voices came from far away.
No, just one voice.
Reading familiar words from a treasured story. Henry, Jess, Violet, and Benny. Four orphans creating a life for themselves.

She could picture the abandoned boxcar in the woods. The makeshift home. The siblings alone and lonely, trying to forge their own way. All the while, there was a real home waiting for them.

They just needed the faith to find it.

She drifted in and out. In and out. Listening to the treasured story.

The voice never stopped.

And then, the light pulled her closer.

She wanted to see it. To see him.

It wasn't easy.

It was almost impossible. But she opened her eyes.

And there he was, sitting by her side. A book in his hand. His cheeks moist.

Like he'd been crying.

She wanted to reach for him. Inched her fingers forward until they touched skin.

His words cut off. He looked up. Gasped. Leaned in.

"Tate."

"Are you...? Are you here this time? For real?"

"I think..." Her voice was scratchy. She cleared it. Tried again, "I think so."

He pressed his forehead to hers. "Thank God. Thank God."

He backed away, just far enough that she could see his face. She wanted to lift her hand, to touch his cheek. There were so many things she wanted to say, questions she wanted to ask, but she couldn't find the words. They were swirling in mist, letters and sounds without meaning. When she tried to grasp one, it floated away.

Tate looked past her. "She's awake."

A figure moved on Misty's other side. She shifted that way. Her head pounded, but she couldn't close her eyes against the pain. She wanted to see them.

Summer. And Krystal.

Summer lowered her head to Misty's shoulder and wept.

Krystal gripped Misty's free hand, her own tears falling.

And then there were doctors and nurses and more people and everyone kept saying it was a miracle.

A miracle.

She didn't know what they were talking about, only that she was there, and the people she loved were there, and everybody was okay.

And there were still so many tears.

CHAPTER FORTY-FIVE

Six weeks had passed since that terrifying night.

Misty still struggled to make sense of it, to understand the events that she'd lived through but would probably never remember.

She'd left the rehab facility in Boston and moved in with her sister in Coventry.

Denise had offered Misty a room in the main house with her, but she'd wanted to stay in the cozy guesthouse with Summer. They shared the big king-sized bed, much bigger than the one they'd shared as kids. When nightmares woke her, Summer scooted close and held her, just like she'd done when they were little.

And just like back then, her big sister's presence calmed her.

Last night's terrors dissipated in the sun shining in the late September sky. The place was small but new and beautifully decorated. Fresh air fluttered gauzy white curtains, beckoning them to take advantage of the unseasonably warm day.

In the yard that separated the cottage from the main house, Denise and Jon and a small crowd of friends were preparing for a birthday party. Their voices and laughter carried in on the breeze.

Summer set a bowl filled with grapes and apple slices on the kitchen table and sat across from Misty. "Help yourself."

She plucked a McIntosh wedge and nibbled.

"What are you thinking?" her sister asked.

"How blessed I am to be here."

"Here," Summer asked, "as in the guesthouse, or here as in...alive?"

Misty's gaze took in the space. The small kitchen might not work for a gourmet cook, but it had everything they needed. When four people gathered at the round table, the small eating area was cramped, but in the way that made you feel like you were home. The living area, with its cushy sofa and loveseat, had seen a lot of rom-coms in recent weeks—and probably too much dropped popcorn on the pretty blue-and-white area rug.

"Both. To enjoy the breeze. The world." She caught her sister's eyes. "The people I love."

Summer plucked a grape. "You ready to do this?"

They went over the events of that terrible night every few days. Misty had recovered most of her other memories. Though she still dealt with headaches—and maybe always would—the doctors were astounded at her recovery. Her vision and hearing hadn't been affected. She could take care of herself, cook for herself. Her reflexes were getting better every day. It was only a matter of time before she'd be able to drive again, though she struggled with maps and navigation. Would she get that back? Maybe, maybe not. But there were online maps.

She would be able to live a normal life.

Yes, there were stories of people who survived being shot in the head at point-blank range. Misty wasn't the first, but that didn't make it any less of a miracle.

"You with me?" Summer asked.

That was one thing that lingered, Misty's tendency to drift away. "Yeah."

"So, you were at the party."

"I remember that, the tent and the music. The tuxedos and gowns. I remember going into the new building. I was with a woman. She had red hair, right? Older?"

Summer's smile always surprised Misty, maybe because she'd hidden it for so many years behind that tough veneer. Summer had been through trauma, and look how beautifully she'd emerged. Healthy and whole and happy.

Misty was getting there. "She was my neighbor."

"That's right. Ruth was the one who gave your lock code to...?"

"Raul Dawson."

She recalled the name but couldn't picture the face. Her short-term memory was still...vapory.

"I went with Ruth into the empty building. She took me to the locker room, where the man was waiting for me. Not Dawson, but he took me to Dawson."

She vaguely remembered a cold walk across wet grass.

"There was a shack. He held me there. Tate was there for a little while, but he left."

She struggled to remember why.

"The other man, the good one..." She closed her eyes, tried to grab the name out of the fog. "Freddy. Freddy burst into the shack because he was afraid Dawson was going to kill me. Tate came in behind him. Not because he didn't want to rescue me, though."

She always got confused about this part. Why had Freddy come in first?

Summer didn't say anything, just waited while Misty tried to pull the story from her head. Words wouldn't come, but there was a picture, one that had been described to her more than once. Lights bouncing in the darkness. And then she remembered. "Tate saw that help was coming. He was going to work with you and Jon and the police to rescue me. But Freddy didn't want to?"

"Freddy didn't see them coming. He was afraid for you. He thought he could take Dawson down himself."

"But Dawson used me as a shield." Misty wasn't sorry she couldn't remember this part. The nightmares were bad enough. "He put me between himself and Freddy and Tate and was going to take me with him. But the police told him to stop. And then..."

She didn't like to think about this part.

Summer reached across the small table and took her hand. She didn't rush her or even prompt her, just waited.

"He fired the gun."

She could hear the sound of it in her nightmares, loud and shocking. "The bullet went into my skull." She touched her head. No longer bald, thank God. Her hair was growing back. Still too short, but soon enough, it would cover the scars. "I fell and hit my head. I was unconscious."

Summer was nodding, lips pressed closed.

Misty figured this part was hard for her sister to remember. "Dawson was shot. Multiple times." She figured Summer had fired at least one of those bullets, but she'd never asked. "And then Tate and Freddy were taken away, and you were with me, and you thought I was dead because I was so still, and there was a lot of blood. And then, I moved."

"That's right. And then it was pandemonium." Summer chuckled and swiped tears away. She always cried at this part. "The paramedics wouldn't let me get into the ambulance with you, so Grant drove us to the hospital."

"And Tate, too."

"Yes. We were all crying. Trying to pray. Tate just kept

saying, 'Please, please, please.'" And by the time we got to the hospital, you were in surgery, which took a million years."

"And they couldn't get the bullet out."

"But they relieved the pressure on your brain. And then you slept for two weeks, and we didn't know if you were ever going to wake up." She swiped at tears. "Tate read *The Boxcar Children* a thousand times." She smiled. "I'd forgotten how much you loved that book."

"How could I not? Four orphaned kids trying to find a way to be happy. And they did it."

"They learned they had a family," Summer said. "They just needed to trust."

Voices carried through the windows, and Summer smiled that direction. "Like we've found a family here."

"More than that," Misty said. "We've found our true Father. A good Father."

"Tate read that book so many times, I'm pretty sure I have it memorized." Summer was gently drawing Misty back into the story.

"He hardly left my side."

"Not for more than a few minutes at a time. He refused."

"And then I woke up."

Summer grinned. "That's his favorite part of the story."

"Because I said his name."

A soft knock on the door, and Tate stepped inside, grinning. He crossed the small space and leaned down to kiss Misty on the cheek.

She took his hand and held it, not wanting to let go. It'd been a week since she'd seen him. A long week. He still had his job in Boston, more than two hours away. He still had a life there. But he came up every weekend. They'd spent hours together, walking the trails behind the house, exploring the town in his car, talking about everything and nothing. Sometimes, they were just together, silently.

She'd known she liked him. She'd felt those first stirrings of love. But what she felt for him now was beyond anything she'd expected. The problem was, he lived in Boston, and she never wanted to go back.

But she didn't want to lose Tate, either.

He squeezed Misty's hand but focused on her sister. "Not that we're keeping score," Tate said, "but she didn't say 'Summer' or 'Krystal.'"

"If she'd seen us first—"

"We'll never know." A teasing argument they'd had more than once. He turned his hazel eyes to her. "How you feeling?"

"Good."

"No headache?"

"Hardly." Comparatively speaking, anyway. She was learning to live with the dull pain. "I'm ready for the party."

Summer pushed back from the chair. "I'm going to see if I can help."

After she stepped outside, Tate tugged Misty to her feet and wrapped her in a hug.

She rested her cheek against his soft sweater. Much as she loved staying with her sister, loved the bond growing between them again, she felt most at home in Tate's arms.

He led her to the loveseat, where they sat side by side. "I have some news."

"Oh."

"First, the bad news. Ruth, your neighbor—she's the one who—"

"I remember."

"She claimed she had no idea that Raul Dawson intended to hurt you and acted shocked when she found out what happened. Nobody believes her, of course, but with no evidence except your spotty memory... She accepted a plea deal. She won't serve any time."

Misty was disappointed but not shocked. It wasn't justice, yet. Misty would leave that in God's hands. "Okay. Is there good news?"

"Damien Humphrey was stopped at the airport yesterday, caught trying to leave the country."

"But I thought he hadn't been charged yet."

"He has now. Multiple charges, including conspiracy to commit murder. He's being held without bail."

"Wow. What about Leland?"

"Leland and Clark Humphrey both maintain they knew nothing about what Damien was doing. They believed the new office building had been funded with company money. As the CEO of Hawthmarks, Clark doesn't have a leg to stand on. But Leland didn't work there. We know he knew about the bribery, but that's not exactly a capital offense. It's possible he was in the dark about the rest of it."

"What do you think?"

Tate tilted his head side to side. "I don't think they'll be able to tie him to any of it. He had an office in the Hawthmarks building, but a search turned up nothing. It looked like he never used it. There's no evidence he was involved in the company's operations. He hadn't gone to a board meeting in years. I don't think he's guilty. And not just because he's my friend. The evidence—"

"I think you're right," Misty said. "I trust your judgment."

Tate relaxed. "It's not going to matter, of course. He's already resigned. The public will never trust him again."

"But he still has his law license. He can go into private practice. Or salvage what's left of his family business. Do you think you'll like working for the new guy?" Misty couldn't remember his name.

He shrugged, looked past her. "I was thinking... You want to stay here, right? In Coventry?"

Here it came.

They couldn't hide from it anymore. They had to face the truth of it. No matter what happened.

"I can't go back to the city, Tate." She studied his hand. The dark skin, the trimmed nails. The strength. How many times had he held her with those hands?

She hated this. She hated it. "I just can't do it." Tears filled her voice. "Too much noise. Too much chaos. It's hard enough to think here, where it's so peaceful. I don't think I could handle it."

"I would never ask you to."

"I know." He was too kind for that. And too kind to end things with her after what she'd suffered, even though it made no sense for them to be together. How could they be when they didn't even live in the same state?

"I'm afraid you're going to think it's too soon," Tate said. "But...I mean, I'm ready. Maybe you're not sure."

She looked up into his kind, beautiful eyes. She must've missed something. "What are we talking about?"

"Thomas was telling me about a job."

Thomas. She tried to think of a Thomas at the DA's office but came up short. The only Thomas she knew...

"Thomas Windham." He clarified. "The mayor."

Of Coventry? "I'm confused. What about him?"

"He offered me a job. I mean, not that it's his job to offer. But he said it's mine if I want it. He has influence. Apparently, they've had trouble finding somebody who wants it, who's qualified. The county needs a prosecutor. I'd be working mostly in Plymouth, but I might need to go to Haverhill sometimes—New Hampshire, not Massachusetts, obviously. Haverhill's an hour from here, but Plymouth isn't that far. I could find a place nearby, for now. While you're recovering. If it's not too soon."

Misty couldn't figure out what he was saying. She tried to make all the words make sense in her head. "You'd be working up here? You'd live...here? Why?"

He blinked. Leaned back a little. "Because I love you." He rubbed his lips together. Swallowed. "But if you don't feel the same way—"

"Just...give me a second." She wasn't following. But she knew there was something very important, *very* important, and she needed to grasp it. As if this might be the most important thing in her whole life.

"You love your job."

"No. I *like* my job." His tone was measured, patient. "I *love* you."

"But you want to be the DA someday. Or..." She couldn't remember what he'd told her. Something big. "You have dreams. Plans. Ambitions."

"Leaving the DA's office doesn't mean the death of my dreams. There are DAs in New Hampshire. There are judgeships. Besides, if I ever want to get involved in politics, New Hampshire is a great place to live. Where else can I hobnob with future presidents?"

"Oh. I see."

He leaned close, his intense gaze holding hers. "None of that is why I want to move here." He tugged his hand out of hers and placed it on her cheek. "I want to move here because I love you. The rest of it—all of it—is secondary."

"You'd give up your career for me?"

"When I thought you were dead..." His eyes turned red at the edges. "I would have given anything, done anything to get you back. At that moment, I realized what you meant to me. What you still mean to me. You're a beautiful gift, one I want to spend the rest of my life unwrapping." He chuckled, shook his head. "That didn't come out right."

Tears dripped down her cheeks. Her heart seemed to grasp what her head still couldn't. "You'd give up your job for me?"

"I'd give up my *life* for you, my love. A job is just a job. But if you think it's too soon... We can keep doing what we're doing. Me in the city, you here. I don't want you to—"

She cut off his words with a kiss. A beautiful promise, not just for this day, but for the days to come.

A throat cleared. "Uh, sorry." Grant was standing in the open door. "The party's getting started, if you two want to join us."

The scents of grilling burgers and hot dogs carried inside. And voices, more voices than before. She hadn't noticed.

"We're coming," she said.

Grant closed the door.

Misty turned back to Tate. "In case the kiss didn't answer your question, there's nothing I want more."

He grinned, then stood and held out his hand to her. "I'll tell Thomas today."

They stepped outside into the bright sunshine.

The backyard was filled with food and games—and a couple of bounce houses. And children running everywhere. And friends.

So many friends.

There was the guest of honor, Ella, her brown hair flying behind her as she dashed across the yard amid a gaggle of girls. It was her ninth birthday.

Her father was holding his baby boy. They belonged to the redhead...

Jacqui. The one with the Boston brownstone. And her husband was Reid.

Who used to be married to... Misty scanned the crowd until she saw Denise, Ella's mom and Jon's fiancée.

Manning the grill was the handsome guy with the longish brown hair, the one married to the woman with the striking blue eyes. They had a couple of kids.

She whispered to Tate, "What are their names?" She nodded to the table.

"Cassidy and James," he said. "Don't ask me the kids' names, though. Wait...the girl is Hallee? Is that right?"

"Yes. I remember. Cassidy and Denise were best friends in high school, and so were James and Reid, I think."

She was glad to know her short-term memory wasn't gone for good.

The guy who looked like Bradley Cooper waved at her from beside a table where his wife, the curly-haired brunette, was painting a little boy's face. Weird names, she thought.

What were they?

Fitz. And Tabby. They had a baby.

A dark-haired, dark-skinned woman helped her toddler climb a tiny slide. The little girl slid down, and her father caught her and threw her over his head.

Tate must've seen her looking that way. "Carly and Braden."

"Carly's the one who makes the desserts."

"And Braden works for Jacqui."

"I wish I could remember."

"You do. It just takes a minute for the memories to surface."

There were older people who didn't look familiar. Probably Ella's grandparents, maybe some of their friends.

Two blondes approached. One had straight hair. The other's always looked windblown, like she'd just come off a surfboard. That image helped Misty remember she was from Hawaii. Why could she remember that but not their names?

The one with straight hair said, "Hey, Misty. It's Grace."

"Oh. Thank you."

The woman gave her a kind smile, then nodded to her friend. "And Aspen."

"I'll remember one of these days."

"It takes time. Are you going to join us?"

"I just need to acclimate to the chaos."

"Makes sense." They moved away. Neither of them had kids, but... Did Grace look like she was expecting? She and her husband...

"Andrew."

She said the name aloud, and Tate chuckled. "Right. And Aspen's with...?"

"Garrett. He's the one who built the guesthouse and fixed up the main one." Oh, and there was the mayor, making the rounds. Unlike Misty, he never forgot a name. He jogged over, gave Misty a quick kiss. "It's Thomas."

"I remembered. This time." Two seconds before, but it counted.

He turned to Tate. "Well?"

Tate beamed at her. "We're good to go."

"Yes!" Thomas high-fived him. "I'll make the call tomorrow. You're a godsend." To Misty, he said, "You guys are going to love it here. It's the greatest place in the world."

He joined his wife, the one who owned the coffee shop.

Misty closed her eyes and pictured the sign over the door of the little café.

"Cuppa Josie's."

"You got it," Tate said. "That's the whole crowd."

Misty watched these Coventry people who'd huddled around her as if she were one of them. They'd brought meals after she'd gotten out of rehab, sat with her, and read her stories when her head pounded so badly she couldn't keep her eyes open. They'd invited her to church and to their girls' nights and parties. They'd welcomed her as if she belonged.

Just like they'd done with Summer, Jon, Grant, and so many others who weren't natives but who'd chosen to make this little New Hampshire town their own.

And now, she and Tate would do the same.

From behind, he slipped his arms around her.

She leaned back against him. "Are you sure you can give up everything for this?"

"You make it sound like a sacrifice. It's like trading chicken nuggets for lobster."

All her life, she'd craved security. She'd tried to achieve it through money, but her modeling career had gotten her kidnapped. She'd sought it by putting bad guys away, as if she could rid the streets of evil, one criminal at a time.

As if it was her job.

But God could find plenty of other people to put bad guys away, people who would be able to keep their perspective a lot better than Misty ever had.

True security didn't come from money or justice. It didn't even come from people, though she did feel comfortable with the friends who surrounded her.

And safe in the arms that held her.

True security came from God, who'd known exactly what she needed, all her life.

She'd been camping out in a boxcar, pretending it was good enough, when He'd had a plan for her all along.

And now she'd found not just a man who loved her, but a community that gathered around her and offered friendship and support.

She'd abandoned her boxcar—and found a home.

The End.

I hope you enjoyed Tate and Misty's story. If you did, you won't want to miss what happens next. Download the *Vengeance in the Mist Bonus Epilogue*. Just click the link, or visit https://dl.bookfunnel.com/izq67kan72 to download it.

And then, turn the page for a sneak peek into the Coventry Saga bonus book. You might remember talk about Daniel Wright, Grant's oldest brother (the hero from *Courage in the Shadows*.) Daniel was murdered four years ago, and his wife and children are still picking up the pieces. When Daniel's killers target Camilla's children, she'll do anything, *anything*, to keep them safe.

Turn the page to learn more about *A Mountain Too Steep*. I think you're going to love this story.

A Mountain Too Steep

A car accident that might not be an accident at all. A murderer bent on revenge. And a woman desperate to keep her family together.

She's already lost her soul mate. She'll do anything to protect her children.

For the sake of her kids, Camilla Wright managed to survive after her husband's murder. When she's awakened in the night with the news that her teenage son and nephew have been in a horrific car accident, she rushes to the hospital in a haze of shock and panic.

The boys were supposed to be skiing in the mountains east of Salt Lake City. What were they doing so far west? More alarming, the wreck might not have been an accident at all.

While Jeremy fights for his life, Camilla is running out of time to discover who lured her son and her nephew into the desert. With each new clue, the terrifying truth becomes clearer.

Her husband's killers are closing in...

ALSO BY ROBIN PATCHEN

The Wright Heroes of Maine

Running to You

The Coventry Saga

Glimmer in the Darkness

Tides of Duplicity

Betrayal of Genius

Traces of Virtue

Touch of Innocence

Inheritance of Secrets

Lineage of Corruption

Wreathed in Disgrace

Courage in the Shadows

Vengeance in the Mist

A Mountain Too Steep

The Nutfield Saga

Convenient Lies

Twisted Lies

Generous Lies

Innocent Lies
Beautiful Lies
Legacy Rejected
Legacy Restored
Legacy Reclaimed
Legacy Redeemed

Amanda Series

Chasing Amanda
Finding Amanda